BLOOD BARONS

A. Dru Kristenev

BLOOD BARONS

A. DRU KRISTENEV

"Blood Barons"
By A. Dru Kristenev
First Edition: 2012

Cover Photo:
  New York Subway
  Courtesy of Angelique Fairbairn
  Design: A. Dru Kristenev

BLOOD BARONS

A. DRU KRISTENEV

WHAT GOOD IS IMMORTALITY TO A DEAD MAN?
DR. ARI

Author's Note...

Science fiction or science fact?

There's some of both in this volume, however the fiction is all soundly based on the facts of where our science community has traveled, may be heading, and where it next could arrive. It's all about the ethical application of scientific breakthroughs, what is the intent of the funding sponsors, be they government or individuals.

Note that I don't claim to be any kind of expert in genetics, medicine or issues of the law, just an outmoded newspaper publisher with a heart for unvarnished facts. In composing this book, and all the others in the Baron Series, I am reliant on the gracious assistance of consultants in all fields of expertise. Yet will I admit to taking literary license in the name of good storytelling and relaying a fundamental and important message, one that I pray will afford each reader an opportunity to consider his or her place in this world and how we, as individuals, may be concerned participants therein. It also behooves me to make note that the most controversial and offensive of statements made within these pages are direct quotes from individuals upon whom those characters are based.

As ever, I must take full responsibility for any mistakes and possible misrepresentations of the good work of others. Here do I give utmost thanks to the diligent study, detecting and discovery of the late Ron Wyatt, whose work has provided a premise for this tale and whom, I believe, God alone could have directed. My apologies to his widow and his legacy if, for any reason, his name appears to be here maligned. Having spoken with him some fourteen years ago in hopes of touring the Holy Land in his company, a hope detoured when family tragedy intervened, I recall him to be a man of integrity and accepting of divine guidance in his quest.

I must also ask law enforcement professionals for forbearance. Protocol differs from jurisdiction to jurisdiction and I have stepped outside the bounds of regular practice to assist the narrative.

My request is that you may read **Blood Barons** with an open and questioning mind, willing to weigh all evidence and regard faith with equanimity. I may be stretching the bounds of the reader's knowledge base and imagination, but there are times in our lives that we must be willing to view the greater universe, breaking down the limiting walls we build.

Having done all within my power to release this fourth book in the **Baron Series** before the 2012 election (as I had done with **Gold Baron**), I may have been unsuccessful in reaching this goal. However, the story told within these following pages are relevant for any citizen of these United States, and may be useful to anyone with a mind for the future of our world, and more significantly, freedom of thought, speech and spirit.

Unending thanks to all who have contributed so much to making this work possible, many in ways that I could not have imagined possible nor be grateful enough for your assistance.

God bless you all on your journey,

A. Dru Kristenev

October 17, 2012
changingwind@earthlink.net
ChangingWind.org

BLOOD BARONS

[18] LET NO MAN DECEIVE HIMSELF. IF ANY MAN AMONG
YOU SEEMETH TO BE WISE IN THIS WORLD, LET
HIM BECOME A FOOL, THAT HE MAY BE WISE.
[19] FOR THE WISDOM OF THIS WORLD IS FOOLISHNESS
WITH GOD. FOR IT IS WRITTEN, HE TAKETH THE
WISE IN THEIR OWN CRAFTINESS.

1 CORINTHIANS 3

BLOOD BARONS

PROLOGUE

This wasn't a pleasure cruise.

The sloop was sliding over fairly calm seas, just enough of a breeze to fill the mainsail and jib, so there was no need to power up the engine. The captain plotted the course to take them beyond the rocky bluffs where the surf continually battered the headland, foaming waters crashing against the breakwater that protected the harbor. Heading out to sea, the 42' craft was manned by a small crew that took their jobs seriously, following the captain's directions as they came about to run north along the shore.

It took a good hour to reach their destination, far enough beyond the shore that it was no longer visible through the fog that drifted between the boat and the land. The spot laid along a sparsely traveled route for day sailors or deepwater anglers, the area being known as desolate of any worthwhile game or good eating fish, having suffered from over-fishing in the last century. The silver-scaled swimmers were just beginning to repopulate the cold waters but had not shown enough of a resurgence for any serious fisherman to bother to cast his line in these seas, making it the perfect spot for today's sailing venture.

Centered on the deck was a rectangular wooden box, rope handles on either end to facilitate its transport. One of the men sat on the crate as the boat rocked in the gently rolling swells, awaiting his orders and watching the shifting mist that wafted between them and the shore, blocking any view of the low cliffs. The captain rechecked his chart to be certain that he'd guided them to the correct spot. Heaving to, he fixed the jib and rudder windward, stalling the ship in the slight chop before following through with his orders.

Nodding to the mate who stood at the base of the mast, the captain silently gave permission to fulfill their duty. The deckhand rose from his perch on the box and, along with the mate, moved to opposite ends where each one gripped a rope handle and hoisted the crate. The captain kept his hand on the helm and watched as the two men moved to the side of the vessel, and carefully swinging the crate over the low lifelines, the cables strung around the boat, they let go. Standing back, the three of them watched the box as it floated briefly on the slight crests forming on the water's surface, then upended and slipped beneath the waves. A swirl materialized in the aqua sea above the box as it disappeared into the deep.

At that, the captain permitted her to fall off, letting the sails out to catch the wind. Turning the wheel to starboard, he brought the vessel about, the sails luffing at first then quickly filling for the run home.

CHAPTER 1

A handsome young man, liquid eyes searching those of a pure, sus - ceptible beauty, the midnight breeze swirling wisps of ebony hair around her porcelain cheek, the trail of a tear rolling to her chin as she tilts it upward. Cocking her head sideways, she offers herself in tribute to an undying love that she knows will change her being for evermore. In acceptance, she closes her eyes and pushes tendrils of hair away from her neck, the pulse of her blood surging beneath the translucent skin, wordlessly urging the man to partake of her gift. A kiss filled both with sweet and bitter essence that will turn to a bite of innocence ended, embodying the epitome of fleshly consummation.

As his lips touch her skin, she swoons in his arms. He holds her, staring at her unprotected neck, the purity of heart that he contem - plates with his own that is tainted by his need. No longer able to restrain himself, he leans over and bares the fangs he has withheld in a valiant attempt to deny himself the taste of her life that will sustain his own corrupt existence.

He sips from her fount, the blind love that will feed his survival.

What utter bunk.

Immediately flicking the channel, Debra couldn't be bothered to check the list of programs, she just wanted out of that saccharine scene of "everlasting love."

Who writes this syrupy claptrap? That kids practically believe this baloney is beyond me. She shivered in her disdain and total disbelief of the illogic that feeds the unrealistic scenes comprising modern film-makers' ideas about tales of *true lo-ove.*

Yup, they feed off the minds of prepubescent morons who eat this stuff up.

She continued to amuse her self-indulgent thoughts with puns on vampire behavior as she searched through the channels for something, anything, that wasn't as idiotic as a fable about the undead and their unhealthy appetites, both physical and emotional. *Who needs a fanciful movie glorifying vampires when we're surrounded by everyday parasites that feed and breed off the sustenance of others? Maybe that's the purpose of this whole falling in love with a* noble *leech is all about? Acceptance of the inevitable bloodsucker, just like the young lovely on the screen.* Debra thanked the Lord for giving her the good sense not to flush any of her hard-earned paycheck on theatre tickets when this film had been such the rage a year or so back.

Maybe it's just because I'm not a romantic at heart.

Ever the pragmatist, Debra shrugged it off as she sat in her own living room, fielding the television remote control with the rough handling more often associated with a sports-addicted male, who'd be stockier by at least eighty pounds, maybe even wielding a beer in the other fist.

As a contrast, Debra Chorister, settled on a national news broadcast that was far more suited to her practical view of life. Not that watching news was a preferred activity since she enjoyed a jaunt through fantasyland as much as anybody. She just saw news more as a necessary component of her life which continually circled around it, particularly working at a newspaper, one of the hard copy dinosaurs still struggling to keep its head above the rising flood of internet newsfeeds.

"A rash of missing persons reports has crossed the news desk of our New York affiliate. This is the third individual to disappear after a recent relocation to the nation's largest metropolitan area..." a cute blonde went into what appeared to be a cautionary tale for singles moving to the big city. Instituting a quirky nod of her head every time she thought to emphasize an important point, she went on to detail how people go missing every day.

"How three makes a "rash" of incidents seems to be a stretch, even for network news," Debra spoke aloud even though she was alone. "I guess I should be glad it's not just another story trashing one of the presidential candidates. That's gotten to be tiresome." As the reporter went on about the disappearances and how these people weren't transients, runaways or prostitutes, Debra changed channels again.

"... awarded a major funding grant for the further development of a bioartificial kidney, opening the doors for dialysis patients to look forward to an implant that will operate just like a kidney, but without the same kinds of rejection problems. New nanotechnology is behind the creation of a "bioreactor" that could help ease the demand for kidney donors which, in 2009, there were only 17,000 to meet a need of 85,000 people on waiting lists..."

Barely listening, though always peripherally aware of stories about kidney failure or diabetes after what a lawyer friend had been going through with her teenage client, Debra subconsciously noted the story. She clicked the remote again, all the while running her own nonverbal commentary tying together odd strands about vampires and, even though the movie was supposed to be a fictional tale, how it paralleled the reality of bloodsuckers in society who just didn't call themselves by those appropriate names. Being a fairly cynical black woman who grew up in some pretty rough neighborhoods in Los Angeles, Debra had the penchant for junking lawyers, politicians (who were usually lawyers) and the nastier side of corporate medicine (that influenced the politicians) together as social vampires. The whole circle having just been rounded out by her last half-hour of television viewing.

Halfway attending to the rest of the newscast, Debra wondered about that story of missing persons in New York. Realizing that people vanished on a daily basis in every big city, this particular city was where her friend and sometimes dinner partner had been transferred. With Allie Maitland, Debra's other friend in what would be considered a mostly companionless life, also now living out of state, evenings at home with the remote as her best buddy had become commonplace.

Debra was never much of a social butterfly to begin with. The friends with whom she'd grown up had never taken much of an interest in the kind of life that Debra had tried to pursue. A few had moved to the outskirts and suburbs working retail and corporate sales, but with her living even further outside L.A., they'd already lost touch before she'd made the leap to Denver once she'd secured a research position at the paper. Even she and her aunt, who was one of the most fun-loving women she knew – they always had a blast together – hadn't kept the communication lines buzzing regularly.

The mention of New York in context to missing people brought to mind the FBI, as often being the agency to deal with that kind of case, and Roy Esteban, golden boy who circumvented protocol in a policy-laden organization. Walking around the rules when he'd been *the* stickler who instituted them, pushed him back down the ladder and booted halfway across country in semi-disgrace. He'd been heading up a big investigation in Wyoming and getting nowhere fast when he made the disastrous career move of drafting some unorthodox assistants into the works. Allie was one and Debra was another.

The whole thing nearly crumbled around his ankles when a kidnapping complicated the investigation, but between Esteban's willingness to forego agency channels and use outside help, he solved the case and was generously rewarded with a big, red target on his back for having ignored the rules. Since then, he plummeted from the fast track of promotion to a sideways demotion back east jockeying a dreary desk in New York.

After all the excitement of that summer running hot on the trail of thugs, even if it was in the cyber-sense as she exercised her remarkable aptitude for uncovering the most deeply buried data, Debra was bored to distraction in her everyday post as computer researcher and data technician. The adventure, throughout which she had actually seen very little real action, had given her a taste of righteous battle fervor, something her everyday life lacked. She missed the adrenaline of hunting human brutes whose purpose was to destroy the lives of others and all for a misguided version of "truth." Generally pretty patient, it didn't take much to light her fuse when diligently trying to deal with plain ignorance. No, make that pure stupidity. Debra wasn't all that charitable with people who refused to use the brains God gave them. And those that were so intolerant of others that they could not listen politely or employ logic were the first to be crossed-off her list.

Returning a modicum of attention to the news, her mind lapsed into autopilot for awhile.

A movie screen dominates one wall of an unsurpassed home the - atre outfitted with every electronic gadget and upgrade available. Capacious enough to seat forty people, only one teen-aged girl is sit - ting down front, practically enveloped by sounds of howling wolves, wind ripping through conifers and labored breathing of the characters dashing across a forest floor. The film's subtle greens and greys create a shadowy nocturnal world, instilling a feral mood that captivates her so much she hasn't noticed the room's door opening briefly, allowing light to spill onto the floor behind the last row of seats.

Her grandfather, in whose house the girl is watching the movie, glimpses her slight figure ensconced in the front row, dwarfed by the giant images racing past her eyes. Not pretending to approve of the fascination she has for the series of vampire movies that has swept the teen scene in recent years, he does understand the consequence of their reception as a social influence. He knows how easily the forma - tive mind is manipulated by peer pressure. Most of the time it doesn't come to the level of "pressure" at all. A need for approval is all it takes to bring a child, and even adults, into line with the perceived majority, the social acceptance that most crave.

His own granddaughter is completely engrossed in the bleeding dry of a feckless youth who, on screen, desperately wants to believe that immortality begins with the death cult of vampire behavior. As young as she is, she's already desensitized to the humanity that should be inherent in the characters.

He fully grasps how these media inferences have helped produce the dependent nature that citizens now have on government, the sub - conscious belief that if you forfeit what you have, by way of taxation and, ultimately individual freedom, an unconcerned life will be "given" you, a life that is blissful with lack of responsibility. The greater "power" will take care of all your ills and tribulations. All you need do is allow it to suck your lifeblood. The programming has been proliferated for so many generations now that the population has become generally unresponsive to what would normally be considered good judgment.

With purpose he guides his everyday business and philanthropic endeavors by such policies, and even sponsors the media that propa - gates films like this one, music, news and social sites, directing the now disengaged, the diverted, up the unobtrusive path toward, basi - cally, operative enslavement.

None of this bothers him one iota. Business is business.

Standing in the shadows, he's convinced that the time is ripe to grasp the power the people have been gradually abdicating for the sake of perceived ease and entertainment. His efforts of destabiliza - tion by generating and disseminating disinformation as educational material, which even his gullible kin buy into so wholly, are coming to bear, leaving him with the only palatable option for his future. He must find a genuine form of immortality to fulfill his ambition; a vampire's mantle suited to the real world as one who feeds on flesh and blood — the labor of others.

He smiles as he leaves his granddaughter to her fantasy. He's halfway there.

CHAPTER 2

Unlocking the front door with fingers barely clutching the key, both arms laden with groceries, the woman managed to pocket it while her hand was sliding off the slick knob. Nudging the door open with her shoulder, she practically lost her balance crossing the threshold, an oversize purse swinging across her back and bags of sundries dan - gling off her shoulders, elbows and forearms at every possible angle.

"Never let it be said that there isn't a crook or corner of the human body that can't be used as a hanger," she said to herself as she ginger - ly lowered one bag after another onto the kitchen counter. Proud of herself for not having dropped a single item in transit from the street, she brushed the imaginary dust off her hands and caught her breath after laboring up five flights of stairs. She turned to view the general disarray in the apartment before unloading the bags, solidly planting her hands on her hips.

"Well, there's still a lot to be done, but the hard work is finished." She was referring to the process of moving everything she owned (everything she'd wanted to keep, really) from one coast to the other. This had been a major undertaking and one of the hardest decisions in her life to sell off half of her possessions, write-off a long-failed rela - tionship and start over. New home, new job and hopefully, some new friends. The old lot hadn't been interested in her plans. Bad habits, every one of the old crew.

She'd made some lousy choices in her 42 years, but finally she believed she had done the right thing. There was a certain peace in her life now even in the midst of one of the biggest cities in the world, and she kind of liked the new landscape. The openness of western cities, like the one she'd just left behind, were a real contrast to the straight up and down of places like New York, the compact humanity that seemed to be everywhere as she gazed out the window of her walk-up.

She patted her hips that had expanded some over the last few years.

"Maybe I'll get a little more exercise. This is a walking city after all, and work isn't so far away that I can't make the mile most days. Particularly after we get a few of the doctor's orders implemented."

Looking over the new furniture that had been a hassle to get moved up the stairs, she was content with the change. Lighter, breezi - er style with softer, more upbeat colors and a splash of deep jewel tones peppering the décor. Yes, this was going to work out just fine. Removing her sweater, she was preparing to undertake the work of getting settled, putting away the groceries and then tackling the chore of finding a place for everything and putting everything in its place.

But before she hunkered down to organizing the new apartment, which she'd only inhabited three days, she picked up the phone to make the appointment that had really kicked her behind across coun - try. Her old job had been so stressful that her health had begun to deteriorate and the benefits were not going to cover what she'd been told was needed. This new employer had been so interested in her hire that they had even agreed to take her on, warts and all, in a manner of speaking. So, first things first... make that call.

After that, there's nothing to hold me back!

CHAPTER 3

Roy Esteban was drilling the computer screen with a lethal stare that elicited no response since the inanimate object didn't blink under his malevolent gaze. As much as some geeks would swear that computers have a soul, Esteban knew otherwise. They were heartless.

It was bad enough being practically invisible in the midst of New York's overpopulated federal building, living half-banished, half-promoted among the Bureau's up-and-coming young stars – one of which he was not, at the ripe old age of 50. Uncertain if he was heading back up the ranks or moving down toward oblivion, Esteban was suffering the ill effects of his combined fiasco and success of the eco-terrorist affair in Wyoming the year prior. His superiors couldn't seem to decide if his handling of the case had been genius or folly, their reassigning him from the top of the totem pole in Denver to the first mezzanine in New York attested to their indecision, and his own frustration.

He knew very well that pulling in amateurs to further the investigation in the plains was probably a bad idea, and he'd struggled with it at the time, but the fruits had been the breaking of a cabal that was on a fast track to blackout the West, and cripple much of the nation's power supply. Would he do it again? Given the same circumstances, even though it came close to losing a life, he would have to say yes, which is just what he told the big boys when he was debriefed. And, which is why he found himself in the virtual dungeon of New York's FBI headquarters.

Nothing more to contemplate on that plane, he turned his attention back to the recalcitrant computer. Zero was coming up no matter what names, words or variables he dropped into the search engine. With his plummet in the Bureau hierarchy he'd been delivered a case that was going nowhere fast. He assumed that was the intent, to keep him in the backwater where the eddy was taking him in circles. That way, no one had to deal with him, kind of like giving a kid a Rubik's Cube that would keep him occupied and out of the grown-ups' hair for a good long time.

Well, the strategy was working, sort of. Esteban was at the point where, unable to make any progress in tracing virtually any information about three missing persons, he was at the brink of losing his cool. The story he was given consisted of a few unattached individuals, recently relocated to the city, who had vanished into thin air. Somewhat enigmatically, the disappearances weren't exactly reported. Because there appeared to be no family connections, there were never any calls from concerned relatives or even friends. Employers began to wonder because their offices seemed abandoned after a couple days, the new hires gone AWOL and no prior notice. Initially interested in finding the new additions to their rosters, the employers weren't about to waste much time or effort on finding people they hardly knew and assumed to be flakes, even though they had appeared to be reliable at the outset. The offices wouldn't stand empty for long in this abysmal economy and the employers couldn't afford to let them stagnate. Too many professionals were on the hunt for not just new positions, but *any* position.

Racking his brain, Esteban had been trying to generate some research assistance, his own resources hitting an electronic block wall, and found that his reputation as a screw-up who got lucky was working against him. No one was interested in what he was working on – a dead-end case for a dead-end career – and certainly, no one wanted to be associated with a downward spiraling agent. Too afraid they'd get caught in the vortex. As it was, so many people drop off the face of the earth in NYC that, frankly, it was hard for the agents to care about every case that came along. The result was that this case of professionals maybe gone adrift was dropped in his inbox without so much as a miniscule lead. Come to find out, there weren't any.

So, what now? I'm the leper at the gate, untouchable and invisible, just like the poor slobs who nobody can find, or seem to be interested in finding.

He'd been scrolling through every database he could conceive trying to piece together the dearth of information that was out there. And it had to be "out there" because he could find damn little of it no matter where he went on the internet or the internal FBI search engines, even the interagency files. These three people were practically enigmas and he didn't believe that it was even intentional on their part. Of the few things he could find about the missing people was that they were not transients or indigent. They were professionals that had relocated to the city for good paying jobs, jobs that were hard to come by in these tough times, which came down to much of his own reason for taking whatever the Bureau handed out in the way of discipline. Work is work. So why would these people, who had uprooted their lives to come to NYC, just up and disappear? It made no sense, another reason why he got stuck with the case. No one else was interested in spinning their wheels and he had no choice but to do as he was told, and man, did that burn in his gut.

Aside from all of that, there were no real common denominators. But it struck Esteban that perhaps there were others with similar stories. The city was overwhelming when you took into account the sheer number of people who traversed these streets every minute, many who were never noticed in their passage. Examining the files he could access on the computer, he was aware of a growing number of cases with a familiar ring, but he couldn't put a finger on what it was. It felt like his brain was going to seed because nothing jumped out at him except that the cases he'd come across centered around those living alone.

Well, that says a whole lot. In a city of loners, what else would you expect to find?

Trying again, he started listing factors that the cases *didn't* have in common.

All the assumed victims came from different backgrounds. Different races, sexes and ages; varied religious affiliations or none. Occupations were all over the board. Economic status diverged some – not all were making six figures but all were in some kind of career track. There wasn't enough personal information to determine if they had similar or differing personal problems, or if they had any at all, so that was no help.

What else was there that could possibly connect them? They didn't seem to run in the same social or business circles or have any mutual acquaintances, school or work history. Politics didn't even seem to be a factor as, from what he *could* get, the individuals were liberal, conservative and apolitical.

Esteban sat back in his chair and crossed his arms. What was he missing? His instincts were telling him that there was something that cross-pollinated these cases. But what?

CHAPTER 4

Esteban hung up the phone after the sixth, or was it the seventh, attempt to reach Debra Chorister. It felt like the hundredth call, leaving messages at the paper, on her home phone and her cell. He was beginning to understand what her level of frustration must have been during the Wyoming incident when all she could get was his voicemail. The difference being that she had been desperately frightened for the safety of her friend who'd vanished in the midst of an investigation. And here he was, hoping to just fly a few ideas past Debra about more disappearances. In this instance there was no emotional connection, these were strangers that have gone missing, not a close friend and confidante. It may have taken more than a year, but he was finally getting it, the near panic that she must have felt when all she heard was a disembodied voice telling her to "leave a message, and I'll get back to you." He shook his head wondering if he'd been as obtuse and unappreciative of her dread as she'd told him after the fact. Probably, much as he hated to admit it.

Not willing to dwell on something he couldn't remedy, all he could do now was go over the same case tidbits. Mulling them over to no avail, he was getting the same non-answers while even more questions popped up.

This is getting me nowhere. I don't know what talking to Debra will do to help, but her input has been a plus in the past, so maybe...

His cell phone vibrated, catching his attention as it gyrated across the desk, creating a buzzing as it slid over the surface. Esteban had muted the ring as being just another irritating noise amid the muffled clamor of the office, which was already disturbing his thoughts as he went over the points of the case, minimal as they were.

Using his thumb to press the "talk" button, he brought the phone to his ear.

"Esteban."

"Chorister, here," answered Debra, replicating his flat business tone, knowing it would tweak him enough to force a smile.

"'Bout time you decided to set aside some time in your schedule to talk to the FBI. You are one difficult woman to reach."

"That's what happens when your phenomenal skills are in demand," she said. Changing the subject, Debra asked, "So this is an official call that I'm returning?"

"Yes, and… no." He hesitated briefly before invoking the negative.

"Whatever that means. Tell me what's up. I haven't heard from you in a while." The statement was made without any rancor or insinuation. It had been months since Esteban had relocated to New York and they had spoken maybe twice since then. She chalked it up to a need to salvage some self-respect, not that he'd ever admit to the demotion as having affected him in the first place. *Men and their bruised egos.*

"They've got me babysitting a missing persons case, three actually, that no one will touch or even bother to hunt up some basic info," his voice carried a shade of disgust. "Can't figure it. Yeah, no one wants to be buried under a dead-end case, drops their closing average into the dumper if there's no resolution, but there are still the victims to consider."

"What about the kudos for closing a mother of a case?" She asked. "Where's the adrenaline rush in pushing papers and pocketing your paycheck?"

"Not everyone joins the Bureau for excitement." Esteban almost chuckled at the thought of how recruiters round up prospects. At one time they did pursue thrill-seekers with a cool head. With the information age, computer skills were more in demand than sharpshooting, even though marksmen were needed for the more radical situations dealing with violent offenders. For that they had the armed response teams.

"How many take government jobs for the bennies, guaranteed retirement and a good pension plan, I wonder."

"A lot more than there used to be, that's for sure. And there are a number in this office who would rather not tarnish their record with what I've been handed," he said.

"So, what *do* you have? Sounds boring."

"Not so much boring as nebulous."

"Even better," Debra's interest had been spiked.

"You may not think so after you hear what little I have," and he went into a brief explanation of the missing persons, the lack of much background on any of them and his inability to find more.

"What are you thinking?" Never one to beat around the bush, which was a quality Esteban admired in Debra, she just cut to the chase. "What do you want me to do?"

"That was easy. No cajoling…"

"No forgotten promises," Debra cut in.

"I forgot something?" He was on the defensive now.

"Nah, just felt the need to put you on your guard because I may ask for real compensation this time," she threw in half-seriously.

"Not that you wouldn't be deserving, but this time you know I'm practically on the bottom rung." It hurt a little more than he expected to point out his change in status, having sacrificed his station to follow his conscience.

"No problem," said Debra. "You know I do this for the fun of it. It's rare that I get a research assignment with any meat."

"This one may be no different. I've used my limited skills to comb the files here and, unfortunately my reputation precedes me enough that no one cares to throw-in with a bumbler. So, not so much help to be had here."

"The commendations you've received would hardly place you in that category," Debra was slightly annoyed at his choice of words, knowing the integrity he always employed in his work.

"Appearances are everything in government, and toeing the line gets more respect than going maverick."

"Let them wallow in their small-mindedness. How can I help?"

"You said so yourself, your prodigious research skills are in demand, and, you don't have a problem with consorting with someone whose rep might cause you to lose yours," Esteban stated flatly.

"Always a pleasure to work with the best. I gather you need more information about these people than has been acquired through the usual channels, is that right?"

"That about covers it. Do you have the time or inclination?" He was hopeful whereas, before, he'd been pessimistic.

"Absolutely! I am on board. No shoot-em-ups though."

"No, no gunplay, car chases or bad guys lurking in the shadows," he laughed. "Just some cyber-sleuthing so we can find out where these individuals went."

⚜⚜⚜⚜

It didn't take much to capture Debra's attention. Give her a mystery and let her do her magic.

All she had were the names, ages, last known addresses and places of work, occupations and… so little else that it wasn't worth mentioning. It wasn't long before she had uncovered limited education records and family contacts, which, for the most part didn't exist. Dead parents and siblings, unless they were only children. No real friends to hunt down, not even much through departments of motor vehicles in their previous states of residence. They were either good drivers with no violations on their records or didn't even carry a license. Debra could see why Roy had been grasping at straws. Nothing was popping on the usual channels. She went to the media for cross-referencing and found nothing there, either.

Scratching her head with the blunt end of a retractable pen, an old habit she'd picked up so she wouldn't disturb her coiffure, she decided to scour the local New York media for mention of similar disappearances. Roy had only given her the three official case names and the minute amount of data in the files, if you could even call them that, they were so thin. Not enough to go on but maybe enough to see if there were other incidents reported in media that had gone unreported to the FBI.

Newshounds always sensationalize accounts of missing persons if they can make the facts sound horrendous enough, thought Debra. From memory lapses and Alzheimer's patients wandering away from home, to runaways and, particularly, if they could find them, the cowardly who faked their death. Could any of the three actually have something in common with others who've evaporated into the city's thick air? Typing with a vengeance, she was determined to find out.

It took some time, but she unearthed 11 individuals who'd disappeared under similar circumstances, or rather, *lack* of circumstances. No surprise, really. In a city of 8 million souls, there had to be any number of people going missing on a daily basis and Debra figured that she may have just scratched the surface of those least expected to slip between the cracks – people living the good, and stable, responsible life.

BLOOD BARONS

CHAPTER 5

"What's the good news?" These were the first words Debra heard after lifting the receiver of her home phone, recognizing the caller identification before placing it against her ear.

"Depends on your point of view as to whether we've got good news or bad."

"And that means…?" Roy Esteban intoned, a little apprehensively.

"It means you've got more than a few odd office workers slipping off the radar over the last 18 months. Taking into account the size of the metropolis and the millions of residents there, it's not much but I can discern a teeny-tiny pattern of new arrivals getting themselves settled in for, what looks like the long haul, and then, poof! Up in smoke, or fill in whatever metaphor that suits your fancy."

"How many you got?"

"Off the bat, including your three, about an even dozen," said Debra.

"All right." He sat back in his chair, stashed behind a mobile wall in his little cubicle. "I'd had a feeling that there were more out there and something told me there was a link of some kind. What criteria do you have that sets these apart from others gone missing?"

"Like I said, it's pretty thin," said Debra.

"Let's hear it."

"The initial thing that popped out was the strange factor that the three files dropped on your desk indicated these people had just transplanted themselves to NYC from quite a distance. They moved everything lock, stock and barrel, making the leap for the benefit of a good paying job with all the bells and whistles."

"Yeah, go on…"

"They unpack, get themselves all sorted out and start working a regular schedule, then, all of a sudden, like I said, poof, they're gone." She went silent for a moment and Esteban waited for the next installment.

"All three of your folks are gone, supposedly without a word to their employers, and nobody calls it in for a bit because there are no close friends or family to take notice. They're barely established in their new homes or place of work. And when the employers finally do report the incident, it's more to cover their behinds than stemming from any real concern. I mean, these folks are new, no one has even gotten a chance to know them yet. Hence, you have no real leads because no one knows bupkis about them except what's on the résumé. The employers have done their due diligence and they are no longer beholden to the new recruits and fill the slots with the runners-up."

"All right. We had all that."

"Yes, you did," she agreed. "What you didn't do was cast a wide enough net to catch all the other cases that sound just like these. That's the slim lead that I found, that there are more of these than you thought."

"The other ones you've tracked down are also recently relocated professionals or white collar types without family, or even much of a past, that have vanished. Is that right?"

"I told you it wasn't much. It's just that these folks are set aside from the druggies, runaways, transients and streetwalkers that are often targets of malicious activity. The fact that they are all pretty stable individuals, albeit without ties or much of a past, is pretty weird in itself." Debra sat back in her chair and sighed.

"What else did you find?"

"Ah, you know me too well. It's not what I found, it's what I didn't find. None of these people worked for the same companies, worked or lived near one another, shopped in the same places even, from what I can see. Thus far, I can find no crossover from one of these independent beings to another. The only thing they have in common, at this stage of our search, is, virtually nothing."

"Progress is often found in the lack thereof when it comes to clues," Esteban noted.

"Talk about putting a spin on finding zip," said Debra. "I'm going to continue hunting for any social media connections, although, so far, that's yielded next to nothing. But you never know when someone has enough of a passion for a hobby, politics or special interest that they contribute to or have their own blog somewhere on the web."

"I heard somewhere that there are over a billion websites and blogs on the internet. How can you possibly find one person's soapbox among all that?"

"Diligence, my friend, and a few tricks," Debra signed of with a sniff.

BLOOD BARONS

CHAPTER 6

Esteban had almost nothing in his arsenal but he decided it was time to take the tidbits he and Debra had gleaned to his supervisor.

Knocking on the office of Harry Bestner, seasoned agent, to which his grey hair attested and what sparse strands that were left combed across his otherwise balding pate, Roy peered in the door. Tall and tending a little toward beefiness, Bestner was bent over some paperwork, signing his life away on agents' reports. He had not been a happy camper about the transfer of the indefinable Esteban to his command. Agents that had gone off the reservation, in his opinion, should be, not only derailed but, permanently retired to the siding. If they'd gone rogue once, no matter how illustrious their career beforehand, they'd do it again. He'd seen the self-destruction of good men in just this way time and again. As a result, he wasn't exactly thrilled to see Esteban standing in his doorway, a few thin manila folders in his hands.

"Problems, Esteban?" Bestner asked with a doubtful tone, barely keeping his disdain under wraps, and not doing a good enough job for his subordinate agent to miss.

"Not a one, sir. Just thought I might run a couple things past you for your consideration." If nothing else, Esteban was always respectful no matter what his superiors may think of him personally or professionally.

Bestner waved an open hand toward the old, wooden guest chair facing his desk. "Have a seat." He sat back himself, hands folded over his midsection. Roy immediately recognized the relaxed attitude that was anything but. He'd used the technique himself plenty of times with informants or agents whom he wasn't about to give any credence. *At least I know where I stand.*

"Since these three cases of missing persons were delivered to me, I've tried every angle of seeking information in an attempt to run down what could have happened to them. I'm sure you're aware of my efforts," said Esteban.

Bestner just bobbed his head.

"It's come to my attention that these are not the only cases with similar profiles." He waited for his boss' reaction, which amounted to a raised eyebrow. "Actually, so far I've uncovered about 12 cases that have parallels."

"Where did the other case files come from?"

"There weren't any files generated on these others. No one had officially reported them."

Bestner hardened his look. "So how do you know they exist?"

"The people who appear to have gone missing were reported as such through the media, although the Bureau wasn't involved in the designation or even case file production," answered Esteban, already knowing where this was going to end up.

"It looks like at least 12 people, who had recently relocated to Manhattan and a couple of the boroughs, have vanished from jobs, good-paying jobs at that, over the last 18 months."

"What else is there to tie these together," the supervisor asked skeptically.

"Not much. Just the fact that these are career types who live alone and have few family or friends. They were offhandedly reported missing by employers who were more interested in keeping the position filled than finding their new recruits." He paused. "That's it."

"What do you want from me?"

"I'd like permission to widen the investigation and utilize more resources, sir."

"Why? It's most likely that these people were flakes that moved on without giving prior notice. I can't see wasting resources on dead-end cases." He sat up and looked hard at Esteban. "I'd suggest that you quit looking for riddles where none exist and just close the cases you have in hand." He directed his gaze at the files in Esteban's lap and gave a sideways tip to his head, indicating that Roy could leave.

Standing, Esteban exited the office without a word, keeping his thoughts to himself.

❦❦❦

Now what?

Already snubbed and avoided by most of the office workers and agents, Esteban was now little better than a pariah. Each time he sought information or answers to even simple questions, the word must have been out to run the other way. As little support as he'd received before, after taking the issue to the supervisor the support tap had dried up to barely a drip.

Bestner was obviously counting on Esteban's failure and had been betting on it from the getgo. Wishing he had a piece of the action, he already knew the outcome without having to study the racing form. What better way to clear deadwood from the NYC office ranks? He'd seen the tactic employed often enough to recognize himself as the target this time around. Trouble was, he was determined to close these cases no matter what the management had in mind for his future, bleak as it seemed.

Since the in-house sources were unavailable, Esteban decided to beat feet, take the investigation to the street and go door-to-door, again.

The three people he had consent to investigate were his starting gate. Checking each of the addresses, he recalled that none lived near one another. No surprise there. The neighborhoods he'd visited were given to the more affluent side of the middle class. These people were not down-on-their-luck or even regular working stiffs. They obviously earned a good wage and as he approached the front door of one building on the upper eastside he was greeted by a nattily attired doorman.

Not too shabby. I wouldn't mind parking myself at digs like this. He'd dropped by earlier in the week but the entry had been unattended and he'd not gotten past the foyer, barred by the lack of a human answering any doorbells.

After taking his information, the doorman led Esteban to the manager's apartment, which was also pretty upscale. Introductions made, the manager guided him into his living room.

Esteban checked out the apartment, which was furnished with some impressive antiques. He was no expert but he could spot the Chippendale and Queen Anne pieces, mostly due to a couple of cases worked over his career.

Although this wasn't a social call, the old fellow, Mel, who appeared to be a spry over-seventy, offered Esteban a seat and iced tea in a cut crystal glass. Esteban held the glass up to the light, watching a rainbow play across the starburst pattern under the lip of the glass, he asked about one of the occupants of the building.

"Have you seen Lorna Truesdale lately? Someone reported her missing and, as I understand it she had just moved into your building not that long ago."

Mel cocked his head to think, as if he had to concentrate on the name to place it with a face. "Oh yes, I remember. I haven't seen her in more than a week. I just assumed that she'd been off early to work every day and that I missed her coming and going." He looked at the FBI agent quizzically. "So, she's been reported missing? How odd."

"Why do you say that?"

"Oh, I don't know. She was so excited about her new job and seemed to be settling in famously, not that I'd spoken to her more than a couple of times over the month or two since she moved in."

"Did she ever say much about herself?" asked Esteban.

"Not really. I did hear her mention that she'd be getting some kind of surgery soon. Didn't sound too serious, though."

"Elective, do you think?"

"Probably. I recall her playing with a hearing aid once when we spoke briefly." He was quiet for a moment while he thought. "Now I remember. She was going to get one of those hearing implants so she wouldn't have to fuss with the contraption – that's what she called it – that she'd worn since she was a kid. Guess she had some kind of hearing loss when she was young."

"Are you sure?"

"Only to a point. I'm conjecturing about the time when she started wearing a hearing aid. Like I said, we only talked a couple of times.

She kept to herself and seemed to be a real loner. Even leased the apartment through other channels. The owner has been working through some online rental agency of late. If I hadn't run into her on the stairs once or twice, we might never have met face-to-face."

Esteban didn't say anything in response, just nodded as he made a couple of notes. "So you don't know anything about where she lived before or where she worked." It was a statement rather than a question.

"Yep. I'm not even sure if she was subletting or going directly through the building owner. All I do is collect rent when there's an overdue situation and watch after the maintenance. You might check with the doorman. He's more likely to have seen Miss Truesdale than me." Mel picked up the cut-glass pitcher, "Would you care for any-more tea?"

"No, thank you. I appreciate your time and the tea was great. You know, you've got quite a place here yourself."

"Yes, indeed. My wife was quite the antique collector. Used to buy and sell pieces. Made a nice bit on the side." He glanced around the room, his vision seeming to cloud a bit. "It's all that's left of her. She passed on just six months ago."

Esteban was sympathetic. "I'm sorry to hear of your loss." He started for the door and paused to ask, "Do you know if Miss Truesdale might have moved out recently, without your knowledge?"

"Anything's possible, I suppose, but I think I would have had some clue if she'd packed it all up and taken off. Did you want to check her apartment?"

"That was my next question."

"All righty, then. Let me get the key in case she's not home, and missing as you believe."

They climbed the stairs quite a few flights and Mel went down the short hall, halting in front of a gaily-painted door matching the color of ripe plums.

"Here it is." Mel knocked and listened, then knocked again, call-ing the occupant's name. After a minute had passed he looked at Esteban and they silently made the decision to unlock the door, even though the agent didn't have a warrant. Mel seemed concerned enough that it was consensual that they should investigate Miss Truesdale's possible disappearance.

Mel opened the door to an empty room. Not a stick of furniture or a scrap of shelf lining paper was to be found anywhere in the apartment. It was clean as a whistle and echoed like a mausoleum. "Well, I'll be damned..."

⚜ ⚜ ⚜

Esteban visited the buildings of the other two missing persons, wondering why it had taken him this long to go back a second time. He'd had the case since the beginning of the week and had dropped by the addresses initially. Receiving no answer, finding none of the neighbors about, or entry of the premises available, he'd let it go while he tried his hand at electronic investigating. But now that the Truesdale woman had obviously vanished along with all her belongings, if you went along with the gasp of surprise Mel had uttered, things were definitely stranger than he'd supposed.

How could someone manage to clear out their apartment without anyone taking notice? What he found when he went back to one of the two addresses was that it too had been emptied and thoroughly cleaned. Neighbors on either side, that happened to be home and in the least bit talkative, denied having even met the missing people or hearing anything akin to the din moving furnishings or scouring an apartment was sure to make. No, no one knew anything.

He wasn't given access to the third flat. The super of that building would do nothing without a warrant, evidently he'd been burned in a lawsuit initiated by a previous tenant, and Esteban's supervisor had vetoed that request earlier. No news there.

All he had now was the fact that two of the three persons were indeed gone along with all their goods, as if they'd never existed. In fact, a couple of the neighbors he had hunted up began to question their memory of the residents down the hall. Not an uncommon problem when confronted with evidence that seems to contradict what they thought they knew. It was why eyewitness reports were so unreliable, people would doubt their own memory if contradicted by accounts that seemed credible, even if they weren't. He'd been a victim of the phenomenon himself.

He came away with just one fact, or assumed fact. Two of the neighbors at two different buildings, Mel and another witness, seemed to recall the missing person mentioning a medical problem that might require a procedure to correct.

And that means, what? Lots of people have health issues. Neither of the remarks seemed to relate to anything else or each other. It was just another unanswered riddle and with Bestner riding him to close the cases, Esteban was in a quandary as to what he could do now that he believed he had a dozen of them rather than the three official files. It was bad enough that the Assistant Special Agent-in-Charge was looking for any excuse to fire him, he didn't need to be handing the guy justification on a platter.

Esteban had assumed that he was being shoved toward the door in order to save department cash on pension and retirement funds. That didn't really compute when government agencies were expanding almost exponentially in personnel costs and program budgets. This Justice Department had already been "under fire," called on the carpet by Congress to offer reasonable explanations for bad judgment calls and exorbitant expenditures on programs like the *Fast and Furious* international gun-walking incident. It didn't make sense that they'd have a bug up their behind to rid themselves of the agent that had busted one of the biggest stateside terrorist rings in years, and one who was Hispanic, at that. What's with that when the White House was constantly invoking race against anyone who challenged the Administration's policies?

Shrugging it off as he walked away, he thought, *Maybe I can get on with the IRS. They're already hiring those 17,000 agents that were written into the healthcare bill.*

CHAPTER 7

Staring up into the glare of an intense light, confusion filtered through her mind as she tried to absorb her situation. The last thing she recalled with any clarity was the doctor telling her to count back - ward as he administered the anesthesia in preparation for surgery. She'd been putting her life in order to be able to take this next step of regaining some normality, the pressure in her chest having grown worse over the last couple of years despite her relative youth. She was laying on a gurney, cold under the sheets as she awaited the surgery, but she knew that she shouldn't be awake, even in this semi-conscious state. Wondering if there had been a problem in the delivery of the medication to take her under, she blinked her eyes but couldn't really move her limbs. The thought crossed her mind about the reliability of the clinic staff if the anesthesia dosage wasn't sufficient at the outset. You can't do surgery of the sort she was awaiting with the patient in a state of clear awareness, maybe even experiencing pain.

As much as she'd been reassured that the procedure was routine, it was still an implant, and she knew that if she were to have an improved quality of life, the stents were a necessity to increase her blood flow to her heart. For that she needed to be knocked out com - pletely. As she batted these things back and forth, the nurse noticed a spike in blood pressure and bent over the patient to check her condi - tion.

"Are you cold?"

She blinked her eyes and moved her mouth ever so slightly to express an affirmative answer to the nurse's question. Noticing every nuance, the nurse retrieved a warmed blanket and covered the patient.

"I'm going to get the doctor. You should be asleep by now." The nurse put her hand on the woman's shoulder and squeezed through the coverlet. "Don't worry, we'll take care of you and get you right back *to sleep. The doctors here are fantastic and you will be good as new in no time."*

A few minutes later the anesthesiologist came in and checked the patient's eyes and vitals, telling her they would just have to give her a little boost before the procedure.

She relaxed and thought about getting back to her new home where she'd settled in so naturally, even in a bustling new city with a new job. It was all looking very rosy and she was anxious to get her life kick-started, build fresh relationships, something she'd never real - ly had before. This was all part of the process.

Health, home, happiness…

Consciousness floated away.

CHAPTER 8

"Well, the leads have turned up nothing."

"All those new incidents I gave you?" Debra was incredulous after fielding the call from Roy. Something had to pop on almost a dozen names.

"Not those. I was given the quick shuffle out of the supervisor's office as soon as I brought up the fact there may be a pattern of missing professionals in the city." A tinge of moroseness entered his voice.

"I don't get it. Why would he turn a blind eye to a possibility of additional disappearances? Does it mess with the official case resolution statistics?"

"More or less. The files I have are proving to be more of a sticking point than expected. The people, at least two of the three, have packed up all their possessions and vacated their apartments, apparently in the dead of night. No one saw them leave and, basically, no one had gotten to know them in the first place."

"And this is news for New York? The place where residents have been known to go out of their way to cross the street in the opposite direction when someone's in dire straits? I guess there aren't that many Good Samaritans around to pick up the pieces that the pious ignore," Debra's disappointment in city dwellers was evident.

"You pegged it. The role of the pious being filled by federal law enforcement leaders rather than Levites."

"Good you know your scripture. Now put it into the further context that the Levites were the lawkeepers, Pharisees, i.e. the lawyers," clarified Debra.

"And the majority of FBI agents are lawyers. Cute analogy."

"When the shoe fits…" she chuckled. "Besides, you're something of an anomaly with degrees in history and criminal justice rather than carrying a bar card."

"Thank God for that. Being a member of the bar association is more like a good 'ol boys club than practicing a beneficial profession."

"Think 'union' and you've got it," said Debra.

"Hmmm. Now you've got me wondering if that could have something to do with my being on the outs with most of the other agents. I'm not in that particular union," he mused.

"Yes, but you are a member of the federal employees union. Face it, you're still the enemy."

They laughed even though he knew she was right on target.

"So, still at a dead-end and the boss isn't happy. Is that it?"

"In a nutshell. And now I'm on his s-list because I suggested we expand the investigation," he added.

"It isn't a matter of the workload, is it?"

"No. The reason I landed this in the first place was the fact that he saw these cases were going nowhere and I'm the expendable one, as in the screw-up nobody needs on their roster." Esteban took an audible breath. "It's an easy way to ease me out the door. I'm not exactly the epitome of a team player anymore."

"Too bad. Rock the boat and get yourself fired, or retired. Is that an option?"

"Could be, though if hasn't been offered… yet."

"So what can I do if your superior isn't interested in running down the other names we've uncovered? And the fact that there are no leads on the three you've got?"

"I'm still trying to work that out." He was mulling things over. "Do we follow-up on the new leads or let them drop by the wayside and just play the game?"

"You're already in the boss' sights and the stories they have me researching at work are less than captivating. This gave me the shot in the arm I could use," said Debra.

He let out a clipped laugh. "Funny you should say that," and he clammed up.

"Are you still there?" She asked after a few moments had passed in silence.

"I'm here," he paused again. "This might be just what the doctor ordered."

"What are you talking about now?"

"There was only one iffy factor that came up regarding two of the three missing persons cases."

After this pause Debra was getting antsy. "Okay, give. What is it?"

"I'm not certain it's even worth mentioning being more off the cuff than anything else."

"Well? I'm waiting."

"You get more impatient as time goes on, you know that?" he said half-joking to which she just huffed into the phone. "In two instances someone said the subject mentioned an upcoming doctor's appointment or procedure."

"Anything more than that?"

"No, and until you said "shot," which made me think of hypodermic, I'd pretty much written it off. But what if there is some weird connection through doctors or health problems, or…"

"A longshot, to be sure, but it's better than nothing to follow-up," she said with more enthusiasm, always looking for another angle to approach a problem, and this was a real quandary. Debra was hooked.

"My other question, then…" he hesitated a bit.

"What?" anticipating a tough query.

"Got any vacation time coming?"

BLOOD BARONS

CHAPTER 9

1985

The archeological team arrived at the small, singular and uninvit-ing hotel in Dogubeyazit, fatigued from the overland trip that had taken days since arriving in Ankara. This was one of many forays the leader had made into the far eastern region of Turkey, it always being a dangerous proposition to visit this province bordering Iran. Settling in for the night, the leader and his cohort, a videographer, stashed their equipment which included a molecular frequency generator and pulse-induction metal detector. They had come fully prepared to trace the remnants of Noah's Ark, a huge boat-shaped structure that lay embedded in the sediment of a mountainside in the Ararat district, just where Biblical tradition placed it, "in the mountains of Ararat."

The team leader had been captured by the playing out of the Genesis drama since first coming across a high-altitude photo, taken decades before, that clearly showed an elongated outline of such great size it was easily visible from thousands of feet above the earth. The picture had appeared in Life *magazine, where he'd initially seen it and been intrigued by the image that had inspired an expedition in 1960. The ensuing controversy had eventually fizzled until this man acted on that interest, sparked by that photo taken so long ago.*

On his first trip to the outlying region in 1977, in his hunt to locate the boat-shaped object he'd seen years before captured in a fighter pilot's photograph, he had been sidetracked by multiple unscheduled roadside stops... the car kept stalling. Deciding to investigate at those inadvertent stopovers, he had encountered local villagers who, after convincing them of his tourist status, became his guide to a desolate site. They first led him to a place where multiple stones of great size stood. They were over six feet in height and had large holes drilled in their cap. Anchor stones, thousands of years old... they could be noth-ing else. And they were carved with eight crosses each. A mystery to the man marveling at what was clearly recognizable from his studies as mariners' gear of antiquity. He logged the placement and pho - tographed and filmed the find.

Further on, his guides brought him to the place of an ancient homestead, the fieldstone fences radiating out from a farmhouse of such great age that the stones were buried in the earth from years of sedimentation. The picturesque setting held little fascination until they pointed out evident gravestones engraved with pictographs of a multi- decked boat floating upon a representation of an ocean wave, and departing from the boat were two large figures of a man and woman, followed by three smaller male figures and three, smaller yet, female figures. To this ark hunter, these monuments could be nothing other than the tomb markers of Noah and his family that had survived the flood.

Through prayer he knew he had been brought to the right place, somewhere nearby lay the giant ship that had ridden the crests of God's flood that scripture described as devastating the face of the earth. Historians and anthropologists who doubt Biblical testimony knew how many cultures worldwide had flood tales among their myth - ic cycles.

After that time, his return trips to investigate had led to the Turkish government officially recognizing the geographical anomaly as authentic, authorities acknowledging that, "it is, at any rate, a ship." The reasoning behind the conclusion that it was Noah's Ark was stat - ed simply as, "because there is no other explanation."

This was the place where, today, eight years following that first visit, he and his team had come to document the metal fittings in the boat-shaped structure. After scanning the perimeter of the snow-dust - ed site, the team revisited the ancient homestead he'd seen in 1977.

Excited to share the wonder of the discovery of so many years ago, he led them to the graves of the family whose tombstones depicted the great ark above the curling wave and the first multihued arc of light, the covenantal sign God gave man that had traversed the misty sky.

But they were gone.

1984

Upon a high plateau of windswept scrub, a stark mountain peak topped with everlasting snows formed a vast backdrop to the boulder-strewn fields of the pillaged farmstead.

The earth around the stone structure, that had crumbled over time into little more than a hovel, was torn and trampled. The walls of the little house had been tumbled and the stones scattered, not by time, but at the hands of greedy treasure hunters, though what fortune was to be found in that bleak spot was uncertain, even to the desecrators of the site.

A rag-tag team had been assembled by a median-level bureaucrat in Ankara whose palm had been greased with an amount that would provide a comfortable income for the rest of his life. It hadn't taken much to locate just the right official willing to turn a blind eye to a project so close to the heart of a feared multinational tycoon. Everyone had a price and in the corruption-riddled intermediate ech-elons of government, there was always someone with just enough influence to pave the way for unethical activities. Particularly when the agencies were promised enormous financial benefits in the form of opening a local office of an international foundation that awards mil-lions in grants each year.

The road had been opened for the odd collection of individuals comprising an excavation team, mostly of unlettered ditch diggers, to be led by a field archaeologist and a laboratory scientist.

The work was quick and dirty. "Go in, dig it up and get out," was the mantra given by the superior overseas and that's what they did, which grieved the heart of the archaeologist. He immediately recog-nized the incredible significance of the target site. The homestead had obviously withstood millennia of harsh weather and geological upheaval. It had hovered under the radar until an amateur archaeol-ogist had uncovered the precious find sitting in plain sight all these centuries. The Turkish government was close to taking unprecedented action of conceding the existence of artifacts that seem to support Biblical accounts, but the personal goals of a powerful money mogul *would not be overridden by a mere national administration, and he moved without hesitation.*

They violated the graves, retrieving what bones were buried there, most that had been petrified through the ages. The sheer magnitude of the site's consequence in the annals of time was viciously sundered, destroying the valuable tracing of historical evidence, never to be reconstructed or recovered. Then they threw down the archaic home and broke and scattered the headstones marking the tomb. The menial workers had no clue of what they destroyed but the archaeologist did. He would have to live with his conscience even as he provided meat for the discrediting of the man who had first located this trove of arti-facts that would now be lost to mankind forever.

They retreated with their ransacked treasure and set the stage for an honorable man's life work and indisputable character to be defamed, even by those he had called friends.

In the tycoon's eyes it was good work for a day's pay.

CHAPTER 10

"I still don't understand why this is necessary." The young woman was a little exasperated at all the back-and-forth between this agency and that organization's interference in an agreement that she'd been told was private. Accompanied by her husband, they had walked into the local Idaho offices of the Health and Welfare Services where their interview had been scheduled weeks ago, which was another issue that had ticked her off. This was being dragged out when a young woman's life was teetering in the balance. Not that any government office worker was beholden to a calendar other than their own. Lainie was usually laid-back in her attitude, especially when dealing with state and federal agencies. It was something you learned if you were ever going to get anything accomplished as a tribal member because the government was part and parcel to just about every transaction or negotiation. But even she had her limits.

For this she'd had to take a day off of work at the hospital, leaving the nurses on her shift short-handed, which grated on her as well. The initial phone calls had not gone well despite Lainie's attempt's to allay the social worker's general belligerence. Because she was afraid this could become an uncomfortable encounter, she'd opted to leave her son, who'd just turned three, with a friend and bring Cisco along thinking his presence might help mellow the interview. People prone to overbearing attitudes could often be cowed by the sheer size of another, it didn't matter that the formidable person in question was actually a teddy bear. Okay, a teddy bear well over six feet tall wearing a uniform. She preferred to stack the deck in her favor.

It had been a couple months since her aunt had called to ask if she'd be willing to get a blood test to check for suitability as a kidney donor for a distant relative. It had taken quite a bit of soul-searching, discussions with her husband and prayer before coming to the decision that it was the right thing to do, but they arrived at a conclusion quickly. Having two little ones now, the prospect of living with only one kidney was daunting, but she also knew that her cousin – she couldn't recall how many times removed – had been living on the brink of losing her life for years. It was a situation that Lainie hadn't even known about until the story had been picked up by a national news outlet a little over a year ago. Some friend of her Aunt Sol's had written the story when all hell was breaking loose in the Plains states with the widespread power outages. The roundabout connection had brought her into the loop when the Lysanders put out a call to anyone even remotely related to the family. They had been logged with the kidney registry and gone through hundreds of potential donors before locating a potential match, and Lainie was it.

The news had been one of joy and concern. She'd be helping Kara, now a young teenager, to enjoy a better quality of life, no longer being tied to a dialysis machine, but Lainie would be sacrificing a crucial part of her anatomy, one that would change her health status, a bit worrisome for a young mother and nurse.

The caregiver in her make-up won out, but for a couple months they'd been dealing with the unwelcome insertion of government oversight, and ultimately attitude, into the mix that should and could have been handled, with the proper medical policy, under independent review. Lainie had no idea how invasive DHHS had become in everyone's lives whether or not they received government assistance. She had been under the impression that unless someone signed up for Medicaid, Medicare or other government programs, the government hadn't any part in their care. She'd been wrong. Then again, she had known that Indian healthcare was a horse of different color, and if you're enrolled as a member of a tribe you couldn't get around its and, by extension, government's involvement.

With the implementation of the Affordable Care Act, which is basically an expansion of Medicaid for which much funding was directed from the American Recovery and Reinvestment Act, otherwise known as Stimulus, in 2009 before the healthcare bill was even passed, came new personal invasions. Lainie came to realize how much she'd been operating in the dark and she *worked* at the hospital, though nurses weren't privy to patients' financial information. What was so surprising about her lack of knowledge was that her own son's godfather was one of the foremost bloggers on the whole Schaalcare scheme, shining a light on the all-encompassing plan long before it was forced through Congress. She was learning the hard way about the changes coming because she hadn't taken the time to log on to ChangingWind.org. Her loss and, unfortunately, that of the country as a whole.

Time to meet the enemy. Lainie wondered where that thought came from. She never used to think that health and welfare was on the "other side." *Go figure.*

Cisco pulled open the oversized glass door to the foyer, past the security guard stationed in the corner, where they walked across to the reception desk, which was walled off by a newly installed bulletproof glass barrier. He raised his eyebrows querulously as he recognized the material.

"You'd think they were a bank," he whispered to Lainie.

"They are. This is what would rightly be called the other 'blood bank' because, among other duties, they dispense life-altering medical decisions. Who gets what procedures, payment for disabilities, hospital care, hospice or sickroom supplies."

"Can you call it 'sickroom' anymore? Isn't that politically incorrect?"

She laughed lightly. "As usual, you get right to the heart of things."

"Yeah, just don't let your heart get anywhere near a government agent who thinks someone could make better use of it than you," he said under his breath.

"Is that your view of Schaalcare's approach to the president's "shared prosperity" vision?"

He just shook his head as they now stood before the polycarbonate shielded receptionist.

Twenty minutes after their names were taken and were told to have a seat, Lainie was called for her appointment. A middle-aged woman in semi-casual clothing directed them through a locked door and down a hall to her office. Not much bigger than a cubicle, it was still a private space with just enough room for two metal chairs facing the desk behind which the social worker settled herself.

Before saying anything, the woman leafed through a manila folder that had been placed in front of her on the blotter. Lainie wondered at that, as to why there would be a file in the first place considering that the donor and recipient had been working through a private arrangement rather than the government directed waiting list, at least that's what Lainie had thought.

"Well, Ms. Rafael," the woman had decided to acknowledge one of the people sitting in front of her, though Cisco was hard to overlook without intent. Opening their conversation without bothering to identify herself she said, "it seems you've decided to be a donor in the Kara Lysander case."

"Good afternoon, Ms. Delmer." The only reason Lainie knew the woman's name was because she read the ID that hung around her neck on a lanyard. "I was unaware that Kara was listed as a case by the department. Frankly, I'm a little confused as to why I've been called in for this interview. Maybe you can tell me." She figured that she could be as cut-and-dry as the counselor, as her title was listed on the tag.

"All organ donors are asked to complete full evaluations before being accepted into the registry program," she began but Lainie interrupted her before she could go further.

"I understood that this was a privately arranged, direct donor done under the auspices of proper medical direction. Is there a reason why my name, and incidentally, my information, is being added to a national registry? I don't get it. I signed up as a good match for my cousin and that's who I'm donating to, no one else."

The woman looked at Lainie over the top of her cheaters perched low on her nose. "That's correct. This is a direct donor case and Kara Lysander will be receiving your kidney."

"So, why all the rigmarole and extra paperwork? We've already been thoroughly over the compatibility, completed all the tests, and had it not been for this delayed interview, Kara would already have had the surgery and been recuperating a month ago. Isn't time of the essence with these things?" Lainie assumed that Ms. Delmer knew she was an RN and not as unknowledgeable about human physiology as most donors.

"There are channels that must be navigated, I'm afraid, no matter how the procurement of a donor organ is arranged. So, if you don't mind we have a further list of information that's required before going forward with scheduling the surgery." She pushed a stapled sheaf of papers across the desk to Lainie who picked it up and started perusing the contents.

"I've already answered most of the questions in triplicate over a month ago." Flipping a page she saw that there was a financial questionnaire that got very personal and didn't seem relevant to the situation at hand.

"Why do you need a financial dossier and tax records? I'm not the one handling the expenses for the procedure."

"Policy. If you don't mind…" and she held out a pen for Lainie's use.

And so it went for the next hour.

⚜⚜⚜

After the so-called interview, which Lainie kept calling an interrogation, she phoned Kara's attorney in Billings, Montana to give her a rundown of the procedure. She called it that, too, when speaking with Yancy because it had been so invasive into their personal lives.

Yancy Collings had been Kara's advocate for a couple of years, pulling every string possible, first, to get a dialysis machine set-up at home and, second, to fight for her life when the EPA, of all federal agencies, interfered with the life-support system operation. The battle with government agencies and their illogical regulatory practices had been ongoing, centering around the denial of service due to policies instituted regarding the phasing out of an old power plant. It had been a real jump from east coast corporate law to defending the rights of underdogs, but Yancy was far more content earning less as an attorney with the Constitutional Legal Fund and serving clients like Kara.

Recently, there had been a number of interesting turns in the legal world that would influence her forward motion in Kara Lysander's circumstances. The fact that the EPA operates according to it's own self-styled rules and independent administrative 'court,' the brakes had been put on Yancy's forward motion regarding provision of adequate homecare. It had even put Kara in a life-threatening situation which widened into a further legal struggle with the agency. However, the United States Supreme Court ruling that came down in the Sackett versus EPA case in March blew the door wide open for redress of grievances by giving individuals the green light to haul federal agencies into court, an option which had been regularly denied by the agencies themselves. This was a game changer. Further, it created a path for challenging *any* federal agency that had previously given itself authority to deny or direct services according to internal regulatory policies. This included the newly implemented Affordable Care Act although most lawyers had yet to think in terms of applying the SCOTUS opinion in this capacity.

ACA had, among its 2,900+ pages, designation of the newly renamed IPAB (Independent Payment Advisory Board) to broach the Medicare expense problem through panel oversight of per capita cost reductions. It is what some politicians and experts that combed the legislation ominously referred to as "death panels." Now that the Supreme Court had also weighed in on the constitutionality of the act, not without a great amount of controversy, the "tax" was expected to be levied against all citizens that had not 'paid their due' by anteing up for either government vetted insurance or the likely sky-rocketed premiums for private underwriters. No wins for anyone, but at least the opportunity to bring action against the multiple bureaucracies, newly-created or sanctioned by the monstrous legislation, was available. What the Sackett ruling handed down was this: "The APA [Administrative Procedure Act] provides for the judicial review of "final agency action for which there is no other adequate remedy in a court." U.S.C. §704." And this was what Yancy was banking on to rectify the appalling treatment her client had received at the hands of the Environmental Protection Agency, Indian Healthcare and a variety of other administrative water carriers and their "final decision."

BLOOD BARONS

CHAPTER 11

Pulling her carry-on down the jet bridge, Debra wondered whether Roy would be able to meet her at the gate or if airport security measures were so strict that he'd catch up with her outside the baggage claim. Not one to travel light, even though she was just here for ten days, she wasn't looking forward to manhandling the luggage off the carousel. The one checked bag into which she managed to pack everything was oversized, and she'd paid handsomely for that luxury. The extra dollars were worth it to make sure she didn't have to purchase anything in the city. New York's reputation for exorbitant cost of goods traveled more miles than the plane she'd just left. She didn't come to spend money and despite the fact that she maintained a stylish wardrobe, shopping wasn't one of her preferred pastimes.

As she joined the weary passengers spilling from the gate, she was pleasantly surprised to see Roy's g-man suit-clad figure on the other side of the glass barrier. Hands stuffed in his pockets, he stood with his legs apart monitoring the area with his peripheral vision, ready for anything. Debra considered how difficult it must be to be prepared for the worst and look relaxed and distracted at the same time. Evidently it was harder than she thought because Esteban wasn't quite pulling it off. The corner of her mouth lifted with the thought of his supposed nonchalance that, if no one else did, she had no trouble seeing through the façade to recognize the vigilance of law enforcement.

Just about the time Debra saw Esteban, he spotted the slight, immaculately attired black woman descending the end of the ramp, gripping her carry-on with long, perfectly manicured fingers. She always managed to look fresh, though he recalled their first meeting where her silk blouse had been rumpled from a long drive and that frustration had charged up with a bulldog attitude. Debra had confronted him, ready to tangle, refusing to accept 'no' for an answer when her friend was in imminent danger. This was one female no one should cross when her fury has been kindled. In her case, he knew size *didn't* matter. He also knew that devotion of that level was what he wanted on his team.

Once Debra had made it through to the other side, she noticed that there weren't that many people enjoying a cheerful reception from friends and family.

"So how do I rate a personal escort when most of the other passengers are going it alone to baggage claim?"

He took the handle of her bag from her and bent down to give her a peck on the cheek. "Good to see you, too." He cracked a smile. "I have influence," and he flicked open his jacket to briefly uncover the badge clipped to his belt.

"I am duly impressed. I suppose you happen to know the way to where I can gather my luggage."

"You have more than this?" Roy was surprised because the carry-on was good-sized. It must have just made the measurement limitation. It was heavy, too.

"Just one bag." She didn't think it was essential to clarify how big it was, he'd find out soon enough.

⚜⚜⚜⚜

Driving back across the Queensboro Bridge in a non-descript, dull blue Mercury sedan that fairly screamed "federal agent," Esteban swept his right hand across the windshield, as if introducing a star… *and heeeere's…* "Check it out. You have finally made it to the Big Apple."

"That's right. Just what I hankered to see more than anything, another big city. The biggest American city, at that," said Debra dryly. It was hard to discern whether she was serious or mocking. He decided to ignore either intent.

"This place is different in so many ways from Denver or even L.A."

"I'll give you that," she agreed. "Didn't expect it to be similar to the west's style of sprawl, not that it doesn't have a certain charm, from a distance, like any city. I will say that the miles of concentrated concrete spikes shooting skyward is dramatic. But there's barely a sprig of green showing between the multitude of greys."

"Central Park has all the green you need, and this town does offer the amenities of having something to do every hour of the night or day, depending on your fancy."

"Sure, who needs sleep?" She turned to Roy, a flash of mischief in her eye. "Maybe that's where the victim's toddled off. They were sleepwalking due to lack of quality REM time? What do you, think? Good theory, hunh?"

"Alleged victims," he replied blandly.

"I forgot. They're just classified as 'missing' for now."

"Afraid that's the case."

"Right. People just fall through the cracks in the sidewalks into the city's underbelly, never to be seen or heard from again," said Debra.

"Yeah, I used to watch that TV show in the '80s, too. "Beauty and the Beast," or some such."

"I'll bet you tuned in for the romance between the girl and the big hairy guy," she smirked a little.

"Yup. Thought it'd be cool to do good under cover of night, disappear by day" he played along.

"I get it, that's why you became a g-man."

"Nope, already was." Changing the subject before they got too far into Manhattan. "You didn't tell me where you were going to stay on your 'vacation.' One of the swanky uptown hotels? Times Square?..."

"With Aunt Ell."

"You have an aunt from Kansas?" he asked, trying to catch her off-guard. No such luck.

"That was Auntie Em and, you may remember that this isn't my aunt, but Allie's."

Esteban tilted his head as if examining the inside of his skull, looking for a connection. "I do remember. She lit into me worse than my boss when it came to having placed her niece in danger. I don't suppose she has a dog named Toto, he could stand between us when we meet. I doubt she's still none too happy with me."

"Last I heard, you were forgiven. Allie's settled down… some, thanks to that little escapade. So, all's well that ends well."

"I certainly hope so, because I don't believe I'd want to encounter her when she's angry," he said.

"Chicken."

⚜⚜⚜

"I presume you have Ell's address," said Esteban by way of asking directions.

Debra opened her purse and dug out a raspberry colored post-it with address and phone number. She read off the information.

"That'd be upper east side. Not too shabby a neighborhood," he looked over at her small frame. "Good thing. Wouldn't want you wandering the mean streets of Hell's Kitchen or even the Village."

"As far as I could tell, just about any place can be hazardous to your health," observed Debra. "How many vicious crimes have been committed in places that we would normally consider *safe*? Look at that theatre massacre not far from my home this summer. If I'd been a Batman fan, I might have been seated alongside those people who were gunned down for no apparent reason."

"Thank goodness you have no penchant for superheroes."

"No, dated enough of them to know better. And none of them could stop someone determined to cause mayhem like that unholy fiend. For that, I call on God as the only superhero that counts." Thinking about the pain that coward had caused, she shivered despite the warm sun coming through the window as they headed up Third Avenue.

"You don't think men have much to do with apprehending felons?"

"Who steers the good guys in the first place? Look at it this way… what guide do we use to write the laws that we live by? There have always been those that argued for universal moral codes but in my thinking, even those stem from God. He wrote them and it would be kind of nice of we acknowledged His influence now and then."

"I hadn't realized this would lead to a sermon," said Esteban with a smile, "but I don't disagree."

"Good thing. I'm not big on helping antichrists." She peered at him out of the corner of her eye just to see his reaction to her choice of words, knowing they were over the top.

"Now, if that isn't a left cross, pardon the pun. I sure hope that I haven't careened so far off course to be chalked up to being on the Big Guy's enemies list."

She laughed lightly, "Not likely. You know what the right side of the Law is. That's why you sometimes manage to end up on the wrong side of your superiors."

They were silent for a bit while Debra craned her neck to look up at the skyline from street level. "Quite a different view from this angle. Not so much a fairy tale vision as looking down from the plane or the bridge."

"Daylight exposes the city's dirty secrets. Makes it easier to find the bad guys. Speaking of which, how are we going to get you on the team?"

"Which team is that? I thought I was on holiday," she feigned ignorance.

"I'm sure that's why you chose this particular city to while away your idle hours."

"You just got finished extolling the wonders of New York and how I can access them at any hour of the day. Was I not to take that under advisement in planning my free time?" He knew very well that she was playing around. She'd let him know that she was more a sun, surf and sand kind of girl when it came to travel.

He decided to ignore that and move on. "I thought I'd see if I can't wangle a way to get you in the door at the Bureau as civilian support."

"Pardon me for asking, but isn't that what landed you in the dog-house to begin with and why you're doing time in New York instead of directing the Denver field office?" asked Debra.

"It's not as bad as being banished to the Alaskan frontier. Generally speaking Wyoming is kind of considered exile and I was brought *out* from there."

"If I remember right, you were due for a promotion until you were sidelined to Cheyenne in a pinch." Not that she enjoyed bringing up the past but she hardly wanted to be the cause of him being ousted for the last time and losing his career, not to mention his pension.

"Depends on your point of view, then. They may have seen New York as a promotion even though I liked Denver. Either way, I'm here now and I could use you on the research team."

"Particularly since you don't really have one," she added. "Which is why I'm here in the vacation garden spot of the world."

"It is. If you visit Central Park."

"Fine, that'll be on my 'to do' list."

"So long as you're not thinking 'bucket list,'" Roy said with his own bite.

"Not in this life."

"No comment."

They sat in traffic for a couple of minutes before she brought it up one more time. "Any errant thoughts on how you're going to get me on the FBI dance card?"

"Not a clue."

⚜⚜⚜

Without any notice Esteban whipped the Mercury into a slot that Debra would have sworn was too small for the dreary blue tank. "We're here."

She was astonished by his skill in locating a spot until she noticed he was in a no parking zone. As she pointed to the sign he pointed to his badge, stuck a placard in the windshield and said, "Privileges of the duly-sworn law enforcement officer."

Raising her eyebrows, she quickly dropped them and figured it to be a gift and decided he had it covered. Parking was always at a premium in New York so she'd take it. He did.

Lifting the bags out of the back of the car, Debra grabbed the carry-on and Esteban pulled what he was calling the steamer trunk over to the stoop. She pressed the button on the intercom while he shouldered the huge duffel, pushing the door open for him as soon as the buzzer sounded.

"Don't tell me she's on the eighth floor of a walk-up," he said as he slung the bag through the door and into the foyer.

"Fourth and there is an elevator. I asked before I decided to pack that suitcase."

"You didn't give it enough consideration, this monstrosity could give King Kong a hernia." Being over six feet and in excellent physical condition, Esteban was well able to handle the bag but preferred to razz her about it.

Overlooking the remark, she stepped inside the lift and made to close the door on him if he wasn't more polite. He slipped in sideways, the bag catching the sliding door before it cleared the threshold. Esteban smiled in validation.

The elevator had seen a long service life and took its time pulling itself up the few stories. With a groan, it halted and the cascading doors slid open for their exit. Two doors away was Ell's apartment and the front door was ajar.

"Come on in!" called out a loud musical voice, one that could easily have carried to the back of an opera house, and would have had Ell found her niche in the theatre as she'd originally planned. Life follows other directions and she never complained or bemoaned the change in hers.

Esteban closed the door behind him, depositing the 'steamer trunk' as far out of the way as he could manage in the narrow hallway. They would need to be careful not to trip over the straps in passing. Ell emerged from her kitchen, full apron draped around her neck and tied loosely around her waist. She was still dressed from the office, smart-looking in slacks, tunic and chicly comfortable slingbacks. Her hair was a coppery shade of blond cut in a bob that was cropped at her nape. It bounced a little as she tromped into the hall to meet her guests. Ell wasn't big, about 5'6" and carrying an extra 25 pounds, but she always let people know she was coming with a solid heel connection to the floor. Esteban, always noticing habits, assumed it might be a practice developed from childhood so she wouldn't catch people unawares. He wasn't about to field any guesses why.

"Debra! It's so great to meet you!" Ell hugged her. "I have to thank you all over again for being there for Allie."

"All done and gone," said Debra, "but I miss her now that she's in Wyoming. Lunch breaks will never be the same."

"I know what you mean, though she is good about calling her old aunt fairly often, despite having a husband now."

"Allie's not about to let contacts go by the wayside. Not her style."

Ell fastened Esteban with a hard gaze as he stood behind Debra, towering the better part of a foot above her head. "You're something else, my boy," hands on her hips she looked fearsome in her protective role, addressing a man less than a decade her junior as she would an errant child. "I don't know how you managed it, but my niece has actually mellowed in the last year."

"Is that right?" he answered, not particularly intimidated.

Ell softened her stance, scowl turned to smile. "Not really. She's just raising hell in a different state. And learning to ride a horse."

"That's what happens when you get hitched to a cowboy," noted Esteban.

"Yup. Come on in," and she turned, beckoning them both with a big swing of her arm toward the living area. "Anyway, you're forgiven," Ell threw out offhandedly.

"It'd be terrific if the Bureau hierarchy were as easy to please," he said aloud.

"How's that?" asked Ell as she showed them to a living room suite, indicating they should take a seat on the couch while she disappeared again into the kitchen.

"Nada. Just an observation on the intolerant nature of government."

"Tell me about it. I'm sure you're talking about office policy but government attitude in general royally stinks," said Ell. "I'd rather deal with a roomful of two-headed rattlesnakes than any administrative employee in *any* government office, be it city, county, state or federal. They're all sitting on their brains."

"I'd hate to think Roy falls into that category as an employee of the Justice Department," said Debra.

"Best as I can see, he was guilty of that last time I talked to him." She poked her head out of the kitchen door. "Isn't that right, Roy."

"In some ways, I'd have to agree with you, Ma'am."

"Look, I know they train you to be polite to people, probably got it from your mother first, but you'd be better off not to call me 'ma'am.' It doesn't draw the expected response from me." She turned back to the kitchen, "Guess I'm not normal." Immediately popping her head back out, "No comment regarding that last comment, thank you."

The guests just laughed along with the raucous hoot that emanated from the kitchen, which was quickly followed by Ell carrying a tray of snacks. "Debra, would you mind grabbing the glasses and bottle of wine on the counter?"

"No trouble." And she hopped up to get the items.

"Hope you're off duty, Special Agent, and can join us," said Ell.

Glancing at his watch as if to ascertain what time it was, though he'd left work a little early to collect Debra at the airport. "Off the clock, as of now."

"Good. I have a feeling that relaxation isn't something you work into your schedule very often."

"Not lately," acceded Esteban. "Good deduction, Ell. Maybe you should consider a career at the FBI."

"I'm too insubordinate."

"Join the club," he said as he held open his hand, wordlessly offering to receive the corkscrew.

As he decanted the bottle and poured, Debra sat back and, accepting her glass, she decided to ask if Ell had been keeping up on the side of the Wyoming story that hadn't made the papers.

"If you're asking about that little girl and how she's been doing since she got home from the hospital, I can honestly say yes."

Esteban hadn't been privy to this story other than what little he'd learned from Debra after the case had been closed, the perpetrators charged and he reassigned to chair-warming in the Denver office. His whole case was hopelessly tied up in politics and he was effectively banished to New York, which may as well have been the North Pole.

He was interested in hearing about this part of the affair that had not involved his agency.

"I'm not up on all the details as things have taken a new direction after that Sackett versus EPA ruling came down from the Supreme Court. It places the EPA decision that shut down my friend's request internally, in a new ball court. Where before she was fighting for the right to take the EPA to court to challenge their decision, now she has precedent allowing her to file on her client's behalf."

"I don't mean to be slow on the uptake, but who is her client?" Esteban needed more information to get up to speed.

"Kara Lysander," Ell said. "She's just turned 14 now but at 12 she ended up in a coma, the circumstances of which could have been avoided had there been adequate power available after the huge out-ages out west - that part of the story you know well. Anyway, she's doing better now and they have finally found a kidney donor, some-thing that had looked to be impossible because of her rare blood type and other factors."

"That is fantastic news. The human interest stories we ran in the paper had generated a lot of attention," cut-in Debra. "That reminds me of a story I saw just a few days ago on a new kidney implant sci-entists have been developing. They called the processor inside a "bioreactor" and talked a little about nanotechnology as being so important to the breakthrough. Do you know anything about that?"

"Me? Are you kidding? I can get any of our company computers working no matter what those numbskulled lawyers manage to do to them but I know nothing about the minute messing around with atoms." Ell looked at Debra and Esteban, "Do you?"

"I couldn't even define the word, except that they build things, machines and whatnot that are so small that I can't conceive of it," said Roy.

"Being a little intrigued I looked up a few things and found that the construction, I guess you call it that, is on such a microscopic level that they are working with molecules." Tapping the side of her head she continued, "One article said that the work is so small the lines between mechanical and biological get blurred. I can't comprehend that but that's how they're engineering this implant and other medical breakthroughs." She shook her head to clear the cobwebs. "Sorry about the sidetrack."

"No problem here." Ell returned to her narrative. "Anyway, they now have a donor and if they can get through all the red tape, they should be able to get her on the road to recovery. I've been told that the longer a patient is on dialysis the less likely it is for success, so we're all praying for that little girl. And for forging ahead to get the agencies that have been dragging their feet to ante up before it's too late."

BLOOD BARONS

CHAPTER 12

The next afternoon, Esteban met Debra on the street in front of Ell's apartment to avoid finding parking for the fed-mobile. He leaned over and pulled the door handle, shoving it open. "Pardon my lack of chivalry in not getting out to do the valet thing properly."

"That's fine. Parking is at such a premium, I'll bet even you could get a ticket this time of day," she said as she pulled the seatbelt across herself and buckled up.

"It is possible if I'm not responding to an emergency. We're not immune from the meter maids, of which I have it on good authority that they eat their young." He pulled away from the curb, "Hope you slept well."

"Good thing you didn't leave me with that thought before bed, because my answer would be different. In fact, I did sleep well, undisturbed and restful. First time for everything."

"You have insomnia?"

"Only when I don't have the comfort of my own bed. I'm really a homebody," she explained.

"I suppose I should apologize for pulling you all the way back east for what may be a colossal waste of time."

"Somehow, I doubt it. You have a good instinct for sorting out the facts, and, like you, I have a feeling that this case is more than it appears to be." Debra settled into the seat. "Besides I got a little sight-seeing in, wandered the streets some to get a feel for the neighborhood. So, where're we going, *kemosabe*?

"Expect that's as good a moniker as any since we may be the lone rangers in this episode." He checked the other lanes, which everyone ignored anyway, the traffic haphazardly staggered across the arterial, before moving over. "We're going to see how far I get with Bestner."

"I won't hold my breath."

"Good, I'd rather not have to resuscitate you."

"You must know your superior pretty well if that's the expectation," said Debra. "So, why are we bothering with him? To confirm his suspicions that you're a rebel?"

"Maybe because I want to know whether he really wants to get to the bottom of this or would rather file it away, unresolved if need be."

"You mean sweep it under the rug, which is where, if I get the vibes right, he'd rather see you... out of sight if you have to be underfoot."

As they drove down Broadway, Debra examined the buildings in downtown Manhattan. Los Angeles was nothing in comparison, the canyons of skyscrapers giving this Western girl a slight case of claustrophobia, but it was undeniably impressive. Traffic was nowhere near as bad as she'd expected and they arrived in the Federal Plaza parking garage within a half-hour, good timing by New York standards she assumed, though she was hopelessly turned around by the time he put the car in 'park.' West coast dwellers often would find themselves thinking "ocean = west" and get themselves turned backward when they visited the eastern seaboard. Having that tendency, Debra had to concentrate to keep her directions straight but driving in subterranean circles didn't help much.

They took the elevator to the 23rd floor and even with a visitor ID and having been thoroughly checked for weaponry of all kinds, Debra felt anything but safe. Probably because she was so unused to the security measures, it had the adverse effect of making her think about all the ways someone could try to take down the New York field office. This wasn't so far distant from Ground Zero where the new monument to all those lost at the World Trade Center was just opening, more than 10 years later. She still wondered what the delay had been, but all she had to do was examine the politics spurring every possible interested party. Being black (the term 'African-American' sort of grated on her, disliking the PC tendency to hyphenation), Debra received more than her fair share of outrageous political spiels from 'brothers,' or what she referred to as minority wannabes. They were the most apt to drive her nuts, the people who, for some reason, couldn't find pride in their own European roots and felt a need to don someone else's ethnic identity. She wondered at people's lack of dignity in dishonoring their own heritage, as if it didn't have the validity of someone else's, especially those of color. *Folks just need to get a grip that this is one nation, of one people, no matter what they look like or where they came from... under God.* She'd stick by that no matter how much her friends, family and some acquaintances liked to malign her conservative views. Hate didn't arise from accepting that they were all Americans, except those who weren't and would do all they could to bring the United States to its knees, and that included terrorists and fanatics of all stripes, like the ones that flew those jets into the Twin Towers on 9/11.

Looking around at the glassed in cubicles and the bustle of agents, she thought gratefully, *this is where they hunt down and catch those bums.* She may have felt like a fish out of water, but Roy and his cohorts were the home team, and she was glad for it.

"Come on this way, Debra," Esteban gently took her elbow and guided her down a hall. "Time to test the waters."

"Whatever you say. Let's go." She pulled back her shoulders and straightened her jacket hoping to make a good impression.

"You're not going to make yourself any taller," he said in a low tone.

"That's what these spike heels are for, and for use as an impromptu weapon. So don't get on my bad side. Things could get ugly."

He laughed, halting mid-chuckle as soon as he reached the door of Assistant Special Agent-in-Charge, Harry Bestner. "You ready?"

"As I'll ever be." Knocking, Esteban opened the door.

❦❦❦

"Should I say it?"

"Go for it," said Esteban, knowing what was coming.

"That went well." He didn't have to strain to hear the irony in Debra's voice.

"At least we gave it a shot," he noted, a little discouraged but not unexpectedly so.

"Come on, you knew it couldn't possibly go any other way. All he was thinking, and you could practically hear the gears in his head, was "here we go again." Bestner certainly isn't your friend, or even slightly in your corner." She sighed. "I'm really sorry to say it, but you've been here before."

They were headed out of the garage and back onto the city streets, pulling into traffic heading uptown.

"It's still hard to understand when we're so short-handed and you're a proven commodity, that he'd be so unwilling to make use of credible consultancy. It's not like it's unheard of and you haven't already been thoroughly vetted."

"That's not the issue. You are. I think he sees you as a threat." Debra pointed out, "Even though you skirted the rules a little, you plainly are capable and get results, which is the bottom line." She looked over at him. "Do you know his history with the Bureau? Is he a producer or someone marking time?"

"Now, he's marking time to retirement, though he was a real cowboy in his day. Someone to emulate."

"Someone like you." She sat back, thoughts running a mile a minute. "You know, you may remind him a little too much of himself and perhaps he regrets that he became such a company man. People do hanker for the old days sometimes and they don't especially like to be reminded that they left their integrity along the way to become paper-pushing empty suits."

"You're being a little harsh in your assessment, but it's possible you've hit close to home."

"So, now what? I'm here with all this playtime and no game on," said Debra.

"Let's take Ell to dinner," he perked up. "I'll bet she could give us a new perspective."

⚜⚜⚜

Always a problem solver, Ell had an answer for everything. To begin with she suggested that they go down to the corner Irish pub and sports bar, O'Roarke's. There were no local teams playing so the place was fairly quiet.

"Don't come here often, but they serve a pretty mean burger, reasonably priced, too." Ell led the way through the entry while Esteban held the door for the ladies. "It's not so loud in the back if there isn't a big game being broadcast."

"What constitutes a big game?" Debra asked.

"Any sport that New York has a team – hockey, basketball, baseball, football, curling," cut-in Esteban.

"No, they can't possibly have a curling team," Debra was unconvinced.

"Actually there are quite a few curling enthusiasts and clubs, though I really don't follow it myself," he said.

"I figured you for a bocce player," said Ell off-handedly. "I'll stick to football. At least I understand it." She pointed across the room. "Let's sit over there. Not so much hullabaloo."

They settled into a booth and ordered. It was fairly low key for a sports pub. Just enough noise to cover their own conversation, not that anyone would really be interested enough to eavesdrop.

After their plates arrived and they were enjoying the fare, Ell got down to brass tacks. "So tell me what's doing with you two. You're thicker than a cabal of Albanian bookies."

"Balkan numbers rackets aside," said Esteban, "we're seeing how we can work an end-game around standard procedure."

"That seems to be your specialty," said Ell between bites. "Tell me."

"I brought Debra out here as an outside consultant to do some in-depth research," he took a drink from his glass. "I got shut-down by the boss."

"That's too bad. Don't you have researchers in your office?"

"We do. However, my superior hasn't deemed this case to be worthy of dedicating any hours, and my skills are limited, so I called Debra for help."

"Not for the first time, if I remember correctly," said Ell.

"No, this isn't the first instance, nor did my boss consider my decisions to be, uh, kosher last time around." Esteban was restrained in alluding to the past. "I was hoping that you might have a suggestion of a place where we can get Debra unrestricted internet access with excellent firewalls and online security. There were limitations at her place of work and I preferred to have immediate capacity to interface, which means having her close by while she does the research." He took a mouthful and chewed. "Any thoughts?"

Ell examined the two people sitting opposite her. She was a shrewd judge of character and despite knowing some of the details of the previous incident, she trusted this man and knew very well how much her niece relied on her friend Debra. In fact, Ell was well aware of the information breakthroughs Debra had made that directed Esteban to apprehend the offenders before they had created more havoc.

"Okay, let me think."

CHAPTER 13

The first day "on the job" and Ell is merrily introducing the new office assistant. A few of the workers were interested in meeting her, a professionally dressed woman with a pleasant but perfunctory greeting. In general, most were too distracted or, when it came to the lawyers, self-absorbed to be bothered with Ell's temp/intern or consultant that she'd occasionally install in the IT department. This was a multinational law firm with tentacles in New York, London, Hamburg, Singapore, Beijing and Bahrain, all designed to serve the international corporate and financial market. It had been expanding until the latest recession that had shaken the global economy, creating cutbacks even in her office. So far, Ell had been immune to the reassignment of personnel from office to office as she was the lead trainer for all the software. She spent more of her time getting attorneys out of computer jams, usually self-inflicted since they were too busy to learn the ropes and relied on the paralegals for most of the data input. Because of the sensitive nature of the work the firm handled, they employed the most sophisticated protection available and Ell was the one to keep it up and running. She had been a trusted member of the company for more than a dozen years so when she brought in an information expert for consulting, or an intern to be trained for transfer, it was just another cog in the well-oiled machine and most paid little attention.

This was Ell's solution to Esteban's dilemma. Debra was ushered in as a temporary consultant. She'd have some in-house duties and Ell would have to actually put her on the payroll as an independent contractor for a few days, but she'd have access to research engines and capabilities that were not available at the average place of business. The electronic security here was topnotch, as impenetrable as they could get, though nothing was perfect, and would allow Debra the ability to get in and out of other data bases without leaving footprints, if that became necessary. Lawyers hadn't earned such a shady reputation for no reason, and, if nothing else, they knew how to cover their tracks. Both Esteban and Debra were hoping that wouldn't be necessary.

Getting settled in wasn't hard. First off, Debra was given some trouble-shooting that anyone with good computer skills could handle to make certain that everything went smoothly. Piece of cake for the temp. She even managed to track down a problem that had been a bane to Ell, not having adequate time to handle all the partner's needs over the last couple of days. Debra was an immediate asset and every penny she'd be paid, which Debra assigned to a women's ministry, was considered to be well-spent if she didn't get anything else accomplished during her short tenure.

She was in like Flynn.

Next up was to track down as much information as she could find about the three official missing persons cases of Esteban's: Lorna Truesdale, a 38 year-old woman from Nampa, Idaho; Elspeth Grigg, 42 from Escondido, California and Harmon Crites, a 45 year-old man from Lexington, Kentucky.

What she did know was that all had relocated to the city within a matter of weeks or months. They had no family to speak of, or that could be easily found and they were practically friendless, having no history of traceable relationships back home or in their new residences or jobs. Loners with virtually no history and all were gone, according to the not-so-interested parties that had reported them missing.

She was able to duplicate the information Esteban had: birth records, marriages – none, thus no dissolutions either, schooling, colleges, occupation training, military – also none, past domiciles, some work history. She even unearthed some past tax records, which Roy hadn't accessed, though it was done through past employers, the few she could find.

With the limited information she was able to compile on these three, Debra delved into the dozen similar cases of New Yorkers that she'd come across on her earlier internet hunt. While she was going through the files she'd brought with her on a thumb drive, part of her mind drifted, remembering another ordeal that happened years ago.

Dina was an exotic beauty. At 17 she was on the cheerleading squad at Compton High, exuding athleticism and poise. But that was just an amusing distraction. A track star, she had secured a scholar-ship to USC where she planned to develop her writing skills, becoming a journalist with a minor in history. Dina was one smart girl. She knew the only way to inform the public about the present was to understand the past that got you there, and she was appalled at the ignorance rampant among her high school chums, and even the faculty, who were supposed to be well-versed in academic studies. Devouring books of all kinds, she was most drawn to biographies of pioneering Americans. Eating up their stories of adversity and triumph over personal and social hardship, she wanted to live that American dream.

Her parents were good workers, struggling to make ends meet. Her dad, never having fully left the neighborhood habits of hard drinking that he grew up with, was still there for the family in need, put bread on the table and loved his kids. Her mom worked part-time in a back office for minimum wage in order to outfit the sons and daughter with uniforms and instruments for extra-curricular activities. They never lacked for much because the work ethic was ingrained in all of them, so much so that Dina was determined to do her part to reach kids from her community with that same ethic her parents had instilled in her.

Her senior year was unfolding with promise and Dina had been enjoying every aspect of it. She was doing well in her classes and having a great time with her friends while preparing to move on to college the next year.

One afternoon, after cheer practice, she didn't come home. Her mother was frantic, dad came home early from his swing shift job to comfort her, and the boys went nuts tearing apart the neighborhood looking for their sister.

They never found Debra's cousin who was only five years her junior. She was at her aunt's house as often as she could during that dreadful fall. Christmas was disastrous and her uncle got so drunk on New Years in despair over the disappearance of his beloved little girl that he walked out in front of high-speed traffic. No one ever knew if it was intentional or not, though most assumed it had been purposeful, he'd needed the booze for courage. As much as she was dying inside for the loss of her granddaughter, his mom called it cowardice.

The funeral for Dina's father was one of the worst days of Debra's life. She felt absolutely helpless, worthless to her aunt who was liter-ally held up by one son at each arm. No closure ever came for her fam-ily, or for her.

With the blink of an eye the whole drama flew by and Debra reliv-ed the whole painful scenario in a flash. Not having dissected it before, the thought now occurred to her as to why she had been so distraught at Allie's disappearance and probably why she was taking such a per-sonal interest in Roy's cases. She couldn't bear to see others go through the same anguish. Although these individuals appeared to have no one, she wasn't convinced that anyone could be that solitary. It only fired her up to dig deeper.

⚜⚜⚜⚜

Debra decided to widen the search. If there were this many people who had melted into the woodwork in New York, where else might similar circumstances have arisen? She decided to go directly to local police agencies first, branching out to major metro areas thinking that if something strange was going on it's most likely to occur amongst a large population base rather than smaller towns where everybody knows everybody's business. She'd call Roy after her cursory survey of law enforcement. It appeared that the Feds might be called in if cases seemed to involve the possibility of interstate interest, drugs or kidnapping. Debra would have to check with him on that as she real-ly didn't know what criteria the Bureau used for acting on missing per-sons reports.

What she'd found is that, although most metro law enforcement use FBI training manuals for department development like missing persons protocol and they were encouraged to upload files to the NCIC (National Crime Information Center) run by the Bureau, some still kept local files for a period of time before uploading to the central databank.

Debra began going through news stories about missing persons who seemed to be lacking a personal history. This was a time-consuming proposition but one that made most sense considering her news connection and familiarity with hunting headlines. It took awhile but she gleaned as many as sixty reports across country that needed to be narrowed down. Even at that, she knew the real number was likely in the thousands. She started going through the factors that they'd punched in earlier, trying to crosscheck possible victims. She went back over occupations – none were really connected; economic status – too diverse, but all earned a decent wage; all had some kind of career track, they weren't day laborers; no political, religious, racial or ethnic patterns; nor was there a relationship regarding hometowns as in size, rural versus urban, etc. Maybe they used the same national moving companies. Nothing.

Debra was scouring her brain for something, anything to connect the people she'd come across thus far. Then she remembered. Roy had mentioned that in two instances acquaintances of the missing people had said something about health issues. It wasn't much to go on, but something was better than nothing.

Let's check healthcare plans. Medical histories, here I come.

Since the inception of the internet, there had been more and more of a move toward taking medical records online. There are still some holdouts as not all doctors are comfortable with private information being accessible to anyone with a password, or who could hack one, but the majority of offices had gone electronic which made it all that much easier for her. Thank goodness for the 'cloud.'

BLOOD BARONS

CHAPTER 14

It was a warm one for a late spring day and the city could be uncomfortable for anyone sensitive to the heat, which included Ell. She avoided outdoor activities if the temperature was over 70°, preferring air-conditioned comfort. When Esteban came by to collect Debra after work, Ell accepted the ride back home but declined to join them for a stroll through Central Park. With the heat index hovering at 85° to 90° she proclaimed it to be "sweltering" and opted for an evening at home.

Finding a parking spot was a chore, but Esteban managed it. The two of them walked up past the Metropolitan Museum of Art passing any number of dog walkers that were practically ensnared by the leashes swirling around their ankles, the mutts coming in all shapes and sizes. They kept their distance from the little snarlers, which were untrained and more than ready to pounce.

"It's been my experience that you have to watch the puny dogs," said Debra. "Cute as they might be, more than likely the owners haven't bothered to do more than house train them, if that." As she finished her sentence, they strolled past a young woman with six canines attached to her like a maypole and the smallest one tried to go for Esteban. "See what I mean? Ankle-biters, every one."

"Have you ever actually been bitten by one?"

"Yes, and I was constrained from hauling off and kicking it only because I was in a so-called friend's house and it was her lousy dog."

"I take it you're not on speaking terms?" chuckled Esteban.

"If you can't control your mongrel and then not even bother to apologize to your guest for it biting them," replied Debra, "then I would hardly call them a friend."

They walked and went into the park, finding themselves about to turn the wrong way on a running track that circumnavigated the reservoir. "This has got to be the first time I've ever come across a track with a clockwise rule," said Debra.

"I never have either," agreed Esteban. "This city has rules that I'd never consider necessary."

"Remember you're talking about a town whose mayor has taken it upon himself to limit everything from salt intake to what size soda pop you can purchase. Frankly, I'm appalled that the people put up with it. I'd be campaigning to throw the bum out and I don't usually get involved in politics beyond voting."

He lifted his brow in skepticism, having heard enough of her staunch opinions over the past year they'd known each other.

They continued along their way and were pleasantly serenaded by a violin virtuoso who'd been reduced to playing for change under the transverse bridge. And as they passed a bronze sculpture of a mounted monarch with crossed swords above his head, they closed in to read the plaque: King Wladislaw Jagiello, "King of Poland, Grand Duke of Lithuania, 1386 – 1434, Founder of a Free Union of the Peoples of East Central Europe, Victor Over the Teutonic Aggressors at Grunwald, July 15, 1410."

"Have you any idea what a monument to a medieval Polish king has to do with New York?" inquired Debra. "An expression of Polish community pride, maybe."

"Let's look it up." Roy pulled out his smart phone and punched in the king's name on the search engine and, voilá, there was the explanation. "The bronze was created for the 1939 New York World's Fair's Polish pavilion and is a replica of a Warsaw statue that the Nazis melted down to make bullets after they took the city. You were on the right track as it was a matter of national pride."

"Fancy that."

They moved through the park past the Turtle Pond through some woodsy areas that were all fenced off, Debra and Roy both commenting on the fact that all the city folk were allowed to do was look at the woods. Both being from the west, they were unused to the restrictions at every turn, pretty as it was.

After noting a sign warning people away from the wildlife, Debra said, "Probably afraid the city-dwellers will try to feed the rabid raccoons. Because then they'd have to sue the city."

"Signs and more signs in order to have plausible deniability. It is about the litigious nature of our modern society," observed Esteban.

"Ah, how we learn to slough off responsibility onto someone else's back."

"The municipality would call it 'expedience,'" he said.

From there they stopped to sit on a bench to discuss what Debra had come across on her first, and hopefully, productive day 'on the job' since he'd been called to assist on another case, his own being relegated to less than urgent. The lack of leads had caused his ASAC to temporarily reassign him assuming that if they're not located in the first 24-36 hours, there's little chance of finding them alive.

Debra filled him in on her efforts to pin down some parallels in the medical histories. So far, no go. Although she'd located the basic complaints of the three and even their diagnoses, she hadn't yet found anything to connect them. All they had in common was that they had developed some kind of health problem. She did tell him that she was widening her search and had located dozens of other locally reported cases around the country that had some comparable characteristics, but not enough to go on yet. Still stumped, she wasn't ready to throw in the towel. She'd pick up the web investigation on the morrow.

As they watched the people on their way through the green space, whether meandering or moving with a mission, Debra had been noticing the photographers, one after another, stopping and setting up their equipment. Everywhere she and Esteban had wandered there was the ubiquitous person with a camera and every kind of high-tech gear, from tripods to telephoto lenses shooting subjects sometimes only 20 feet away.

"Does everyone need to take thousands of pictures?" asked Debra. "You'd think it'd be easier to download photos from the internet rather than haul all that equipment around."

"Who do you think posts all those photos?" Esteban paused for a moment. "These are the guys who trademark the images and charge royalties that people pay to download their works of art for a fee."

"Only goes to prove nothing in life is free." And she pointed her phone to capture a shot of the rolling greensward upon which everyone else had focused their pricey cameras. Pocketing it, she gave Roy an impish grin.

CHAPTER 15

The morning had been spent in attempting to zero in on anything that might come close to a common denominator among the growing number of assumed to be missing persons, not only in New York but around the country. For many she had been able to target medical records and X-off things like drug or alcohol abuse if she didn't find them to be a reported factor. But then, the major criteria she'd set-up for these apparent victims was that no one really knew them, so no one had any idea other than an impression as to whether they drank or shot-up on a regular basis, if at all.

What kind of search criteria is that, when you think about it? That no one knows anything about the people in question. They're on the list because no one knows anything about them. Aye-aye-aye. Who's idea was this? It just qualifies them as one big, super-sized question mark.

That afternoon, Debra decided it was time to get away from the fruitless merry-go-round and tour one of the city sections where two of the people she was trying to track down happened to live within a five-block radius. Giving Ell the hi-sign after e-mailing her intention to take a break, Debra consulted a map she'd downloaded and caught the subway for the first time.

She determined that this was not her favorite thing after figuring her way through ticket purchase, descending the escalator and waiting beside the tracks in the well-lit tunnel for the train to arrive. To her way of thinking, it didn't matter how much candlepower you threw down these subterranean passageways, they could never be wide enough or bright enough for her. They were still dark tunnels and she was claustrophobic enough to find it uncomfortable.

By the time she emerged into the sunshine she was ready to walk for a while and breathe in the outside, unfiltered air. It wasn't hard to locate the first of the apartment houses. The entry was on a side street in a nicely kept block with colorful spring blooms abutting the stone steps that she climbed up to the stoop. Finding the button for the manager by the door, she depressed it. Instead of hearing a buzz indicating that she could enter, the door was opened by an older woman, outfitted in designer active wear that was a little faded but neat and still relatively stylish. Her hair was short, grey and fashionably spiky. She gave Debra the once-over, noting her own tasteful clothes and coiffure. She added a smile, deciding that Debra wasn't a solicitor and asked what she could do for her.

"Thank you, Ms.," Debra glanced at the name on the button again, "Prentiss, is it?"

"Yes, I'm Mrs. Prentiss. And you are?"

"Oh, yes. My name is Debra Chorister and I was interested in seeing if Ann Garner is home. I don't see her name on the list by the door but this is the address that I was given."

"Ann moved out less than a week ago," replied Mrs. Prentiss.

"I didn't know that," Debra was genuinely surprised. "Do you happen to have a forwarding address? It's very important that I speak with her."

"No, I'm afraid I don't. In fact, I don't actually know when she moved out, just that I tried her door one day to look in on her, she'd not been feeling the best, and everything was gone," explained the manager.

"That's part of the reason I'm here, is to see how she's doing. I knew she wasn't feeling really well, but she hadn't said why she was ill. Did she tell you what was going on?"

"It's not so much that she was sick, just her knee had been giving her a lot of trouble. She was preparing to have a knee replacement, which was really quite miraculous because until recently they'd been telling people that they have to wait until they were older for that kind of reconstructive work. I guess because there's a limit to how long the implant will last and they don't want to do the work twice." Mrs. Prentiss was getting into the swing of the story. She liked to gossip if the opportunity arose.

"I'll bet sports professionals never get the kind of runaround average citizens do," Debra played into the drama. "Tear up your knee or your shoulder and you're taken care of immediately. So under the circumstances, that is wonderful news that she was getting in for surgery right way."

"You bet. As it was, the poor girl was suffering, but that was the last I heard. You can see for yourself, the place was cleared out, and I had no idea she was gone."

Debra followed Mrs. Prentiss through the door, deciding there could be no harm, she hadn't misrepresented herself as anything, let alone law enforcement. She assumed that she looked like some kind of trustworthy acquaintance who'd come to check on Ann's wellbeing. "So you think her family came and helped her move?"

"I would except, from what I could gather, Ann didn't have any family and not in the city, at any rate. She'd just moved here from Des Moines for a great job in computers and the knee surgery was part of the package," filled in Mrs. Prentiss as she opened the door of the empty apartment.

"Do you have any idea where she went? I do need to get in touch with her."

Mrs. Prentiss shook her head. "I'm afraid not. She must have gone in for the operation and for some reason, had someone come and get her stuff, deciding not to return. But you'd think she'd give some kind of notice," she added a little petulantly.

"Perhaps there was a complication and she couldn't get in touch with you."

"I hope not but then you'd think the clinic, or someone might have called me."

"Do you know what clinic she was going to?" Debra was hopeful maybe she'd hit a lucky streak.

"Not exactly," the older woman tilted her head and tapped her temple, mentally reconstructing the conversation. "I believe she mentioned something like the Midtown or Midcity Orthopedic Partners… something like that. No place I'd ever heard of. Wait, I think 'Scarsdale' was somewhere in the name. Scarsdale-Midtown or some such." She shook her head. "Or I might not even be close. Sorry, I'm not much help."

"No, no, Mrs. Prentiss, you've been a great deal of help," said Debra, smiling. "Every little bit will help me reach Ann, so thank you for your time."

With that, Debra turned and trotted down the steps and headed toward the other apartment only to find no one at home and no way to talk to anyone regarding that tenant. As she was leaving the building she saw an old man with a walker coming out of a street level apartment next door to the building that she was leaving. Knowing that older people can be very observant, oft times out of pure boredom, she decided to give it a shot.

Meeting the elderly gentleman as he slowly moved up the street, she asked if he happened to know the tenant she was looking for in the neighboring building.

"Not really, I've seen him and spoken to him once or twice. He wasn't a real talkative fellow."

"Oh," Debra paused briefly, "I've been trying to catch up with him for a while." She held out her hand, "I'm Debra Chorister... and you are?"

"Abe Ulitsch, with a 'u'," he said, emphasizing the vowel.

"Nice to meet you Mr. Ulitsch,' she said as they completed the handshake. "Do you happen to recall what you did speak about?"

"Actually, it was a little hard to have a conversation with him because he had a hearing aid that didn't work real well," he said. "I did gather that he was going to have one of those new-fangled implants put into his ear, one of those that you can't see and are supposedly miles ahead of the old-fashioned aids. I'm lucky... still got my ears," he added with a wink.

"How fascinating! I've heard advertisements about those. Did he happen to mention his doctor's name or where he was going to get the implant installed?"

Old Abe's eyes took on new hint of suspicion. "Are you from the IRS or something?"

Debra laughed. "Oh no, I'm just trying to find him and connect him up with an estranged family member. The both of them are pretty much alone in the world and his distant cousin has been looking for him for a long time."

"That's good. He seemed a lonely kind of guy but looking forward to being able to hear his music again. Seems he was a musician, and a good one from what he said."

"That sounds just like him," encouraged Debra. "So, did he happen to mention anything about his doctor or clinic?"

"Not so's I can remember." He thought a little more. "That's right, his appointment was out of town, someplace on the Hudson I think."

"Not Scarsdale, is it?"

"You're not from around here, are you?"

"No, I've come from out west to find him."

"Scarsdale isn't on the river. I think he might have said Nyack. Yes, a clinic in Nyack."

"Well, Mr. Ulitsch, you've been tremendously helpful. With luck we'll be able to find him and get him back in touch with his family. No one wants to be alone in this world," said Debra as she shook his hand again.

"No, no we don't. I thank the good Lord every day for my daughter and son-in-law. Godspeed, dear lady."

"And God bless you, Mr. Ulitsch." She turned and walked back to the subway.

With this much information, Debra bubbled with anticipation. It wasn't much but it was an improvement over the crumbs she'd gathered before making this little foray. She couldn't wait to get back online to corroborate her finds. Even though the medical problems had been different, the clinics may have something in common. That is if she can figure out which clinics they are or if they actually exist. Thinking that Roy will be impressed with her deductive skills, she began to wonder how much of the information she garnered was really valuable. Shrugging it off, she thought any tidbit must be useful. She now had far more admiration for detectives and investigators on the street, having to make something out of virtually nothing.

Debra and Roy were now a little further along than they'd been this morning… she hoped.

BLOOD BARONS

CHAPTER 16

Sterile walls, sterile fixtures and a sterile atmosphere. Masks, scrubs and gloves are the uniform in this laboratory and everything must be sanitized. He is pursuing groundbreaking research within this disinfected room and nothing can be allowed to compromise the irre - placeable specimen that has been in storage for decades, waiting for science to catch up with the benefactor's expectation.

The scientist swathed in hospital green has been developing this project for much of his professional life, moving at a snail's pace from the conceptual to the functional. He has been over and over the ana - lytical chemistry, studying and contemplating the forthcoming process until the time that facilities and instruments would permit him to move forward. Now is that time.

Technology enabling researchers to dissect the secrets of the DNA double helix has only come into its own in the past 20 years. Science fiction and science fact have overlapped for centuries. The most recent example being the commonplace, erroneous assumption that genetic testing was instantaneous magic long before months of testing had been whittled down to weeks, the immediacy that television proliferat - ed still an illusion. The human genome project took 13 years for the majority of DNA to be mapped and there is yet ongoing research to fine-tune the designation of genetic properties. In this day and age, enough progress has been charted that the project work in this private laboratory is finally moving ahead at an accelerated pace.

While science was catching up with theory, the host specimen has been stored in a specialized facility, kept in an ultra-hygienic, mois - ture-free environment with a highly sophisticated monitoring system operating 24-7 to be certain nothing contaminated or compromised its integrity. After years of consulting, training, and doing theoretical research on the cellular level and fabricating instruments to handle the final stages of the project, the scientist is viewing the specimen through a special lens suited to examine subjects on a molecular scale.

Isolating the cells that had somehow evaded petrification within the host bone has taken years of tenacious labor. They were initially identified when the fragments had been delivered to the laboratory, gingerly handled with the utmost care and caution once they had been exhumed, immediately being deposited into a controlled atmosphere container. This one small section had inexplicably escaped the process of organic cells being replaced by water-borne minerals over time, yet it was completely surrounded with petrified osseous tissue, i.e. fos - silized bone. The mere notion that this miniscule bit of biological his - tory had come through tens of centuries basically intact has continu - ally enchanted the researcher throughout the development of the proj - ect.

It has also taken years to sort through and classify the associated broken, twisted and nearly disintegrated items that had been extricat - ed from the site along with the precious specimen that has been the focus of his study. Those included potsherds, well-crafted iron tools and an astonishing swatch of fabric with a parchment-like quality that had adhered to the bone segment he finds to be so incredible. The archaeological side of the project verifying the antiquity of the speci - mens has also spanned more than a dozen years but it is imperative to reliably identify the specimen's age, for which the applicable science of credibly doing so was only replicated as recently as 2000 using ultrafiltration in radiocarbon dating.

Peering through electron, scanning tunneling and atomic force microscopes he is amazed at the ingenious design of the human cell on the molecular level; consistently awed as he has dissected the chromo - somes and split the DNA for experimentation using the natural scalpels, restriction enzymes, to do the work.

The researcher's greatest fear has been whether there was enough genetic material for him to successfully complete his experiments and create the expected outcome, for which he is being well-compensated. At times, he has been flooded with the ethical argument of whether he should have undertaken this work at all. He's had to tamp down his conscience, allowing it to compete only long enough to be over -

whelmed by his professional curiosity. Personal integrity had to be set on the shelf.

Only within the last three years has a variation of the FOXO3A gene been confirmed among centenarians by a study at the Christian-Albrechts University in Kiel, and the findings are promising. Getting to the hub of the research, he is comparing DNA from a donor with a trace of the ancient DNA obtained from the specimen, looking for the specific gene for cross-referencing. The outcome of his project centers on what he will find.

Looking closely at that explicit gene in the antediluvian specimen, his eyes widen in bafflement. Sitting back, he stares up into space, his mind spinning around the divergence of attributes from the modern DNA sections he's been poring over for years. The implications could be earth shattering.

⚜⚜⚜

Flipping through the pages of the lab report, he halts when his eyes focus on the newly discovered data. It has taken years of prelim - inary studies and prep before the genetic scientist he has been funding could get down to basics.

Not a man to get excited about any prospect, this is as close as he can come to exhilaration. The work is plodding and meticulous, but there is no other way to approach it if he is to see the result that he, and his father before him, have been so handsomely bankrolling.

It was government that had underwritten the human genome proj - ect and not long into the development, the molecular biologist that had made such great strides at the outset of the project at the National Institute for Health, James D. Watson, the co-discoverer of DNA struc - ture with Francis Crick, found himself on the outs. Watson was replaced by someone who didn't have a conflict with the new NIH director over the issue of patenting gene sequences, calling it an assertion of ownership over the "laws of nature."

This financier, like that NIH director, doesn't see any conflict with the idea of patenting gene sequences and, although the subject is still a grey area in regard to U.S. law, he is not only entrenched in funding private research labs to that very end, but expects to keep this partic - ular study completely confidential. No one but the scientist who has compiled the report now in front of him, has full understanding of the research potential and his ultimate expectations. Everyone else involved has limited knowledge, including the head of the archaeolo - gy arm. His plans are to keep things as 'need to know' and his team splintered. They are paid for discretion and the less information any - one has of the overall scope of the project, the better off they are.

His life's work hinges on the success of their genetic investigation and it has involved decades of effort to conceal the origin of the spec - imen that his research scientist is using. Only two other men alive hold that key, and only one beside himself understands the repercussions that could ensue should the general public become informed.

Every means available has been utilized to destroy the reputation of the man who had originally located the site before the significance of the find had been verified. It left the financier's raiders in the clear almost 30 years later, the region's antiquities officials having attrib - uted the destruction of an old farmstead to that of treasure-hunters that sold whatever artifacts they'd found on the black market. Had that original archaeological detective not done such a thorough job of exploring, receiving the attention that he had from Middle Eastern authorities in many countries, this whole scientific venture would never have been possible, not that the financier is troubled by his slan - dering that man's character. In the benefactor's view, it is all to good purpose. The fountain of youth is not a fairy tale to be hunted by a Ponce de León, the secret of it appears to have been buried in the vol - ume millions read for spiritual guidance.

Smirking in derision of the God-worshippers, he thinks, They've no concept how much myths derive from fact, which led us to this lit- tle hiccup of history. Gods are for the making by anyone with the sin- gle-minded courage to do so.

CHAPTER 17

Traipsing through midtown from one apartment house to another, pursuing what little she could find of her quarry – the missing people who may or may not want to be found – Debra was raring to head back to the office to check out the new leads.

Checking her watch, she had a good hour to make it back and get something done, so she hustled to the subway station, to catch the next train back to "work." When she looked at the schedule, she saw that the train she needed didn't come for another 15 minutes. It was going to be close, but she should be able to make it no problem.

Debra paced the tile floor of the platform while going over in her mind what she'd uncovered. Fifteen minutes had come and gone and still no train. She'd not been paying attention to the announcements, her thoughts taking precedence over everything else, so she stopped to listen. Sure enough, the voice over the PA system was saying that the train was slightly late due to a stall further down the line. Not knowing what else to do, she waited, assuming that a taxi would take as long or longer anyway, the surface traffic being backed up this close to rush hour.

Before long the right train pulled into the station and she hopped aboard hoping to make it back in time. Slowly, the beast moved out and up to speed. There was stop after stop but Debra figured they'd get there, then she'd only need to scamper two blocks over and up the elevator. There was time.

There had been time, until another train (or was it the same one?) stalled and halted the line one more time. Debra just slumped back into the bench and gave up on the idea of getting to the office before closing time. *Bummer.*

When she finally exited from the deep, it was after hours by ten minutes. She was out of time and out of luck. And just when things looked so rosy. She had a couple of leads!

Looking around at the bustling streets, Debra felt disconnected to the hubbub. This wasn't her town or even anything resembling the familiar streets of a western city. All of a sudden she felt as if she were floundering in unfamiliar seas. She'd have to get back to Ell's but wasn't enthusiastic about taking the subway again. This time, without the giddiness of looking for leads and then having them in hand, the claustrophobia came rushing in almost to the point of paranoia. She'd always felt relatively safe in Denver or even L.A. because they were her cities. When she'd make her way home from a football game at the Coliseum, which was in a fairly dangerous part of town, she never felt threatened. She chalked it up to knowing her way around, being in a comfort zone even in a lousy neighborhood. *The devil you know...*

Physically shaking her head to lose the unwelcome sense of being watched, which was how far her discomfort had degenerated, Debra started to retrace her steps, reaching a decision not to take the underground this time. Her skin crawling with the idea of being followed, she kept to open spaces where the crowded sidewalks were filled with distracted people making their way home after being boxed up in offices all day.

Eyes or no eyes observing her every move, she pulled out the phone with the intention of calling Roy. *He's an FBI agent. I'm only play-acting detective and obviously failing miserably right now.* Scrolling to his number, she touched the screen and dialed. *Got to have some good advice for an anxious out-of-towner, maybe even come to my rescue. Yeah, why don't I just act like a frantic female...* She almost hung up in chagrin when it immediately rolled over to voicemail.

Not again! She flashed back to when she had first tried to reach him in a real crisis, as Special Agent-in-Charge of the case where her friend had stopped answering her phone too. One too many unsavory memories.

Well, can't get him so I'll hail a cab. That was easier thought than done. It seemed every available cab had been commandeered by someone else in dire need of reaching safe harbor, so she kept walking and the feeling of being followed grew stronger with each step.

A taxi came around the corner, no passenger in sight. Throwing caution to the wind she stepped out in front of him to make him stop. As he slammed on the brakes, cussing her out for the unsafe maneuver that almost caused him to run her over, Debra pulled open the door and jumped in.

"Are you nuts, lady?"

"No, just desperate. I left my insulin at home and I need my shot, so get me there before I go into shock." Deciding it'd be better to fib than tell him what she was really thinking, she gave him the address and he took off.

"Wouldn't it be better to get you to a hospital?" He asked as he darted in and out of traffic that was thick at this time of the evening.

"No, the emergency room protocol would take even longer, not to mention the outrageous cost. Don't worry, you'll make it in time and I'd much rather give you a good tip than take my chances with a swamped ER," she said as she slumped back in the seat feeling better already that the eyes were gone… she hoped.

CHAPTER 18

Coming out of anesthesia was like floating to the surface of a placid lake, calm and dark enough that she had no concept of width or depth, just a slow emergence from water. Her eyes barely slit open in the muted light of a strange recovery room, still too bright to attempt to view her surroundings with any concentration, or in fact real inter - est. What she could make out of the room, in her semi-conscious state, was unusual, not that she was sure what she expected to see. She did recall going under, tempered by a fleeting thought of having needed more anesthesia. But she didn't remember enough, nor did she truth - fully care. Tilting her head slightly side-to-side, she recognized the intravenous tubing and the electrodes that were attached to her chest, though the gown covered most of them, aside from the wire leads strung to the monitors.

For a few seconds she listlessly watched the spikes that jumped up and down on the display screens as they followed her heart rate, which she remembered was important because the procedure had involved her heart. No, the arteries. That's right, they'd installed stents to help her blood flow to the heart.

Assuming that everything had gone well, she had no misgivings about the clinic, it had all seemed clean and professional when she came in and this room seemed a little off, but so what? She was feel - ing pretty good although concentrating on anything was sort of diffi - cult; she was still too loopy. Loosely trying to corner her thoughts about her job and her home, she found that recollections of either were ephemeral, more dreamlike than anything. Any details about her life were cloudy so she left the whole process alone, supposing that every - thing was fine.

Her eyes flickered open one more time and noticing no one else in the room, she began to slide back into oblivion, unconcerned about where her home was or when she'd get there.

CHAPTER 19

A key turned in the front door and it whooshed wide to admit the owner of the comfortable abode. Ell swept in with her usual energy bubbling, plopping her purse on the hall table, a nesting stack of lacquered Oriental design. Walking her groceries to the kitchen she plunked the bags on the counter.

"Where'd you get to this afternoon?" She opened the refrigerator and began emptying the recyclable sacks that she was forced to use due to the standards set in place by city government decree. An ordinance that absolutely drove her up the wall. "Got your e-mail but it was too cryptic to get a sense of purpose."

"I imagine that I can't exactly describe all my doings to you over the internet, or even in a phone call. I don't want to get you in any hot water."

"To wit, I am greatly appreciative. So, where'd ya go? What did ya do?"

"There's only so much that I can do on the computer so I decided to do a walking tour of the city and despite my best intentions to get back to the office before quittin' time, I was forestalled by a stalled subway train."

"I like the way you put that," she said, her head buried in the vegetable bin.

"So, I beat you back because once the subway finally pulled into the station by your office, the doors were locked and I had no recourse but to head back here. And, as I see, you went shopping on your way home. Get anything good?"

"If you consider a nice table red and a couple different kinds of cheese and prosciutto, plus pesto, for an after work appetizer as 'good.'

"Hmm-mmm. How'd you know that I'm a woman who can appreciate a full-bodied red wine?"

"Family connections." Ell closed the fridge. "I talked to Allie. She says "hi" and don't get in any trouble."

"Like I'm the one." Debra clucked her tongue. "Who was it who got herself in a bind last year? Wasn't me."

"Nope. So, what else happened today?"

"Not much. Like I said took the subway to midtown."

"And?" Ell was insistent for more.

"Checked out the neighborhood where a couple of our 'subjects,' for lack of a better word, reside. Or used to reside. Depends on how you look at it."

Before she could continue, Debra's phone rang. Looking at the display, she saw it was Roy. "Pardon me, I need to get this."

"Go ahead. I can hear the rest later."

"Hello Roy."

"You tried to call me earlier." It wasn't a question though he expected an explanation.

"Obviously. Where are you now?"

"Downstairs at Ell's, as I presumed that since it's after hours, you might be back by now."

"That's either a good guess, you are a gifted detective or you have my person bugged with a locator," she jibed.

"All three. Now, can I come up?"

"I'll ask the landlady."

"Ell, Roy's downstairs. Do I have your permission to grant him admission?"

"Sure. I don't have anything against him anymore."

"That was a nice qualifier," said Esteban when Debra returned to the phone. "I must be growing on her."

"You keep thinking that. I'll let you in."

⚜⚜⚜⚜

Esteban had made himself comfortable on the couch as they munched on the pre-dinner snack that was so plentiful it ended up substituting for the meal. Debra occupied one end of the sofa, feet curled up under her. Ell presided over the little confab from her favorite perch, an overstuffed recliner tastefully upholstered in shades of jade, mahogany and ochre, like the rest of her living room suite. She was so fond of those hues that she almost melted into the furnishings most days, preferring to wear outfits with the same color schemes.

Prodding Debra to impart the tale of her afternoon adventure wasn't too difficult, though she held back any reference to her brief bout with paranoia. At this point, after a glass of wine and some hearty hors d'oeuvres, the episode seemed silly and she was profoundly grateful that she hadn't left a message on Roy's phone, giving her plausible deniability later. She went through her conversations with Mrs. Prentiss and Mr. Ulitsch about the two people on the expanded "victim" list.

"I didn't get to the one other person whose address was in the same vicinity," said Debra. "It would have taken me too long to get over there and then back to the office before closing. Not that it would have mattered since I didn't make in time anyway. Hindsight."

"We'll finish up tomorrow. We closed the case that I was assisting on, and this one needs cleaning up," said Esteban. "Though, as far as my boss is concerned, it's a done deal anyway. Almost a week gone and no resolution in sight, nor much hope of one."

"He's written it off?" asked Debra.

"Looks like. Why else would I be tagged as back-up on someone else's case?"

"To mess with your closure percentage," said Ell. "It's all about performance, isn't it?"

"'Fraid so."

"Sounds to me like someone's got it in for you." She took a sip from her glass.

"Could be," he acknowledged.

"I'd say 'absolutely.' You've probably ruffled a few too many feathers during your illustrious career. Tell me I'm wrong."

He was staring out the window framing a view of the street, the building across the way and the single sycamore on the short block, branches full with broad, hand-sized leaves. Sitting back into the cushions he said, "Can't get much past you."

"That's right, observant and insightful to a fault," she laughed. "Everyone worth their salt makes enemies because they won't bow to stupidity or laxity. You're one of those with a little integrity tossed in."

"I'm speechless," he grinned. "And I thought you didn't like me."

"I haven't been a real fan." She laughed again. "But you kind of grow on people."

Debra had nothing to add to the dialogue so she kept her mouth shut lest she be called upon for an opinion that she was unprepared to offer.

Esteban asked Ell, "Can the office live without your consultant for a few hours tomorrow?"

"After her brilliant showing on the very first day, my 'consultant' can pretty much write her own ticket."

"Good. We have a little more leg work to do."

CHAPTER 20

Next morning, Esteban and Debra were heading to a neighborhood not far from where she'd been the day before. When she gave him the address, he recalled it as one from the original trio of his missing persons.

"I checked this place out a few days ago."

"And what happened?"

"Nothing. Nobody answered and the super wouldn't let me in. No warrant, so no entry." He turned the corner and hunted for a place to park.

"So, no conclusion to be reached, right?" she asked.

"Yes. Nothing concluded." He found a tight spot and slid the blue tank into place without much jockeying. "Bad enough that you're dogging my case, now you're hauling me along for the ride."

"Thought that's what I was here for," Debra poked fun as she unbuckled her seatbelt. "And, as far as I can see, you're the one in the driver's seat."

"Good enough," he yielded with a sideways half-grin as he climbed out and opened the door for her. "Let's do a double-check, shall we?"

They retraced his steps of the few days before and knocked on the door that, following their other encounters with empty apartments and enigmatic occupants, neither of them expected to be answered.

When the door was pulled open by a woman in her early forties dressed for a day at home in a casual lounge suit, Debra started in surprise while Esteban was as stoic as ever.

"Hello?"

"Good morning," led Esteban. "Are you Elspeth Grigg?"

Her eyes hooded with slight suspicion. The man had an official air, but she couldn't get a feel for the elegant black woman who was with him. They didn't quite look like a pair.

"Yes. May I ask who you are?"

"Certainly, my name in Roy Esteban, FBI," and he showed her his credentials. "This is Debra Chorister. May we come in?"

"Well, I'm not exactly feeling quite up to par, but, I guess so."

"Sorry to hear that you're not feeling well. Have you been ill?" he asked as they followed her down the hallway and into the living area.

"I just got home from having a medical procedure and I'm recuperating before going back to work."

"So you've spoken to your employer lately," said Esteban.

"Of course. When you're out for a week or so for surgery, the first thing anyone would do is inform their employer. Kind of hard to keep a job if you don't communicate about things like that."

"Well, you see, Ms. Grigg, we had a report from your employer that you're missing."

"Missing?" She was shocked and became concerned. "That makes no sense. I spoke with them weeks before I took medical leave. When did they contact you?"

"Less than a week ago. Said you hadn't come to work, didn't answer your phone and no one had any information on family or friends to call, or where you might have gone."

Debra looked intently at the woman who was obviously worried. She couldn't see how she could be faking her confusion.

"That's crazy. I just talked to my supervisor day before yesterday after I returned from the clinic. They said everything was fine about the leave and there was absolutely no mention about being reported as missing." She shook her head.

Esteban pulled out a pocket notebook and flipped it open to a page. He had an iPad but didn't like to carry it around everywhere. Even the electronic notebooks could hamper an agent's quick response when they were in the field. "Let's go over a couple of things so we can get this all straightened out, since you're obviously here and appear to be well. We received the call from Carson and Holt five days ago. They said you hadn't been in for three days and no one could contact you."

"What's Carson and Holt?"

Esteban narrowed his eyes as he observed her reactions. "The advertising firm. Your employer."

"I don't work for an advertising firm, and certainly not for the company you just named. I've never heard of it."

"According to our records, the human resources director at Carson and Holt completed a report, verifying that you worked for them as an executive assistant, giving all of your vital information including your social security number, address, age, etc. They said you just moved from California two months ago explicitly to take this position." He turned the book around where her stats were written down. "Is this information correct?"

She looked at it, in thorough disbelief. "Yes, that's me, but, like I said, I don't work there. Never have."

"Then why would they call and make a report that you had disappeared?"

"Disappeared? That's nuts. I didn't disappear, I've been here all along, just gone to the hospital for a few days for a surgical procedure."

"May I ask what kind of procedure you had?" It was the first time Debra opened her mouth.

Elspeth looked at her oddly, then seemed to decide there was no harm in telling them. "I had to have stents implanted. I have a congenital heart problem and they were finally able to take care of it. It's one of the reasons I took this job, for the medical benefits for pre-existing conditions."

"And which job is that if you don't work for Carson and Holt?" asked Esteban.

"That would be Health and Human Services. I transferred out here for an administrative job."

"Would you mind giving us some information about your office address, supervisor and where you were hospitalized for care?" Debra asked, really intrigued by the situation and wondering how Roy was going to deal with what seemed to be a false report. The whole thing was very strange.

"Don't see why not." She gave them the address of the HHS office and her supervisor's name. The clinic was called Darrington Surgical

Center outside of the city.

"Now, if you don't mind, I'm still recovering from the procedure and I'm really very tired." She directed them to the door. "I hope you find out who pulled this ridiculous joke, because I don't find it to be the least bit funny."

"Thank you for working with us and we're sorry for the inconvenience, Ms. Grigg. Heal quickly."

"Thanks," and she closed the door behind them.

As they left the building, Debra couldn't hold her peace any longer. "What was all that about? She didn't work someplace where they swore she did? We find one of your missing persons, but we don't?"

"Beats me, but we're definitely going to find out if this is an intentionally filed false report or?" his misgiving showing through. "Frankly, this is a new one on me."

CHAPTER 21

Esteban turned off the main drag and circled the block of urbane addresses, each accommodating thriving businesses that catered to high-end clients. Leaving the car in the underground garage, he and Debra caught the elevator up to the eighteenth story where Carson and Holt Marketing Associates' posh offices occupied most of the floor.

The receptionist guided the two back to human resources to speak with the department director, Joy Matteo. This was the second conversation Esteban had with her but the first time they met eye-to-eye. A phone interview would not serve when she could be facing a criminal complaint for making a false report to a federal agency.

Ms. Matteo was a dowdy appearing woman at first glance. A double take showed her to be large but attired in a costly suit that was definitely not purchased off the rack. Around her neck dangled a dramatic suite of padparadscha sapphires, the pinkish apricot color sparkling across the top of her blouse. It was evident that this was a successful business and Ms. Matteo, one of the partners according to file briefs, was enjoying the proceeds thereof.

The receptionist deposited the two at Matteo's desk with a polite introduction before retreating to her post. The HR director stood and cordially shook both proffered hands, waved them to be seated and retook her own chair.

"How can I help you today, Special Agent? I assume this has to do with Ms. Grigg. Has she turned up?" She was professional in her attitude but didn't give an air of unconcern.

"Thank you for seeing us, Ms. Matteo. And yes, to both questions. Elspeth Grigg has surfaced. In fact, she says that she's been here all along and has been in contact with her employer, as well," said Esteban with a blank expression.

"I don't see how that's possible," the partner in Carson and Holt creased her brow in doubt. "We've tried consistently to reach her for a number of days before throwing in the towel. At this point, we assumed that she had simply decided this was not her cup of tea and had moved on. You have all the information that we gave you, correct?"

"Yes, we do. The odd thing is, ma'am, that when we spoke to Ms. Grigg yesterday, she said she'd never heard of your office and had never worked here."

"What? How could she possibly make such an assertion?" Ms. Matteo kept her wits about her though she was obviously taken aback at the claim. "Elspeth Grigg worked here for over a month before disappearing into the ether."

"Strangely enough, Ms. Grigg said she works someplace else and that not only had she never worked here, but she never heard of Carson and Holt." Esteban leaned forward and speared the matronly woman with a deliberate gaze. "You do realize what the penalties are for filing a false report with a law enforcement agency."

Ms. Matteo, dropped back into her plush chair, instantaneously deflating at the insinuation that she had done something unlawful. She sputtered a little as she answered the FBI agent seated in front of her desk. "This makes no sense. We reported her missing because of our concern for her wellbeing. She had a heart condition that was going to need attention soon and we were waiting for her to inform us as to when the procedure, which is fairly routine, would be scheduled."

"That is interesting because she said she had just returned from receiving three stents and was recuperating. You were unaware that she had undergone the procedure?"

"No, indeed! She was hired despite the problem because we felt that her résumé was so superior it was worth extending the benefits for a pre-existing condition." She looked at Debra and Esteban with confusion. "I am utterly baffled."

The HR director turned around and, opening a file drawer, pulled out Elspeth Grigg's personnel records. "Here is her file. It contains everything from print-outs of her online communications before hiring, to her résumé, W-2, and all relevant forms." She opened the file and pointed out a few things. "Here is the confirmation of her employment, the dates, her personal information, including address and phone number. It should all be in order."

Esteban leafed through and compared the information with what he had obtained from Grigg upon their visit. He noticed just one discrepancy, outside of the obvious fact that she denied having worked at the marketing firm – the phone number was different from what he'd received from Grigg. "Did you try reaching her at this phone number?"

"Why yes. That was the number she gave us when we first began the hiring process. It's a Southern California area code. When we last called we were told that it was no longer in service and took that to mean that she was no longer interested in returning to work here."

"I expect that was a little upsetting considering all the hassle you went through to hire and train her," said Esteban.

"I wouldn't be truthful if I told you otherwise," said Matteo. "We were very disappointed as well as considerably alarmed at her disappearance. Understand that we knew she had a heart condition that needed correcting, though we understood that there was no immediacy. All things considered, that's why we made a missing persons report."

"I do understand."

"To be honest, I am stunned at the whole situation. She appeared a most efficient and reliable woman, no history of mental illness, and didn't show any sign of inconsistency or anxiety. I would not have hired her otherwise."

"No, I imagine not," said Esteban. "All that I can tell you, is that this appears to be the same woman; the photo matches the woman we met. She has no recollection of working here, and under the circumstances, has no plan to return."

"I am forced to say that it is just as well if she is indeed unstable." She looked at Esteban with a touch of sympathy, "although I am saddened at the situation." She shook her head and gave him and Debra, who hadn't uttered word one, an expression that bordered on entreaty. "I do hope that there will be no consequences for our firm for conscientiously reporting Ms. Grigg as missing. It was done out of concern and now that you have located her and she appears to be unharmed, may I assume that the matter is closed?"

"I don't see what else we can do. There was no crime committed unless you wish to bring charges for any losses Carson and Holt may have incurred."

"Absolutely not," Ms. Matteo was emphatic. "Please excuse me if I sound heartless. I have a business to run and am very glad that you found her to be safe and sound. However, we represent too many high profile clients and certainly cannot afford a scandal."

"Thank you for your time in helping to clear this up," he again offered his hand, which she accepted.

"I must admit to never having come across anything so odd in all my thirty-five years in the business." She turned to shake Debra's hand also, quizzically considering the speechless woman who had accompanied the federal agent. "Miss? I'm sorry, I didn't retain your name..."

"Chorister. I'm just an observer in the field. Please pardon my intrusion in this delicate situation."

"Certainly. And I wish Ms. Grigg the best."

As they showed themselves out the front door of the offices of Carson and Holt Marketing Associates, and sauntered down the hall toward the elevators, Debra asked, "What do you do now? This just gets swept under the rug?"

Esteban shrugged as they watched the door slide open.

"You have a woman who relocates all the way across country to take a dream job with a great business that seems to actually value their employees. It even sounded as though she really liked it there, if you read between the lines of Joy Matteo." Debra continued, "She checks into the hospital for a procedure, apparently without informing her employer (if you believe her ex or supposed boss, and oddly enough, I do) and, when she comes home, there's a new phone number and no recollection of her most recent past. The last two months described by Matteo never occurred. Grigg's memories are completely gone, as if wiped clean, and she begins a new life with a different memory of that period." Debra paused for a moment as they descended to the garage level. "I don't know about you, but how can that be and why does no one care?"

"Because the question has been answered in the basest sense. The missing person is found, is okay and phhhtt… the problem goes away, saving the Bureau any more expense on man hours." Esteban looked at her as they exited the elevator car, "details aren't vital as long as no laws were broken, no charges filed and the victim is fine."

"But is she?"

❖❖❖❖

All that their interviews accomplished was opening the hatch for more speculation. Esteban decided on revisiting the places of interest that Debra had gone to the day before. She'd told him how Ann Garner's place had been cleaned out, just like the apartment uptown that the super had shown Roy. There, he'd been able to get the Evidence Response Team to send in a member for a quick once over, which did not make Bestner happy at all. In the end, the ASAC felt he'd been vindicated when they found nothing, not a paper scrap, carpet thread or fingerprint anywhere. Which meant that Esteban was going to get nothing if he requested ERT support to check out this empty unit.

Because Debra had represented herself to Mrs. Prentiss as an acquaintance of Garner's, Esteban explained their presence there as a follow-up to her worry for the former tenant. The apartment house owner scrutinized them, trying to decide is she'd been "had" by the black lady or if this was a legitimate concern for Ann Garner as having disappeared. Making the decision to be cooperative, mostly because the big good-looking guy in the suit had the proper official air, and Dara Prentiss relied on her ability to gauge character, she relented from blocking the doorway and invited them inside.

Mrs. Prentiss hadn't leased the place yet, weighing whether or not to paint first, so the apartment was exactly as the last renter had left it – clean as a whistle.

Entering through the door and peering into the front room, Esteban was disappointed to see that the place was immaculate.

"Have you been in here to clean?" he asked the landlady, who was tidily wrapped in an aqua velour athletic suit, grey hairs gelled in that bristly style that had become vogue among aging hipsters.

"Not a whit," she said, leading them through the apartment, room by room. "Didn't have to. If nothing else, that girl scrubbed this place inside and out before leaving."

Or someone did it for her. Aloud he said, "Has anyone else been inside the premises since Ms. Garner's departure?"

"No. I've been toying with the idea of painting it a nice soft ecru using peach tones for accent." Forgetting the reason for their visit, she automatically turned to Debra for an opinion, recognizing the woman's flair for fashion. "What do you think?"

Taken off-guard but not wanting to appear aloof, Debra answered with approval. "It would brighten it up, I think."

Roy gave her a querulous flash before continuing with inspecting the residence. He couldn't find anything and decided it was probably a waste of time to ask Bestner for the ERT to take a look. Thanking Mrs. Prentiss for her time, they walked down the front steps and toward the car.

"Well, not a dust bunny in sight," remarked Debra. "What are you going to do now?"

"See if that fellow down the street has returned yet."

As he spoke, their ears became more attuned to approaching sirens. In New York, the noise of car alarms, sounding horns, screeches in the street and emergency vehicle sirens almost become background noise, so ubiquitous are they amid the condensed blocks of humanity. As the screaming of the first responders' trucks and police cruisers turned the corner just blocks away, Esteban and Debra's attention followed their route.

"That's where the other apartment is, right near there," observed Debra. "We're going to have a tough time getting in to check it out now."

"We'll just have to leave the car here and walk over. It may be that it's a few buildings down and we can still get inside to see what happened to the deaf musician." He relocked the Mercury's door and started down the street, keeping his strides in check so the much shorter Debra could keep up in her heels.

"Glad I chose a good walking shoe today."

He looked down at the three-inch heels she wore. "You're not serious."

"Of course I am. These have a sturdy, broad heel. Good for pounding the pavement."

"Whatever you say," and they hurried their steps toward the address in question.

⚜ ⚜ ⚜

It didn't take but a few minutes to cover the blocks in between the Prentiss building and that of the missing musician. Nor were they able to gain access to the residence. It was the one burning so hotly that the buildings on either side had been evacuated.

Debra recognized Mr. Ulitsch standing in the street, clutching the handholds on his walker, fear in his eyes as he saw the fire flicking up the outside of the apartment house adjacent to his own.

"Mr. Ulitsch, are you all right?" Debra asked the elderly man as he stood frozen watching the destructive flames coming close to taking all that he had in this world. His dread was palpable.

"What?" he started, unnerved to find someone at his elbow. "You scared me. I didn't see you come up, Miss... I'm sorry, I forgot your name."

"Debra, Debra Chorister. I was here yesterday to see if your neighbor was home."

"I remember," he forced a laugh amid the chaos of the firemen trying to douse the flames. "I'm not *that* old."

"You most certainly are not," she replied with a smile. "I was just coming back here to see if Mr. Arance was back yet."

"You mean "Ah-rahn-che." He was real particular about pronouncing his name correctly. An *Eye*-talian, you know how they can be."

119

"Yes I do. Like all Latin men," she said in earshot of Esteban, just to make him smile a little despite the possible tragedy they may be witnessing. She'd seen enough heartache in her lifetime to know a little levity in times of distress could relieve the pressure of a tense situation.

Mr. Ulitsch may have been old, but even he caught the aside and grinned at the joke made at the man's expense standing next to Debra. "So, who's this? Your boyfriend?"

"No. This is Roy Esteban from the FBI."

Mr. Ulitsch's eyes widened considerably. "Is Arance a mobster? Maybe he lost his hearing from shooting guns. Like a hit man for a crime family? He kind of had that look."

"Oh, no. Nothing like that. Mr. Arance is a musician, just like he said."

"Well, I wondered, because it's his apartment where the fire started."

Esteban cut into the conversation. "Is that right. What else did you hear?"

"Well, the manager next door called 911 and got everyone out of the building before the fire took off like you see it now. Most of the people were at work so it wasn't hard. Of course, I heard the explosion in the first place and had already come outside to see what was going on," the story tumbled out as Abe Ulitsch became involved in the telling. "Seeing how the flames were taking off, I decided not to go back inside. Turns out the firemen started clearing everyone out of their homes anyway."

"You said there was an explosion?" asked Esteban. "Have the authorities mentioned anything about what caused it?"

"No. I heard a couple of rumors from the other residents that it was a gas build-up or some such, but nothing official."

"And you're sure that it started in Mr. Arance's unit."

"Oh yes. No doubt about it. Heard it from both the manager of the building and the fireman who came to talk to us because he wanted to know what we had seen, too," said Abe.

Esteban thanked the old man and excused himself to go talk to the supervisor of the fire scene.

"You must be getting tired," said Debra. "Let me see if I can scare up a chair for you while Agent Esteban talks to the authorities."

"Thank you, miss. This is a little bit too much excitement for me."

Climbing back into the car, Debra was both exhilarated and tuckered out by the tension. She and Roy had said hardly a word as they walked the few blocks back to the blue tank parked in an illegal spot. Even though Esteban had left the official business notice in the windshield, the meter maid had ticketed him anyway. Toying with the idea of tearing it up and tossing it in the street, he set aside the inclination, mostly because he didn't want to litter, having more esteem for the sanitation workers than the meter maid, whom he wanted to strangle. This would be just another hassle with the City's finest which seems to employ gene pool rejects for the parking authority. The drivers in those little go-carts were notorious for piling violations, one on top of another stuck under the wipers, when the driver had been dead behind the wheel for days.

"Just another day in paradise," he said stuffing the ticket in his pocket, despising the fact that it was going to take time out of his day to deal with something so inconsequential.

"My thought exactly, especially after watching the neighborhood burn down."

"Not quite. Though it would have been a boon if they'd been able to save more of the unit where the blaze initiated." He was emotionally run-down more by the misfortune that the residents had suffered than by any physical drain. It was also disappointing to watch the furnace gut the one floor of the building that he needed to examine, knowing that he wasn't going to get the answers he wanted about the apartment's occupant. The information that he had been able to glean from the fire captain was that the unit had already been thoroughly emptied of all furnishings before the explosion had occurred. Though they were still investigating the cause of the blaze, they were able to inform Esteban that no one had been inside. In fact, he was relieved to hear that no one had lost their life. All the apartments on that floor, however, were pretty much a total loss and the rest of the units had not fared well either.

The good news was Abe Ulitsch's place had been saved; all the mementos of his wife of sixty years were still secure to be handed down to his children and grandchildren.

"So, we've got zip. A gutted apartment and no clues, just another missing person," he said as he drove off.

"Does that mean he makes it into the case file?" Debra asked, referring back to how the ASAC had refused to take the extra disappearances seriously.

"Your guess is as good as mine. Bestner is not to be underestimated."

⚜⚜⚜⚜

A crowd had formed beyond the yellow tape that had been pulled across the street to take the onus off of the firefighters trying to quench the stubborn flames flaring from the windows of an apartment, working their way up the outside of the building. Their rapt attention was centered on the smoke billowing from the aperture and the bustling activity surrounding the fire. Police had rushed to the scene to prevent the onlookers from encroaching on the emergency crews, a couple of cruisers at either end of the block. By the time one man filtered through the crowd, keeping his distance from the fireline but moving in close enough to get a bird's eye view of the commotion, he noticed the black woman and her escort speaking with an old man leaning heavily on a walker.

The number of spectators had already grown substantially at that point, masking his presence as he mingled with them, drawing as little attention to himself as humanly possible. From his standpoint he could watch the little black woman who stood out from the crowd with her Italian pumps. Most New Yorkers were shod with sensible walking shoes when on foot. This gal looked like she wasn't prepared for the sidewalk, which was broken and irregular even in this modestly upscale neighborhood. Even so, he hadn't seen her trip or twist an ankle. She was poised and steady on her feet.

The sight of her companion was a surprise. He wasn't aware that she was working with anyone in her snooping. It had been a fluke that he happened to be on the block when she came by the first time, but after following her downtown on the subway, he'd reported the incident to his boss. That had been enough to trigger this response though he thought it was going overboard. He'd already done an exceptional job as a cleaner on more than one level and his feeling was, why take the chance of creating a situation that requires inquiry? Sometimes the smarter you think you are the dumber the decisions, and working for people with too many letters after their name was a guarantee of fiasco.

But, what did he know? He was just the hired hand and now there was a big guy with a badge palling around with the little investigator, though, by the looks of her and her actions he figured her for an amateur. Maybe that's why she brought in the gun, who he watched flash his creds and cross the police line.

He must be a detective with the force. Though after studying his mannerisms when he talked to the fire captain and the uniforms he changed his mind. *A fed. Great. I told the guy not to do this, but no. I'm the one with nothing more than street smarts and a BA, so I could - n't possibly be as clever as him.*

The observer shook his head as the thoughts filtered through his mind. This was a good paying job in an economy that was so busted his college degree got him nowhere but in debt. He'd been glad to put some of his studies to use, but this was just an exercise in stupidity and now there's a fed on the case.

It was time to call it in.

CHAPTER 22

Back and forth, back and forth... Deep in the night and Debra's thoughts were all over the map, sleep absolutely unattainable as she went over and over the outcome of the Elspeth Grigg case. Knowing that the FBI will probably shelve it as solved, the fact that this woman evidently began a new life then turned around and junked it without a thought was something Debra couldn't let go. Somehow she had been robbed of those recent memories. But why would that happen? Debra had heard of different types of amnesia before, even some forms that affect the most recent memory and nothing else, but those were so rare that it was really only used as a plot for the crime programs that abounded on television. This was a true story and she was profoundly disturbed by Grigg's experience. What could possibly cause this kind of blanking out of two months of a life?

Some details just didn't hang together, either. Such as her not notifying Carson and Holt of the procedure date, though she swore that she did notify work. Trouble was, her work was at another completely different office doing a job that was totally unrelated to the position she had held (or not held, by Grigg's telling of the story) at the marketing firm. Roy did do a follow-up call to the supervisor at the HHS office where Grigg said she was employed, and, believe it or not, all of her records confirmed what she said. Though he didn't go into specifics with the government office workers as to whether they remembered her. HR wasn't related to her actual co-workers. He'd have to check into that on his own time because Bestner gave orders to close the book on Grigg. No harm, no foul, basically.

What Bestner was going to rule on the Arance situation was another thing altogether. Roy hadn't been disposed to press it more than informing the ASAC of the development in the invisible case, realizing he could be shut down with a sneeze if it looked like he was giving it too much time.

There were too many unanswered questions and it was messing with her beauty rest. She wondered if Roy was bothered by it too. Knowing him, as she had come to after the Wyoming affair, she believed that it did.

So, the next question was, what was she going to do about it? She had the research base still available to her at Ell's law office and she planned to make good use of it in the morning to delve into more of these other cases that were, more or less, non-cases according to police agencies. Now, it was 2 a.m. and she couldn't sleep, but she had a cell phone and she knew someone else who rarely slept and might have some insight. Besides, he was two hours behind the east coast. Midnight.

His wife, and her friend, Sol, would probably kill her but she resolved to give Toddy Littman a call. If there was ever someone who thought outside the box, he was that guy.

⚜⚜⚜⚜

The phone rang, and rang, and rang. Finally, a distracted voice answered, "Hello."

"Hello. I'm so sorry to call so late but I was hoping to catch Toddy," said Debra beginning to regret having placed the call so late. *This was a stupid idea.*

"This is he. What's up?"

"Toddy, this is Debra. Did I wake you?"

"No. The baby's been cranky all day. I had the dog watch, Sol took first and now I've got middle watch."

"What are you talking about?" Debra was confused.

"Sailors' watches every four hours. I got stuck with the midnight to 4 a.m. She's teething and we break it up so somebody gets some sleep sometime, we hope. In answer to your question, I am awake and relatively alert. What do you need? You're up kind of late, too."

"Later, or earlier, than you think. I'm in New York and embroiled in a quandary that has really muddled my head." She was tired but still needed to talk things out. "And I figured the only person to call at a

126

time like this is you."

"I think I'm flattered since I seem to be sharing the pedestal with ghostbusters."

"In a way, this isn't so different. I've been assisting Roy Esteban on a missing persons case that has developed a really strange twist." She hoped that she could hook him. "A number of people disappeared but this one person was found, and, in the meantime managed to start a whole new life, or maybe a double life, that no one knew about, not even her."

"This sounds as if it needs some explanation. Take your time, I have plenty to spare."

Debra presented an overview of the cases on which she'd been called in to assist and how she'd just unearthed another 30 or so across the country that fit a specific criteria: that no one really knew they were missing, or, for that matter really even knew the individuals.

"Then how did you find out about them? No, never mind, it's probably not relevant." He paused a moment. "You have 30 or more people who've gone missing, or you suspect are missing, but you really don't know because they have no family or friendly ties, just a hint somewhere that they haven't returned to where they live. They're not transients, prostitutes or drug addicts, had really good jobs before they *may* have disappeared and, basically they just dropped off the face of the earth. No bodies, no nothing… yet."

"I'd say that sums it up."

"So, what's the problem?" He asked semi-interested.

"We finally find one and she can't recall anything about the employer who reported her missing."

"You got my attention," Toddy perked up a little.

"I'm concerned that all these other folks are still missing and only one showed up but without a memory of where she worked, and with an attitude of who cares what anyone thinks. You know, "I'm here, I'm fine, now go away." In fact, she's gone to work with another agency, a government agency, supposedly while she was still arriving every day at the previous employer's place of business." Debra sighed with fatigue. "How does someone show up at work every day – until they don't – where it's all documented, and then have another job that says she's been logging hours there the whole time? Either the woman can split herself in two, has an evil twin or was cloned."

"Probably none of the above. What other pertinent facts have you glossed over?"

"Oh, right. The reason she supposedly disappeared is that she went in for a medical procedure. According to the *new* employer, she gave ample notice, though as yet, Roy hasn't talked to anyone who actually saw her. According to the employer who described her as missing, she didn't inform them, hence they considered her missing," explained Debra.

Ignoring the part about who was notified and who wasn't, Toddy went directly to the medical part of the account. "What kind of procedure did she have?"

"When we saw her at her apartment – same address and different phone number, by the way – she said she'd had three stents put in her arteries around the heart."

"Interesting," said Toddy thoughtfully.

"This isn't an ancient rerun of *Hogan's Heroes*, Toddy. What do you think?"

"I think this might be the forerunner of a trend."

"What kind of trend would that be?" Debra didn't get it.

"One that involves implants of all kinds, but mostly replacement and enhancement of body parts," he said.

"Which would you classify a stent under?"

"This isn't a medical term, but I'd call it enhancement or, if you prefer, this is a corrective measure that includes a foreign object, something unnatural to the body, but helps it regain proper function."

"Okay, I understand that, but you think this has something to do with the gal's odd behavior?" asked Debra. "Like the use of drugs as causing some strange reaction that would cause her to lose her memory?"

"Kind of but not really. I'm thinking that the implant may have had some other component to it."

"Now you're losing me. Like what?"

"Well, I'm not sure," he stalled. "I have to do some hunting around. I'll get back to you."

"What, no instant answers? I had hoped for more than this," disappointment descended on Debra despite her joking. He obviously had an idea but was unwilling to elucidate, leaving her hanging, and unhappily so, at 3 a.m.

"Hmmm, I have to be certain before I leap off this cliff," said Toddy. "Make sure there's a net to catch me."

"Some superman."

"Not the first time I've had to refute that contention," he chuckled. "Talk to my wife, she's knows there is no such thing, and if there were, I'm as far from it as you can get."

⚜⚜⚜

Toddy had a few hours left of his "watch" and the baby was finally slumbering peacefully so he decided there was no time like the present to pull so many threads together, at least in his mind. One of the threads had to do with the decision the Supreme Court, which he referred to as SCOTUS, had just rendered on the Affordable Care Act. He'd been following it closely since the March arguments that really made it appear that SCOTUS might rule against the constitutionality of the bill that the president had signed into law. The main claims, that the "individual mandate is not a valid exercise of Congress' power under the Commerce Clause…," and that the same mandate that every individual must purchase insurance or suffer the levy of a penalty was not within Congress' constitutional power, had been decided by the court.

On the first question, the court ruled that, "even if the individual mandate is "necessary" to the Affordable Care Act's other reforms, such an expansion of federal power is not a "proper" means for making those reforms effective." Yet on the second question regarding the imposition of a penalty for not purchasing coverage, instead of ruling upon the constitutionality of the mandate, the chief justice opted to rule it a "tax" despite the legislation naming it a "penalty" and, in effect, send it back to Congress for further determination on that argument.

Another question was answered by SCOTUS and that was the point that this Medicaid expansion, which is how the court viewed the ACA, was not within constitutional application in threatening states with the loss of federal Medicaid funding if they did not knuckle under and "comply with the expansion."

There were a number of points within the ruling that had Toddy's back up, particularly in the usage of the "general Welfare" clause in that, although they quote it correctly as the "general Welfare of the United States," (Article 1, Section 8, Clause 1) they do not return to the original intent of the Framers. Toddy had typed until his hands ached and talked on the radio until he was blue in the face explaining that, if only people would regard the words as they were written, withholding their own modern, mis-educated interpretation of what "general Welfare" is, the country wouldn't be in this mess and we could actually climb out of the deepening debt hole. Again and again, he had pointed people back to the Federalist Papers and President Jefferson's second inaugural address where he clarified concisely the "Welfare" as being only a benefit of the State, not individual citizens' comforts, relief and indulgence to which he exclusively named education and arts. He refuted the whole concept of these things as being ascribed to the "public" domain, making clear it is anathema to the Constitution despite what later became institutionalized as a corrupted and incorrect governmental definition of "Welfare."

Out of this whole misanthropic application of the general welfare clause in respect to what people casually called Schaalcare, came the establishment of the exact opposite of the majority party's characterization of the act as bighearted. Selling the country on the concept that the ACA would care for more people's medical needs was a doozy that Toddy's nature wouldn't allow him to let slide. And the Supreme Court ruling did nothing to help the average citizen understand the complexity of more than 2900 pages of regulations, immense bureaucratization and impersonalizing of their care. If anything, there were now more hoops than ever to jump through and committees like the

IPAB (Independent Payment Advisory Board) were commissioned to dole out care according to their willingness to pay for it. Simple as that, these boards would be picking and choosing winners and losers, and no one elected any one of the individuals vested with that power, which he found in §3403, stating *"(b) Purpose. – It is the purpose of this section to, in accordance with the following provisions of this sec - tion to, reduce the per capita rate of growth in Medicare spending – "* The first salvo fired by the administration was to raid Medicare of $716 billion to fund the non-funding of Medicare patients in the ACA.

Toddy was spent from the fight but unwilling to give it up yet, particularly when he saw the trend toward modern medical devices or "enhancements" that may or may not actually enhance lives. His perspective was a little peculiar by some standards, but it was only his ability to step outside convention and look in that gave him that unique ability to see what others refused to see. And what he'd hinted at to Debra was exactly one of those close-to-the-edge ideas, which meant that he wanted to cover his bases before prognosticating, and scaring the hell out of her.

CHAPTER 23

"Okay. One down, eleven still to go." Roy picked up Debra from the office, Ell having declined the offer of a lift home. It was still early enough in the workday that she couldn't call it quits yet.

"Much as I hate to burst your bubble, I don't have a choice," said Debra as she buckled herself in.

"Would you like to explain that remark?" he said, fearing the consequences of his asking.

"Not really. However, under the circumstances it behooves me to inform you that our inquiry has now turned up more than 30 people who seem to have evaporated into the general atmosphere."

"Here in New York?" Esteban was incredulous and not in the least bit thrilled to hear the news.

"Uh, no. On a hunch, I plugged in the general parameters to a couple of search engines and located these," she pulled a folder from her chic but capacious handbag. "They're from all around the country… St. Louis, Detroit, San Francisco, etc."

"Great. You weren't satisfied with the dozen that were already lost right here in our own backyard?" he snarked, knowing that he'd get no support, let alone recognition of the problem, from his office.

"That would be *your* backyard. I'm just here on vacation, remember?"

"Yes. But, damn, you couldn't leave well enough alone, had to go looking for more trouble," he said glumly. "Not that I want to avoid my duty or the Bureau's to check out any possibility of foul play, wherever they crop up, or don't, as the case is here. It's turning into something I had hoped it wouldn't."

"You couldn't live with your conscience if we didn't look into every corner regarding these cases, and you know it."

"Too bad it's such an easy call for the ASAC," said Esteban acidly. "Back to the dilemma at hand. The locales that coughed up more names were all major metro areas? Places that have lots of homeless?"

"Yep. But in order to qualify for this exclusive group you can't be homeless, if you'll recall," said Debra, going back to the intriguing part about the whole investigation.

"Great. Now what should we expect? A whole population will show up as no-shows at workplaces nationwide? We are screwed, blued and tattooed."

"In a manner of speaking."

"No buts about it, my own agency isn't interested in the few we had to start with."

"Maybe you'll be able to get through to them now that there appears to be a pattern developing across the country," Debra said.

His reaction was more of a disgusted grumble than anything else.

"Don't think so, hunh?"

"Not really. Flesh it out," suggested Esteban. "These individuals have fallen off the map but so far as we can tell, they haven't actually gone missing." He looked over at her. "Has anyone made a stink about their disappearance? Because I have seen nada, zip, zilch at the Bureau. All they had, as far as I know, were these three cases they tossed at me and, as you saw, they were thoroughly disinterested in the others you uncovered. Realistically, what have we got?"

"A big, fat enigmatic zero that could also be morphing into more than 30." She was beginning to lose heart too. That all of these people may be lost, hurt or victims of some dastardly crime was more than she wanted to deal with. And because the information Debra had compiled was so elusive, the authorities would rather shuffle it away than cope with the possibility that there were people out there who might need help. "Budgets are the key, aren't they. Unless there's a solid evidence trail to follow or someone has a vested interest, nobody will stick their neck out. They have to protect their administrative funding, and if a few people get thrown under the bus, well, that's the way of it." She clucked in distaste.

"You know, it took a lot of digging for me come up with this list of possible missing persons, the similarities are enough that it should raise eyebrows. No one's really sure what happened to them."

Esteban hesitated as he mulled over the consequences. "Maybe we should find out," he said finally.

No time like the present.

With that thought, after dropping Debra back at the apartment, Esteban used his smart phone to locate the most local of the clinics that had been mentioned during her solo foray the day before. All he recalled was Scarsdale-Midtown something or other. He did a search and found the office within a mile of Ell's place. *How convenient.*

He was off to the races, literally. Feeling a crunch for time since these alleged victims had already been out of contact for a week or more, he was inside the offices and standing before the petite blonde receptionist within a quarter hour. Timid by nature, the girl was practically tongue-tied when the FBI agent displayed his credentials and asked to speak with a supervisor.

"Uh, I'll see if she's s-still here," stammered the girl, and she shot out of her chair with lightning speed. Esteban wondered at the reaction, assuming that his general appearance was nothing out of the ordinary. Happening to catch his reflection in a mirrored etching of a cityscape, the scowl inscribed on his brow made him wince enough to make an effort to soften his expression.

The young woman returned with another woman probably 20 years her senior who matched Esteban frown for frown. He tried to lessen his harsh look even more, reminding himself of the old adage that you can catch more flies with honey than vinegar.

The office manager didn't reciprocate. "May I help you?" It was a cold query.

A ton of honey couldn't win over this horsefly. "Yes, ma'am. We've had a request to check into the circumstances regarding a woman, one of your patients."

"You know that we can't divulge any information about patients, Agent..."

"Esteban, Roy Esteban." He replied, adding a slight smile, giving the honey strategy a further boost. "We're not interested in any specific information, Ma'am. All we need is a confirmation whether or not an Ann Garner may have come to this facility. What kind of treatment she may or may not have received is not within the scope of our concern."

"As I said, it isn't something that I can authorize, Agent Esteban. I'm sorry." She started to turn her back on him.

"Ma'am, at this point it is only a single question we are asking. I assume that you would prefer to avoid a full investigation employing warrants to probe operations."

He got her attention enough that she turned around, a trace of indignation exaggerating her crow's feet.

"This is all we need." He widened the smile a bit more, but now it held the slightest hint of a threat behind the white teeth he exposed.

"Let me see what I can do," she replied, turning to exit the lobby once again.

"Ms.?" He caught her before she disappeared through the door.

"Tarr," she supplied. "Yes?"

"Ms. Tarr, will you please take a look to see if a Mr. Vincent Arance may also have made an appointment and whether he followed through? I'd greatly appreciate it." It struck Esteban that there might be some connection between the two missing individuals although the witnesses had recalled different facility names. There was always a possibility that clinics referred patients back and forth.

"No problem," she grumbled, as she made certain to quickly close the door behind her before he could add anything else to his request.

It wasn't but a few minutes later that Ms. Tarr emerged from the recesses of the office complex. "I'm sorry, Agent Esteban, but we have no record of either of those names in our files, check-in sheets or telephone messages."

"You are thorough," he said while thinking that it wasn't likely they could have scoured all those files as rapidly as she had done, digitized records or not.

"Are you affiliated with any other clinics that perform surgical procedures?" He knew there was a satellite office in Scarsdale from his online check. He just wanted to see how Ms. Tarr would field the question. Would she admit the obvious or not?

"We have the actual surgery facility in Scarsdale, per our name. The doctors in this office are more like the triage end of our service. They see patients and then refer to our facility out-of-town, or wherever else their diagnosis necessitates treatment if the procedure prescribed is beyond what we provide."

"Did you cross-check with the Scarsdale facility?" He assumed she would say yes, though he doubted that jived with her true actions while she'd made her brief search in the back office.

"Certainly. All of our records interface." Her features hardened at the questioning of her conscientiousness.

He'd noticed the ubiquitous spiral-bound telephone message book, the kind with NCR paper, on the reception desk, evidence that their phone message system was still manual. Leafing through scores of pages would take time, time that could not have been sufficient to complete the task which would have included the pad sitting in plain sight.

Removing a small brass case from his jacket pocket, he opened it and handed her a business card. "In case you think of something regarding these two individuals, here's my card. Again, thank you for your time," and he pushed open the glass doors knowing full well that nothing Ms. Tarr said was credible. Her obdurate attitude, and the nervousness of the receptionist, was all the substantiation he needed.

Outside the Scarsdale-Midtown Clinic, he consulted his phone one more time, pulling up a search application for medical clinics to locate any private surgery centers in the Nyack area. Walking over to the car, he placed calls to the three that came up, not including the hospital. Considering the hallmarks of the supposed vanishings, a hospital that answered to an elected regional board wasn't likely to be involved.

The second call to a surgical center hit paydirt. The Nyack Central Surgery Center had an affiliation with the Scarsdale-Midtown group. Only handling outpatient procedures, it had a referral relationship with the clinic that Esteban had just visited.

He checked his watch and asked how late they were open. He was in luck. Thursday evening was their late night, they would be open until 7 p.m. Revving the big engine in the dinged-up Mercury, he pulled into traffic and drove upriver to Nyack, New York hugging the Hudson River.

⚜⚜⚜⚜

Traffic was a nightmare but he made it to the clinic before they closed their doors for the evening. This time his reception was congenial, an agreeable middle-aged woman manning the post.

"Hello! May I have your name and what time your appointment is tonight?"

Esteban read her nametag... Jeanne McIntyre.

"Good evening, Ms. McIntyre."

"Just call me Jeanne. We don't stand on ceremony around here," she said smiling broadly.

"Well, Jeanne, my name is Roy Esteban and I'm from the New York field office of the FBI," he offered his badge for her to inspect. Her eyes widened a little, the surprise then instantly subsiding.

"My goodness. The FBI. Is there anything wrong?" she asked, the brief alarm gone as if it had never occurred. It wasn't unusual for people to assume there to be a problem when law enforcement officers approached, so he let it go.

"No, Jeanne. I'm just making an inquiry about a possible patient," he said reassuringly.

"Oh, of course. How can I help?"

"We only need to know if you've had a Mr. Vincent Arance here for consultation or treatment. Do you think you can find out for me?"

"I don't see why not. It shouldn't be a problem to confirm someone having visited the clinic, but I'll go check to be sure."

"Thank you."

She left her station and was back in less than two minutes. "Agent Esteban? Dr. Slauson said he'll be right out."

"Great."

A few moments later, an older, slightly stooped man in a spotless lab coat came through the frosted glass French doors partitioning the front office from the back. He reached out to shake Esteban's hand.

"Agent," he nodded his head. "What can I do for you? Jeanne says you wanted to confirm something about a patient?"

"Yes, Doctor. It's important to find out whether Vincent Arance had an appointment here not too long ago. Do you recall the name?"

"Yes, I do. He was a very interesting character. Traveled all over the world as a musician but had lost most of his hearing. Made a joke about not having the gift of Beethoven and hoped to get an implant that would make it possible for him to return to work."

"How long ago was he here?" asked Esteban, careful to mask his jubilance at finding a lead of some kind.

"About two weeks ago. His procedure was going to be a little more complicated than what our office could handle so we referred him out," said Doctor Slauson.

"Can you tell me where you sent him?"

"Certainly. A very good clinic of excellent reputation, Scarsdale-Midtown."

BLOOD BARONS

CHAPTER 24

The phone rang numerous times before the man at the desk emerges from his reverie enough to recognize the insistence of the tone. Checking the readout on the digital display, he punches the speaker button knowing that the last person he wants to deal with at the moment is on the other end of the secure line.

"Lab." He has no interest in encouraging a conversation when he knows the caller will want answers he doesn't yet have.

*"Update me." No pleasantry to begin with, but then the research center proprietor hadn't expected one. His benefactor is all business. He suspects that there is no such thing as recreation in the caller's life. Perhaps business **is** his idea of rest and relaxation.*

"Thus far, it's hard to quantify the results of the most recent reports. The anomalies in the bone specimen aren't many but they are significant," says the scientist.

"How so?"

"I've been poring over the latest lab tests and it's a lot to digest." He's been staring at the mapping of the one gene section that simply has him scratching his head in wonder.

"Give me something to substantiate your extravagant salary." The disembodied voice is as adamant as the ringing phone had been.

"The specimen's genetic qualities are so rare that I've never encountered them before. In fact the DNA disparities between it and other comparable human DNA of this particular gene are revelatory. But the conclusion as to what those factors represent, I haven't been able to pin down. It will take more time to conduct some other tests." He knows this is not going to satisfy the caller who has actually been patient when one remembers how long this study has been in the works.

"You know better than anyone how fragile and limited are the samples, their great age and irreplaceable nature. I am compelled to

be judicious in the cell dissection. Once the sample is used, it's gone forever."

"Yes, I do understand the circumstances," the caller agrees. "However, time is growing short. The theoretical research must catch up to the tangible application. The only thing that matters now is the product. All the experimentation in my other scientific research invest -ments are coming to fruition but this one, and yours is by far the most vital. The rest will have no purpose if this genetic parallel is not made."

"Which is why there can be no mistakes and no wastage. We are making great progress. The deviation of known chemical bonds in this gene must be resolved to the modern specimen in order to create a result that will fulfill your requirement." He takes a deep breath and releases it. "I believe we are nearly there."

"That's what I expect to hear." The connection goes dead.

Having to clear his mind of the intrusive call, the biologist stands up and walks away from the troubling but captivating reports. He is too distracted to settle back into analyzing the genetic correlation between the two specimens, whether he can make the experiment work, because he is only going to get one opportunity.

Instead, he is drawn into the fascinating quandary that is posed by the ancient bone DNA. He stops in front of a tall cabinet, opens the door and extracts a fat expandable folder that holds photo after photo of an excavation that had all the hallmarks of sloppy, substandard and absolutely unprofessional work. That was done intentionally. He should know, he was there.

Most of the shots are of the tumbledown stone house, which they now know to be thousands of years old, and the open graves of equal age. There are a few handcrafted trinkets on the sides of the dirt piles, tags attached for follow-up documentation, one of them a staff of great size that has the look of belonging to a shepherd. Many of the photos show the archaeologist tenderly sweeping earth from the bones that had been laid to rest many centuries before.

The scientist pulls two photos from one of the albums. They are buried in the center of tens of pages, easily overlooked if one isn't *aware of their existence. But he is, and he now holds them in his hands that are trembling as he sees the images with new eyes.*

In both photos there is a figure on the right flank of each shot. The person is seen in no other picture taken during the exhumation of the bones. These two photos are focused on the ribcage of the body that lay in the grave just where there is one portion of one rib that is par - tially obscured by a fragment of fabric that has taken on the texture of parchment. This is not the facet of the photo that his eyes are now scrutinizing. For the first time he is examining the blinding white gar - ment that the figure on the right is wearing. It appears to be typical Middle Eastern garb. That makes sense to him as they were deep in Asia Minor and many of the indigenous people wore this type of out - erwear.

What draws his eye even deeper into the image is that, after searching through all the other photos, he notices that not one of them captures an image of this man but these two pictures. Not even in the few photos where all the crew had lined up for a group shot, all the names designated for records, does this man appear. At closer inspec - tion, the scientist sees the blurred edges of the man's image as he appears to be looking down on the bones just before they were removed from their ancient resting place. The robe is glistening white making everything else fade into the background, dimmed by its bril - liance.

Placing the album onto the desk next to the lab reports, his mind is taken to a new level of speculation. Whose bones are these? Who would have been buried in the far reaches of an obscure mountain range in eastern Turkey?

Pondering the implications of the gravesite, which had been left to look as if marauders had raided the earthen tomb in search of artifacts to be illegally sold to the highest bidders, he is struck again by the anomaly in that small portion of bone... and the presence of a strange man at its disinterring.

Placing the photos back in their folder and into the cupboard nook, he practically falls back into his chair, pondering if he should copy or pull those two photos into his personal keeping for protection.

There is only one other person with authorization to enter this inner sanctum and that is his benefactor who has yet to come anywhere near the workcenter, his only interest being the ultimate results. The biolo - gist leans back, and staring at the ceiling, wonders what he has real - ly become involved in, this DNA having all the characteristics of humanity but with this one particular trait that deviates from modern man. Does this support the idea of evolution? Of this he is completely unconvinced, instead he is beginning to see something more along the lines of supernatural occurrences that may lead to an utterly incon - ceivable revelation, a staggering discovery that could knock the world on its ear. Except that he has signed non-disclosure agreements so air - tight, no lawyer could crack them. He has to accept that this break - through will never be published, never see the light of day.

CHAPTER 25

The desk is piled high with financial statements from every one of the clinics involved in the study, and the trustee feels overwhelmed by the reams of useless paperwork that is constantly required to fulfill funding guidelines.

This is the problem with government programs; it's about how many written reports are generated to substantiate their theory. Doesn't really matter if there's any actual success.

She couldn't be any more disgusted with the endless reports, let - ters of support, subjective surveys, interviews and unending stacks of documentation, real or misleading that do little more than justify the need for bureaucratic paper-pushers. All of it does little to ascertain a constructive outcome.

She slides down in her executive chair, the leather slipping under her linen suit, having worn something light in the stifling summer heat that, even with the air conditioning on, blasted through the floor-to-ceiling windows overlooking the sludgy waters of the Big Muddy. The trustee runs her fingers through her loose hair, uncaring as to whether she's mussed the chestnut layers. There's no one on her schedule of any real consequence today.

Recalling that fact, she kicks off her shoes before beginning the paper shuffle, which is still mountainous in the digital age, making no difference whether she scrolls through the computer files and data tables or leafs through the physical documents. It's all the same story, how much can you generate? Nobody really reads it all, they just like to have it as backup in case they get called on the carpet. Of course, once it's reached that point you can lay money that something in those ridiculous stacks of papers or archived e-mails will nail you to the wall.

She learned that by watching the downfall of her predecessor. Now she dots every 'i' and crosses every 't' to make sure her butt doesn't get caught in a sling, which is why she's saddled with the other part of this... the endless paperwork.

Sitting up again, she opens the files that are on her desk blotter and reads through them once more. The discouraging results coming from more than one clinic involved in the trials is disheartening for more than one reason – her job being top on the list.

And I worry about others relying on the endless sea of paper to validate their position. Guess who's in the same boat?

The statistics are not lining up the way she wants them with a mis - erable 3% success rate over all. It is her job to do whatever she can to boost that number, and manipulating them to represent a triumph in the world of medical devices is the first option. Technically, the study requires proof of technology advances, not survivability, so they are already on the right side of the equation. The grant guidelines expect documentation on the development of the technology. The government agency with oversight of this project doesn't have the least interest in application, only the theoretical improvement in assumed care by developing better devices.

Typical of government-implemented programs, they only require information that implies success without actually providing it, data that supports the theory without delivery of results. And, that, we have by the bucketful.

During her earlier conversation with the private fund manager, he reinforced their expectations for medical device application outcomes and he stressed the tightening timeline. She was reminded that it's the business end of this organization that necessitates better results and that is where failure is untenable if she wants to keep her job... which she does.

CHAPTER 26

This is an election year and the incumbent's polling numbers were slipping despite the constant barrage of ads assailing the challenger, a high-profile businessman wielding a success portfolio, public service and charitable giving history that would shame the most prestigious money moguls. Known as likeable and, by all media accounts, above average in the department of intellect, Cameron Van Schaal was not faring as well as his backers wanted to see.

The fact that the country was sliding deeper into a double-dip recession was becoming a real concern for the President's campaign, the passing of all the massive spending bills that were touted as designed to reduce the deficit having no effect. His stimulus had not reduced the unemployment rate as he promised it would. In fact, billions of dollars were still unaccounted for as unspent for the President's "shovel-ready" projects. Among which billions had been squandered on 'green' energy loans to companies like eTec, Tesla Motors, the now bankrupt Solyndra, and others; as well as programs to provide earth-friendly home improvements that produced nothing but a few hundred jobs at about half a million dollars apiece in California, and so few homes upgraded in Seattle that they could be counted on one hand.

All these programs and numerous more adding to the escalating government deficit spending, the greatest example being the unpopular boondoggle Schaalcare that encompassed one-sixth of the national economy, were beginning to resemble an albatross around the president's neck. Over a thousand large businesses, including the big labor unions, had already been granted waivers by the President's HHS Secretary from the Schaalcare requirement to participate in the new healthcare plan, demonstrating undeniable cronyism throughout the administration's policies when added to the renewable energy, and other union favoritism.

When the decision came down from the Supreme Court about the Affordable Care Act, otherwise known as Schaalcare, pundits waffled between it being a brilliant decision to a bogus judgment. The ruling that the so-called penalty was indeed a tax, fed a new firestorm of roundtable discussions. Did the chief justice cross the line in this singular decision, which disturbed both the conservative and the liberal sides of the court? No one had been able to pin down the rationale behind the decision except, perhaps, to avoid ruling on the actual issue of constitutionality. This included the manner in which the bill was passed by a single-party majority in Congress, bypassing numerous required congressional reviews and was a direct abuse of the Reconciliation rule by the U.S. Senate to purposefully skirt the 60 vote requirement, which proved unnecessary but was done anyway.

This was a fiercely contended issue and Ell, who boisterously voiced her opinion on politics in general, was railing against the failure of the court to do its sworn duty.

"The proof is in the pudding," said Ell hotly. "Here we are with a mandate that clearly steps outside the constitutional intent, even if you call it a tax. Personally, I'd call it a hatchet job on the individual's right to choose what kind of insurance they want, or none at all and just keep a safety net called *saaavings*," she sang the word with a musical lilt. "Not that that's so feasible the way this president has gutted the economy. Grrrrr, it just infuriates me!"

"I see what you mean. Having to research all these news stories that so many of our do-gooder journalists slant into a 'poor me' issue for the uninsured is just plain ridiculous." Debra and Ell were trying to enjoy an evening but the constant yip-yap about the recent ruling was all anyone was talking about. While at the office, Debra had downloaded the full Supreme Court opinion and after coming back to Ell's apartment, she finished reading all 193 pages of it.

"It's obvious that most of the talking heads have only read the few pages of the syllabus because once you get into the dissenting opinion a whole 'nother world unfolds in terms of logic," said Debra. "Probably the only part of the treatise that holds any logic at all.

"Here's one for you. The dissenting opinion points out that the penalty for failure to buy insurance is unlawful in itself," Debra looked over her page of scribbles taken down as she had read the slip opinion. "They also say that the exemptions of prisoners, illegal aliens, Indians and the poor require that it not be considered a tax because the exemptions are not consistent with the tag. Quote: *"But varying a penalty according to an ability to pay is an utterly familiar practice."* Unquote. Unlike a tax, or how taxes are supposed to be levied, only now, about half the population is exempted from paying income taxes. No wonder these people can't keep it straight. And if you get into what Toddy brings out in so many of his articles, going back to the Federalist Papers, you see that the whole income tax business is a sham that goes against everything the Framers intended."

Debra looked at Ell. "I'm no lawyer, just some little number cruncher turned researcher, but it is clear that someone avoided their duty in this whole Schaalcare matter."

"You can bet on that, and the Supreme Court is supposed to be above politics. That's why they have lifetime appointments, so they aren't beholden to any transient office-holder." Ell began to clear the table and went into the kitchen grumbling at everything political and Debra couldn't blame her. As she re-emerged she said, pointing at the TV, "and listen to that turkey of a president who went right back to calling the mandate a 'penalty,' completely ignoring the decision by the court that it's a tax. It's almost as if he agreed with the dissenters while whooping it up as a win."

After dinner, Ell decided to switch to a network drama or two, take the weight of the world off her shoulders and give it to some imaginary characters, telling Debra, "at least when they do something stupid it only affects the other dolts who play along with the idiocy. Lets me release the real-life foolishness to the fools who would be king. I just hope we can rein in these nincompoops in office before it's too late."

While Ell settled in for a little mindless entertainment, Debra decided to make another call to Toddy, see if he was ready to reveal his hypothesis about the missing patient case, as she was beginning to refer to it. The label made sense as she dug further and further into the

30-odd MPs she located, only to find that there was some mention of an upcoming medical procedure associated with most of them.

Before she could even open the subject of the missing people, Toddy overrode her with a running commentary which was difficult to interrupt once he was on a roll. Usually, if you let him go, there'd be some enlightening tidbit that would come forth, taking the listener off-guard in its brilliance because, although it looked like a small morsel of truth, the fact of it could rock the nation. All we had to do was put the information into context and apply it.

"I was reading through Federalist Papers 78-80 and this jumped out at me. Blew me right out of my seat. This is what SCOTUS said regarding the Affordable Care Act: *"When a court confronts an unconstitutional statute, its endeavor must be to conserve, not destroy the legislation."* They got it backwards. According to Alexander Hamilton, they are beholden to put the Constitution first and foremost! Impeachment of justices is possible for *not* putting the Constitution *first* in adjudication of questions of legislation and its application, rather than what the chief justice wrote in the ruling. The whole of it goes to the misappropriation of duty, and when it first occurred that the judiciary started applying case law instead of the actual Constitution to a question placed before the court, I don't know. But it definitely has something to do with the fact that the Senate no longer represents the States but is just another popularly seated chamber of the Congress since the passage of the 17th Amendment. This completely changes the balance of power within the legislative branch and, ultimately the whole of the national government... the States no longer have proper standing, because the 17th Amendment changed the Senate from State Legislative appointments to a popular vote!"

There was a slight pause as Debra digested the information. It was nothing along the lines of what she had expected to be discussing, but the import of it smacked her sideways. "The Senate had been an appointed body? I didn't know that."

"Most people don't. There were two amendments rushed through the process in 1913: the income tax and this one to substitute election to the office of senator rather than appointment by the Legislature.

Think about it… there are 29 Republican governors. That would be 58 Republican senators. And then the independent governor of Rhode Island served in the Senate as a Republican. Do the math. This Senate is upside down in terms of it representing the States as it was intended by the Framers," Toddy stopped to take a breath.

"So all we really need to do is repeal the 17th Amendment to assure as close to a balance as we could get. Nothing's perfect but it sounds to me like those who wrote the Constitution had a much better idea than we do," said Debra.

"Damn right! Although it would actually mean that we need to pass an amendment to nullify the 17th, just like the 18th Amendment was repealed by the 21st Amendment. That's how it works. *AND* it can be done from the States. Don't let anyone ever tell you that it needs to go through Congress first. All they have to do is read Article V. Of course, it means paying attention to the commas and semi-colons to see how three-fourths of the States can ratify an amendment *telling*, and I dare say dictating to, the Congress what will be added to the Constitution."

"How is it I never heard this before, or understood it?" She was surprised at the information.

"Because of our NEA education. It's been a steady change of direction in how civics is taught in schools," said Toddy. "The intent has been leading us away from the founding merits that this country is based upon and trending toward a collectivist belief of share-and-share alike."

"Guess you have to start somewhere to get the concept of private property excised from the minds of the citizenry."

"Now you've got it. By the way, I've written four articles on this whole thing and they're posted at http://repeal17.ning.com. Take a look sometime."

"I will. To get back to my initial reason for calling…" said Debra.

"Right. What's up?"

"I was hoping you had something to reveal about the missing patient cases we're working on."

"Are you familiar with nanotechnology?" asked Toddy.

"Only that it involves mechanisms on the molecular level. What kind of mechanisms, I'm not really sure, though I came across a news story referring to nanotechnology in relation to an artificial kidney. Not that I understood what they were talking about." This conversation was beginning to take its toll on Debra who was already exhausted.

"Good enough. Let's talk about an artificial organ. The kidney they were referring to is created using components so small that they are a cross between a machine and an organism. It's taking the 1960s movie, about miniaturizing people so they could go into the patient's bloodstream and correct a physical problem by using microscopic medical instruments to a new plane. At the time instruments of that scale didn't exist... nanobots are that instrument today."

"Nanobots? Come on. That sounds like the movie you're talking about, science fiction." Debra had a lot of respect for Toddy but she was beginning to believe that he'd gone over the edge here.

"It was science fiction at one time, but not anymore. They are developing nanomedibots that can repair tissue damage on the cellular level, nanopharmaceuticals that can deliver meds directly to the affected cells without bothering the surrounding cells. Think about targeting just the cancer cell and no others and what a boon that would be to medicine."

"That sounds like an incredible application of technology," said Debra, excited at the concept. Then she thought more about who she was talking to. "Okay, what's the downside..."

"The downside is that nanobots have already been conceived that replace cells such as neurons. What they can do is great in that the rejuvenation of nerves can occur, helping people to be able to use limbs that were otherwise paralyzed. But it can also mean the replacement of neurons in the brain, which could potentially change the way one thinks or *remembers*. Like cloning, there are infinitesimal lines drawn between the ethical and unethical use of groundbreaking technology." Toddy exhaled, gathering his words to express himself without being misunderstood. "Nanotechnology creates the ability to build all kinds of incredibly helpful mechanisms, like an artificial kidney, or maybe a lung that can be implanted rather than being the size of a dresser like a dialysis machine that operates on the outside of the body. But it can also introduce the possibility of evil intent, which most scientists would never conceive of, but there are a few financiers with bottomless funds that would pay anything for just that capability to rule another's thoughts and actions. Imagine what these people could accomplish if they also had a great influence on the government with this new health care law and its mandated participation. When you think about it, this may be a great reason for the waivers and carve outs for those groups who already support centralized government, so the target is everyone else."

"You're talking about crazy people," said Debra thinking he's really walked into unreality now.

"Do you recall the kind of inhumane experiments Hitler was fueling with his concept of an *uber* race? The ghastly medical "research" he inspired and commanded from Dr. Josef Mengele and his so-called scientists? Attempts at having a controllable people under the thumb of a dictator have already occurred and man doesn't change. Evil still walks the earth."

Debra was speechless for a brief moment while the idea sank in. "You think we may have stumbled across something that unspeakable?"

"I don't know. I'm just saying…"

"Right, just saying and giving me nightmares," said Debra.

"Go to our website, ChangingWind.org, and type "nanobot" into the search engine," said Toddy. "That'll give you more of an idea of what I'm talking about. It also takes into account how this Schaalcare works into it. It's definitely outside the realm of conventional thought."

"I'd expect no less," she said in closing.

BLOOD BARONS

CHAPTER 27

Before going to the website, Debra decided to ferret out as much information as she could relating to the thirty-odd people that were missing, if you considered the lack of a report called a "report" as amounting to anything notable. The whole concept of going missing, but not, was really messing with her mind. That still didn't deter her from delving deeper.

Something is seriously out of whack here, and I'm going to find out what it is.

Having the tools at her fingertips while settled into the ergonomically designed secretarial station at Ell's workplace, Debra widened the search in earnest for clinics or healthcare providers treating any of the individuals that might have *anything* in common. It meant gaining access to some of their personnel and medical files, which wasn't exactly proper being a tad outside legal limits, but it was the quickest way to get answers. The FBI was unwilling to take action, leaving her feeling that she had no choice and it allowed Roy to turn a blind eye to her online machinations.

Hours later, having accumulated list after list of doctors employed at any number of healthcare facilities, Debra uncovered a loose connection of names associated with more than one clinic. All of the facilities were privately owned and had boards of directors or trustees where a few names crossed-over from one entity to another.

What difference that makes, I have no idea. At least it's a connection.

The more she combed the background of each clinic or surgical center, the more she found an intricate interweaving with a few individuals showing up on their boards as well as associated with a couple of private insurance companies and hospital boards.

Paring it all down, there were six clinics nationwide that met the criteria of possible connection with five individuals holding positions on one board or another. Although some of them were tied to a number of other healthcare facilities outside of these six, one individual appeared on every one of those six boards of directors, trustees or advisors. Debra found them in Grosse Pointe, Michigan; San Rafael, California; Santa Monica, California; Scarsdale, New York; Jacksonville, Florida and East St. Louis, Illinois.

Strange choices for locales. They're spread all over the place... but what do I know about prime real estate?

⚜⚜⚜

Connecting the final dots between the clinics in far-flung cities was tossed back into Esteban's lap. As much as Debra had some compunction about crashing the gates of semi-private websites in order to help people who may or may not be in distress, she was unwilling to chance taking a backdoor into the FBI search engines.

First thing he noted was that most of the municipalities had kept a reasonably robust economy and thus a highly mobile employee base in these tough times. Detroit seeming to be the exception, from what he understood.

Working together over the phone, the two typed in tandem to gather more information from these medical facilities. Each clinic had a private surgical center, which was a point of interest to them. The little bit they'd been able to garner about some of the individuals still missing, and one that had been found, included the detail of expected implant of a medical apparatus.

It took quite some time, but between the pair of them they were able to hone in on two individuals that fit the same profile of Elspeth Grigg in New York.

Trey Thompson, a computer engineer concentrating in the field of artificial intelligence was on the leading edge of research in the Silicon Valley. They tracked his employment history to find that corporate headhunters had him securely in their sights. Having a weakness for extreme sports and amassing big boy toys, he had a predilection for changing jobs whenever a sweeter deal came along from a high-tech competitor. 'Loyalty' didn't seem to be in his vocabulary. After trashing his hip in an accident incurred during a helicopter drop while skiing the Canadian Rockies, he had let it be known he was due to go in for joint replacement surgery. He scheduled the time off for the operation and rehab, but subsequently never returned to work. His employer chalked it up to *Trey-time-off*. It was a term that had been coined in some of the industry stemming from his occasionally ditching one job to take another in order to get an extended vacation before arriving at the next workplace. Apparently, the only reason employers put up with his eccentricities was because he was so good and in such demand that he could write his own ticket.

All of this information was collected through a few phone calls to previous employers, many who wished aloud to have him return as it boosted their financials when he was working a project. The last place of employment, however, had given up after a brief attempt to get in touch with him about returning to work. They assumed that he'd jumped ship once more. The exact words of his supervisor had been, "Much as I enjoyed Trey, and his work was superlative – he had an ability to practically become one with the machine he was developing – at some point we had to move on. We were very fortunate to entice another boy wonder straight out of MIT to fill Trey's spot. Wherever he is, we wish him well."

And that was that for Trey Thompson until Roy Esteban tracked him down, assuming that this was the same man. The social security number, date of birth and some other identifying information was the same, but he was no longer working in the forefront of computer geekdom. Esteban located him in a San Francisco city government office. His new position? That of a workplace advocate for transgender employees.

"You're kidding," said Debra. "This is a sought-after computer engineer and he's now holding the hand of someone looking for a sex-change operation, or a hall pass to the women's room?"

"Hard to believe that this could possibly, by any stretch of the imagination, be the same dude, because he had been known to state, among friends – not at work, that the behavior of cross-dressers, transgender, et al was "aberrant." Not exactly sympathetic to the population he now is supposed to serve," filled-in Esteban.

"Well that is San Francisco, where the bizarre is the norm," she added.

"Maybe after his hip replacement he had to give up high altitude skiing and sky-diving, did some soul-searching and turned his life around to help others," Esteban couldn't help being snide.

"Right, and that coming straight from the mouth of a public servant," she shot back.

"Well, ya got me there." Switching gears, he said, "So this is the other fella I tracked from what you gave me. From San Francisco to Detroit we go."

"Both super-liberal cities just like New York."

"Hey, don't dis my city," he laughed.

"That'd be the farthest thing from my mind," she feigned contrition.

The hunt had turned up Bill Porter, a conservative entrepreneur who had been making money in spite of the economic devastation that had torn through Detroit, leaving parts of it a virtual ghost town… his own black neighborhood a victim of the times. Porter had risen from poverty to building a profitable consulting firm, providing business and industrial growth plans that had proven their worth, and his, over time.

An auto accident that resulted in a radically progressive hearing loss had decided Porter to take a hiatus from work, closing the office for almost four months. He had informed his clientele that he was taking time for himself, previously unheard of being a workaholic who had never set aside time to have a family, and he began investigating state-of-the-art hearing augmentation devices. Not one of his clients ever heard from him after that, as months of silence ensued. A couple of his customers had tried to reach him, only to find the office dark and locked up with a rental notice posted on the front door. He had virtually dropped out of sight and one of his associates had become concerned, placing a missing person report with the local authorities. It never went anywhere, the officer on whose desk it had landed telling them that he's a grown man who might have just decided to go on vacation permanently. The officer also said something to the effect that he'd heard Porter had plenty to retire on. End of story... until now.

Esteban discovered the whereabouts of Bill Porter in the last place he expected to find him – processing disability claims for a welfare office in Lansing.

"These people we're locating seem to be so different in character from those who disappeared that it makes you wonder if we're dealing with identity thieves. Except after follow-up on the Grigg case, we *know* that's the same woman," mused Roy.

"Aside from aliens entering human bodies..."

Roy cut in on Debra's thought. "You mean, like the Planet Dracos lizard-people theory that that radio nut, provocateur promotes?"

"That's the first I've heard of that one, thank goodness. But no, I was just thinking how weird is this whole thing. Granted that we've only found three people out of 30 so far..."

"Not so bad, ten percent..."

"Okay, like I was saying," she went on, "the ones we've found have just flipped their personalities, working in places that in another life, literally, they would have nothing to do with for personal moral reasons, disagreeing with the lifestyle, be it sexual orientation or economic."

"No question it's screwy," said Esteban. "These people completely dismantled their lives, dropping everything that made them successful, for what? A government paycheck? Not that I'm knocking it. I'm on the same payroll."

"You're hardly the automaton that so many bureaucratic workers have become. Look at all the trouble you cause doing what's right rather than what's expedient. You can go back to Paul's epistles in the New Testament where he says, "All things are lawful unto me, but all things are not expedient..."

"I hadn't thought of it in those terms before," he said.

"You might want to crack your Bible once in a while. Generally speaking, it won't turn you into a frog. In fact, it might bring out the inner prince," she teased.

Ignoring the comment about the frog becoming a prince, he went on. "Whatever the case, no one who knew them – not that they had developed many personal relationships for their own reasons – had any notion of their career swap or they wouldn't have tried to find them."

"As far as I can see, none of it makes any sense. There has to be a rational answer," said Debra.

"Maybe not so rational… to our way of thinking," and he fell silent.

CHAPTER 28

Finally, Debra pulled up the website that Toddy runs and where he posts the results of his research, putting it into context for anyone who has enough imagination to absorb the broad frontier that stands beyond conventional "wisdom." Typing in the term 'nanobots' she was thinking, *How off-the-wall could this be? Well, no time like the present to find out..."* And she pulled up an old article that looked like it spoke directly to what they'd been talking about.

"Nanobots & Healthcare Reform
Posted by Toddy Littman | Posted on 10 Jan, 2010

This article has proven to be hard for me to work on.

Imagine for a moment appreciating some little thing, be it from a friend or loved one, maybe a fond memory that brings a tear to your eye.

Now, imagine not feeling anything from it. So now let's say it's something big, say a child getting married or the birth of a grandchild. Just imagine feeling nothing from it, or even anger toward something about it.

Imagine a variety of memories you once had, gone, just vanished because they do not make you more intelligent. But you don't care since you no longer even remember them, the neurons that made them exist are no longer present in your mind.

These can easily be the results of nanobot technology that the 18 intellectuals who can have the most influence on policies worldwide have suggested "to make people think more intelligently." Anyone who knows someone with Alzheimer's knows how heart-wrenching this is to consider.

And, apparently, according to a group of experts, intelligence is a static set of values, ideas, knowledge, etc., there is no variance, no other activity but that which is identified by these people, or others like them, that is intelligence. "One size fits all" is apparently how intelligence is determined and the idea of sanctity of ones' own thoughts to themselves is no longer valid.

Here are links to articles about nanobots as a real, tangible, design to be in our midst in less than 20 years. And you wonder why government wants to run healthcare.

http://www.nanobot.info/
http://www.youtube.com/watch?v=R-2Xw-GNkUQ
http://www.scienceahead.com/entry/artificially-intelligent-nanobots-in-human-brains-by-2029/

Gene therapies are good, but programmed bots that replace the neurons in your mind, now that puts an end to a variety of troubles for government and the minions of bureaucrats who want the public to "just comply," to "just obey." Imagine being hacked through wi-fi or voting for someone on the basis of what the program in a group of nanobot neurons tells you is right, and not due to your mind's own knowledge, life, and experience. This is what is in store for us all, and a damn good reason so many in government voted for healthcare this time around, the price they pay for their vote will be temporary. Hell, there are people in Prince Edward Island who are sure there are nanobots in the H1N1 shots (Comments under article at http://www.the-guardian.pe.ca/index.cfm?sid=303591&sc=98)

So while we are sold the idea on the basis of the cost to us of the uninsured, let's not kid ourselves into believing government isn't doing what is in THEIR best interest, and with this nanobot technology where you will "think more intelligently" according to government. Once there is this government healthcare in place, irrespective of 60% of Americans not wanting this bill, it's very obvious this bill is being done for purposes the government has in mind, nothing else.

Thank you for reading,
Toddy Littman

Why have I not seen this before? Because it sounded just like the sci-fi movies he was talking about... but, in God's name, what if???

She began thinking about Elspeth Grigg, and now the other two people who have so utterly upended their lives after undergoing the implantation of medical devices that are designed to make your life better. How is it that Grigg, when they interviewed her, had so completely forgotten about her recent past? Because now it looks like there are others who may have undergone that same kind of amnesia and answers aren't falling out of sky. The thought that there could *even* be such an outlandish solution was more than she wanted to contemplate yet she knew that now she would.

⚜⚜⚜

Debra went ahead and forwarded the article to Roy's personal e-mail.

This shows up on his work e-mail and they'll boot him for sure.

She depressed the send button anyway, knowing that he was definitely going to believe she'd crossed the line into mental psychosis, though she was already questioning herself on that issue. Then again, Toddy was not nuts. He just had that unlimited ability to see beyond the walls that average people build over their lifetimes, brick by brick.

That done, she realized that they'd uncovered enough information for her to have at it and start finding the ties that bind – the money connections.

We've got the actors in this sordid drama, now what about the cash?

The questions that trammeled her thoughts while she began the process of backtracking financials were countless. What is it that they might be doing that's just not above-board? Is this some kind of conniving to do illicit, or maybe beneficial, research or experimentation? *And if it is, are the patients aware that they might be guinea pigs?*

It all led to Debra's consideration of what exactly human nature is capable. To this she already knew the answer. She no longer bought the prattle that everyone is good at the outset, that they are turned into malcontents by society and thus the enigmatic 'society,' being the basis of all evil, must be transformed. All you had to do was observe the beautiful, innocent child in its crib, crying for what it needs and thinks that it wants… self-centered from the get-go – it doesn't yet know any better. But that is the reason to love, hold and coddle the helpless baby, teach it the way of a giving heart which is the imparting of a parent's love.

As much as many of Debra's acquaintances eschewed the idea of God, she enjoyed reading scripture and finding truths that were so eye-opening to her that she wondered how so many others glossed over it. In many places throughout, it is clearly stated that the heart of man is, well, no way of putting it delicately, deceitful, and face it, the truth of it is plain everywhere one looks. So, how hard is it really to imagine that there are fellow human beings that would devise evil against their neighbors?

Guess we're gonna see just how bad a person can be…

CHAPTER 29

Guinea pigs. Or are they hamsters? President Cameron Van Schaal could never tell the difference between the rodents that, for some incomprehensible reason, youngsters kept as pets. But that's what was running around in the cage that his grandchildren had hauled with them on vacation to the summer White House on the exclusive island of Nantucket. Letting them have their fun, he recalled his own childhood in South Dakota where they had a dog at some point in time, not that it had been of that much interest to him.

He grew up in a working class neighborhood, always planning his way out and into the majors using the navy as a jump-off point for college. Then on to work in politics, which at the time, meant democrat connections. There he set his sights on making it to the top. Though as a washed-up, and washed-out by a republican successor, senator, he literally fell into the big dog's seat when his ship came in with flying colors during the last election. You could call it a fluke but he preferred to apply 'destiny' to his good fortune. Either way, he was sitting pretty, surrounded by the opulence of the Camelot legend, the American dynasty owning choice property just down the road, across a few miles of Nantucket Sound on Martha's Vineyard and on the Cape.

It took some doing to land hip-deep in riches, far beyond the means of his modest upbringing. He thanked the good ol' boy network of union politics that took him to the top and settled him in the comfortable chair of administering an environmental advocacy think tank before being chosen from the vast field of vice presidential potentials to be added to the 2008 ticket. From there, who'd a thunk?

Van Schaal initially had thrown his hat in the ring for a presidential bid those four years back, dropping out when he didn't receive the support he rightfully deserved. Now look at him. A little tragedy leading to his good fortune, bumping him to the top of the ticket. Yup, enthroned in the catbird's seat and enjoying every bit of it, from end-less golf to handing out government cash among solid supporters, bol-stering his base.

The stimulus bills had worked out perfectly, giving the president the opportunity to dole out funds as he saw fit. The lion's share went to prop up alternative energy enterprises that really didn't fit the capi-talist label as most were better described as shell operations promot-ing fiscally untenable technology. Unfortunately, the fact of it was becoming evident to the public when he couldn't gloss over the demise of some of his buddies' companies. It pained him to see how ineptly they'd covered their tracks in applying the loans and grants he'd gifted them. And they had called him a financial bungler.

Van Schaal knew well that the appellation was misapplied to him. No bungler could have pulled off the coup that was the success story of General Motors, which he engineered precisely. With nary a whim-per, he had pried the business away from the parasite investors and delivered it into the hands of his minions - the government and dili-gent union workers. Not until this year had any journalist really gotten the lowdown on how he had manipulated the bankruptcies of both GM and Chrysler, propping up the union pension and retirement funds, like the Voluntary Employment Beneficiary Association. Paying off the $29.9 billion owed to the other unsecured creditors with 10% of the New GM Corp. and warrants for 15% more to be bought at preferred prices when it went public in 2010, VEBA was over-generously awarded 17.5% along with $9 billion more in preferred stock. The unions walked away as major stockholders of the brand New GM, which his administration created to swallow up the old GM, and the creditors who had sunk vast amounts of dollars into the auto giant were rewarded an insulting pittance of what was owed for their real debt. VEBA would continue to give retirees in their mid-50s nominal payout service for healthcare throughout their lives at the expense of the taxpayer, the whole of which was expected to top $27 billion, com-pleting Van Schaal's ideal of redistribution. And he made sure the same thing occurred for Chrysler, which he peddled for a song and a dance to the Italian carmaker Fiat, which even Van Schaal remembered calling "fix it again Tony" back in the 1970s.

All in a days work was Van Schaal's motto. He was using all the weight of his office to keep the transformational dream afloat. Thank goodness for the continued backing of groups like buildingbridges.org, his union buds and the financial resources of David Scirras that propped him up, ensuring his impending return to office this year. He was still a little clueless as to exactly what Scirras expected in return for funding the campaign so heavily, both in 2008 and this time around. Sure, Van Schaal was a shill for the alternative energy and environmental super-protagonists, which Scirras formally promoted at every turn. But this economic Goliath had fingers in every pie, manipulating markets in energy, currency and commodities to pave philosophic inroads of education and healthcare in over 50 countries. Whatever could influence the perspective of Americans to match that of the rest of the world seemed to be where Scirras infused cash, and the president's overall attitude, that the United States was too big for its britches and needed to be taken down a notch, fit Scirras' bill.

What troubled Van Schaal most was that he simply wasn't certain where this guy would stop, or if he would. The ruthlessness of the hedge fund tycoon was immeasurable, and the president, ambitious as he was, felt eyes burning into the back of his skull at every turn. Confident as he appeared before the public, Scirras unnerved him.

Now that the chief justice of the Supreme Court had given the president a win in allowing the Affordable Care Act to slide into home base, was it really a victory or could it play to Van Schaal's deficit when it came to counting votes in the end? The controversy still raged as he refused to call it a tax, no matter what SCOTUS ruled, even though, in reality, it was by far the biggest tax known to mankind, let alone the USA, ever to be levied. This was going to be an uphill battle trying to maneuver voters to overlook the cost of his healthcare law, let alone these penalties which practically triple the amount a family already pays into health insurance, and believe the story that the ACA will provide for more individuals' coverage. Between putting a positive spin on healthcare to keep the populace overlooking the lack of job creation, despite his continual tallying of nonexistent millions of jobs generated, and pointing out how the wealthy aren't paying their fair share, Van Schaal was betting on inattention to detail and pitting the people against themselves to win the day. Why change a game plan that worked in 2008? The republican nominee, Garvey Pilot, former governor of Florida and immensely successful businessman, may not be the darling of the tea parties but thus far, he's touted a very different outlook for the States.

Guess we'll see how much of a threat he really is, and, how much of a threat Scirras is, for that matter.

Van Schaal leaned back in his chaise, drinking in the sunshine, listening to the coos and squabbles of the grandkids, contemplating whether his future would be a rosy renewal of power or lavish retirement. He smiled. He'd done the main work to modify the nation with the institution of healthcare and the stimulus bills. Either way, life wasn't half-bad for an ideologue from South Dakota.

He glanced at his watch as he noticed his assistant approaching. It was time to meet his golf partner on the links.

CHAPTER 30

On its face it may have looked like a coincidence, but the fire that just happened to erupt at an address of one of the missing 'patients' was enough to drive Esteban back into the office of his ASAC. He wasn't expecting a cordial reception and Bestner didn't disappoint him. The ensuing conversation turned rancorous with little help from Esteban.

"What now?" Harry Bestner was seated behind his desk, attention directed at the computer, with two mounds of paperwork flanking either elbow. "I'm in no mood to hear about mysterious disappearances, alien abductions or demonic possessions."

"Well then, lucky for me, that's not the news I bear," said Esteban as he went ahead and sat in the chair facing Bestner, legs outstretched in as relaxed a pose as he could muster despite the roiling in his gut. He knew there was something nasty going on which he couldn't pin down, and he knew his boss wanted to hear none of it.

Looking away from the computer screen where he'd been reading through one of many reports that had been delivered electronically, Bestner answered, "Okay, what do you have this time?"

"By the standards you've set, probably not much, but being duty-bound, I felt I needed to at least bring it to your attention."

"I'm all ears," which he obviously wasn't as he kept glancing back at the monitor.

"I was double-checking on a couple of the addresses, one that had been emptied, in connection with the missing persons case."

"What did I just say?" The ASAC was in no mood for more of this case. He'd already relegated it to the dead file.

"Under the circumstances, I'd be derelict not to report the fact that while I was in the vicinity at one vacated apartment belonging to an alleged victim on the expanded list of missing persons…" Bestner was opening his mouth to object when Esteban just kept going, "and the other residence that I had been preparing to visit went up in smoke."

"Meaning?" The boss wasn't hiding his exasperation.

"I was walking down the street toward the address when firefighters arrived on the scene of a blaze at the location in question." Esteban raised his hand to forestall the coming objection as the ASAC's jaw clenched. "And yes, it was confirmed that the fire had started in the precise unit that I was going to check." In all of this, Esteban felt it was better to leave any mention of Debra Chorister out of the narration. He was under fire enough as it was, and dragging his impromptu research partner into range would be doing nothing more than drawing a nice, round target on her forehead, too.

Bestner sat back and folded his hands over his growing paunch. Peering at his subordinate with a sigh of exasperation and minimal interest. "So you were investigating something that I had deliberately told you to disregard as inconsequential to your case and, in so doing, one of the houses catches fire. Is that right?"

"That's about it. The fire was no coincidence. The occupant, Vincent Arance, has not been heard from in more than a week. The fire scene investigator said the premises were completely vacant before the fire was set, although the arson was a conjecture on his part until further investigation. It appeared that the gas stove might have been rigged to explode. The conclusive report is pending." Esteban had gotten it all out. Now he waited for the explosion of his ASAC that he could see building by the reddening of his complexion. *Here it comes.*

"Interesting as it all appears, I still cannot authorize an expanded investigation. There is nothing to warrant it beyond, as you say, conjecture on the part of the fire authorities." He sat forward with hands clasped in front of him on the desk, knuckles whitening. "You knew what the answer was going to be, so why are you here?"

Esteban got up from the chair and, standing respectfully, a touch of defiance in his carriage, he replied, "I think I made it plain as I initiated this conversation, that I felt compelled to make the report as being suspicious in nature, feeling that you would wish to be informed of any developments that may, or may not in your opinion, affect the case that you have assigned to me." He shrugged as he made his way to the door. "Simple as that."

"Duly noted," said Bestner as he returned his attention to the computer station.

Another perfect day in the city and Central Park lent itself to the tête-à-tête that Debra and Roy were having as they strolled down one of the shaded paths. Determined walkers and joggers trotted past, as well as mothers with perambulators and the occasional romantic pair holding hands as they meandered under the cooling boughs, bristling with green leaves. The Great Lawn was spotted with blankets and lounging figures taking in a little sun in the city's oasis as the afternoon waned. Coming upon a secluded bench, they settled into it to continue combing through the results of their research thus far.

"So what have we got?" Debra watched a couple of mourning doves flitting back and forth among the branches of a maple, the propeller seedlings hanging by the dozens.

"Let's summarize," said Esteban. "Six clinics in six widespread cities that specialize in, what? They appear to be linked, maybe, by a couple of doctors and board members. They're owned by, whom? All by the same organization or different ones that may or may not have crossover shareholders? The cash comes from, where? We need more in-depth information on that end. And then there are the patients. Is there any connection between them and the doctors other than the usual patient-medical professional relationship? And then there's the really strange question regarding how many patients went in for surgery or some kind of procedure only to exit with a new identity, for all intents and purposes." He sucked his upper lip between his teeth. "What could possibly be behind that little oddity?"

"And those are just the ones we could track down. What happened to the other 27, and maybe more, missing people? I'd really like a better look at the clinic records, see if any of these were also admitted for procedures. What we have are just suggestions that some of these individuals may have consulted with them, nothing else."

"If there are records of these people at one or any of the clinics, they're not open for our perusal. At this point we don't have cause to get search warrants," remarked Esteban.

A mischievous glint flashed in Debra's eye. "Why does that have to be a roadblock? I mean, if there's the least possibility that a connection exists between any of these entities, and it could lead to locating someone who would otherwise be written off by the authorities, isn't that incentive enough to go ahead with a little, uh, unorthodox investigation?"

"And since when did you decide to go rogue?"

"Since I started associating with the king of the mavericks," stated Debra straight-faced.

"Are you referring to me?"

"I don't see anyone else in the general vicinity fitting that description, so don't give me that innocent act. I've known you long enough and seen you in action too many times to know exactly what you're capable of, officially sanctioned or not." She practically harrumphed, which was a stretch for such a small woman, it being a response more suited to the girth of a Sydney Greenstreet type. "Look, we've got more questions than we can reasonably answer, or even speculate. There's nobody else looking for these people who may or may not be alive. The way I see it, we've been tagged "it" and it's up to us to take this to some kind of conclusion, good or bad."

They both sat quietly for a while watching people promenade down the park trails, some hurrying to reach their destination, others taking their time, walking at a leisurely pace. Debra broke the silence.

"I don't think we've been given a choice about this. You had a feeling from the beginning that this wasn't a cut-and-dry case. And now we know it isn't. People are not only missing but they're changing their personalities. How, for one question."

"Oh right, the invasion of the nanobots," said Esteban facetiously.

"You read the article. Didn't you check out those links?" Debra shook her head. "Some scary stuff, if you ask me."

"It's out there, all right. But no, I can't write off any possibility… yet." he conceded.

"Okay, then let's consider why. Who could possibly benefit from this?"

"There's the rub. What advantage could it be to anyone for people to shirk their successful lives, ditch their personal drive, their go-getting lifestyle and settle for a government job?" Esteban was perplexed.

"With bennies, don't forget the bennies," she added.

"Yeah, that's why I work for the government. For the benefits," he said sarcastically.

"It *is* why so many people do take government jobs, though. We both know it. AND it's much the reason why the country's in such deep doo-doo. The federal employee unions and their unreasonable demands are bleeding the private sector dry. Not that this is any reason to hunt down personality chameleons."

"Your last statement aside, you make me sound like some kind of twisted, self-centered porker slurping at the public trough." He was a little miffed at the characterization of public employees.

"Don't take it personally. Gee, I thought FBI agents had thicker skin than that. Besides, you know there are those in the employ of Uncle Sam who are little more than vampires sucking the lifeblood of the hard-working private citizen." She looked at him. "Do you like that comparison better?"

"You mean a vampire over a pig?" He considered it with playful gravity. "Sure. More romantic."

Debra rolled her eyes before continuing on. "Then we have to think through the next part... what made these driven individuals change directions midstream?"

"We need to find out," he allowed.

"Damn right, we do."

⚜⚜⚜

From the relative serenity of the park on a sunny morning to a compact cubicle at Ell's office, Debra slid behind the computer and started typing away on the keyboard. She may have been fast as a ten-key operator in her old life of keeping track of accounts receivables, but when she was fired up to find information to prove a case, her fingers literally flew over the keys, clacking away at a mile a minute.

Ell was down the hall at another attorney's station trying to straighten out a program crash caused by his attempting to upload something he shouldn't, a popular computer game. He could have landed himself in big trouble but Ell, as usual, pulled his fat out of the fire while extracting a sincere (*if attorney's could ever be sincere,* thought Ell) apology and promise to never do it again.

"Right," she muttered inaudibly as she trekked back to her own office to find Debra, head buried in the research she was collecting.

"Got anything yet?" asked Ell as she closed the door to the IT suite, allowing a little bit of privacy for a chat with Debra.

"Yes and no," she replied. "I gave Roy the heads-up that I was going underground with some of this, and, frankly, you're better off not knowing details either."

"This isn't anything that they can trace back here, is it?" Ell answered her own question. "Of course it isn't. You wouldn't jeopardize my position, let alone yours."

"No way, no how. I'm just perusing the greater internet for info scraps here and there. You know, feed the data dog I keep under the desk."

"You almost had me looking for a mutt down there," said Ell, laughing. "I must be losing it."

"No, I think it's the tales you hear from these lawyers that make you doubt what's in front of your own eyes," encouraged Debra. "Hard to know who to trust."

"You got that right. Okay, I'll let you do your thing. There's nothing else pressing around here today. Tomorrow is another matter. I have to train three new hirees on data entry."

"Hah! Piece of cake," said Debra. "You do that with your eyes closed."

"Not around here, you don't. This is a law office, remember?" With that, she settled herself behind her own desk and started buzzing through prep work and answering calls.

Debra proceeded to finesse her way into the online files of the clinics that she and Esteban had winnowed out for scrutiny. Finding her way inside was, surprisingly, nowhere near as difficult as she had expected. Their protection levels were adequate but relatively wimpy by her standards. Particularly since she had been assuming that these medical offices might be a little dirty, the fact that their firewalls were so ineffective against an amateur, albeit first-rate, hacker like her was a cause for unease. As careful as she was in tracking others and avoiding leaving a trail of her own, the relative effortless access to their files was a little alarming. If they were really trying to protect their patient records, or their financials, the security should be much more difficult to penetrate, at least enough for her to sweat it a little.

So, maybe we were wrong? Everything's legit and there's no mon - key business? There's only one way to find out. And she dove in.

With little to worry about from her end, the law firm's system being secure from reverse hacking on top of her additional efforts, Debra now had free rein perusing the clinic files. Government sites were another ball of wax, which is why she'd had Esteban doing that checking from the inside. At least she thought she wasn't getting into government files until she ran up against an odd program that *was* linked to a federal database, and it wasn't the Department of Health and Human Services, which is what she would most expect considering the nature of the business whose files she was riffling through.

Trepidation set-in when she realized it was a tracking program inserted by everyone's favorite spy organization, the IRS. What troubled her was that the program didn't appear to be chasing financial information. It was monitoring patient files.

Now why would the IRS be interested in the patient information?

She was cautious about wading into an IRS program, but it was a foot in the backdoor of the clinic's system and it's own security was easily breached, perhaps because of the nature of the program they hadn't been as diligent about protecting it since nobody would know it was there in the first place.

That sounds pretty stupid to me, but then we are talking about gov - ernment work, and I've seen too often that that means 'only do what you have to.' If I'm maligning some diligent worker bee, then, my apologies guys, but for whatever reason, looks like you gave me a secure view of what somebody wants to keep secret.

Following the tread of the stealth footprint, she found the program led her back to a special office somehow connected to the Treasury Department, something Debra had never heard of before - the Agency for Healthcare Research and Quality.

What in heaven's name is that? Deciding that there was no time like the present to find out, she opened another window and did an online search for this subsidiary related to the overseers of all things monetary in government. What healthcare research had to do with Treasury was another quandary to which she hoped to have some answers double-quick. She knew that the new healthcare law had pro-visions in it for the assessment and collection of a 'penalty' that the Supreme Court had just ruled to be a tax, and thus the IRS would of course have an interest in anyone's insurance procurement, but this wasn't connected to that, from what she could tell. It was looking like she'd have to go to the source, the 2900 pages or more of legal mumbo-jumbo that was the Affordable Care Act.

Oh no, not that...

Having no choice, she went back to the law and pulled it up in order to do a search for this AHRQ, which she located in Subtitle F – Healthcare Quality Improvements, on Page 1035.

Debra read, *"(a) Purpose. – The purposes of this section are to –*

"(1) enable the Director to identify, develop, evaluate, disseminate, and provide training in innovative methodologies and strategies for quality improvement practices in the delivery of health care services that represent best practices (referred to as 'best practices') in health care quality, safety, and value; and

"(2) ensure that the Director is accountable for implementing a model to pursue such research in a collaborative manner with other related Federal agencies.

"(b) GENERAL FUNCTIONS OF THE CENTER. - The Center for Quality Improvement and Patient Safety of the Agency for Healthcare Research and Quality (referred to as the Center), or any other relevant agency or depart - ment designated by the Director, shall –

"(1) carry out its functions using research from a variety of disciplines, which may include epidemiology, health services, sociology, psychology, human factors engineering, biostatistics, health economics, clinical research and health informatics;" etc., etc.

What is health informatics? Curiosity getting the better of her, Debra did the search thing online and found that it's a computer information science. Basically, collecting and deciphering health and bio-medical data for research using computers and other technological tools, to oversimplify the definition. Or so it appeared at a glance. They even named one of the programming systems after a childhood disease. MUMPS. *Bet Mass General thought that was cute. Nothing like taking the humanity out of human maladies. But it looks like, were the bottom to drop out of the news industry, I could do a little retrain - ing and go into medical information gathering and sharing without much strain. Might not be a bad idea considering how the US econo - my is going full-bore toward healthcare as the new growth industry.*

Back to the Agency for Healthcare Research and Quality. *What are they researching?*

"(2) RESEARCH REQUIREMENTS.—The research conducted pur - suant to paragraph (1) shall—

"(A) address the priorities identified by the Secretary in the national strategic plan established under section 399HH;

"(B) identify areas in which evidence is insufficient to identify strategies and methodologies, taking into consideration areas of insufficient evidence identified by the entity with a contract under section 1890(a) of the Social Security Act in the report required under section 6 399JJ;

"(C) address concerns identified by health care institutions and providers and communicated through the Center pursuant to subsection (d);

"(D) reduce preventable morbidity, mortality, and associated costs of morbidity and mortality by building capacity for patient safety research;

"(E) support the discovery of processes for the reliable, safe, efficient, and responsive delivery of health care, taking into account discoveries from clinical research and comparative effectiveness research;

"(F) allow communication of research findings and translate evidence

177

into practice recommendations that are adaptable to a variety of settings, and which, as soon as practicable after the establishment of the Center, shall include—"

Blah, blah, blah, blah, blah.

Here we go, thought Debra. *Funding. That's what we're looking for… who's funding what to what end. As they say, follow the money…*

"(g) FUNDING.—There is authorized to be appropriated to carry out this section $20,000,000 for fiscal years 2010 through 2014.

"SEC. 934. QUALITY IMPROVEMENT TECHNICAL ASSISTANCE AND IMPLEMENTATION.

"(a) IN GENERAL.—The Director, through the Center for Quality Improvement and Patient Safety of the Agency for Healthcare Research and Quality (referred to in this section as the 'Center'), **shall award—**

"(1) technical assistance grants or contracts to eligible entities to provide technical support to institutions that deliver health care and health care providers *(including rural and urban providers of services and suppliers with limited infrastructure and financial resources to implement and support quality improvement activities, providers of services and suppliers with poor performance scores, and providers of services and suppliers for which there are disparities in care among subgroups of patients) so that such institutions and providers understand, adapt, and implement the models and practices identified in the research conducted by the Center, including the Quality Improvement Networks Research Program;* **and**

"(2) implementation grants or contracts to eligible entities to implement the models and practices described under paragraph (1)."

Debra noted that funding began in 2010, but from what she knew, were mostly unallocated for the programs. So, where'd the money really come from? That question required that much more digging until she found herself at the website for stimulus spending, otherwise known as the American Recovery and Reinvestment Act. Aside from the $20 million noted in the law there was $300 million set aside for research through AHRQ for grants. This is where she found what they were researching:

"§399HH. National Strategy for Quality Improvement in Health Care.

"(a) Establishment of National Strategy and Priorities. –

"(1) National Strategy. – The Secretary, through a transparent collabo -
rative process,"

We know how that works, Debra thought...

"shall establish a national strategy to improve the delivery of health care
services, patient health outcomes, and population health."

Now she was getting something of a picture as to the barn door
that had been opened when the Affordable Care Act had been signed
into law. She had to draw back as she realized that this was a drop in
the bucket of "change" because, according to this insignificant snippet
of an overbearing 2900 pages of legal maneuverings and elitist over-
lordship, Debra wondered if the regulations could be harnessed at all.
Just going over these few pages and understanding how the ACA
referred back and forth to other titles in the U.S. code, such as Title 42,
Title 4, Title 2, Title 26, and on and on, it was obvious that this so
entangled the whole code that it would become almost impossible to
extricate the American people. *If,* she thought, *we don't do something
soon. Like Toddy advocates, flourish our colors, affirm our power as
the founding documents made clear. Government is our servant and
may be whipped, chastened and simply run out of town if those in
office refuse to perform their duties according to the will of the People.*

Just reading through this and page after page of restrictive policies
laid out with flowery language that absolutely obscures the mal-intent
of the law in general appalled her. Debra also understood how citizens
would simply accept the governmental spin on the content of the legislation instead of even attempting to comprehend the language. *But
this is how we're losing the nation. All due to complacency.*

Her train of thought brought her back around to focus on the bill
before her eyes, the references to this section and that which pulled it
together began to take on a fiendish quality. Debra had to pose the
questions of what the IRS was surreptitiously monitoring at these clinics. *Perhaps it's about new methodologies. The legislation certainly
proposes the development of such for the* "improvement of healthcare" *and research includes experimentation.*

Mulling it over, Debra considered that the patients – *maybe they are victims* – had undergone treatment for some kind of implant. Perhaps the research was to test the efficacy of the new and improved devices? It says that the AHRQ was all about improving delivery of healthcare. So what would be the purpose of the kind of experimentation that induced the strange results they've encountered? Could behavior modification be a side effect? At this point, it crossed her mind that this idea kind of fit the "bill." *Legislatively speaking, that is.*

CHAPTER 31

Another Saturday night but this one was far different from any the three cohorts had experienced in the past. They were confronting something that, before this week, none would have conceived possible. Though dinner started out with the mundane.

The weather was cooperating so well, Ell was opining about the ridiculous laws that virtually banned outdoor grilling without actually doing so.

"You know. There was a time when I could have a barbecue on the balcony and enjoy the evening air… as much as you can in a big city. But then the nannystaters took office and prohibited having a grill within 10 feet of anything combustible. That effectively makes anyone living in an apartment or condo in the city a criminal for setting up a hibachi. *And*, you can't transport propane, so that's out." She went back to her little rangetop grill that produced a tolerable facsimile of barbecue but without the fun or flavor. "Much as I love this city, I have gotten fed-up with the absurd regulating of everyday life. No wonder tea partiers are taking it to the streets," she said as she turned the steaks. "Now, if only the media would cover them with the respect they deserve instead of trying to equate them with the complete imbeciles that took over Zucotti Park, trashing it and closing businesses. Could there be anything so opposite as those two groups? Not to mention the fact that tea parties outnumber the Occupy Wall Streeters by the tens of millions."

Ell's diatribe concluded for the moment, Debra and Roy helped her load the plates and take them into the living area to enjoy the meal, peering out the glass pane instead of trying to sit three chairs on the balcony. "If it even smells like I grilled, the neighbors would bust me without a second thought." Ell settled in and took a bite. "This is what we have to look forward to, people turning in their neighbors for implied lawbreaking. Ya know," she said as she chewed, "lately things have really gone south, people not trusting anyone and ratting out neighbors for the most moronic things."

"Have you thought about moving out of the city?" Debra asked between bites.

"I have, but I'd miss all the amenities I've come to depend on, like the fantastic restaurants, shows, movies. And I don't need a car."

"Okay, you don't have to spend on parking or the manipulated, outrageously overpriced gas, but then," Debra made her point waving her fork in the air, "you can't even buy a big Coke at the theater."

"Give a little, take a little," said Ell.

"Are you hearing yourself? You can't stand the regulation but even *you* are taking a futile attitude." With a playful air of scolding, Debra shook her fork at Ell. "You disappoint me. Look at what Roy and I have run across. This kind of potential for evil is only empowered by an attitude that accepts what's unacceptable. And that's not the Ell I know."

"Point taken. Sometimes you just lose the will to buck city hall, literally."

"Exactly," said Debra.

Roy thought this was as good a time as any to jump in. "Since you said we've run across something, I'd kind of like to hear the details, be in on what I'm already supposed to be in on." He cocked an eyebrow at Debra.

"I was planning on giving you the rundown after we'd eaten. It might spoil your appetite."

"Good enough," he put down his plate, which he'd already cleaned with some alacrity, charbroiled or not. "Talk."

"Yeah, talk girl," chimed in Ell. She was ready to change the subject knowing she loved this town but, like so many who lived there, she was beginning to feel oppressed and practically helpless to do anything except kvetch. Maybe giving Debra a place to do research would assuage some of that guilt.

"All right," said Debra as she also laid her plate on the coffee table.

"Just don't tell me where any of this came from. I need deniability," cut-in Ell, half-jokingly.

"Okaaay..." Debra hedged a bit before diving in. "Where to start. Hmmm, patient files. That's about the best place to begin as any. I stumbled across an interesting intruder into a couple of the clinics' online files while I was wangling my way..."

"Nope," Ell cut her off. "Stop with where you were going or how, etc. I don't need to know details, remember?"

"Right," and Debra bypassed that part as she explained about how befuddled she was at the healthcare facilities' lack of armor and the backdoor monitor that traced back to Treasury.

"I don't get it, what's that got to do with medical clientele?" Ell was with Debra in thinking, at first, that it made no sense.

"That's what I thought until I found the trail of the gatecrasher leading back to something called the AHRQ."

"That sounds like air quality control, taking me totally off course and back to thinking about the outside grilling no-no in New York," said Ell.

"It isn't air quality, but you got one of the words in the acronym correct. It stands for Agency for Healthcare Research and Quality."

Esteban reclined into the sofa, hands clasped behind his head while he silently absorbed the chronicle of Debra's inquiry. Ell's response was the opposite. "What the hell's that? It could be ominous or nonessential. Knowing what I do about attorneys and their penchant for candy-coating something nasty, I'd go for the first option."

"You may be right. The major purpose that I could see for the agency was to fund research for, let me see if I can find it, I wrote it down." And she dug into her purse for a mini legal pad with her scribbling across it.

"Here it is..."The central goal of our research is measurable improvements in health care in America, gauged in terms of improved quality of life and patient outcomes, lives saved, and value gained for what we spend." So, they are spending, as just one of 12 agencies in the Department of Health and Human Services, uh, $405 million dollars budgeted for 2012 on research for whatever they consider to improve quality of delivered healthcare. And that's up $28 million from the year before."

"I'd love to know what the AHRQ and DHHS consider to be 'improvements'," said Ell.

"That seems to be part of the quandary connected to all of this. So, I had to comb through parts of the Affordable Care Act..."

"You poor thing," commiserated Ell.

"Uh-huh, my favorite thing, to read through endless pages of lawyer-speak. Anyway, this is what I found," and she pulled a file out of the same handbag that was on the end of the coffee table. "I traced the possible relationship between the medical facilities to what they call "technical assistance awards" and what are probably clinical studies. According to section 934(d) in the bill, the AHRQ matches funds to grants at a ratio of one dollar of private funds to five dollars of federal money, but, and here's the rub... the funding is actually from the American Recovery and Reinvestment Act of 2009. This is money that was allocated for the healthcare bill before the bill was passed, *and*, the ACA didn't really have any funding within it." Debra looked up at Roy and Ell. "If you remember, this was one of the conservative arguments about this bill and their supposed ability to make it ineffective because all they had to do was keep it unfunded. Well," and she pointed to her notes, "how much of the funding had *already been passed before the ACA was ever introduced on the floor of Congress?*"

Roy raised an eyebrow but Ell was fuming. "What an utter crock! Can we trust no one in office?"

"No, not really," said the otherwise silent Esteban. "Even the best of politicians who start out with the right attitude get turned once in D.C. simply because they don't understand the Constitution to which they've pledged to uphold."

"And you'd know. You take the same pledge," said Debra.

"Okay, I'm digressing some," and Debra returned to her narrative. "The AHRQ awards all kinds of grants that come inside their broad guidelines, which you heard, to colleges, hospitals and research facilities. The funding, however, isn't overseen by any actual administrative office other than, you guessed it, the White House. It's a "special projects fund" so, I presume that means it gives money to whatever the

White House deems to be a special project. At least, this is how it looks but I don't pretend to be an expert.

"This is what it says at the AHRQ site, which I could find through the ARRA website but had trouble locating through DHHS:

"The Agency for Healthcare Research and Quality (AHRQ) has opportunities under the American Recovery and Reinvestment Act of 2009 (Recovery Act) to provide patients, clinicians, and others evidence-based information to make informed decisions about health care. The Recovery Act contains $1.1 billion for comparative effectiveness research. Of the total, $300 million is for AHRQ to build on its existing collaborative and transparent Effective Health Care program."

"This is where you find the funding for what may be a research grant to these clinics that we're checking into," Esteban sounded more like he was reiterating the information for himself, to see correlations in his mind.

"It appears to be pretty obvious," Ell added.

"Yes, and when I went to see what kinds of grants they were handing out, I came across the "comparative effectiveness awards," which, if my surmises are anywhere near accurate, fits like a glove to what could be happening as in they're trying out newly engineered medical devices for "comparative effectiveness." And, that's a pretty wide catch-all, don't you think?"

"Oh, I think," agreed Ell.

"This definitely is looking very possible," said Roy. "Let's go back to the matching funds. Did you find anything that indicates who the private financier is for these, I guess we can refer to them as studies?"

"Fancy you should ask, because that brings us to the fun part."

"I'm glad to hear that there's a little entertainment involved in all the drudgery of reading through congressional legislation," he deadpanned.

"I did track a couple of the names on the boards, including the one who sits on all six in some capacity or other, and it led back to the Scirras Foundation," said Debra expectantly.

"Somehow I think I should be able to place that name," said Ell, scouring her memory.

"I know that you're familiar with the name. Grigor Scirras was the major financial source for the democratic ticket in 2008 and this election cycle as well. He and his heirs fund buildingbridges.org and the left-left-left blogs that have the audacity to call themselves journalists. The Scirras Foundation is also a key backer of the largest, most radical progressive environmental activists from EcoEarth Legal Center, Conservation Society, Protect Our Planet – which was caught red-handed committing eco-terrorist acts – and, not to forget, the international tentacles of the Free States Foundation which promotes and undermines governments with its progressive agenda." Debra took a breath.

"Say it like it is, because now I remember, the guy is an elitist tycoon turned socialist who got his and wants to ensure no one else has the opportunity he did," said Ell. "The old, 'I got mine, now the rest of you can do homage to me.' In other words, pound sand."

"You pegged him. This is one of the biggest hedge fund guys around," added Esteban. "It finally started coming out a couple of years ago."

"The person who really blew the lid off the progressive democrat politics-Scirras connection and his so-called philanthropy, which we know as involving himself in more than 50 nations' politics, especially Eastern Bloc, previously Iron Curtain countries, was Toddy Littman," explained Debra. "Everyone had been late to dinner when it came to identifying Scirras and his leveraging ways in the currency market until Toddy took him to task through his website, ChangingWind.Org, before the 2008 election. Trouble is, no one listened until that radio and cable personality started blowing his own horn a couple years later and taking a lot of flack for it, too. Enough so, that he packed up his toys and left, setting up an internet television network. He's been exceptionally successful and thank goodness because no matter how ahead of the pack Toddy is, not enough people are taking him seriously. If we'd listen to what he blogs on regarding the sovereignty of the people, this country might have a chance. No one else is reading the Federalist Papers or seems to understand them in today's application."

"I know that I couldn't wade through them. The language is so antiquated it would take me forever," said Ell.

"You know, if the Federalist Papers were mandatory reading in high school instead of some of the questionable novels that are required, this country would be in far better shape. We might even understand the Constitution," said Esteban thoughtfully.

"All right, so now what?" asked Ell. "Not like I know anything about any of this, which is precisely what I'd answer to anyone who asks."

"Now," said Debra, "I think we have to tidy up the origin of cash contributions, the research entities as in who applied for the grants, assuming there were grants awarded, what outcomes they're trying to achieve and who all are receiving the reports. That last one will tell us everything about who has an interest and why."

"With luck, it will lead all the way back to finding the people who dropped out of sight. Their disappearance is the trailhead. Once we make connections between them and the clinics, the types of surgical procedures performed and if they're related to any clinical research, we may have some answers," said Esteban.

"Then, maybe we'll solve the crime, if there is one," added Debra.

Roy sat up and started to collect his dishes. "It's time to get inside the medical admissions records."

"Already done." Smiling demurely, Debra handed him another folder she promptly produced from her designer purse.

BLOOD BARONS

CHAPTER 32

Sunday morning and it was another bright and blessed day, the way Debra saw it. Their investigation may have been shrouded by strange circumstances and stranger links to government institutions and financial figures but she stashed it away, having determined to go to church. Unfamiliar as she was with the local church scene, she decided to attend a Catholic church within walking distance from Ell's.

Debra had grown up in the Catholic tradition but more recently had found a nondenominational church that suited her. Spending time reading the Bible had become more of an interest, particularly as so many people were likening the current social troubles to end-time prophecy. Her personal viewpoint was not to expend excess energy on what might happen but place emphasis on what will help her live better, applying more effort toward service than worry. That attitude had a tendency to get her in hot water with some evangelical camps but she figured Scripture is Scripture and she'd follow that rather than a particular individual's teaching, though she found all of it fascinating. Occasionally she still enjoyed going to mass, finding solace in the ceremony that had been part of her upbringing.

Before Roy had left Ell's Saturday night she'd made mention of her plan, hoping to get Ell to come along. Debra didn't really want to miss church two weeks in a row since the last Sunday she'd been busy preparing to catch a flight to New York. Predictably, Ell declined, not having any inclination toward organized religion.

The firebug incident at one of the locations Debra had visited alone the day prior to the blaze they had witnessed, prompted Esteban to insist on escorting her. He'd given up on church years ago himself. Figuring that God had taken a hike, he'd directed all his energy into his job, probably one of the factors that had led to his wife leaving years ago. Catholic-raised like Debra, he'd just shrugged and decided it couldn't hurt to go light a candle.

He arrived to pick her up and they turned up the street, out of sight of Ell's front porch when someone else spotted them taking a Sunday stroll. He decided to tag along, at a distance.

⚜ ⚜ ⚜ ⚜

Walking down Third Avenue was relatively quiet for such a wide and usually bustling boulevard. Trees were at a premium in this part of town, but there were some spreading their limbs across the sidewalk, broad leaves creating small oases of shade in the dazzling morning sun. It didn't take more than 15 minutes to amble down to the 19th century church, the architecture reflecting the time of its construction, traditional yet not overpowering, the vaulted roof inspiring awe yet not overwhelming the penitent.

Debra and Roy climbed the steps to enter the church and found the pews well filled for the 11:15 mass, which, for some reason surprised Roy. Having settled into the Big Apple, the majority of people he met day-to-day were secularists who gave faith short shrift. It taught him not to assume too much from limited experience, which, oddly, he carefully avoided on the job. *Goes to show how prejudice can slip in anywhere.* He was impressed with the showing of the faithful, although a fair fraction of them may be Sunday Christians it still demonstrated an effort to do the right thing.

Pervading memories of his childhood, holding tightly onto his mother's hand as she towed him into their hometown cathedral, came flooding back as he gazed upward. As a toddler he'd experienced an earthquake where the roof had partially collapsed. After that, his young mind always pictured the soaring ceiling of intricately carved clouds and angels holding aloft what had to be heaven, falling down around him. The childhood dread that he'd felt each time he'd come to mass swamped him as he first set foot outside the narthex, the foyer, feeling the room open spaciously to house the parishioners. The feeling quickly vanished as he walked down the center aisle with Debra to find a pew halfway down the nave. Taking a seat, he recalled the points of the service, having been ingrained in him at a young age. The familiarity of the mass brought an ease that he assumed had dissipated with time, and he gave in to the surrounding peace that caught him by surprise.

⚜⚜⚜

Mass had been refreshing and the handshakes that had been offered in welcome afterward had restored hope in Roy that the city wasn't the desolate place he saw most of the time. Dealing daily with criminals and individuals, including some fellow agents, struggling with life had jaded him more than he'd realized. It was a wake-up call that he'd abandoned prayer, replacing it with mental gymnastics that rarely gave him answers, let alone a calm perspective, on which he'd prided himself as a professional problem solver. *So much for that assumption. We've got a problem now with so many questions, resolu-tion isn't looking so good.*

Half a block from Ell's was a nifty little joint that served a hearty breakfast and Debra and Roy decided to stop and eat. Sundays were a big day for the brunch crowd and they waited for ten minutes before procuring a table outside where they could drink in some sun along with a full-bodied cup of coffee.

"Hmmm, aromatic Kona will sweep all your ills away," Debra held the mug under her nose and just inhaled the rich scent of freshly ground beans. "Didn't think you could get such great coffee in a little sidewalk diner."

"Are you going to drink that or cherish it?" Esteban sipped his own coffee. "This is New York. You can get anything here, legal or not, which is why my office is so busy."

"Well then, some Jamaican Blue Mountain would hit the spot even more than Kona. That would take some hunting down, but, hmmm is it worth it."

"Worth the price?"

"Oh yes. Which is why I can just be wistful about enjoying it rather than procuring any," said Debra. "Outrageously expensive for the real stuff. Like gold."

"This'll have to suffice," he said.

"I will enjoy every swallow," and Debra did exactly that.

"Now that you've exhausted the subject of superior coffee, I need to make some tough decisions and I need your help to do it."

"Me? I know nuthin' from nuthin'. I'm just the researcher, here on holiday and enjoying a exceptional cup of joe." She peered at him over the rim of the mug, huge brown eyes deeper than wells, lightheartedly questioning his need to consult her, an amateur.

"You've proven your own worth, far more than that Jamaican Blue you prize so highly," he winked, but the solemn nature of his thoughts underlaid the jocular banter.

Catching his drift, Debra put the jesting aside. "So what more can I possibly help you with? I thought I did what I was here to do and now it's back in the FBI's court."

"It would be if the big and semi-big boss were interested in following up on what you uncovered," he assumed the official agent persona for a moment, getting serious. "After the last encounter in the ASAC's office, it's more than evident that no one in the Bureau wants the headache."

"How disappointing that federal law enforcement would look upon the disappearance of dozens of people as a mere 'headache,'" she said with a sniff.

"But there you have it and thus, my predicament."

"What predicament is that? They shut you down," Debra's voice raised some in vehemence as she clunked her mug on the table and made an effort to mellow her tone. "I don't get it, but that's the size of it as far as can see."

"It is," Esteban concurred. "So. I'm weighing my options."

"I didn't know you had any… unless you're toying with mutiny again."

Shrugging his shoulders, he gave her that penetrating stare. Debra sat back in her chair and lifted her hands up to the sky in exasperation.

"Figures. Still haven't learned your lesson, huh?"

"Depends on how you look at it. Do a rundown of what we've

got."

"You mean, what we haven't got, don't you?" She was wondering where this was going.

"Perhaps," and Esteban persisted in evaluating the evidence, ticking off points on his fingers. "One: Thus far we've identified approximately 30 missing people with special circumstances who law enforcement has written off for one reason or another. Two: All were pointed toward some rehabilitative surgical procedure at one of... Number Three: Six medical facilities cross-pollinated by five individuals – three doctors and two businesspeople. Four: Funding in some measure has been traced to two entities, the Scirras Foundation – by way of multiple auxiliary organizations or corporations – and the Agency for Healthcare Research and Quality. Five: The funding appears to be related to grants for unspecified research awarded by point Four A under titles like, "Comparative Effectiveness of Common Surgical Implant Procedures – In-patient to Outpatient Facilities."

"You have been studying," said Debra, impressed by his rattling off a title like that.

Ignoring her, he went back to his enumeration. "Six: Three patients have been located of the 30. Seven: All three have undergone some kind of personality modification." He relaxed back in his chair for a moment before moving ahead with the big questions. "All these apparently connected facts still leave us with these unanswered points. Where are the others who have supposedly gone missing? Last we see them they are preparing for surgery and we only have a few patient files that indicate admission to any one of these six clinics for procedures. Lastly, how do we find them and how does that concern the evident research studies or clinical trials?"

"You're the professional detective here. So, what's your suggestion since the answer is not to be found going back through normal channels? How many times do you need to be cut off at the knees?" Debra became pensive. "And if you sidestep the Bureau that's got to be the sunset of a remarkable career."

"Yeah, I'd be out the door with a bootprint on my ass."

"Well put," she said ironically.

"Which, the description of my retirement or the bootprint?"

"Both," she looked at him hard. "All right, cowboy. I know I'll regret asking but, what's your plan?"

"To find out why the Scirras Foundation is interested in hip and knee replacements…"

"Don't forget artery fortifiers and hearing aids," she cut-in.

"And why, with all their dough, are they getting federal funding?" Esteban placed his napkin on the table and stood up. He took cash out of his pocket and counted out the bills to pay the check.

"Time to get some answers." He held out his hand for her to take. "Coming?"

⚜ ⚜ ⚜

Although the formidable looking agent was asking his lunch partner if she wanted to accompany him, another patron, who had been sitting right inside the restaurant at a window booth, also decided to take him up on the offer.

Keeping a healthy distance behind the odd pair, the fed about a foot taller than the black woman who was dressed for church, which he hadn't guessed at having tailed them there, he was forced to stop when they went no further than the apartment building where he'd picked them up earlier. They both went inside and he deliberated his options.

Hanging around on the block wasn't one of them. He'd be spotted for loitering or recognized from previous instances and the number one rule was "don't take chances." So, he didn't, but he'd heard enough to report in and take the rest of the day off.

Heading toward the subway, he pulled his cell phone out of his pocket and placed a call. It rang so many times he was preparing to just shut it off rather than leave a message, which was rule number two: "don't say anything unnecessary." Leaving a recorded message came under that heading as providing information when they were adjured to say as little as possible in any public forum, and voicemail could be accessed by unknowns. At times he found the whole, "don't do this or that" annoying beyond belief, but it paid the bills and he was whittling away at the school loans, which was the worst of his debts.

As his thumb hovered over the screen to touch 'end,' the line was picked up. *So much for a quick out.*

"Yes?" was all the answer the doctor gave.

"It's Shep," which wasn't his name, just an identifier for the man in charge who 'Shep' wasn't sure was really a doctor. That's just what he'd been told to call him. "I have some information that I wanted to get into your hands."

"Is this from your task this morning?"

"Yes. I just left them and I'm heading home."

"That's fine. What information do you have for me? I'm interested," said the doctor.

"I was lucky enough to grab a table close to them at Cluckster's and overheard quite a lot," said Shep.

"How do you know it's reliable?"

"I don't, but they didn't appear to be concerned about being overheard. Most people wouldn't have made head or tails from it anyway."

"You think so, eh?" Skepticism was a natural sense with the doctor. He didn't trust anyone, let alone a hired hand. Never did he count on mercenaries, especially the amateurs. "Go on."

Shep detailed the major points of the conversation and when he reached the highlights of mentioning Scirras and the Agency for Healthcare Research and Quality, the doctor knew they had to watch their back.

"Good that you contacted me," said the doctor. "Go ahead and take the rest of the day for yourself."

Shep hung up, already thinking about what he'd do with his Sunday. With luck, his girlfriend would be home. He came to the subway station entrance and hopped down the staircase anticipating a pleasant afternoon.

The doctor, on the other hand, had just been handed notification that the threat quotient had increased. Now he had to weigh his choices with extra caution because they had just dwindled by half.

BLOOD BARONS

CHAPTER 33

The last thing on Roy Esteban's wish list was approaching ASAC Harry Bestner on this case of the missing patients. He'd given in to using Debra's label for the ever-growing list of disappearances that, by law enforcement standards, were classified as not having actually vanished. He knew what he had to do. Nothing in this case, or cases, was as it appeared and despite his boss' expectations of having Esteban neatly tie this up in a bow, the tails were getting longer and leggier with each passing day. There was nothing neat or tidy about the whole mess, particularly when it looked like the fraying ends led back to a powerful money mogul and government involvement. He was not looking forward to what he knew would be an unpleasant confrontation.

Suck it up, compinche. Knocking first, he opened the door to federal hell.

"Again?" Assistant Special Agent in Charge Harry Bestner's scowl couldn't have been any more pronounced. "You're here less than a year and it's been nothing but a tug-of-war with you, Esteban."

"Not intentionally, sir. I'm just being diligent as has always been my habit."

"Diligently digging a hole for your career is all that I can see." Bestner sat down behind the desk. "Your performance rating rises for a couple of years, commendations and promotions, then you crash. Up again and down. How many times have you done that, Esteban?"

Roy had to think before he answered. He hadn't put it in quite those terms before. "Two or three. Circumstances are what they are."

"They are indeed," said Bestner. "Believe it or not, I'm really not out to sideline you. You've earned your retirement and it's coming up soon enough. Thirty years is a good long haul in the Bureau. So why are you jeopardizing your pension with this penny-ante case?"

"It's not a matter of risking my retirement, you know we all have sworn to perform our duty and when I'm confronted with the possibility that what looks like a dead-end case may have resolution, the choice seems obvious." Esteban continued to stand, figuring he'd be kicked out of the office as soon as he planted his behind in a chair. "At least, to me it is."

"Look, you had three people to locate. You found one. Job well done. The others probably don't even want to be found, like that Grigg woman. They just want their privacy and to be left alone. They're grown-ups and can do whatever they want."

"You know and I know, real grown-ups act like it and don't fall off the map. Sure, there are irresponsible bums that would put their friends and family through hell just to scrap their unhappy lives. But those are few and far between. From what I've discovered about the two still missing from the original case, is that they weren't flakes," Esteban was near pleading for an ounce of compassion for the victims.

"You have found nothing other than empty apartments, and some-one had to authorize the thorough cleaning that you observed after they'd gone."

"Who's to say that it was the alleged victims who did the authorizing?" Esteban wasn't giving up yet.

"No one, but we have no proof that anyone else did, either." Bestner exhaled, "You've got to let this go. At this juncture, it's best to close the cases."

"What about the pattern that's formed?" asked Esteban.

"I don't see a pattern, and like it or not, I'm not blind. I assume that you're talking now about the other so-called missing persons cases you've come up with. What I see is an assertive effort to make these unrelated cases appear to be associated, but you've got to recognize that it's a stretch at the very least," said Bestner.

"Let me give you some of the facts that have come forth. Most all of these individuals were preparing for surgical procedures at one of six clinics nationwide. There appear to be close ties between all of the facilities, linked by management personnel, financing and the fact that potential patients have gone missing. There's also a strange connection to a federal research agency." Esteban did his best to lay out some of the most persuasive of his arguments. And even as he stated them, he knew they were so tenuous that he'd never receive the sanction to investigate.

"You've got to understand what it looks like from my side of the desk and no matter how passionate you are regarding these people who no one can find, or has even really tried to find, from what you've told me, this is the bottom line. I cannot authorize any manpower to investigate something as nebulous as a handful of people falling off the grid in major metro areas that are famous for disappearing acts." Bestner had been trying to be calm about the whole thing but he was rapidly losing patience with the constant argument from a subordinate.

"I've identified the underlying ties that make this case a viable one, and as such I know it can be solved, bringing a lot of people home," said Esteban.

Bestner became wary about Esteban's research claims. "How was the information obtained and how reliable is it?"

"An anonymous source of impeccable character. The information is rock-solid."

"How can you assert that if it's an anonymous informant?" The ASAC shook his head. "You're heading right down the same old rabbit hole, Esteban. You know I can't authorize this. I have to have more confirmation.

"We both know this is nuts." Bestner shut him down in every direction, tired and irritated by the whole continuing argument. "Close the files on the three cases on your desk and you'll receive a new assignment tomorrow." He waved his hand, angry that he couldn't get this agent to play nice. "Get lost. I don't want to see you in here again."

⚜⚜⚜

Esteban had to make a judicious effort to close the door behind him without slamming it, his frustration level was so far off the chart. Deliberately walking past his desk he found himself in the elevator and heading to another floor. He punched in a number and tried to keep his temper under control when his inclination was to plow his knuckles into the metal sliding door of the lift. Esteban had more common sense than to purposefully maim himself and restrained the impulse, forcing his hands into his pockets. Reining in his resentment, he managed to plaster a reasonable facsimile of a half-smile on his face, one that always seemed to affect women in such a way that they were amenable to his practical requests. He was going to need it as he calmed himself to wait until the elevator door opened completely, allowing him to exit on the floor where human resources was located.

❧❧❧❧

Later that day, Esteban arrived at Ell's before she'd come back from the law offices. Debra was already there, packing up her monster suitcase in preparation to catch a flight home. She buzzed him in and when she opened the door to admit him he spied the activity.

"Leaving so soon?"

"I've had my fun, done my duty and cornered the bad guys in cyberspace. Now it's up to you lawmen to catch 'em and throw 'em in the clink for the rest of their miserable lives," she said as she walked back to her job of folding and stowing articles of clothing.

"What, without my trusty sidekick?"

"Tell me, am I Lois Lane, Batgirl or Nell Fenwick?"

"Never Nell. Railroad track rescues aren't in the plan and I'd like to think Dudley and I aren't intellectually equal."

Debra gave him a sidelong glance. "Don't start playing the horses, Do-right went to any lengths for justice, smart or not."

"You got me there. But as a crime-fighting partner it would have to be Lois Lane for all her news know-how. So how about it?"

"How about what? I thought I'd done all the damage I could and am being cut loose to actually go enjoy a few days of real vacation," said Debra.

"How can you possibly enjoy your holiday without me?" And he slapped on the engaging half-smile that had already worked once today, hoping for a second bonanza.

"What in the Lord's name are you grinning at? And what do you mean about vacationing without you? Why would you be included?" She quirked her brow waiting for a sensible response.

"These," and he pulled airline passes out of his jacket pocket. "Two tickets to paradise."

She'd had enough of his cat and mouse and whipping around on her heel, she placed both fists on her hips. "What *are* you talking about?"

"Well, you're already packed and I have a week off so I figured we'd go sleuthing."

"In paradise? Unless you have a case in St. Lucia…"

"Not quite. Would St. Louis suffice?" he asked hopefully.

"That's about as far from a Caribbean resort as you can get, but, okay, give me the particulars."

⚜⚜⚜

When Ell walked in the door, she found Debra's bags packed and obstructing the hall. Debra and Esteban were seated on the couch, heads together going over something that sounded important.

"All right, what plot are you hatching now?" she asked, reaching over the pile of luggage and dropping her handbag on the hall table.

"Us? No conspiracy here," Debra playfully waved her hands negating the idea of concocting surreptitious plans.

"After this week, I don't really believe you," and she came into the living room, plopping into her favorite chair, dangling her hands over the armrests in the picture of exhaustion. "Now tell me what's going on."

"When you're caught in the act…" Esteban leaned back into the sofa and tried applying the grin once more for the day.

"Wipe that smile off your face," said Ell. "You're not about to charm this old spinster. Seen too much to be hornswoggled by the likes of you. Besides, it doesn't fit the all-business federal agent guise you wear like one of those government-issued suits."

"You don't like my suit?" Esteban gave in to Ell's hard knocks. He respected her experience and her sense of humor.

Debra jumped in, "And I'll defend the smile. It's a nice change from the gruff stuff."

"Have it your way. Tell me what's up." Ell was done with the chitchat.

"Looks like we're taking this show on the road," replied Debra.

"You're what?" and she pinned Esteban with a glare that could cut steel. "Did you learn nothing from the last escapade? First, my niece, now her friend? You're running out of susceptible women to do your bidding. Who will you haul into one of your felon-fetching schemes next time?"

"Let's not go overboard here," Debra said to calm the flare of indignation. Ell was very protective of her chicks and Debra was now one of them. Esteban was the strutting rooster who needed to have some tail feathers plucked. "I'm not going undercover. All we're doing is visiting a couple of cities and asking a few questions about people no one can find. Nothing risky."

Ell sat back, mollified some. "That's what they all say." She looked at Esteban. "You'd just wormed your way into my good graces. You'd better not blow it."

"You have my word," he was somber and started second-guessing his idea. How crazy was it? Not like the last one that sent his career down the tubes, in this he was certain. *No, we'll be okay. I'll be with her every step of the way and all we're doing is asking questions.* Though he fully realized that a simple question asked of the wrong person could cause trouble, he was confident that they'd be fine, and he was going to need someone who could get inside databases if it came to that.

"So, what's your estimated time of departure?"

"First thing in the morning we're flying out of La Guardia," said Debra.

Ell got up and went toward the kitchen. "We may as well send you off right. I'm going to rustle up some vittles and you need to hear what Allie and Yancy had to say today. In another way, it has bearing on the Schaalcare baloney you've been digging through."

As she went into the kitchen, Esteban asked Debra, "Who's Yancy? Is he a colleague of Allie's or Ell's?"

"Yancy's a she. And she and Ell got to know each other when they worked in the same law office here. Since then, Yancy's gone out to Montana to take a job with the Constitutional Legal Fund as an advocate for individuals fighting for their rights, most often against heavy-handed government agencies, like the EPA."

"She's a lawyer? I thought Ell didn't like lawyers."

"Depends on the person. Yancy wasn't cut out for corporate law and she couldn't handle the liberal tactics of the defense fund she'd worked for in Boston. Said they were all cannibalistic sharks," explained Debra. "She wasn't so far from the truth when you think about it. You talked about meter maids eating their young? Attorneys swallow them whole."

"But Yancy isn't cut from the same cloth," said Esteban.

"No, she has a conscience."

Ell came back into the room with a huge platter of nachos, convection-oven style, and a pitcher of margaritas. "They're virgin. You'll need your wits about you."

They dug in with enthusiasm while Ell went through the interesting conversation she'd had with Yancy earlier in the day.

"I know you remember, Debra, but Roy, you probably don't know about this one case Yancy has been working on for a couple of years. Kara Lysander has been struggling with the effects of juvenile diabetes which was misdiagnosed for years, ending up with this little girl depending on dialysis. I won't go into details but the family has wrestled with first, under-funded Indian Health, she's Crow, and then, of all things, the Environmental Protection Agency."

"How does the EPA come into a healthcare issue?" asked Esteban.

"It's convoluted but it came down to receiving a dependable power supply to their home in a small town in Wyoming to make sure the dialysis machine was always working. You were deeply involved in the investigation into the power plant explosions there so you know what was going on with the old plant being shut down, etc. etc."

Roy nodded. "Go on."

"Setting aside the battle with the EPA, this whole deal has come down to the family finally locating a kidney donor, only this time it's a different government agency sticking its nose in what should be private business," Ell took a break from her narrative to nibble on some nachos.

"You must mean DHHS," said Debra. "Who else would insert themselves into a healthcare issue, particularly since the Schaalcare bill empowers them with all kinds of sway over individual medical decisions."

"You got it," said Ell, swallowing. "Kara's folks found a distant cousin who was a match. In fact, it's one of your friend Solana's nieces in Idaho. Talk about one big circle of relationships."

"They say you're connected to every sixth or seventh person on earth. In this instance it has a lot to do with the fact that there are around 11,000 tribal members. So it's a strong possibility that if you have Crow blood, you're related to other members somewhere down the line."

"How would you know that trivia?" asked Ell.

"I work as a researcher for the Denver Post and it has stringers in Crow country." She shrugged as if to say, 'part of the job.'

"At least now I understand the population dynamics better. I still get that it was a longshot because Kara has a very rare blood type. They were very lucky to find her cousin. Anyway," and Ell waved her hands through the air melodramatically. "This young lady, who was contacted directly by the recipient and the agreement reached as a private donor, was practically harassed by the state arm of DHHS, the Health and Welfare office, to set an appointment with one of their case workers."

"Why are they even involved?" Debra asked rhetorically.

"You got me. This was a transaction between private parties and there was nothing regarding exchange of funds. It's not like Kara's cousin was selling her kidney, which would be against the law..."

"And involve the FBI – crossing state lines in perpetrating a crime," said Esteban distractedly.

"Like I said, there's no money exchanged. All I can figure is that because Indian Health has been part of the conversation it draws in the whole Medicaid question, i.e. federal healthcare. Who funds Indian Health? Congress, and it's all funded through the House Energy and Commerce subcommittee. Now doesn't *that* make you think."

"Yes, since energy and commerce is the subcommittee that doles out DHHS funding, consider the connection between health and energy or EPA funding, since they oversee that too. Puts another spin on things," said Debra. "There are no coincidences that Yancy is fighting with the EPA and is now watching the Medicaid watchdogs weigh in, which Schaalcare is an expanded version per the Supreme Court."

"No kidding. Like sumo wrestlers only moving at the speed of a banana slug," said Ell disgustedly. "Health and Welfare have held up the surgery for months now while Kara's cousin *waited* for these jokers to make an appointment which *they* had insisted on. And once you're on dialysis, time is of the essence."

"What's the situation at this point in time?" asked Esteban.

"The donor has *this week* met with the case worker, who incurred the delay because she couldn't fit the appointment into her schedule until now! That poor girl is on pins and needles waiting while this bureaucrat is sitting on her thumbs, the kidneys she has deteriorating by the moment. But the point is, the agreement was private and the government waltzes in and forces the donor into the national registry. Why?"

"I'm sure we could track it down, not only in the Schaalcare bill but previous Medicaid regulations to which the more than 2900 pages constantly refers back to, along with the IRC, Social Security and other parts of the U.S. Code. It's a monstrosity that's eating us alive," Debra responded with dejection because this whole investigation that she and Roy were following up was all about sucking people into a merciless system.

"All this does is demonstrate just how vital it is that we find out what really occurred with these 'missing patients," ruminated Esteban aloud. "Injecting government control over citizen's physical bodies..."

"And maybe even their mental faculties," interrupted Debra.

"...is not only unacceptable, it's beyond the pale by destroying individual freedom in the most sacred of places, our persons."

"Well, drink up my friends. You have one helluva job ahead of you," toasted Ell as she raised her glass.

CHAPTER 34

They flew in to St. Louis International Airport at noon, almost on the dot. Debra gazed out the window of the plane as it came in for a landing. Being one of those individuals who wanted to know something about every place they visited, she'd researched the airfield on the internet before leaving New York. Now as they descended, feeling the clunk of the landing gear being lowered into place, she remarked on the history to her traveling companion. "Imagine watching Lucky Lindy taking off from this field to fly east on his way to make history in his monoplane."

"I thought he flew from Roosevelt Field on Long Island," said Roy.

"He did, but why do you think they called it "The Spirit of St. Louis?" This was where the trek began, Lambert Field. The non-stop part was from New York to France. I can't imagine what an intrepid will it would take to jump off into the known but unknown, leaving your support on the continent behind you – he didn't have a radio."

"That is why they dubbed him the Lone Eagle. A venture like that takes the kind of heart that you rarely find these days."

"Yet Lindbergh might not have hazarded the solo flight across the Atlantic if it hadn't been for the $25,000 prize offered by private enterprise, and the businessmen who backed him by building that special plane. If that isn't a tribute to the American way and capitalism, I don't know what is."

They landed soon after and deplaned, Esteban and Debra hauling their carry-ons down the jet bridge and on to catch a shuttle to the car rental kiosk. It had taken both Ell and Roy badgering Debra in tandem before they could get her to leave her mammoth suitcase at Ell's. She was reticent to do so, assuming that she'd just go with Roy for a couple stops then finish her trip by going directly back to Denver. They had convinced her to do the round trip, not only because it was more cost effective, but for the fact that dragging that monstrosity from city to city would be a burden. Esteban had been forced to play the age card. At 50 he said he was too old to be a full-time baggage handler. Though she didn't buy his argument, she finally relented, but not before stuffing the carry-on to the point of bursting, she was not about to travel practically shoeless. Esteban had since christened her "Imelda."

Loading the luggage into the trunk of a midsize Buick SUV, Debra couldn't resist comparing the more stylish ride to the blue tank that he'd left parked in the federal building lot. "This time they won't see you coming."

"Who?"

"Any suspicious types. You won't be tagged as a fed before you even open the door. This car isn't the typical gas hog that federal employees always seem to drive," said Debra as they climbed in.

"That's because there's a need for plenty of horses under the hood. You never know when you're going to need the power to overtake a vehicle in a car chase." Esteban put the car into gear and they headed for the interstate.

"If you ask me, that Marquis would be hard put to outmaneuver a bicycle."

"In New York you'd be right. Didn't your mother tell you never to judge a book by its cover? That Mercury may look like a dinosaur but it moves like a rocket when required."

"You're sure," she was dubious of his description. "You've put that thing to the test?"

"Unfortunately, yes."

"Never mind, I don't want to know the why behind the 'unfortunately.'"

"Good, because I really didn't feel like discussing that incident," he said.

"Another time when I need a bedtime story." She realized what she said. "Don't get any ideas, that was a figure of speech."

"Got it, mademoiselle."

She just nodded her head with approval that they'd straightened that out.

As they drove into downtown they saw the Gateway Arch, designed by Eero Saarinen, reaching up and curving across the skyline. "I guess you call that a lifer," said Debra. "I remember studying the architect in school but this is the first time I've seen the arch other than in photos. Pretty impressive."

"Agreed. There's the Gateway Geyser across the river now, too. I haven't seen that yet."

"Geyser? St. Louis is an odd place for a geyser. It can't be natural," assumed Debra.

"And you'd be right. They built it in East St. Louis on the other side of the Mississippi. Maybe Illinois wanted to cash in on some tourism dollars. Though spending millions of dollars to shoot water hundreds of feet into the air seems on odd allocation of tax dollars. But, hey, what do I know about civic budgets."

"I wonder who came up with the idea? It never would have crossed my mind as a plausible plan to entice visitors," she replied. "Though I'd be interested in seeing it spout off. Since they spent the money may as well have a look."

It was still early in the afternoon but they went ahead and checked-in, parking their bags in adjacent rooms. After freshening up, they left their overnight accommodations to visit the residence of one of the missing patients from the St. Louis area, which meant turning right around and leaving town immediately after arriving.

⚜⚜⚜

Heading back the same way they'd come from the airport, Esteban took Interstate 70 to I-170 north. The individual they were looking for had just purchased a home in the Fleur area. The woman had recently transferred to a local food distributor as a middle manager and looked like she was settling in, getting to know a couple of people but hadn't become well connected yet. It turned out that she hadn't had much of a personal life in the state she'd left, either. One of the reasons she ended up on Debra's short list, the woman was practically a phantom outside of work and she hadn't been at this job long enough to gain notice or make friends.

Locating the house, they saw that someone was inside, cleaning and packing up personal items, keepsakes and a hodgepodge of knick-knacks, creating a showplace that was devoid of personality. Esteban and Debra had arrived before all the individuality had been stripped from the walls and shelves, stashed in boxes to be moved out.

The door had been left ajar and Roy pushed it wider to see the bustling of a sturdy woman dressed for housekeeping duty. Emerging from the kitchen, she brushed highlighted bangs out of her face with the back of her wrist.

"Good afternoon! What can I do to help you?" Debra could tell right away that this was a professional woman taking a day to do the heavy lifting in a job that generally entailed dressing out to impress clients.

"You must be the broker for this property," said Debra before Esteban had a chance to introduce himself and his companion.

"Yes, I am. How did you know? I don't even have the sign up yet." She was mystified but jubilant that she had a potential buyer before she'd even listed the property. The two seemed mismatched by their appearance, the woman appearing demure and the man commanding attention, inducing apprehension if you had reason to fear either the law or lawless. She had no reason for anxiety in both cases and began to stretch out her hand to offer welcome when she looked at the dust and pulled it back.

"Sorry about that. Trying to get things in order to show the house." She swept her arm wide as if to encompass the whole floor plan. "Great place isn't it? My name is Ardith Swanson, Grand Acres Real Estate. Are you interested in the nickel tour? It's a little discombobu-lated, but even at that, I think you'll like what you see."

"It's good to meet you, Ardith. I'm Debra and this is Roy. We'd love to take a looksee."

"Great! Let me just wipe my hands and I'll take you through." Ardith grabbed a clean rag that had been sitting on the counter, dry-scrubbed her hands and waved them to follow her into the main rooms.

"So, Ardith," said Esteban, deciding that it wasn't essential yet to inform their hostess of his law enforcement status. He was officially on vacation, so it couldn't hurt to play the part of househunter. They might get more information that way. "We've been looking through the neighborhood for awhile and noticed that this house hasn't been off the market for that long."

"Well, the wonderful gal who had moved in had to leave the area suddenly and escrow was never completed, putting it right back into the 'for sale' category."

"Was it a lease with option, then? That's a pretty nice deal," observed Debra.

"You got it. She came in to work with one of the big companies and, though I don't know the details, circumstances changed."

"Then you were the agent on the original sale," stated Esteban. "You must have some insight into the buyer's leaving on such short notice. It didn't have anything to do with some problem with the property, did it? You know, something overlooked in the disclosure agreement that was just going to cost too much for her budget, anything like that?"

"Oh no! Not at all. The house is in terrific condition, new roof, treated for all the pests – termites and such – all upgraded plumbing… the works! She actually fell in love with the place, which is why she put in to buy it as soon as her job was confirmed as permanent. Evidently, she had a health issue that needed to be handled."

"Was it so severe that she was unable to keep her obligations? I don't understand," said Debra.

"Frankly, I'm not sure." Ardith wondered about giving so much information but thought that these were real prospects and divulging the truth was more likely to hook them rather than glossing over facts. "It looked like it was all a 'go' and then she didn't come back. Didn't even collect her earnest money. Because I was worried about her and she didn't really have much in the way of acquaintances yet, I also understood that she had no family, I checked into it as best I could."

Esteban and Debra put on their concerned faces. "It sounds as if the health problem could have been more severe than she let on, poor woman," said Debra. She was getting good at this, which was beginning to worry Roy. But it seemed to elicit the response they'd hoped for, more information.

Ardith turned to face them with an expression of worry for her client. "All I know was that she was going in for back surgery. These days they do such amazing things actually replacing discs with artificial ones and I think that's what she said she had scheduled."

"Any surgery is major surgery," offered Esteban. "I've been through back surgery myself and they almost lost me on the table. A reaction to the anesthesia."

"Whoa, that's hard on the family. In this instance, I simply have not been informed of anything and the owner couldn't wait any longer on the sale since the paperwork was never completed."

"So, you're forced to pack up her personal possessions and put them in storage, is that right?" asked Esteban. He even managed to soften his usually austere demeanor, establishing some trust. "That has to be rough."

"It is, actually. I really liked her and just pray that she's okay and I'll hear from her soon." She looked at the couple beside her. "You know, you just want the best for your clients. There's no reason to be in the real estate business if you don't want to see people happy in their home."

"That is *so* important." said Debra sympathetically. "Were you able to check with the hospital facility where she had her surgery, see what happened?"

"You know, I tried every avenue to reach her, including going to the Fairmont Clinic over in Illinois, where she told me she was scheduled for the procedure." Ardith's indignation came through. "It's a bit of a drive, and do you know, they refused to give me any information, wouldn't even recognize that she'd been there. They said, because I wasn't family. Like I told you, she didn't have any family that could be there for her, and they blocked me from doing that when there was no one else. I felt just awful."

"There are times that I wonder about how far we take the privacy laws. My goodness, even to the point of denying someone compassion. It's enough to make you crazy," Debra said, sharing Ardith's anguish.

"It does. All I can do is hold her furnishings and pray I'll have the opportunity to get her into another home when she comes back."

They walked up the hall in silence when Debra began to ask a few questions about the property, showing interest to lighten the atmosphere. It didn't take much to get Ardith to open up, pointing out all the amenities of the house and compact, well-maintained yard. The summer blooms dominated the borders, lavender, golden yellow, scarlet, deep purple interspersed amid the bright green foliage.

It was a pleasantly appointed property but they had achieved their goal – the collection of information about one of the missing patients. Taking Ardith's card, they told her that they were only in the looking phase, awaiting confirmation of Roy's new position.

Getting back in the Buick to head back to town, Esteban caught Debra's attention, looking at her out of the corner of his eye.

"What?"

"You're enjoying this too much," he said.

"I'm just getting the hang of it. Seemed like we'd get more if you didn't flash your credentials and intimidate her."

"I don't think she's the type to be put off by a badge, but you may be right. She was far more relaxed giving the story to potential buyers rather than a federal agent," he agreed.

"Who's on vacation," stipulated Debra. "Are you even supposed to be identifying yourself in an official capacity being this far off-duty?"

"Technically? Probably not. But this is why we're here so, let's get to the next place."

"Which is?"

"Fairmont Clinic."

BLOOD BARONS

CHAPTER 35

Things are getting heated. With the benefactor breathing down his neck, the scientist is burning the midnight oil trying to get a grip on the genetic composition of this mysterious bone fragment. Although he's about isolated the sequence that houses the FOXO3A gene he is still hunting for the proper amount of mitochondrial DNA in the spec - imen cells. The fact that it is missing is inexplicable. This is the DNA that is the easiest to locate in any cell, but there is almost none in any of the cells from this ancient bit of bone. Why and how can that possi - bly be? mtDNA comes exclusively from the egg, which even an ele - mentary schoolchild these days knows is contributed by the mother. But the normal amount of a million mtDNA molecules is almost com - pletely and utterly absent. He can find less than .001 percent of mtDNA indicating that the male's mitochondria made it through rather than the female's, or that it had once been there but somehow has been destroyed. Whatever the case, it's just gone, for all intents and purposes nonexistent.

Again, he goes back to the age of the bone fragment. They have done all the tests and the closest they can come to an age determina - tion, using the radiocarbon and fluorine dating processes, is that it is over 5000 years old, and he suspects that it is much older than that. That still doesn't account for the mtDNA deficiency, and how the per - son functioned without it. What it seems to point to is that the person to whom this bone belonged must have had no mother.

This is simply a preposterous assumption that he can't find any reason to accept, except what the evidence seems to be saying. Getting up from his work, he begins to pace and think. Recalling something he'd seen years ago. Another idea, which also makes no sense, is infil - trating his mind.

This video had been of a student of archaeology who was explain - ing an incredible discovery he had made. One that was so outrageous, in fact, that the scientific world had instantly derided him rather than listen to the process that led him to his conclusions.

The scientist stops his pacing and walks over to his desk and open-ing the internet connection, he begins an online search for this ama-teur who had an incredible story. It isn't long before he finds the exact video for which he is searching.

Uploading it, he watches it with new eyes, listening to the hypoth-esis again. Radical as it sounds, it makes him reconsider the possibil-ities. Here he is staring at a cell that has virtually no mitochondrial DNA while listening to someone claiming to have found cells in a blood sample taken from a secreted spot in the Holy Land, dating back to the first century. The sample was determined to be alive by the Israeli lab, an impossibility first of all, then they confirmed there were only 24 chromosomes in the cells, 23 contributed by the mother and just one Y-chromosome. There was not the full contingent of 46 chro-mosomes as humans normally have, seeming to indicate the lack of a human father.

The concept floors him. IF this guy wasn't off his rocker, and the independent laboratory that did the testing of the specimen could sup-port the conclusion, and the scientist is familiar with that particular facility, then he had found blood from a man who had just the one Y-chromosome. And now, he's sitting in his own lab with a human bone specimen that has so little mitochondrial DNA contribution that it indicates the opposite, that this man had no earthly mother.

The implications are beyond his comprehension of possibility but as a scientist who is continually baffled by the incredible design of minute organisms, let alone the galaxies, he falls back on that very ter-minology, "design." That alone is indicative of the exact opposite of random creation.

Today his understanding is being stretched to the very limits. He keeps coming back to one question, whose bone is this?

CHAPTER 36

It took less than an hour to drive the 40 or so miles across the state line, circle East St. Louis and out I-64 to reach Fairmont, Illinois, pulling into the parking lot of the medical facility.

Esteban and Debra may have been heading to Illinois to follow-up on the woman's disappearance, but because the case, which wasn't a case, originated in Missouri, Debra had first come across it through an initial report made to that state Highway Patrol's Missing Persons Unit. What had gained her interest was the fact that nothing ever came of it. The real estate agent had submitted the information to the unit but then no one ever came forward with anything more and the whole thing faded away. The one lead that they received from Ardith Swanson, that the woman had scheduled an appointment at the Fairmont Clinic, was all they had left. It just happened to jive with the list of clinics Debra had compiled, and here they were.

This interview was going to be conducted in an official FBI fashion with Debra in the role of observer only. Debra understood her part walking by his side as they entered the comfortably furnished lobby, designed to ease the anxiety of anyone awaiting surgery. The two were duly impressed by the atmosphere of caring and attention to detail, which became obvious when the receptionist flashed a brilliant smile, asking what she could do to help them. Her teeth were so dazzling that Debra had a stray thought, perhaps they'd read the sign wrong, this had to be a dental office.

Esteban stepped forward, telling the young woman who he was and that he'd like to speak to the office manager. Her smile dimmed momentarily as she abandoned her post without adieu to collect the person whose presence he requested. Turning to face Debra, he displayed his own pearly whites before rapidly replacing the grin with a more serious demeanor as the receptionist returned to her seat, her own smile properly affixed once more.

"It will be just a moment, if you'd care to have a seat," she offered pleasantly.

Esteban thanked her and they both sat on a cushy couch awaiting the arrival of the person in charge. A few minutes later, a young man in a smartly tailored suit accented with an understated violet tie, if purple could ever make a modest statement, entered the lobby with hand outstretched.

"Good afternoon, Special Agent and Miss?" He was smooth, slicker than a snail-trail, thought Esteban who answered for her.

"This is Miss Chorister, a consultant," he said as he shook the man's hand with a sturdy grip that could have been construed as intimidating. "Mr.?"

"Riley Gregson, I'm the clinic manager."

"Should I address you as doctor?" asked Esteban.

"Oh no, I'm a numbers guy. Anymore, a medical office has to watch its pennies, so that's me," he said with a self-confident grin. "So, what can we do for you today? I assume that this is a business call and not a medical visit. You look to be in excellent health," he attempted joking to lighten the mood.

"Well, I do have this rotator cuff injury," Esteban went along with the tone while rolling his right shoulder with some stiffness.

"Hah! I'll bet you do. Taking down all those malefactors over the years of fighting crime."

"Yep, that's it." Esteban then slid into a more sober mood. "Actually, Mr. Gregson…"

"Just call me Riley."

"All right, Riley," continued Esteban. "I'm trying to gather a little information on a few people who might have visited this facility either for consultation or procedures." He quickly added, forestalling the expected reluctance to disclose patient information, "I realize that there is a doctor-patient privilege and I don't wish to breach that. We just need information as to whether these individuals have had any contact with this clinic."

"I don't see how that could be a violation of privacy in that you aren't asking anything regarding their inquiry, diagnosis or treatment," said Riley after weighing his options. He swiftly assessed the situation. Having already been notified of a similar visit to another clinic in their network, he was aware that the belligerence had backfired. It was imperative that he handle this as delicately as possible. "Why don't you give me the names and I'll do a cursory check. It will take a little more time to go through all the phone records if nothing turns up at first glance."

This guy is shrewd. He's already got a bead on me... probably via foreknowledge. Esteban caught on fast. Debra and he had already connected some of these clinics through individuals serving on multiple boards, and although Riley Gregson wasn't on that exclusive list, he had just confirmed the connection in his roundabout way. Both of them realized they'd come to the right place.

"That would be very helpful. Here are their names," and Esteban handed him a sheet ripped from one of his pocket notebooks.

Gregson read the names, showing nothing to indicate recognition or otherwise. "May as well make yourselves at home. I expect this will take a little while though I'll be as speedy as possible."

Esteban nodded his acceptance and reclaimed his seat. Debra wandered around the office, examining the artwork while Esteban watched her and the comings and goings of patients to the front desk. The office wasn't overly busy as closing time approached. More patients exited the back offices, stopping at the desk to ante up and schedule their next appointment, the receptionist beaming through each encounter. *She must suffer facial fatigue at the end of the day.* The idle thought popped up while he observed all the activity in the lobby, including Debra's apparent meandering.

After some 15 minutes, Riley reappeared from a closed office designated "Employees Only." His expression seemed congenial, but Esteban detected a tightness around his eyes and a little less ease in his step.

"Special Agent Esteban. It looks like only one of these names had contacted us, evidently to first make an appointment and then to cancel it. The other two don't show up in our records anywhere that I can find, but I'll continue to check. We do have a referral office that may have something on record, which we'll also look into," he said as he reached the now standing FBI agent, Debra approaching from the side. "Here are the dates of the call and cancellation, and also the scheduled appointment in case that is of use." He handed the sheet to Esteban and glanced at Debra as she assumed her position at Esteban's side.

"Thank you for your cooperation," said Esteban. "What is the name of the referring facility?" He was going for a pen in his breast pocket.

"I've already written it on the reverse side of the sheet, along with one other office that refers a high number of patients."

"Great." Esteban shook his hand, giving him one of his cards, he said, "If you come up with anything else. Much appreciated," he said as Debra nodded her thanks before they headed for the door.

"What was so fascinating about the artwork?" Esteban asked Debra as they walked out to the parking lot.

"Didn't you notice?" she was surprised that it had missed his powers of perception. "They were all technical drawings of different medical devices, artificial joints, replacement spinal discs, synthetic apparatus or enhancements, implants of all kinds. Fascinating stuff and really amazing when you think that these unnatural objects are inserted into bodies every day."

"I suppose that makes sense in this kind of clinic that seems to deal mostly with orthopedic surgery." He looked down at her, noticing that there was something else. "What else did you see?"

"All of the art pieces had a company name somewhere incorporated into the design, GSF Research, LLC."

"And what do you think that stands for? It's obvious you have a really good suggestion and I'm all ears."

"Grigor Scirras Foundation, of course."

Immediately the sky opened with a crack of thunder, the deluge soaking them as they ran for the car.

CHAPTER 37

Taking matters into his own hands, Riley Gregson immediately told the receptionist that something had come up and he had to leave early, grabbed his rain jacket and fled out the side door soon after the FBI agent and his associate exited through the front. A downpour kept the pair occupied as they dashed for the car, the business manager going unnoticed as he ran for his own car. Slipping into the driver's seat, he activated the Bluetooth attached to his ear, placing a call to the doctor.

Keeping his eye on the road and hanging back far enough that he blended into the stream of traffic, Gregson trailed the agent's vehicle by a wide margin as he spoke to the project coordinator, filling him in on the latest visitors to his establishment.

"I may have jumped the gun here, but what would you do? Especially since you'd informed us about the New York incidents," Gregson calmly kept a bead on the SUV while getting an official opinion.

"Under the circumstances, probably the same thing as you since there was no one else to send. But don't do anything more than find out where they're staying and I'll handle the rest."

"I just want them to go right back to the hotel so I can make my report and go home," he said, following Esteban onto the interstate. "Somehow, I don't think I ought to lay any bets," he added.

Keeping tabs on the Buick through rush hour in East St. Louis was a challenge for an amateur. It always looked so easy in the movies, but he soon found that tracking a vehicle required concentration and swift reflexes; it simply is not what he'd trained for.

MBAs don't play cat and mouse with cars. Numbers, yes, he thought miserably as he somehow managed to stay out of view as the FBI guy and the girl decided to do some sightseeing. Wondering where else he'd have to hover in the shadows, he was glad for the periodic rain showers that commanded their focus rather than a sporty compact that seemed to be going everywhere they went.

The cloudburst was short-lived. Having exhausted their leads in the St. Louis area, with only speculation to keep their minds busy, Roy drove the rental down to Malcolm W. Martin Memorial Park on the east bank of the Mississippi. The idle conversation circling around watching the man-made geyser erupt before making the hop to the next city in their investigative expedition, he pulled into the parking area in time for the 6 p.m. waterworks.

"I've been to Yellowstone and waited for Old Faithful to make its scheduled splash but this is strange, kind of abnormal," mused Debra aloud. They had stopped to read some of the information about the mechanical geyser's inception and construction. "Six hundred feet is quite an upward blast. Think of the force it must take to push water that high. I remember that it weighs more than eight pounds a gallon."

"How is it you always have these odd bits of trivia buried somewhere inside that clever brain. At any given time, a tidbit pops out, enlightening the rest of us ignorant Neanderthals still roaming the earth."

"It is a wonder that you haven't gone the way of the wooly mammoth or triceratops," she tossed back. "Can't help it if odd information captures my interest here and there. The weight of water I know from hauling gallons of drinking water back to my apartment in the old days. That way I could figure whether or not I'd gotten enough of a workout. Better than free-weights."

"And purposeful," added Esteban.

"There is that."

The time was closing in on the fountain's scheduled spout into the sky and, although they knew this was a man-made marvel, there was still some anticipation. When the water exploded upward, Debra snapped a photo on her phone.

"It'd be useful if I had a Facebook page."

"You must be one of the nominal few who don't," he said as they walked back to the car, the sky threatening to let loose with more showers to compliment the one they'd just witnessed.

"Come on, don't you do any of the social networking?" she asked, beginning to run for the car to avoid getting drenched for a second time that afternoon.

"Only what's necessary to do my job, which means viewing other's sites. I'm not about to waste time on one of my own."

"Bet you get on the nieces' and nephews' pages, though, doncha," said Debra, opening the door and hurriedly sliding inside.

"You know that because you do the same thing." Esteban plunked down beside her in the driver's seat. "So much for sightseeing, let's get some dinner and get our plans organized for the next stop on the tour. I know a great place for barbecue across the river."

"Works for me."

CHAPTER 38

Another phone call. This time the report wasn't as succinct as expected.

Hanging up after hearing what he hadn't wanted to hear, he sat back and contemplated the mildly disturbing report. This was going to make things more difficult. As cautious as he'd been in keeping a tight rein on the operation, this latest in a series of accounts from separate operations had increased the need for tightened safety measures, turning down the spigot on communications between establishments. The fewer contacts, the fewer possibilities for security breaches, and right now, that was going to be his major focus.

Generally, there was no need to have internecine information exchanges between facilities. They were independently operated and, for the most part, owned. The loose confederation had only to do with the autonomously conducted studies being carried out on implant procedure and post-surgical function. Each facility fulfilled the guidelines of the research without interfacing with any other clinics, keeping all statistics and data compilation independently for more complete and comparative findings. The surveys hinged on avoiding data contamination, which could occur through cross-referencing with other study participants. The practice is common in double-blind studies and the project coordinator, who was also a board member at each facility, was meticulous in follow-through, delivering data sets to the director at the home office.

At this moment, it was his job to calm the clinic managers that there had been no security disruption despite the fact that an odd pair consisting of a diminutive black woman and a sometimes officious federal agent have shown up at a few locations where they should not have been.

He slumped back in his chair, Morrocan leather molding to his back, easing his stiff muscles that had been tightening with each call and e-mail. These two people were just that, two people who, from all he could discern, were operating on their own. He even had ears in the field office where the Hispanic agent is based, and had assembled a dossier on him, now knowing the man's history to a tee. In fact, in each of the cities that quarter one of the network clinics, he had been careful to contract a willing contact inside the Bureau satellite or field office. The information he acquired never overstepping any legal line, but was always relatively benign, meaning little to his insider but much to him.

Today, he was satisfied that everything was contained and even the odd arrival of Special Agent Esteban and his unsanctioned aide, Miss Chorister, were nothing to cause alarm. And that is precisely what he was about to report to his superior at the home office.

No damage had been incurred, just a few questions had been asked, and, as far as he could see, answered to the agent's satisfaction. But he was also authorizing further tailing of the two, fully realizing that circumstances could change at any time. Questionable files had already been deleted from the mainframes and individuals whom he was asking after were locked out of the information stream, both in the digital world and, for those that were reassigned, in their own consciousness.

Punching in a phone number on his secure line, he was ready to speak with the trustee.

Let the two investigators hunt all they want. There's nothing to find.

⚜⚜⚜⚜

She fields the call while gazing across the river as the geyser shoots waves of water skyward during its daily evening blow.

This is the first she's hearing about any inquiry, authorized or otherwise, into the web of medical clinics within her purview. After scrutinizing the individual reports submitted by each facility, which she compiles and synthesizes to meet the grant agency's periodic update requirements, the data sets aren't instilling great confidence. But that was all she assumed to be worrisome... until now.

The circumstance prompting the project coordinator to place this call is underscored with slight misgiving in his voice and, then, in her own churning gut. For herself, the unsettled feelings are as much related to her inclination toward worry as the odd information he's imparting. Until now, nothing has crossed her desk regarding an inter - est in the facilities other than grant related and she questions him on the purpose of the couples' visit to the clinic closest to her own office.

"As far as the business manager could tell, they were looking for a couple of individuals that may have received treatment at his facili - ty. Neither the woman, who apparently said very little, and the FBI agent..."

"FBI? I thought you said this was a minor issue? I'm sorry, but I'd hardly consider a visit from a Bureau agent to be something of negli - gible concern," she is beginning to think that she isn't being given all the facts.

"The agent didn't give any particular reason for asking questions regarding the individuals, except what I've just said. We have no rea - son to believe that anything has been handled improperly, and the managing personnel answered truthfully according to their records, most of the names did not appear within their files." He is unwilling to say too much himself as the project coordinator. In the end, he's the one with oversight of research guideline implementation, the trustee handles the finances and the AHRQ contacts and reporting. The only reason he is placing the call to her at all is the fact that, since the study is federally funded, it behooves him to inform her of a possible feder - al inquiry, which frankly, he doubts. The results have not been any - where near as positive as they have been hoping, which is the trustee's main concern, but that will not jeopardize the continuation of the pro - gram and it is his job to ease her mind on that matter.

"Doctor, why would the FBI even show an interest? This is boring, though groundbreaking work, yes. Obviously the outcomes are disap - pointing in that there has been such a small rate of total success in all areas, but that should not precipitate any inquiry. Everything is being executed strictly according to prescribed procedure, is it not?"

"Absolutely. I am as baffled as you and the only reason I called was as a courtesy. And in case you may receive some type of call at your office, though that is highly unlikely."

"Good. I don't need any surprises here, except that you see meas-urable improvement in the success ratio of these new generations of devices." The trustee tries to sound encouraging but the fact that any-one would have need to check into one of their facilities while they are undergoing such sensitive research, she finds disquieting. "Is there anything else that I should know?"

"No, and I wasn't really sure that it was all that necessary to have bothered you to begin with."

"That's all right, Doctor. It's best I be kept abreast of any events that may be out of the ordinary."

Closing the connection, she runs her fingers through her hair as she considers something else he said. Did I hear him say personnel, files and records, as in plural? Did he mean this has happened at more than one clinic?

Shaking her head to clear it of cobwebs, she looks across the river to see that the geyser was again quiet, and works to convince herself that she only thinks he alluded to multiple events.

⚜⚜⚜

"Those were by far some of the best ribs I've ever had," said Debra as they exited a homey restaurant packed away in an unexpected cor-ner of downtown St. Louis. The fare had been exceptional and filling, served in an atmosphere saturated with delectable aromas tempered by mellifluous blues that set the mood to enjoy good food and genial company.

"Those were my exact words when I first ate here. I've heard peo-ple say Midwest barbecue has Texas barbecue beat, hands-down. This place is so good that I'm inclined to agree."

"I wouldn't say as much around any well-armed Texans. They might take offence," she noted as they walked down the block.

"Individualists and armed, God bless 'em, every one. Down there,

228

the guns are generally in plain sight and it's no surprise who's carrying, so I'd be less apt to provoke anyone I shouldn't."

"You might like to apply that piece of advice toward your immediate superior," snickered Debra. "As much as you've ticked him off,
he may be the one most likely to shoot. Texans are circumspect."

"Point taken. However, he's not here and I'm on vacation, having
a fine time in the heartland with a lovely lady by my side."

"Somehow, that comment makes me feel as though I should be
wearing petticoats and twirling a parasol. Thank goodness modern
streets are paved rather than the muddy ruts of a hundred years ago.
My shoes would be ruined."

"That'd be disastrous." They reached the rented Buick and he
assisted her inside, walking around to the driver's side, he strapped
himself in before broaching the subject most on his mind. "We didn't
get very far today."

"No, so what's next on the agenda? I'm running out of vacation
days."

"Catch a flight to another garden spot in these United States," he
said as he pulled into traffic.

"Please don't tell me Detroit is on the tour. As it is, I can only
afford one last stop. This traipsing across country has deflated my
bank account enough that I need to return to my desk so I can pay for
my cat."

"You don't have a cat."

"Not anymore," she said. "I used to and I'm considering getting
another one for company. Cats cost money."

"Not if you visit the local animal shelter. Pay for the shots and
voilá, cat custody." He added, "but I don't see you with cat hair on
your fashion duds. What's the real hurry?"

"Got another call from Gleason, the news editor. They miss me
already and are asking when I'm due back," she looked over at Roy,
who had one hand on the steering wheel. "Seems they can't do without my genius."

"Neither can I," he said, keeping his eyes on the road as he made
a turn on their way back to the hotel.

"Really, this is adding up and I don't see that we're making any real progress, do you?"

"Not exactly. We're still pretty much at square one. Missing people and clinics that deny having had any contact with most of them." He sighed as he considered his next words. "Are you ready to give up?"

"Just because we have no official sanction and are running around the country assuming something will fall into place if we just ask the right question at the right time to the right people?"

"Sounds like a fool's errand when you put it that way," his outlook was taking a dismal turn.

"It is, but no, I'm not ready to blow it off. I know that we've stumbled across something that feels fiendish," she shivered in spite of herself. "I don't know what it is but I know we can't let go yet. So, I'll give you one more city, as long as it isn't Motor City."

"What have you got against Motown?"

"Love the music and the history but I am not going to spend my vacation in a ghost town, courtesy of our present administration. I don't think I could handle the depression."

"Think how the residents feel," he noted. "San Francisco and then back to New York. Okay by you?"

"Sure, who wouldn't want to visit the Golden Gate? Haven't been there since I was a young'un."

"Pray for rain, then," he said obtusely.

"Rain?"

"We need to be flooded with good solid information so we can put this little mystery to rest," he answered.

"Then rain, it is."

CHAPTER 39

The idea of dealing with Bay Area traffic by flying into San Francisco International didn't appeal to either Debra or Roy, and the cost being substantially less, they opted for Sacramento instead. Debra hadn't been back to her home state for a couple of years and advocated the plan as a chance to enjoy a taste of California summer before returning to Denver.

A few hours later they were ensconced in the front seats of another rental car, this time a Ford Explorer. Esteban's preference for SUVs became obvious with his choice of vehicles at each stop. When Debra questioned him on it, he allowed that he favored roomier cabs. Turned out his one idiosyncrasy was being slightly claustrophobic.

"I don't like tight places," was his explanation.

"Slept in a coffin sometime in your distant past?"

"Are we back to the vampire thing?" he laughed.

"Whoops, unintentional word association. It's what comes to mind when I think small, cramped places."

"Not a closet, trunk, old refrigerator or maybe a vault?"

"Now that you mention them, any one of those would work," she considered. "So which one was it?"

"Was what?"

"Where you were locked in?"

"None of the above. Accept the fact that I enjoy having ample leg room."

She just *hmmmed* as he merged onto the freeway to travel the 80 miles to San Francisco.

⚜⚜⚜⚜

The drive hadn't taken much more than an hour to reach their destination, which was on the east side of San Pablo Bay. Neither one of them had any inclination to spend the night in a big city and Vallejo was a practical starting point for their plan of action, as much as they had one.

That in mind, Esteban figured they'd begin with the flighty persona of Trey Thompson, one-time computer wiz and recent Silicon Valley dropout. Still wondering if this guy was the real deal or a Trey impersonator, they moved in to their rooms and mapped their route, beginning with visiting the career chameleon at home right there in Vallejo.

Arriving at a modest condominium complex bordering a browning, grassy hill on the north side of town, Esteban and Debra hunted through the building numbers to find the one where the new and improved Trey Thompson had set up housekeeping.

"Nice place for a nine-to-five bureaucrat, but a far cry from the million dollar property he sold in Sunnyvale. Wonder what he did with the extra cash?" observed Esteban as they found a parking space close by the four-plex.

"Charity? Now that he's more interested in serving the public, maybe he gave it to GLAAD hoping to lessen the denigration of the gay and lesbian population? He does work as an advocate in his reincarnation," allowed Debra, considering the new circumstances of the subject's life.

"We may be assuming too much. It could be the guy just got sick of the fast-living or was given an ultimatum to cool things off if he wanted to live longer."

"As in, he should quit jumping out of perfectly good aircraft or snowboarding off the side of cliffs as being life threatening activities? I'd say that's a given," she remarked sarcastically.

"Time to find out."

As they were standing at the door of the person of interest, Debra wondered aloud about the new position this man occupied in government. "I'd never heard of a job as a workplace advocate for transgender employees. Do you think it might be an addition that grew out of the new healthcare law? No race, color, creed or sex left behind?"

Esteban stifled a laugh as the much maligned and also admired Mr.

Thompson answered the door. Or so they assumed it to be the same man. In the Grigg case, the person was physically the same, but the personality had undergone a total makeover and the two were most interested to know whether he had been through the same wringer.

Palming a previous photo of the subject, Roy glanced at it to compare it with the man who opened the door, satisfying himself that it was the same person, with the addition of 20 pounds or so.

"Mr. Thompson?" he asked as the door swung wide.

"That'd be me." He looked at Esteban and Debra with a puckered brow, "and whom might you be?"

"Roy Esteban, FBI, and Debra Chorister, my associate." He gazed over Thompson's shoulder to see if anyone was with him. "Would you mind if we came in for a few minutes?"

Thompson continued to look at Esteban, concern dusted with distrust creeping over his features. "I can't imagine why you would want to speak with me," he said while blocking the door with his body.

"We have something of a mystery that we were hoping you could help us solve."

"Me? I don't know anything except go to work and come home, so it's doubtful I'd know much about your "mystery.""

"In an average situation, I'd have a tendency to agree, however this particular mystery revolves around you," said Esteban.

"I'd say 'me' again, but that would be redundant. I still don't get it," said Thompson, as yet unmoving from the doorway.

"If you wouldn't mind allowing us entry, we could explain how you can help," nudged Esteban.

"I suppose, but let me see your credentials first." In answer, Esteban pulled the wallet out off his pocket so Thompson could examine it. "Well, it looks real. Okay, come in but I have someplace I have to be soon."

"I thought you said that you "go to work and come home" as your routine. Is this something new, then?" Esteban asked as they came into the living area.

"I suppose you could say that. One of the guys is trying to get me out to be more physical, so I've joined the bowling league." He pinched a growing roll of fat around his waist. "Put on some weight after surgery and I need to start watching it."

"What kind of surgery did you have, Mr. Thompson? I hope nothing drastic," Debra asked as she positioned herself on the sofa.

"Depends on what you call drastic. I had a hip replacement."

"That's not a usual problem for someone of your age. Did you have an accident?"

"Actually, Miss, I did."

"May I ask what kind of accident? It must have been pretty horrific for you to receive an injury that would require joint replacement."

"You know, I don't really remember the accident, though I was told that I was in car three of a major pile-up on the 101. It's strange how it seems to have wiped out the majority of my memory, even to the point where I couldn't testify in the case. They've made sure that all my medical bills are covered and I'm getting a very generous settlement, but it hardly makes up for a life lost, you know? I can't recall anything in between high school and now. That's ten years in the dumper," he ended on a morose note.

Debra glimpsed briefly at Esteban trying to keep the incredulity from showing on her face. Basically, this man had just told them he recalls nothing of his past life as a computer engineer in artificial intelligence. At the least, Grigg remembered her life up to the point of moving to New York. Thompson just said that he didn't remember a whole career, which Esteban decided needed a test.

"Have you ever worked in computer engineering, Mr. Thompson?"

"I sincerely doubt it. Though I'm good with electronics and even some programming for the office where I work, I haven't been involved in the industry," he spoke without conviction.

"What happened to the property you owned in Sunnyvale?"

"Did I own property there? I frankly don't remember. It must have been worth something. You can't find squat in that town even to rent, let alone buy." Now he was becoming confused. "But I don't know why I'd own anything down there. It's too far of a schlep to the job in the city, and Vallejo is enough as it is."

"Do you know if you have any assets other than this condo?" Esteban was really in a quandary how, whoever it was that engineered this whole lifestyle change, they'd managed to dispose of property without the patient knowing what was going on.

"Like I said, I'm receiving a very generous payout from the accident. It's already being disbursed and it comes to the neighborhood of $1.6 million. Enough to give me a comfy retirement if I invest well."

"Trey, do you have any close relationships?" Debra was getting concerned for this guy as well. First, he's a go-getting top-flight engineer who loves the good life then, in a flash, he becomes a stick-in-the-mud government minion who questions nothing. The pattern that it inferred was that the surgical procedure somehow involved a grand scheme that replaces a person's self-determination and drive with acceptance of a complacent life, doing what you're told, for lack of a better analogy. That brought to mind a Peter Gabriel song from the '80s... "We do what we're told." Scary.

"There are a few guys I hang with from work, but I don't have any family, not that I can remember or could find, and none who have come forward after I lost my memory. Why?"

"Just curious. You seem like a very nice young man. I hope that you continue to do well after your surgery and all," Debra was at a standstill, not really knowing what else could be said to a man who had lost his life but had no clue it had happened.

Gaining his feet, Esteban thanked Trey for his help and took leave for himself and Debra.

As he was walking the FBI agent and his associate to the door, Trey asked, "Well, did that help?"

"Help?" Esteban was unsure of his allusion.

"Yes, did I help you solve your mystery? The one that revolves around me, you said."

"Yes, yes you did."

"And how did it have anything to do with me?"

"We found you."

Trey mouthed, *found me?* His voice was inoperative as they walked down the front steps without looking back.

❧❧❧❧

"What few answers we got from him equals one drop in a thousand gallon bucket," Debra bemoaned the lack of explanations still plaguing them.

"Who could possibly engineer such a major change in someone that includes everything from blocking out their entire adult life to selling million dollar real estate without the knowledge of the owner? The magnitude of re-fabricating a career and memories on top of absconding with their property is mind-boggling," the thought was forcing him to consider the implied scope of a really strange scheme.

"They didn't exactly abscond with the property, they just readjusted his gross income," she grinned, using euphemisms the architects behind the "readjustment" might employ. "I imagine the $1.6 million actually came from the sale of the property," she paused a moment. "No matter how you look at it, we have walked into something so weird that I can't see any sense behind it, can you?"

"No." Esteban didn't know what else he could add because, as far as he could see, *nothing* added up. "That's the problem, of course. None of it makes sense because we have no motive."

"Then we'd better look at what we *do* have to see if we can find one."

"How many times do we have to rehash this?" He was fried from racking his inadequate grey cells. "Don't answer that."

"We have this… and I'm writing it down for my own clarification." Marking bullet points before each assumption, she began scribbling her conclusions as he drove back to the hotel.

"One: People disappear after they have some medical device implanted.

"Two: Some of them are found but have changed their occupation, interests, friends (if they had any to begin with) and in some cases, home addresses.

"Three: All those located after surgery have some kind of memory loss.

"Four: The clinics that provided the service deny having treated most of the subjects.

"Five: All of the subjects had indicated contact with one of six clinics. Okay this is four and four is five. I need to rearrange the order. Also, all six of the clinics are related somehow by board members and personnel, with one that serves on all boards.

"Six: One of the clinics had artwork that tied the preferred medical devices to GSF Research LLC which is mostly funded by Grigir Scirras Foundation with Herculaenea Fund money."

"Where'd you get that information?"

"A little off the chart treasure hunting. Actually, it wasn't hard. All I had to do was go back to the research Toddy had done on Scirras years ago. He was thorough. Too bad no one paid attention because we wouldn't be doing this investigation now if they had," Debra was almost fuming by the time she finished the last sentence.

"So much for 'coulda beens.' What else you got?"

"If it all comes down to the GSF Research LLC, then we need to find out if all the clinics use their devices. Maybe that's the connection, that the devices are at the crux of a research grant from the AHRQ and why Scirras' name has come up regarding private support. We've been skirting this thing from every direction, but it could be that it all comes down to what they're studying." She paused, rubbing and pinching at her chin, stroking a non-existent goatee.

"Well, Watson, how hard can it be to find out if GSF Research has received a grant?"

Debra came out of her reverie, immediately dropping her hand into her lap. "Not hard at all. It should be posted on the American Recovery and Reinvestment Act website. That is, if it's an above-board funding and not a "special project" allocation directly from the White House. Those are not usually published for the general public even though we pay for them. Through the nose, I might add."

"What I gather, they're often related to the dime-a-dozen executive orders that this president signs every time he turns around," appended Esteban as he pulled into the parking lot of the motel. "Let's order out, stay in and do some homework, what do you say?"

"That we need to compile all our facts before we head out for another sortie." She gathered up her notes and squirreled them away in her purse. "I think we should be properly armed and carry plenty of ammunition."

"That's my girl," Esteban tipped his head, acknowledging her wisdom with a wink as he adjusted the gun in his shoulder holster for emphasis.

CHAPTER 40

Beginning by going north to see a woman from Santa Rosa, this was the first of three more names from the Bay Area on their list.

"This is turning into quite the tour of four-star American cities," said Debra offhandedly as they drove through wine country, taking the scenic route. "You miss driving through real country, don't you."

"Since when does California qualify as "real country"? This has got to be the most plastic state in the union."

"It is if you reserve the plastic part for L.A. and San Francisco... okay, and some of the coast communities," she qualified. "The rest of the state is mostly populated by what I would call real people, meaning they have a grasp of reality, they just don't have the majority of votes."

"That, I assume, is allotted to the certifiable fruits and nuts by which the state is so fondly referred by the rest of the union."

"Can't argue there. But I still love the land, and you've got to admit, the beauty has it's own hold on you," she said wistfully.

"Sounds like projection, Debra, when it's you that misses this place as opposed to my driving the countryside."

"Yes and no. I can't elaborate any more than that, it wouldn't make sense."

Roy let the subject lie as they continued driving through drying hills crowned with California live oak or the occasional stand of redwoods. Water in the meandering creeks was dwindling as the summer came on strong. Still, there were tall green grasses and punks by the streambeds, waterfowl along the banks, squawking and flapping their wings. It was a pleasant change from the grinding sounds of the city streets to which he'd become accustomed over the past year. In noting Debra's remembrance of a different life, Esteban had the insight to recognize how much he preferred middle America to urban sprawl whether it went up or out. It made him consider what was next in his future, the NYC field office roster wasn't likely to include his name much longer. Not after this cross-country ranging against orders, vacation or not.

They rolled into town just as regular office hours commenced. It didn't take very long to locate another government institution where one of the medical device recipients was listed as working.

It was a community college financial aid office where they had located this "disappeared" individual. The woman was in her fifties and had undergone the implant of two artificial discs in her lumbar spine, according to the medical files they were able to retrieve, unofficially. She'd been a successful impresario who had dropped out of sight after retiring from a regional opera company. Theater people, being what they are, generally short-sighted when it came to anyone's well-being but their own, didn't keep in touch and her previous acquaintances wrote off the silence to quiet retirement. As a result, no one from her past had any idea what had become of her and, as Esteban and Debra were to find out, she had recall of that life though not much interest in it.

Arriving at the college, they found her installed behind a desk in a small cubicle, going through files in preparation for her next appointment with a student. When Esteban and Debra sat in front of her, peppering her with questions regarding her past, she had virtually nothing to say. She recalled her career as a producer in the theater but said she didn't miss it at all. Her job, counseling students in scholarship and loan applications, was more her style now, the flamboyance of the opera and the egos that crowded it were taxing and better left to the past.

They thanked her for her time and moved on.

"It may be that wasn't such a big leap, and as such she seemed more suited to the lifestyle change," observed Debra as they walked back out to the Explorer.

"I don't get you. Explain." Esteban was interested in her take on this particular "patient."

"You know, these days in the arts almost everything is tied to grants and grant-writing to get anything produced, whether it's a touring art exhibit, a children's theatre group or a ballet company. Everything is tied to private philanthropy or government grants in the arts."

"I must admit to my ignorance of arts funding," said Esteban. "Sounds like a royal pain to get anything done."

"It is. It's a constant merry-go-round of grant cycles, applications and reporting. Nothing I could deal with. You're always operating at the behest of the person holding the purse strings," she said.

"Ah, like what Congress should be in relation to their constituency."

"Exactly. So, for someone like this woman, going from constantly seeking funds for whatever the theater group needed to a staid job with a steady paycheck may not be such a difficult hurdle. Aside from the fact that she may have been burnt out by the grant-seeking rat race, she's already inducted into the concept of government doles."

"I would never have put it into that context," said Esteban.

"Here's another thing, though it's kind of off-the-wall when it comes to context, but think about this… we're looking into stimulus money being funneled into the healthcare act with a possible research connection, right?" Esteban only nodded in response to Debra's question.

"We just visit someone who may have been part of the ostensible research study who is deeply involved in handing out government grants, including Pell grants." She pointed into the air to punctuate the next statement. "The thing about those educational grants is that $17 billion of it was also part of the American Recovery and Reinvestment Act of 2009, but, get this, the reason the grants have been cut dramatically to students in need this year is because the money was redirected to Schaalcare as part of the Reconciliation Bill that pushed the behemoth ACA through Congress."

"Talk about a convoluted web of legislation and funding." He contemplated the whole circle, or twisted intertwining threads, more like. "Going back, the fact that she is indoctrinated into the grant mentality, that all you need to do is apply and, abracadabra! money appears. Looking at it that way, it kind of makes sense in a nonsensical way that her memory wouldn't be wiped like some of these others. The transition was almost natural, which doesn't completely line up with what could be a motive."

"You have a theory," stated Debra.

"Not yet, it's only in the development stage."

"Ai-eee. You sound just like Toddy," she grumped. "What is it with you guys and putting the brakes on sharing your thoughts?"

"I just need more info. When, no, *if* it makes more sense to me, we'll discuss it," he was implacable.

"Brainstorming can be the best thing you can do to get a grip on an elusive idea," she cajoled.

"No. It's too out there. I think it's because the insinuated premise makes absolutely no sense to me."

"Probably because you're not psychotic enough to get inside the heads of the crazy people masterminding whatever it is they're cooking up," said Debra, hoping to crack him open.

"I know I'm not schizo enough, that's why the motive isn't congealing." Changing the subject, he said, "Let's go see the next *victim*." There was no extricating anything more from him.

⚜⚜⚜

The next two stops weren't any more enlightening. If Esteban thought he was stumped before, these interviews weren't helping narrow anything down.

The first individual had been a nanny who was in such demand with the upper crust that she charged an outrageous salary and enjoyed luxurious vacations in exotic locales, sometimes traveling with the families who employed her. It was on one of these holidays where she encountered a parasite that devastated her alimentary system, the infection induced by the parasite literally eating through part of her stomach. She had been flown back to the States from the Caribbean paradise to immediately undergo a less drastic version of sleeve gastrectomy, a procedure usually performed on the morbidly obese, to remove the ravaged portion of her stomach. Despite being an active young woman in her late twenties, she carried an extra 40 pounds and as much as this procedure was out of the ordinary, having been developed for weight loss, it served the purpose in this instance. What occurred next is what had landed Christy Han on Debra's missing patient list.

Christy didn't return to the family compound in Montecito, the community with one of the highest per capita income levels in the United States, let alone celebrity-saturated California. Her employers tracked her to a hospital where she went AWOL after reportedly leaving of her own volition *before* the surgery. The family was told that they had no idea where she went and they, devastated – mostly inconvenienced, though that's not what they said – by Christy's apparent disappearance, scrambled to replace her, abandoning their search as useless.

Christy Han did turn up, but nowhere that anyone expected. She was now occupying an administrative position with Head Start in Richmond. The benefits couldn't compare with the perks to which she'd become accustomed, and she wasn't even directly involved with the children anymore, instead manning a desk as assistant manager for the program.

When Debra and Esteban walked into the building, they found a wan young Asian woman whose energy level was obviously lacking. The malady and surgery had taken its toll on her system and her attitude seemed placid as she finished placing a call, hanging up the phone as they entered her compact office. Who they encountered exhibited none of the bustling, bouncy personality that the Montecito family had described. All Esteban had to do was glance at the photo from the file they'd compiled to confirm it was the same woman.

The interview was brief, Han had duties that required her attention and she was disinclined to spend much time with her visitors. The two managed to find out the basics, that she'd received her degree in early childhood education, which matched up with her history, and to her recollection, she'd been employed at her current position for some months. She recalled having undergone surgery at a center in San Rafael after a visit to Ensenada in Baja where she'd contracted a parasite, though she admitted her memory was sketchy. "I was told this kind of illness can affect your brain, leaving you with a patchy memory," she explained.

Esteban asked if she had been employed as a nanny before coming to work at Head Start. The answer was puzzling in that she referred back to jobs she'd had right out of college but not the nouveau aristocracy that had kept her in designer clothes for the last few years, clothes that she certainly hadn't donned this day. Debra noticed that fact instantly, being one who was fond of style and paid attention to personal appearance. There was no recollection of the St. Bart's vacation or even the family that she'd accompanied to the exclusive island. Getting nowhere with their questions except the name of the facility that had performed the surgery, they moved on.

"Here's another one experiencing the lavish life who dumped the bonuses to go on the government payroll," observed Esteban as they trotted down the front steps.

"Not to denigrate the good work Christy did… I mean, just listen to the glowing testaments the families gave, but you can't have it much better than enjoying an opulent lifestyle on someone else's dime, essentially."

They walked in silence, mulling over the contradiction that was, not only Christy's story, but the other individuals that they'd managed to locate. And those numbers were few. They could count them on one hand.

CHAPTER 41

Curiosity was getting the better of him.

His benefactor is on tenterhooks waiting for the final product, which is in the final stages of development, but the quandary that is invading his every waking thought and keeping him from sleep has to be answered.

Leaving his bed, he settles himself behind the computer monitor to do as thorough a search as possible. Combing every site he can find on the subject, he even scrutinizes official Turkish websites where he can only pick out a few words here and there, having forgotten the smidgen of the language he'd acquired while there over 20 years ago.

Finally, he finds what he's hunting. Information on the national park located 10 miles east of Dogubeyazit. It even has a visitors' cen-ter that is open regular hours this time of year, if, of course, the fre-quent skirmishes between the indigenous Kurds and regular Turkish forces don't close down local tourism. Tribal allegiances still reign supreme in that part of the world.

He doesn't hesitate and immediately books a flight to Erzurum via Paris and Istanbul that is scheduled for departure tomorrow at noon. It's a hassle but he's determined and manages to get all the short hops in order within a couple of hours. Having made his decision, he e-mails his superior, knowing that there will be unrestrained fury shoot-ing from that office once the news is received that he's skipping town for a week. But his conscience is unrelenting to the point that he has no choice, and it doesn't matter how much it costs to get to the further-most eastern province in Turkey without delay.

He has to know and he's praying the answers are there.

BLOOD BARONS

CHAPTER 42

There was no forward motion in trying to nail down the last person on the list. All things considered, Debra and Roy felt fortunate that they'd actually tracked three of the "missing" here in the Bay Area. Trouble was, they weren't any closer to pinning down solutions to the dilemma of why some were unaccounted for and others were locatable but still gone, for all intents and purposes; the lives they had led relegated to the rubbish heap.

"The saddest part of this whole episode," lamented Debra, "is the huge potential that these people had. Their abilities, and for some, their innovative genius, are gone to waste while they twiddle their thumbs in monotony that was anathema to who they really are... or were. I'm getting more confused by the day rather than enlightened by this, this exercise in futility."

"Don't let the frustration get to you," said Esteban, "though I'm probably the last guy to offer encouragement. It's nothing new, landing a case that looks like a total dead end and then you practically trip over a lead that takes you right to the source. That's what I'm banking on. Luck." He paused for a moment. "I have to."

"Nothing like throwing in all you've got."

"Have you known me to do things any other way?" He slid a sideways glance at her while they drove to one last destination. As much as Debra had called it a fruitless task, he'd enjoyed spending the time with her, the mental sparring, raking over every tidbit of information they could uncover in an attempt to reach the truth, maybe even restore some people to... he didn't know what. Most of them hadn't had any family or even friends. What they had were prolific lives of invention and productivity, something that their new incarnations utterly lacked. As he thought about it, he realized that what had been stolen was not just their personal existence but their prospects of contributing to a more vibrant society. Instead, they were now cogs in a bureaucratic wheel that went in circles producing nothing.

If that isn't a bleak picture of where this nation is headed, I don't know what is.

With that clanging through his brain he almost missed the exit from the northbound 101 into San Rafael. They'd made the most part of a grand circle through the vineyards of Napa and Sonoma Valleys, down a dogleg to Richmond, crossing the northern arm of the bay, whitetops on the water flicking beneath as they twice traversed the bridge. Driving the final miles back up to the northwest side of San Pablo Bay, the popular clinic would be the last stop on this peculiar carnival ride.

It was late in the day, getting on to closing time when they pulled in to the parking lot of an exclusive medical facility landscaped with bright bougainvillea and lacey mimosas. The San Rafael Surgery Center.

"Looks like a classy place to get a new hip, couple a discs or a redesigned stomach, if you ask me," said Debra as she climbed out of the Ford. "Don't know that I'd mind having a tuck or two done here if I had the cash."

"If you needed plastic surgery, which you don't." He couldn't imagine a beautiful woman like Debra even making an offhand remark like that. Then he remembered that this is California where surgical augmentation is performed for every reason under the sun, including on a whim. Watching her climb the steps to the front door where she turned to wait for him, her pumpkin-colored linen suit encasing a per-fectly petite figure accessorized with cannily matched pumps, he knew her to be too smart to go under the knife unless it was absolutely unavoidable.

"Who knows what I might entertain 30 years down the road when I'm crumpled up from wear and tear," she grinned as she allowed him to open the door for her. To Debra, chivalry was not dead and though she was used to doing for herself, she accepted being treated like a lady, and Esteban was gentleman enough to pick up on the fact. He winked back at her as she glided through to the glassed-in foyer, an etching of redwoods climbing the floor-to-ceiling windows on either side.

"This facility carries a rating for excellence that even Thompson seemed to endorse. The mystifying business is *how*, or even more importantly, *why* ten years of his life went up in smoke. To what purpose would anyone be engineered to forget his previous life? And it can't be by accident, the details of a memory cover-up entail too much. So, what else do they do here besides drop in new body parts?" Esteban asked as he let the door whoosh closed at its measured pace.

Lowering her voice and stepping to the side to look at some of the artwork while the front desk personnel dealt with a number of patients, Debra referred to the e-mail she'd sent Roy days ago. "You read up on the nanobots, didn't you?"

"It sounded completely unbelievable, but yes, I did," he kept his own voice down and directed her away from open ears.

"Truthfully, I can't conceive of any other explanation except the idea that they're experimenting with more than just the replacement of worn-out joints. Think about it, maybe there's something added to these fancy medical devices," as she said that she pointed to one of the framed pieces hanging right in front of them. As she spoke, Debra drew a line with her finger around the inscribed letters, 'GSF Research LLC.' "Perhaps they're replacing neurons, like Toddy described."

"Now, that is hard to believe," Esteban said, unconvinced.

"Consider each one of the patients we've been able to locate and interview. How many is that? Six altogether? All but one has incomplete recall or truncated knowledge of their lives before surgery. Can you come up with some other explanation?"

"What about drugs? There are pharmaceuticals that can wipe memories, aren't there?" He was pulling at straws.

"I can't completely refute that, but I believe they would destroy much more than just the memory. Drugs affect the whole body because once they're introduced they go through the whole bloodstream. It's why chemotherapy is so dangerous even when it's applied for a good cause, and many don't survive the cure. The toxin meant to kill cancer, or other organism, basically attacks everything. It can't discern the difference between good cells and bad, the same as any pharmaceutical."

"But, according to what we read in the linked websites from Toddy's article, nanobots are being developed that *can* target organs, cells or, what you're saying, even neurons," he became quiet as the concept sank in.

"Hmm-hmm. Bio-mechanical neurons that would insinuate themselves into other operating parts of the body or brain." Debra thought a minute. "Ten or more years ago, Michael Crichton wrote a book that described the possibilities of nanotechnology gone haywire in a similar way to what we may be observing. "Prey." It was a fascinating book and scarier than all get-out."

"Great." He was beginning to feel like he'd been drafted into a bad sci-fi movie, and his features darkened with a glower that was almost as scary as the scenario she was painting. "So what happened to the people that haven't surfaced? That's the other part of the $100,000 question."

"You're getting cheap. This one's more than two billion dollars. Maybe they didn't survive the implant surgery, or whatever reconstructive procedure they underwent. But I think all of them required some kind of device, from a stent, staple or disc to a full hip replacement," and she jabbed her finger at yet another of the prints on the wall. They were all stylized drawings of the type of medical devices they were talking about.

"I don't know if I can buy that. These procedures are practically routine, in fact, that's what you hear all the time."

"Which is perhaps why whoever is "researching" this is using everyday replacement parts, like knees, hips and hearing implants. Maybe even metal rods and screws to patch up shattered bones?" Debra's eyes had gotten so wide in describing something she considered unspeakable that the fear showed in them as liquid, dark chocolate pools.

"We have no proof, just a truckload of conjecture. What we need are the files. We've been finagling every which way to get our grubby paws on them…"

"My hands are anything but grubby," she interrupted for the sake of defending her nimble, impeccably manicured digits.

"Figure of speech, and you know it."

One corner of Debra's mouth lifted in an attempt to draw herself out of the state of foreboding she'd painted herself into.

"Point is, we can prove zip if we have no evidence," said Esteban.

"We know the files existed. We've backtracked through the Agency for Healthcare Research and Quality to the "non-existent" files," Debra said.

"Yes, but that's as good as having nothing. We can't prove any-thing… legally. What we kinda sorta suppose will not get anywhere near a courtroom." Esteban grew pensive, his brow furrowing.

"Not that we have any kind of evidence, as you say, but if we're on the right path I think invasive nanotechnology experimentation with neuron replacement in the functioning brain is more often fatal than successful…"

Esteban broke in, "What could possibly be construed as "success" in research like that? That's where I can't find a motive, without one we're batting blindly in a black-out."

"Talk about striking out," Debra added to the baseball analogy. "But it looks to me like if it's not "successful," whatever that is, then they're stuck with a study subject that is no longer viable. These peo-ple did not fall off the face of a flat earth, I think the researchers are being forced to dispose of their mistakes."

"Whoa. That's a leap," Esteban wasn't as surprised by her surmise as he sounded. He'd long thought that the "missing patients" were no longer among the living. "Could it be a reasonable assumption? Maybe."

Esteban turned to check the line at the reception desk. When they'd arrived, the sizeable lobby had been filled with patients and family members waiting to see doctors for preliminary appointments, pre-op prep or post-op follow-up, but the crowd had since thinned out. He and Debra took that lull as an opportunity to approach the desk to see what they could pry out of the help. They weren't overly opti-mistic.

❧❧❧❧

Debra and Esteban were met with a chilly reception at the front counter. Cold and sanitary as any operating room should be, and an appointment desk for a healing center that collected millions of dollars from its patrons should not. The staff went beyond professionalism to frosty. Not that their welcome had been the warmest at the Illinois clinic, the administrator a picture of phony cordiality. All the pleasant impressions at their first arrival at San Rafael Surgical Center were instantly crushed, changing Debra's mind about the clinic, outward appearances belied what she now expected was a surly bedside manner. It made her wonder why the place had such a sterling reputation. *Sterile rather than sterling, I'd say.*

It also fortified Debra's thinking that this is just the type of attitude that could cart off "mistakes" without compunction. No personal involvement, no remorse. Just a business transaction, which is precisely how the clerks manning the front desk made her feel, like a credit on the balance sheet. Oh, they smiled and were pleasant enough, but their heart wasn't in it. Good thing she and Roy were only there for business.

The questions they had for the staff were about ten names that she had corroborated with missing individuals through the AHRQ back door and whether or not they still had records at the clinic. They didn't have much hope for receiving straight answers; nor did they.

Esteban weighed the fact that he was investigating without the full weight of the Bureau behind him. If the management for this facility was the inflexible type, which Esteban suspected it was after dealing with the staff it had hired, it was wholly possible that a call might be placed to the regional field office. Not a happy prospect. It'd get his carcass hauled before the SAC without delay. The road rash would be painful. As he extracted his credentials from his pocket he prayed that the clinic manager would be arrogant enough to assume he could handle a lone FBI agent with ease. That was the only chance for Esteban's dodging discipline that would end in suspension.

The cool smile offered by a plump Hispanic woman in her thirties, who was tastefully attired in summer colors, a silk scarf with a poppy motif tied stylishly around her collarbones, created a barrier on the first level. She agreed to tell the administrator that they were in the waiting room and would deliver his response shortly.

"Guess we'll see if he thinks he has the time to talk to us," said Esteban unenthusiastically. "I have no illusions regarding the likely answer."

"No kidding. He trained the staff so their attitude is an extension of his own, crisp and dry, which is good for bacon but not a reception-ist," observed Debra, which brought an unbidden smile to Esteban's face. The administrator appeared just in time to see him wipe it off his mug.

Turning to fully face the doctor, whose nametag, pinned to the man's pocket, published the fact of his title, Esteban greeted him with a serious air hoping that his forceful bearing might encourage cooper-ation. Scanning Dr. Abed Parven's features dispelled that idea. His coloring and name indicated Middle Eastern origin, which could mean anywhere from Persia, to Turkey or Pakistan among a plethora of other nations. Wherever he called a birthplace, he wasn't in the mood to play nice... and neither was Esteban.

"Thank you for taking time out of your busy day," Esteban made the effort to start out on the right foot.

"Yes, Agent, I believe Julia said it was Esteban?" His voice was lilting, confirming Esteban's guess that the doctor wasn't American born, but without welcome. He didn't offer his hand, keeping both of them tucked in his lab coat pockets "How can I help you today?" The offer lacked sincerity and if there could ever be a brush-off in a greet-ing, this was it.

"We need to verify information regarding a number of individuals who received treatment at this facility." He decided not to supply alter-natives. If the good doctor didn't want to participate he'd have to say as much without being given a polite option. It may have been the end of the doctor's day but Esteban's patience was wearing thin. For the last couple of weeks he'd been chasing his tail following ghosts from one coast to another.

"It isn't our policy to disclose personal information about our patients," Dr. Parven revealed nothing by his words. He was as clipped as the clinic staff he'd instructed.

"I understand that. We are not asking for any personal information, just corroboration of their having been seen by your staff. The request does not breach doctor-patient confidentiality."

"To what purpose are you making this inquiry?" He delivered the question flatly, devoid of any real interest.

"I'm afraid that I can't discuss the details of an ongoing investigation. I can tell you that it has no bearing on your facility. All we need to know is whether these individuals came here for care and when. That's it, nothing more." Esteban planted his foot in a way that was a subliminal message of his adamancy. He was not going to let the doctor off the hook, they'd come this far.

Debra watched the face-off with fascination. Neither man was backing down and Esteban was in the weaker legal position, not having a warrant to support his request, let alone *any* law enforcement agency. Waving a badge wasn't carte blanche and savvy citizens knew it, but if they had something to hide, giving a little to defer deeper probing was a sensible alternative. His extra couple of inches of height didn't cow the doctor, but his obstinate stance made the clinic administrator take an involuntary step back. Esteban had won.

"As this appears not to be an intrusion into any patients' files, I will have one of my staff look up the information you require. Please wait here." Dr. Parven accepted the list from Esteban, turned briskly to face the reception desk and quietly gave instructions to Julia, who had initially fetched him.

Debra moved closer to Roy's side as his frame relaxed imperceptibly. "That's one for our side," she whispered.

He didn't respond at first, keeping his eyes on the doctor and Julia as they disappeared into the inner recesses of the clinic. "That's yet to be seen."

The lobby had mostly cleared before the confrontation. One couple was consulting with a specialist on the other side of the great room, too busy with their discussion to take notice of the subtle battle that had ensued. The consultation concluded and the last patient having emerged from the treatment rooms, the doors were locked behind them as Debra and Esteban continued to wait for the results of the database search.

It took a half hour for the task to be completed and Julia, the last remaining staff member on duty, the others having gone home exiting through the back, came out front with a file in her possession. She handed it to Esteban with a brief "thank you" for having waited so patiently. She didn't describe what the results were or offer any commentary at all. Instead, she guided them to the front door and thanked them again as she turned the key in the lock to let them out.

Before stepping through the open door, Esteban tucked a card in her hand saying, "Thank you for your assistance, Julia. Should you think of anything more that you believe is important, give me a call." The look on her face changed from the mildly concerned mask she had worn since re-entering the lobby, to surprise and back to a worried frown. Her mouth opened briefly, rather like a fish as she debated asking a question that didn't come. Nodding instead, she ushered them out and locked the door behind them.

Not feeling compelled to leave right away, Esteban walked Debra toward the Explorer, which was parked around the side of the building, away from the front entrance. But he didn't go to the vehicle. He skirted the clinic to take a look at the layout, check the entrances and whatever else that presented itself as interesting. As they rounded the back, Julia pulled out of her parking space and drove around the lot to exit in the other direction, the pair escaping her notice.

"What are we doing," Debra asked as they milled around the grounds, benches situated adjacent to a fountain, the soothing water sounds creating a park-like setting for patients and staff to take advantage of on their breaks. Esteban spotted a picnic table and led Debra there to sit for a few minutes and take in the surroundings as the sun began its descent. He opened the excruciatingly emaciated manila folder on the table to examine the paltry contents. He hadn't been expecting much but this was pathetic. There were two documents inside. The doctor returned Esteban's original list and the other was one sheet of paper reiterating the list of names that he had supplied. That sheet addressed the two questions Esteban had asked, no less, no more. Next to the list of potential patients was another column, which indicated the date they had been seen at the San Rafael Surgical Center. Nothing else. The results were also as expected. The only people that the clinic confessed to seeing, not if they were admitted for surgery, were the three people they'd already found and spoken to: the computer genius, the opera impresario and the nanny.

"Looks like you get what you ask for," commented Debra as she read the results alongside Roy, sitting in the little paradise of waterfalls and tropical plants. "I know I've asked this before, but, what now?"

"Frankly, I'm fresh out of ideas. Back to the motel and fly away home, is my guess." He looked over at her, brown eyes luminescent in the ginger light, sunset hovering an hour away. Debra's expression reflected disappointment as she caught his eye.

"This isn't what I came here for, to get kicked back home empty-handed. There has to be something we can do yet."

"Well, if you think of anything, let me know. I'll be the first one on that bus," his frustration was as tangible as hers.

"If nothing else, they've landscaped this place as a relaxing escape, the exact opposite of the feeling you get when you're inside the building." She leaned back against the picnic table with her elbows perched on the flat surface, legs stretched out and crossed at the ankles. "What a contradiction. The environment out here is more refreshing than the inner sanctum, and after meeting the head guy, who reminds me more of a witch doctor than a healer, I'd take my chances with a rain dance rather than letting him touch me," she snorted her disapproval.

Bending at the waist, Esteban leaned over and placed his own elbows on his thighs, he folded his hands together and contemplated the view that looked away to the blue-grey waters of the bay. They sat like that for five or ten minutes allowing their minds to run in whatever direction they would, for the first time in two weeks letting go of the investigation that led nowhere. They'd been stonewalled at every turn and all that was left were a few moments of serenity framed by blue sky and open water dotted with sea-going craft of all sizes.

They were brought back to reality by the sound of an approaching vehicle. "Probably security to chase us off," said Esteban, rising. "We might as well leave."

"Right, another day, another adventure," chimed in Debra, also getting to her feet and brushing the wrinkles from her skirt.

Although they heard the vehicle, they couldn't see it from their location at the picnic table. Curiosity egging them on, they edged around the corner of the building to peer at the back entrance. It wasn't a security vehicle they saw but an oversized van.

Something told Esteban to keep out of sight and he held out his arm to block Debra from going any further forward.

"What? The logo says it's a medical waste collection vehicle. See? Got the hazardous material insignia on it and everything," she said glibly.

"Shhh. I don't know why but this bothers me. Why didn't they come during business hours? There's no one else here to let them in." He looked down at her. "What collection agency, garbage, laundry or even armed guards transporting valuables do you give a key to for facility access on their own?"

"None that I can think of."

"Me neither. So who are these guys and what are they collecting?" Esteban leaned out a bit further to gain a better view of the van, Debra at his shoulder. As they watched, two men went into the building through a man-door adjacent to a freight entrance, both of who were wearing uniforms with the same logo printed on their backs that appeared on the van doors. A moment later the rolling steel door retracted into the building, exposing a large storage area with room enough to back in an oversized van the size of the medical waste vehicle. But they didn't bother to back the van into the space. One man walked back out to the vehicle and opened the rear cargo door then went back inside. The next thing the observers saw were the two guys carrying a heavy wooden crate out to the vehicle where they loaded it into the back without any regard for the contents.

They do *work for a waste disposal company,* thought Debra whose mind jumped to the obvious due to the size of the container and deciding not to voice her opinion. *So why would they care how the cargo is treated?*

As the workers locked up the facility, Esteban motioned for Debra to follow him. He sprinted ahead to get the car and she ran along slightly slowed by her heels, though the length of his legs accounted for more of his speed. She was fast even in fashionable pumps. He'd just pulled the Ford out of the parking space as Debra jumped in and fastened her seat belt.

"What do you say let's go for a ride," said Esteban as he drove around the building, hanging back enough that the van driver didn't see him follow them down the hill.

"So what are we doing here," said Debra, "trailing a trash truck."

"It may seem like a new low in FBI policy if it's nothing, but if it's something," he raised his eyebrows at her in expectation, "then we got us a lead."

"You said you were relying on luck, let's hope this is it," and she settled back in her seat, letting him do his cop thing. "You don't think we could get ourselves into a tight spot, do you? Like they see us, turn on us with AK-47s or something?"

He gave a look that said, "get real." "The likelihood that there's even anything improper with these dudes is slim to none, so I don't expect to be ambushed. But then, I'm not going to get close enough for them to see us. We just want to keep our distance and watch. Maybe we *will* get lucky."

The van followed the main drag through town giving Esteban lots of wiggle room to conceal his pursuit, keeping between three and five cars between them. Tailing was a cinch, the van looming over most all of the other traffic. Eventually, a food service tractor-trailer nudged its way into line ahead of them where Esteban lost sight of the van until he saw it make a right turn. From there, following to a commercial warehouse district was painless, where he watched them pull into a lot by a building with the same logo emblazoned on the door. This is where it got a little tricky.

The sun was just beginning to set, still providing plenty of light to see the action of which there wasn't much. Esteban had found a spot kitty-corner to the building right in between two other vehicles that veiled his presence but gave them a great vantage point. Once installed in his position, he decided to go online and check out the medical waste company using his smart phone. He couldn't find any reference to the company through any of the available search engines.

"What are you looking for?" asked Debra from the passenger seat, keeping an eye out for any activity across the street.

"To see if I can find any information on this company. Nothing so far."

"It doesn't look like a facility equipped to handle biohazard disposal to me. But then, what do I know?" Debra was half joking.

"I'm not familiar with disposing of medical waste, what it entails. My guess is that you *do* have an idea."

"All I know is that there are a few ways of rendering the material inert, but first of all, the crate isn't an acceptable disposal container. Not only wasn't it marked as a biohazard but it's obviously not an airtight container or bag which are very recognizable. Secondly, after you transport it in a sealed and marked container, the facility is equipped with an incinerator, steam or chemical processor. I don't see anything about that warehouse that looks like it's outfitted for any of the above, do you?" she looked over at him as he pondered the information.

"There are no chimneys, exhaust or ventilation systems on the roof that would indicate the presence of anything like an incinerator or processing system. Dry cleaners have more junk on their roof than this building," he returned her gaze. "You may be on to something, girl."

"That's what I'm here for, to be the voice of trivia."

They continued to watch until the daylight had almost gone, a mercury vapor lamp the only illumination of the parking lot where the van sat idle, the two operators having gone inside. After another five minutes a heavyset fellow with a hardhat under his arm left the construction office next to where they were parked, paying them no heed as he climbed into the pickup next to them and driving off. Esteban wasn't worried about losing any cover by the loss of neighboring cars, dusk was falling and an extra car parked across the street was of no interest in an industrial area where people came and went at all hours. Next to the construction business was a newspaper distributor who had workers and deliveries coming and going day and night.

"Looks like this is going to take awhile," said Esteban. "Are you game?"

"Sure. Any idea what we're expecting?"

"Won't know until it happens."

So, they waited.

CHAPTER 43

The night descended with quiet encompassing the Explorer, the two figures occasionally lit by the ghostly glow from their cell phones. Nothing was happening at what they'd decided was a faux medical waste facility and they were beginning to wonder if they were twiddling their thumbs.

"How long should we give this surveillance?" asked Debra.

"Depends on whether we think we're right about that company, that it isn't anything but a front for something so nefarious you and I can't wrap our heads around it." Esteban looked over at her indistinct silhouette backlit by the parking lot lights. "What's your gut say?"

"That I can wait longer. There's something wrong with this whole scenario," she dropped her head back on the headrest. "What a day."

Esteban was about to make another comment when the dark was creased by a stream of light emanating from the door opening across the street. A man walked outside to smoke, the end of his cigarette glowing in the shadows.

"Nicotine break," Esteban made the casual remark. "So much for excitement." Just as he said that, a weather-beaten pickup came down the street, slowing in front of the warehouse they'd been watching and parking next to the van. The fellow who had been leaning against the exterior wall, puffing on his cigarette, dropped it and ground out the butt with his heel. Standing with his hands in his pockets, he waited for the truck to pull into the spot that, it was now obvious to the two observers, had been left clear for its arrival. The driver snugged the truck next to the van, the tailgate right by the van's rear door.

"What do you think," asked Esteban rhetorically, "transfer time?"

"Could be. If so, are you going to follow the truck?" Debra's eyes widened with anticipation after enduring a couple hours of doldrum.

Esteban didn't answer more but kept an eye on the activity by the warehouse. "Maybe there's another way to dispose of medical garbage," he finally said as the back of the van was opened and the two operators from the pickup, who were dressed in jeans and windbreakers, shifted the crate into their vehicle from the other. There wasn't much contact between the van driver and the truck occupants other than the completion of the goods transfer. No handshake, pats on the back or laughter. The medical waste driver saluted the pickup operator, whether in jest or out of respect couldn't be determined by the surveillance team situated 50 yards away. Esteban had come prepared with pocket field glasses, but watching backs of heads and guarded faces didn't edify emotions, or lack of them.

Business accomplished, the two men from the pickup hopped back in their vehicle and spun out of the lot, making enough noise that neighboring building occupants would notice, if anyone happened to be around. The van driver shook his head in obvious irritation as he went back inside, there being nothing he could do about someone else's stupidity.

As the medical waste employee disappeared into the warehouse, Esteban immediately fired up the engine and rushed after the truck before he lost him. There were no other vehicles in between them and the pickup, which had to slow for an intersection, rolling through in a classic California stop.

To keep the guy in his field of vision, Esteban had no choice but to copy the pickup and blow the stop sign, praying there were no vigilant police units in the vicinity. It was in their favor that the pickup's driver and passenger seemed to be more in a hurry than concerned with traffic, lessening their notice of what was behind them. They turned onto a thoroughfare that ran alongside the estuary out of town. Being early in the evening still, traffic was abundant enough to impede the truck's haste to get to their destination.

As the road curled around the inlet of the bay, traffic eased up, cars pulling off to neighborhoods or into restaurants and marinas that dotted the shore. Esteban continued to follow the truck at a comfortable distance, the driver easy to keep in view by his erratic behavior.

"Can't imagine what his hurry could be," said Debra.

"Maybe they need to catch the tide," Esteban mused aloud.

"You think they have a boat to catch?"

"Don't know why else they'd be blasting around the corners toward the sea. There isn't much else down here except for a few marinas. I only hope that when he turns off the road we can keep our anonymity."

"You mean that they don't spot us," she dropped the euphemistic language.

"Yeah. I don't want Ell as an enemy for putting one of her chicks in danger."

"*Again...* I think you meant to add," said Debra good-naturedly.

"Right." He concentrated on staying with the truck while hanging back far enough to evade detection.

"Somehow I doubt that those two are paying attention to anything other than where they need to be."

"I sure hope so," he used a grave intonation that made her think twice about the possibility of real risk in what they were doing. *What did you expect if you're gonna pal around with an FBI agent in inves - tigation mode?*

Less than a mile later, the pickup turned down a road that led to a harbor where, once they came around the bend, Esteban and Debra saw there wasn't much activity. The slips accommodated everything from fishing vessels to a couple of yachts, but the majority of vessels were mid-range pleasure boats. The truck pulled up to a floating dock at the end of the line. Parking by the gate, the passenger impatiently jumped down before the driver had put the truck in park, after which he cut the engine and walked around to the tailgate and dropped it. The other guy had already unlocked the gate at the top of the dock and swinging it wide, he went through and climbed into the driver's seat of a motorized cart used to transport cargo to the slip.

Esteban turned off his headlights before coming into the parking lot and slid into a place a safe distance from the head of the dock, where the banging around of the two guys in the truck would muffle the Ford engine's whine. They were a loud pair, obviously not concerned with being seen or heard.

The man drove the cart out the gate, positioning it where it would be easy to load the crate and a few other items, including a black plastic container that *was* marked with the biohazard emblem, something they'd missed in the cargo transfers.

"When did that get loaded?" asked Debra.

"Probably at the clinic. We could see the crate because of its size and it needing two men to move it, but with the doors open and the way the van was positioned near the cargo door, we could have missed it," explained Esteban.

"You don't think it came from somewhere else and was already in the van?"

"That's possible, too. Which would mean there are other places illegally dumping medical waste." Esteban huffed. "Just what we need, to trip over a criminal disposal scheme." He paused for a moment. "Come to think of it, it could be a boon to us, give us a back door to catching the clinic in the act of illicit practices."

"Particularly since no one seems to be in the least interested in missing patients. This could force an investigation." She looked over at Esteban. "You're getting photos of this, aren't you?"

"Have been all along. Phones with cameras are real handy. This fancy piece of technology even has a zoom feature."

"Good thing, 'cause it looks like you're going to need it," said Debra as she watched

the one fellow drive the cart halfway down the dock, stopping in front of an ocean-going sport fishing boat. There was a man standing on the flying bridge, a baseball cap with an extra long bill shadowing his features, waiting for the cart to park at the gangway.

The driver had climbed back in the truck to park it on the other side of the lot from where Esteban had chosen his perch. They both heaved a sigh of relief, worried that he might pull close by their vehicle. From there he trotted down the dock to help unload the cart, after which the other guy drove it back to the head of the pier to park it. The cart jockey then ran back to help his partner stow the cargo at the direction of the captain. Tying down the crate, they then cast-off and motored down the estuary to the bay, Debra and Esteban losing sight of them as they rounded the breakwater.

"Well there goes the evidence," remarked Debra.

"Evidence to what, do you think."

"One of the missing patients. You don't agree?"

"Could be, but we'll never know," Esteban was deflated. "We have evidence of something stinking to high heaven on a fishing boat that isn't fish." He put the SUV into gear, "But it'll soon be fish food."

"Yes."

No hello or appropriate greeting other than the blunt affirmative, not that that bothered the caller, he was also a no-nonsense professional. His answer was just as concise. "We have a development of which you should be aware."

The doctor instantly recognized the caller's voice. He detected the slightly singsong accent with ease as belonging to one of his clinic administrators', the Persian physician who had long ago immigrated first to Britain, where he received his primary education, and then to America to train in medicine. Dr. Parven was his most businesslike and dedicated of all the clinic managers, and the least likely to panic under stress. Hearing from him was usually a pleasure but with a preamble like that, the doctor knew that a situation of some urgency had come up.

"Go ahead."

"This evening, just before finishing clinic hours, the couple you'd warned of came in requiring information that I was loathe to provide." Although Abed Parven had seen disturbing events in his youth before escaping the religious regime of the ayatollahs, he was not completely inured to alarm, especially if it threatened his livelihood. Islam had been left far behind in the dingy back streets of Tehran. Parven was a secular Muslim who affected the rites and ceremonies, even celebrating Ramadan with his observant brother who had run to England with him, but he was more concerned about serving the greater good, and that included cutting edge research. He was committed to bettering lives even if it meant that a few lost theirs in the quest. This was the reason why the doctor, to whom Parven had placed the call, trusted his judgment.

"What exactly did they request." This was not a question but an order for information.

"The FBI agent, Esteban, was almost belligerent in his probe for confirmation of whether some names, that he provided me, were those of patients at our facility."

"Go on," he prompted.

Although Parven wasn't frightened, self-preservation trumped all else. He'd learned that lesson the hard way as a youth, and he knew that how he had proceeded with this situation would shape his future with this research group. "There were ten names on the list, of which I verified three, all of which have returned to jobs in the region."

"Were the other names of any import?" the doctor needed to know all the possible consequences.

"Other than the fact that they corresponded to individuals that are not in our databases."

The doctor fully grasped what Dr. Parven was telling him. These are names that had been purged, just as this FBI agent had asked about similar patient names at other facilities in their research network, personally arriving in New York and Illinois and phoning inquiries to Grosse Pointe, L.A. and Jacksonville. He was beginning to wonder how this Esteban had put together the puzzle of their group. They weren't affiliated in any way other than receiving grants for device research through his funder, and that information was not public. Nor was the fact that he served with every one of those boards of directors in different offices.

"Do you think that you satisfied his interest?"

"I do not have any idea. I felt the circumstance was better served if I left the premises before the information was placed in hand, to remove myself from immediate access should he be unhappy with what we provided. I allowed my office manager to deliver the file and she is not privy to the research study."

"I would concur with your handling of the situation," said the doctor. "Is there anything else that you can add?"

"No. Due to the fact that I was no longer at the clinic and Julia left soon after, I have no knowledge of what he did with the information, or if there was anything that he could do." He was silent for a moment while he decided whether to add the information that just occurred to him. Choosing to be forthright on all counts, he added, "I suspect that this will have no bearing, however, tonight medical waste is scheduled to pick up material for disposal. They arrive long after closing when there would be no one present."

The doctor didn't answer right away although a pang of misgiving shot through him. *Would the FBI agent have waited around and seen a waste removal?* He relegated the unwelcome thought to the back of his mind as being thoroughly unlikely. There was no reason on earth for him to hang around.

Dismissing it, he told Parven to have a good evening, that there was nothing more that he could do.

After ending the call, the doctor went through all the reports he'd been receiving over the last week. No matter how many mental gymnastics he did, not a one provided any solutions, and he was forced to set the problem aside until he had more facts.

BLOOD BARONS

CHAPTER 44

Reading through the latest lab report from the researcher, the benefactor's eyebrows rise noticeably, furrowing his already craggy forehead. He is rarely impressed by anything. If an alien spaceship were to land on his front lawn, consuming all 80 acres of it, it would - n't give him pause, he'd ignore it as much as he does the average human. But this information, this is inconceivable.

His understanding of biology is limited, even he would acknowl - edge this to be a subject outside his expertise. A genius in business, proven by his ability to manipulate currencies and national economies, exploiting commodities and the populations dependent upon them, this information has him floored.

Understanding that everything is dependent on organization, even chaos being an outgrowth of organization as a rebellion from it; and entropy is reliant on a system in which it is the disordered element, this lies outside the laws of nature. In all, order is all and overrides all. Randomness is manipulated by order, thus comes his father's theory of reflexivity as being a manipulation of reflexive action against order. So how the doctor could possibly arrive at a conclusion that contradicts order is implausible to him.

But here it is. An organism that lacks the part that orders it, that communicates how and when and what to build. DNA is essential to all living beings, the informational code, in effect, the business plan of the cell. There can be no organization without an organizer, there can be no functioning organism without DNA, the building blocks of life. And here he finds mitochondria – of which he realizes he must refresh his memory on its function – that effectively has no DNA.

Reading further into the report he sees that mitochondria is an organelle, a separate component within the cell that already possess - es DNA within the chromosomes hidden in its nucleus. Yet this little organelle has DNA of its own. Or is supposed to. Why does a part of a cell have DNA outside that of the host cell? He naturally questions something that is beyond his knowledge of genetics.

Science is science and every organism is organized, that's the basis of the term from which function derives. He understands this, it's how he runs his empire, even when organization is used to incite anar - chy, which then allows organization to take advantage of the lost with - in the organism.

This report is telling him that there is no mtDNA, which to him ends the viability of the organism, and in this case, it obviously did not.

There must be an explanation. Perhaps the mitochondrial DNA was destroyed in the petrification process, the water flowing through the grave and washing it away. But this made no sense either as the part of the bone from which the cells were extracted was not petrified, as was the surrounding bone.

Placing the report on his desk, he massages his temples, dumb - founded by the confusing information. He decides he must have answers now. After already waiting twenty years, what he gets are deeper mysteries that it appears could bring all this hard work and millions of research dollars to naught. The money means nothing, it's the research and the anticipated results that have the most signifi - cance for him. This is research begun by his father for a great purpose which he is determined to fulfill.

Lifting the handset of the phone, he punches the speed dial to the lab only to have the answering machine come on, prompting a mes - sage to be left. Not a man to express anger, he presses the speed dial for the research scientist's cell phone and is immediately switched to voice mail.

Fuming, he recalls that his personal e-mail, to which very few peo - ple have the address, had indicated that there were some new mes - sages. Striking him that the scientist may have chosen that method of communication, he opens his mail. There, amid a number of unimpor - tant notices, he sees one from the researcher and immediately opens it.

The e-mail answers the question as to why he can't reach the *man... he's taken a leave from the lab for the next week, citing an emergency, though he does not explain the nature of said emergency.*

A master of containing emotion, he instantly drops his irritation, realizing that the overall purpose of the research may not be tainted by this discovery. Reaching for the report once more, he immerses himself in the study results that matter most to his objective. He will deal with the doctor upon his return.

Frantically, the research scientist had packed his bags and made a dash to Reagan International Airport. He'd cut it close but had dropped into his seat, already bushed from night after night of sleep-lessness, the mystery of the ancient bone sifting endlessly through his mind. Yes, he'd been at the excavation of the gravesite, had even wit-nessed some of the desecration of it in the name of what he thought was legitimate science 20 years ago. He knows now that he'd deluded himself, all for the false promise of being the first to uncover the secret of eternal life.

What kind of fool is he to have been so blinded by his own ambi-tion? Generous compensation has continued to flow into his bank accounts over the years, but to what end? The secrecy to which he has been bound ultimately destroying his marriage and dismantling his family. Signing the non-disclosure agreements, and he recalls how there were many, a new one each time a breakthrough was made, he was told they would just be a temporary restriction until the research is completed and fully patented. Then he will be able to publish and all will be made right.

Now, as he hovers on the brink of finalizing the product that he originally had been hired to develop, the full weight of his complicity in hiding truth is crashing down around him. His conscience is not allowing him respite until he lays his questions to rest, assuming that there are answers still to be found after so many have trampled, including his own interdisciplinary team, what he now understands to be a momentous discovery.

The first leg to Paris is utterly without sleep, every detail of the last year, when the research broke wide-open, filter past his eyes, whether or not they are closed. When he lands at Orly to change planes, he is no better than a zombie going through the motions to reach the terminal for his flight to Istanbul. Fortunately, his one bag is checked through and he operates on pure trust that it will reach Turkey along with him. His carry-on has all his absolute necessities and his smart phone, when it works, will be his lifeline.

As he boards the flight to the ancient capital of both the Byzantine and Ottoman Empires, one religious power having crumbled beneath the overwhelming strength of the next rising force – the Cross suc-cumbing to the Red Crescent – he recalls his first venture to this part of the world. Then, he had taken the time to visit a crucial symbol of the tide of Islam that had spread from the south, one of the greatest Byzantine cathedrals, the Hagia Sophia, which no longer displayed any Christian icons, the Ottoman sultan having plastered over all the imagery of Christ to remake it into a mosque. Today, the secular world has overtaken even the religious fervor of Islam, as the revered church-become-mosque now serves society as a museum.

This, to him, represents what he is now a part of, the destruction of the Church, the relegating of God to nothing more than an impotent bystander as men like his benefactor design their own rise. Theirs is a grasping for an irrational attainment of what they believe to be god-like attributes, attributes that are not available to man in the temporal plane. Yet, he is a collaborator, a role that he now rues.

Thoroughly exhausted by the continual rerunning of a suspense movie in his mind where he keeps missing the ending, his head lolls to his shoulder and he falls into a fitful slumber.

⚜⚜⚜

Even in these technologically advanced times, it has taken him two days to reach the last stop in the airborne portion of his journey, Erzurum, a city of over 300,000 people in the eastern provinces of Turkey. The flights have taken all of the 48 hours between time in the air and layovers and he is anxious to reach his ultimate objective, refusing time to lollygag by visiting the local tourist attractions. From the airport he takes a shuttle to a hotel that is part of an internation-al chain, assuming that they deal with all kinds of tour groups and business people. Once inside, he checks in and immediately goes to the concierge to book land transport to the town of Dogubeyazit, deep in Kurdish territory and practically bordering Iran.

The concierge is hesitant, informing him that lately there had been upheaval in the area, but he is insistent and the hotel employee con-cedes, calling a tour group that is headed there early the next morn-ing.

With the next leg of his trek arranged, the research scientist is utterly done in and heads up to his room, collapsing in a heap on the bed, snoring softly fully clothed, his gear unceremoniously dumped in a pile by the door.

❧❧❧❧

The next morning, he wakes only partially refreshed, his sleep fit-ful despite the fatigue of travel. But he is fed and packed, standing with the other passengers prepared to board the van that will take the five travelers beside himself to Dogubeyazit, and closer to his goal.

The driver wends his way along E-80, a two-lane macadam high-way, for more than four hours through wide, dun colored fields. Boulders that appear to have tumbled from the surrounding highlands are scattered across miles of open land. Villages dot the countryside, some with modern conveniences but most without, those living outside the towns settled in mud-daub houses lacking electricity. The moun-tain slopes are home to families that raise livestock, the dry grass of the plains providing the fodder.

There is much of the landscape that hasn't changed over thousands of years, let alone since the scientist had visited twenty years ago, the passing views rewinding his mind to that time. He has packed along the photos that had captured the ephemeral image of a man in white and he pulls them from his breast pocket to examine them once again.

Although he has kept to himself throughout the road trip, the other couples on trek to see Mt. Ararat jabbering around him, one of them peers over his shoulder as he looks at the photos of the excavation.

"What have you got there?" asks a young man in his twenties, long hair reaching his collar, his soul patch growing out to a full beard as he has discarded use of a razor for this trip. The others are nattering between themselves and pay no attention to the college student on holiday and the misplaced research scientist.

He is taken by surprise, dragged out of his reverie almost violently he is so involved in his own thoughts. At first, panic flows over him, these are photos of a sacrosanct expedition that no one beyond the benefactor and those who were present know anything about, and the local workers saw nothing to arouse their suspicions at the time or since. He feels like a child caught red-handed with his fist full of grandma's cookies.

Calming himself, he calls up his voice that has been used so rarely for the last two years that at first he croaks in delivering his answer.

"A sacred sepulcher," he answers without agonizing over his words.

"Oh yeah? I'm an anthro student from the University of New Mexico. I'd love to hear about this. It looks like there's a good story to go with those pics," he says excitedly.

"What do you know about the Bible?"

"Only that it's a collection of hand-me-down tales from ancient times, kind of like the spoken history cycles among cultures before they had written language. The tale of Gilgamesh has fascinated me forever as the first written tale in one of the oldest scripts known, Cuneiform."

"Are you familiar with biblical archaeology then?"

"Sure. It has to do with biblical scholars attempting to prove the veracity of stories in the Bible by locating and excavating the sites mentioned in the books," says the young man. "I'll admit that I haven't studied much of it. Most colleges don't offer that option, writing it off as unproven."

"Don't you find that to be somewhat hypocritical?" asks the

researcher.

"*How so? It's religious hearsay that serves the purpose of provid-ing answers to unanswerable questions about, well, anything and everything to do with life.*"

"*Look at it this way. You are fascinated by the Epic of Gilgamesh which is what?*"

"*A myth,*" the student readily supplies.

"*So, using your own criteria for following up on a lead, if you will, for a dig, aren't you then attempting to corroborate something that you consider to be an unsubstantiated fantasy?*" The scientist was begin-ning to understand more of his own quest as he posed queries to the young man.

The student considers the premise and finally has to concede the scientist's point. "*You skewered the argument I've been fed for three years with one sentence. How come none of my professors ever thought of that?*"

"*I assure you they have. The problem is that most educators find the very concept of faith to be anathema to their theory of the universe, and its appearance out of the void,*" explains the scientist. "*What I hold in my hand is a precious memento of an excavation, an exhuma-tion in truth, that held answers to questions science is unwilling to ask.*"

"*Now I'm totally in. You have to explain more.*"

"*I don't know that I can until I've reaffirmed my hypothesis, which is why I left my lab to come out here.*" He turns to look at the young man over the back of the seat, "*Why are you and your friends travel-ing this far from home in a volatile district of the Middle East? Particularly so close to the Iranian border after that incident last year with those three young people who were captured as spies? It seems you're far afield in a dangerous age.*"

"*As I said, I'm obsessed with the Gilgamesh story and out here to poke around as close to the origins of the epic as I can get. The oth-ers? Friends and thrill-seekers we met along the way.*" He looks at the scientist with a quizzical eye. "*What is it you do?*"

"*I'm a biologist, genetic engineering.*"

"And you were at an excavation of an ancient site? Where?"

"Somewhere in the neighborhood. The site was destroyed long ago by vandals," he will not admit that it was his own team that had con - tributed to obliterating the evidence. *The guilt now ran too deep in his veins.*

"Can you tell me what it is you were excavating? And who that strange figure is in the photos? He doesn't look like he's even really there, sort of floating." The student gives him a skeptical look. *"Is it photo-shopped?"* he practically accuses.

"I can assure that it has not been tampered with, and, if you want the truth, I don't think that you will accept my hypothesis of who that is pictured in the photos. Because," and he pauses to take a breath and slowly exhales, now knowing that he is certain who it is but also cer - tain that the student will reject his conclusion, *"it takes absolute faith to accept what cannot be confirmed by our five senses."*

The young man looks at him askance, caught between wanting to believe this self-proclaimed scientist and completely eschewing what he thinks the man is trying to say. *"What you're telling me is that you're a Christian, and you believe this to be an apparition of Christ."*

"Not an apparition, and until now when you voiced it, I did not know that I was a believer. Thank you, son. You have seen and stated something that I have been avoiding for years. All the evidence I have uncovered points to your deduction, but I didn't have the courage to admit it."

"What evidence?" The student was hungry to know. *"You're a geneticist. You've found something."*

"If I have, I am not at liberty to divulge it. I am constrained by unwisely signed contracts."

"Tell me anyway. I won't let on. I give my word."

"Young man, I believe you are sincere, and if I were able to tell you any more than I already have, I would. Know that there is proof of a first Adam and a second Adam, which if you read your Bible you will know is Christ. That much I will tell you. Faith will take you farther than any archaeological dig." He pauses again. *"It will truly set you free."*

Approaching Dogubeyazit, 60,000 souls situated in a city straddling the main road between Erzurum and Iran, all the passengers strain to see the famed heights of Mt. Ararat rising to the east, the peak capped in everlasting snows. Here is where these travelers are going to find their own version of the Great Flood, which, as university students, they recognize only from the multiple cultures that have legends of vast floods told over millennia. They will hike the steep slopes, seeking evi - dence that the researcher knows is not there. It is miles distant, near another village close by where he and his cohorts had plundered the resting place of an historic figure many in the earth do not recognize as having existed.

He is here to reconcile his intuition with the science. The facts he has uncovered in the laboratory are incontrovertible.

He is here for resolution.

BLOOD BARONS

CHAPTER 45

Hyped from the reconnaissance mission, Debra was revved up and bummed at the same time. Her initiation into the drab world of surveillance had garnered only the knowledge that something wasn't quite right in the cities by the bay. She thought Roy had hit the nail squarely on the head when he said something was fishy about the whole operation. The sanitation unit they'd followed was definitely not operating within the guidelines of a slew of alphabet soup governmental agencies from OSHA to EPA to California Department of Public Health, even to the DOT... *Ya gotta transport the stuff if you don't handle it onsite*, thought Debra. The only thing they'd left out was the Acupuncture Board, and, come to think of it, she added them onto her mental list, too. *There have to be regs for disposing of the needles.*

At times, the concept of all the regulatory agencies that have their fingers in the revenue pie was beyond disconcerting, the level of insinuation into everyone's lives by charging for fees and licenses had approached the level of outright thievery in Debra's estimation. Before her thoughts traveled any further down this unending road of which bureaucracies should be stripped of authority, she pulled hard on the reins to center on the here and now.

"A little adrenaline pumping there?" said Esteban.

"Should there be? All we did was sit and wait and watch helplessly as these *guys,* whoever they are, flaunted the law – not that I'm exactly against that, mind you, when it comes to ham-handed regulators – but if they were indeed disposing of some-*one* rather than some-*thing*, then we've got us a problem."

"One with no evidence... and thus, no problem when it comes to law enforcement."

"What a crock," she spat. "Aren't a couple of eye witnesses worth something?"

"We'd have to convince an officer of the court that we witnessed an illegal act." Esteban went quiet as he drove along the north side of the bay back to the hotel in Vallejo. It was getting on to 10 p.m. and they were winding down from more than 12 hours of tackling witnesses that weren't and tracking evidence that wasn't. Both of them were frustrated knowing they had just observed the commission of a crime but were powerless to do anything about it.

"We can submit a report to the local authorities and hope that they follow-up on it," said Esteban. "You know that if I go into the SF field office with the whole tale they'll howl all the way to the airport before shoving us on a flight out of state."

"I don't get it. How can you have gone from the FBI's golden boy to the boy who cried wolf in a matter of a year?" Debra was amazed by the contradiction. "And they talk about politicians being flip-floppers."

"Who do you think runs the Bureau? Politicians, every one of 'em. And if you don't play by their rules, you're out on your keester. Which is why the seat of my pants have been so dusty of late. I can't brush 'em off fast enough before I'm booted out the door again." He gave her a rueful smile. "I believe that I will be on a new career track before the week is out, at this rate."

"Don't be so certain," she said, tapping her chin while a thought took form. "I think we should make a statement tomorrow to the health department in San Rafael. Not bother with the police. They won't have any idea of what our purpose was in visiting the clinic. We can just say we were concerned about a friend and there to check on their care." She looked across at him in the glow of the dashboard lights. "It's not too far from the truth."

He glanced at her, wary of what outlandish story she was concocting.

"And we tell them, when we couldn't find out anything, not being family, we camped out at the picnic table, worried and wondering what to do, when we saw suspicious activity after hours." Debra waved off his head-wagging as her tale grew longer. "You being an officer of the law felt compelled to follow your intuition and then, tell them what we saw."

She tilted her head forward and gazed at him, keenly awaiting his reaction. "It could work, right?"

"They'll ask why we didn't just go to the police," he said flatly.

"That one's obvious. Because we weren't sure if a crime had been committed, just a violation of health regulations, which they could investigate and enforce. Particularly since we clearly saw the loading of a biohazard container onto a sport fisher. And... you have pictures to corroborate our statements." She sat up proudly, believing this could open a door that had been shut tight. "What do you think?"

"I think, young lady, that it could work and we might be able to wedge a foot in that door before it's padlocked."

"Good. That's what we'll do first thing in the morning," she yawned. "Right now, all I want is popcorn, a glass of wine and bed."

"Ditto. But I'll pass on the popcorn."

⚜⚜⚜

Next day, they'd followed through with their plan. Driving back to San Rafael, they located the county office for Environmental Health Services and presented their story.

Esteban (and Debra, though she wouldn't admit it) was doubtful that the clerk would take them seriously, but he was pleasantly surprised by the office's willingness to accept the report. Like most governmental agencies these days, the personnel were steeped in the 'green' political narrative, and the thought that their revered waterways could be sullied by illegal garbage dumping, especially biological waste, was despicable and well worth checking out.

The clerk, a nice young black woman with quarter-size golden discs in her distended and distorted earlobes, took the name of the medical waste disposal company and checked their current license information. She found that there was a company by that name, but they were located on the other side of the bay in San Mateo County. They did not list a local address, which made her carefully painted eyebrows slowly creep up her forehead as she realized this could be a major violation. She looked at the odd duo standing at the counter and asked them to have a seat, she was going to fetch her superior.

Esteban gave Debra a wink as they sat on the bench until the clerk returned with a manager, a man in his forties with a short-sleeved dress shirt and skinny tie left over from a previous life or purchased at a retro shop. He carried himself with a serious bearing, evidently the prospect of health violations of this type were a rare occurrence in his office. When they'd been introduced, he said as much.

"Darren Gillespie," he offered his hand to Esteban. "Leslie said that you witnessed a possible act of improper disposal of medical waste last night. That's not something that happens much on this side of the bay."

"Yes, it appeared to be an illegal dumping, so we've come in to make a statement for your department to follow-up," said Esteban.

"Good. If you will, we have an area over here where you can fill in the correct forms and I'll get them through the system right away." He looked at Esteban over his shoulder as he walked them to a cubicle with a couple of desks and chairs. "This is a serious situation so we appreciate your coming forward, Mr. Esteban."

"No trouble. We need to get this finished and I can provide you with a few photos taken of the transfer at all of the locations."

"That will help us complete a complaint that can be investigated as soon as possible. We have an inspector available."

"Great, Mr. Gillespie. Let's get this done."

Within a matter of half an hour, both Debra and Roy had completed the forms and transferred photos via e-mail to the EHS office to supplement the report. They thanked the clerk, who smiled widely at Esteban as they handed over everything and made their way out the door and back to the SUV.

"Didn't know you still had it with the young ones, didja?" jibed Debra.

"Probably has a daddy issue," he said, flicking the comment aside as uninteresting. "Women with problems are not on my list of worthy pastimes." He opened the door for Debra.

"So, was this the best option for siccing the dogs on the clinic?"

"Best idea you've had, coming to EHS instead of the police," he said.

"Why is that?" Debra was puzzled.

"Because law enforcement doesn't have the time or manpower to chase down every possible clue about an infraction or misdemeanor. But government agency bureaucrats, they're another story. They will zealously hunt down Fido to enforce their regulations."

"At the risk of repeating myself, why is that?"

"To collect the *fines*," he said with emphasis on the last word.

"Right… revenue is what makes government go 'round," she nodded her head. "I am smart, aren't I?"

"No one sharper, which is why you're my partner," and he put the car in gear and drove toward the freeway.

"Time to pack up and get out of dodge, wouldn't you agree?"

"Heartily."

⚜⚜⚜

Midnight had come and gone by the time they arrived at Ell's front stoop. The flight from Sacramento had deposited them at La Guardia where they caught a taxi into Manhattan.

"Home again, home again…" said Debra sardonically, having just flown over her own home in the center of the country some hours earlier. Esteban instructed the driver to wait, then walked Debra up the steps, carrying her bag for her. She unlocked the front door and he followed her up the stairs to deposit the one piece of luggage inside the door of Ell's apartment.

"Thank you, sir, for walking me to my door," she said turning to face Esteban after dropping her handbag next to Ell's on the hall table. "I don't know about you, Roy, but I am bushed. As soon as you're gone, I'm going to crash."

"If that's a signal to get lost, I can do that," he said and stepped back to make his escape, taking that as a dismissal.

Debra swung around, realizing that her words might have been hurtful she caught him by the arm and pulled him back to plant a kiss on his cheek. "Thanks for the adventure, Roy. Luckily, it was pretty tame. Your work is way out of my league."

Surprised at the spontaneous kiss and placing his hand over hers, not allowing her to escape, he smiled then became somber, "Most days are full of the boring stuff and I thank God that we never came close to anything that might place you in danger. I'd never forgive myself."

"You managed to keep us both out of trouble and bring us back safe and sound," Debra was unable to suppress a yawn.

Esteban let her go, "Speaking of sound, you need a sound night's sleep so, good night, Debra. I'll call you tomorrow." The statement was half a question.

"Yes, tomorrow we'll... I don't know what we'll do. You'll think of something. Good night," she smiled shyly as she closed the door. When he heard the locks set, he loped down the stairs to catch the taxi home and some essential shuteye.

CHAPTER 46

Taking the day to check back in with work, Esteban compiled all the notes and "evidence" that he and Debra had discovered in their multi-city investigative tour into a folder and backed it all up on a thumb drive. Two actually, one for his ASAC, who would be livid when he received it, having refused Esteban the authorization to expand his inquiry. He was also adding digital tapes of phone interviews with the Grosse Pointe, Santa Monica and Jacksonville clinics along with photos to the hard copy folder. The phone conferences and photos he digitized and included on the jump drives to make sure he had multiple copies of everything. The methodology for obtaining access to some of the information, he did not allude to in any of the files, hard copy or computerized. If, and he prayed it would happen, the Bureau decided to move ahead on what he'd collected, they'd have to recreate the sequence through proper channels with warrants. The hardest part about all of it, in eventually turning it over to his superiors, was knowing that the access may have been dissolved, or files scrubbed by then. Time was of the essence but government did not work in that world, it dragged its feet at an interminably slow pace. There were times that he believed it was complicit in ensuring that any proof of illegal activity disappeared into the ether beyond the best forensic computer expert's ability to reconstruct. It was cynical to the core, but by now after more than a quarter of a century working at the FBI, Esteban no longer trusted any of the politically motivated hierarchy, which was the majority of them.

Hours later, a thumb drive in his pocket and one plus the file locked in his desk, Esteban called Debra to make a dinner date.

"Do you have plans for the evening?" he asked as soon as she picked up the phone.

"Only repacking the "trunk" for the trip home. Did a little shopping today with Ell to get it out of the way, because tomorrow we're going to do the last bit of sightseeing," she chattered a little self-con-sciously, though, for the life of her, she couldn't understand why. This is Roy whom she's known for more than a year and just spent almost two weeks working intimately together, whether or not they'd been successful in getting the gears of justice to move. "Gotta have a little vacation on my vacation, ya know."

"Well deserved, too. Allow me to treat you to dinner tonight. It's not much compensation, I'm afraid."

"Enjoying a meal without having the case hanging over our heads at every turn would be a delight," she said. "I'm ready for a little R and R, even if just for a day."

"Great. Tell you what, how about I pick you up from the bistro in the middle of the block across the street. They have a nice bar and I'll meet you there as a starting point," he suggested.

"That'll fit right into my schedule," said Debra happily.

"See you at seven."

"Looking forward to it."

⚜⚜⚜

Anticipating an evening without dredging through file after file to pinpoint leads and possible evidence for the missing patient case, Debra was excited to spend time with Roy on a different level, a more personal one. They'd been traveling together for days and meeting almost daily the week before that, but all of that time was geared to solve a mystery that, although they had a good idea as to what was happening, they were still unable to prove anything. Justice was not in the offing thus far. The opportunity to be just Debra and Roy for a few hours was appealing to her and, even after working so closely with him, she was experiencing a touch of nerves. *This, I don't get. Hours on end talking over theories and computer traces and* now *I get the jit - ters.*

She shook it off and dressed with care, planning to enjoy a plain old date. Something she hadn't had since the last time they'd been out together before he was relocated to New York. She'd had plenty of offers but no one had really sparked her interest and she wasn't one to go out just to go out. She'd had too many guys get the wrong impression simply because she'd sit down to dinner with them. Wild imaginations, most of them, thinking they were irresistible. And then there were the metrosexuals who were just too involved in their own primping to be worth her time. Boring. If she wanted to go out and talk about clothes, hair and skin moisturizers, she'd have a night out with the girls. Even that was a rarity. Her best friend Allie didn't come into town but once a month for meetings at the paper. Though occasionally she'd be there with her husband on ranch business.

Face it, girl. Your life is duller than dull. Until these last couple weeks. It's been just plain fun, exhausting, but fun.

Around her shoulders Debra threw a handcrafted shawl of glistening yarns and threads artistically woven together in a summery collection of lavender, persimmon and pistachio that complemented her sundress. Caparisoned for a warm summer's eve on the town, she grabbed her clutch and stepped out the door, calling goodbye to Ell who was enjoying a night in with a good book open on her lap.

"Have a terrific time! And remind Roy that he's not out of the woods yet. I'm keeping my eye on him!"

Debra shook her head and smiled as she closed the door behind her.

⚜ ⚜ ⚜

Esteban decided he'd try to make some inroads with Debra. Since the first time he'd met her when she was desperate to find her friend in Wyoming, he'd been fascinated by her passion and generally modest personality. She had a sharp wit, and a tongue to match when she was provoked, but most of the time Debra was an introvert who rose to the occasion when necessary. Esteban had been surprised by her ability to roll with the circumstances, no complaining, just jumping in and even taking the initiative, reading the situation like a pro. The case may have been one with a tragic twist as people had lost their lives literally and figuratively, but the pleasure had been in having a partner who could grasp the gravity of the subjects' condition, or possible condition. Someone who had the intellect to take the clues they had and go that shrewd step further, advancing a theory that he'd overlooked for the outrageousness of it. This whole investigation had been one of revelation after revelation of what man can be capable, leaving him in a quandary as to what the outcome will be… justice served or amorality condoned.

Tonight he was going to arrive bearing a simple and elegant bouquet in appreciation for an elegant and remarkable woman who he truly didn't want to see leave. For the time being, and he acknowledged that that time may be short after this last independent foray across the country, he was stuck in the city and Debra was due to leave for Denver. He was going to miss her profoundly. Shrugging it off he thought, *I can't wait to see what Bestner is going to do when I dump the next batch of data on his desk. Maybe I should pack my bags, too.*

Esteban had opted for taxi service rather than messing with parking, which could put a huge damper on what he hoped would be an evening of companionship that could develop into a closer relationship. He and Debra had been skirting the issue ever since that initial meeting. The few dates they'd enjoyed together just before he'd been bumped to the eastern seaboard had only whetted his inclination to get better acquainted. These last days had just served to prove that he was correct in his first response about Debra, that she was a unique and very special woman, unlike anyone he'd met since his divorce years ago.

As the driver headed down the avenue, an ambulance sped away in the opposite direction, sirens braying and lights flashing. They pulled aside, as much as New York taxis do, making a nominal attempt to clear the center lanes, as the blaring bus fled to the nearest hospital. Re-entering the flow of traffic, the taxi went a few more blocks and pulled up to the curb, dropping Esteban across the street from the rendezvous point. Trotting across the road with the spare but striking spray of lilies in hand, he pushed open the door to the quaint little bistro that was across the way from Ell's. The place was buzzing with chatter, but he was oblivious to the gossip filling the air, his mind on laying eyes on the lovely lady with whom he was looking forward to passing a pleasant evening. Examining all the patrons of the restaurant, it was obvious that Debra wasn't among them. Checking his watch, he saw that he was late, the extra time he'd taken to purchase the blooms and the emergency vehicle flying by had added an extra 30 minutes onto his travel time. He'd expected her to be a little late, she was a woman after all. Although most women prefer to be theatrical in courtship, he hadn't supposed Debra to be of that mindset. *Every woman's a surprise*, he thought, sitting down at the bar to wait. *Debra should be here any time.*

Debra had arrived just a few minutes late, but even at that she had beaten her date to the appointed place. Feeling comfortable with herself and having paid meticulous attention to her appearance, she had hoped to make something of an entrance for Roy's benefit, wanting to impress him just a little. Missing the boat on that prospect, she settled herself at the bar, self-consciously arranged her skirt to create the most artistic effect, and ordered a cocktail. Not one for passing wine fads among the popular crowd, the currently fashionable reds, though she appreciated them well enough, merlot or pinot noir held little interest for her. She stuck by her favorite varietal, California Chablis.

A few minutes later the bartender brought a long-stemmed white wine glass and set it before her. She clucked at the half-filled glass wondering at the outrageous charge for beverages in this city. *Probably regulating this like they are soda. Can't have anything bigger than 16 ounces so why not limit service to three or four ounces of wine.* Denver was expensive enough, but the West still made an effort to provide value for the dollar. Setting aside her initial peeve, she heard the front door open and turned to see if Roy might be entering the establishment. No, instead she saw an interesting looking couple dressed in bike leathers. Not the usual attire in this part of town. Parking for motorcycles wasn't much more readily available than for cars, despite their more compact size. Evidently, these two managed to wangle a spot and, helmets tucked under their arms, bellied up to the bar right next to her. Turning her attention back to the door, after a moment she reached over and took a sip of her wine. It left the slightest of an acrid aftertaste, which she chalked up to toothpaste residue and tried another drink. It seemed a little better and she swallowed, keeping her eye on the front door, to forewarn herself of Roy's arrival and alter her manner to appear more relaxed than she felt. Okay… was feeling, because all of a sudden she was light-headed and beginning to gasp for breath. Before she knew it, she was down for the count.

Esteban was beginning to get concerned. He'd been there ten minutes and still no Debra. He'd called her cell phone and it went directly to voicemail. Finally, he called Ell to see if she was still at the apartment. Maybe she'd stuffed her phone someplace where she couldn't hear it ring.

Ell answered the call.

"Hello Ell. It's Roy. Is Debra still there?"

"No. She left at least a half-hour ago, why?"

"I've been here for a while and she hasn't made it to the bistro yet. Could she have stopped by the drugstore on the corner for anything?" He didn't want to appear alarmed but when Ell said it had been over 30 minutes, that news did not sit well with him.

"I doubt it. She was going minimalist tonight, just a clutch. She wouldn't want to be lugging a sack around." Ell was no slouch when it came to family, intuition and sniffing out a problem, and she was smelling a foul one. Before she could add anything more, Esteban cut the contact with a quick, "Thanks, I'll get back to you."

He turned to look at his beer on the bar and noticed a quarter glass of wine that had been sitting there the whole time since he arrived. Finally attuning his ears to the jabber around him, he realized that the excitement that the clientele had been yapping about was an emergency that had happened *here, in this restaurant*.

How had he missed the constant rumoring about the patron who had collapsed at the bar? Wanting to slap himself, he leaned over the bar and nabbed the server's attention.

"Tell me what happened here. Did someone have a heart attack or something?" His attitude was authoritative enough that the man, a dark, good-looking guy in his thirties, answered.

"A pretty lady sit right where you are now and just fall down," his English was a little stilted, sounding like an immigrant, probably from Italy. "We don't know what happen. She got sick and we call nine-one-one. The amboolance come right away and take her to hospital."

Esteban's heart was in his throat. He had just passed an ambulance going the opposite direction not 15 minutes ago. "Was she a petite black woman?"

"Yes, yes! Do you know her?" The server was appalled and excited at once.

Esteban didn't answer directly. Instead he asked, "Is this her wine glass?" instantly recognizing the white liquid when most everyone else was ordering the stylish reds.

"Oh yes, I nearly forget. I need to clean it up." And as he reached for the glass, Esteban immediately snatched it away from him.

"What? What are you doing?"

"I need to take this as evidence," said Esteban, pulling his credentials out and displaying them briefly before stuffing them back in his coat pocket. "Get me a plastic ziplock bag right away."

The server looked at him for a moment, confused.

"Presto!" Esteban ordered and the server jumped to fulfill the command.

Esteban saw another man, professionally dressed, standing aloof behind the bar and watching the exchange. Assuming him to be in charge, Esteban gestured him over. "Are you the owner?"

"No, I'm the manager."

"Tell me what happened, quickly, and don't leave out any details."

The man explained what had occurred and that the woman was taken by the EMTs to the hospital.

"Do you know which one? There's more than one in the area," Esteban was trying to keep his cool but he was rapidly losing his composure knowing that Debra was alone in some strange hospital in a strange city, possibly unconscious and no one to help her.

"They didn't say. I haven't had to deal with emergency techs much and I didn't think to ask. I had a restaurant full of shocked customers that demanded my attention. There wasn't anything I could do for her besides call for assistance."

Esteban grabbed the baggie from the server and gingerly lifted the glass with a clean napkin, depositing it inside, liquid and all, forcing as much air out as he could and sealing it. He looked at the patrons closest by him and asked what they had seen or noticed. One mentioned the motorcycle couple that had come in just before Debra had collapsed, sitting right next to her.

He looked over the clientele still in the restaurant and didn't see them anywhere. Turning to the manager, he asked, "When did they leave?"

"I didn't really notice, there was so much commotion. But they were gone about the time the ambulance took off. Dropped a couple bills on the bar for their drinks."

"Do you still have their glasses?"

"No. I don't even remember picking them up." He looked over at the server, "Gianni, did you clear the glasses for the couple that were wearing the leather outfits?"

"No, I did not see them after they left."

"Was anyone else behind the bar that would have taken them?"

"No, no," said Gianni. "Just me here."

"Okay, thanks," said Esteban as he took the bagged glass, hauled his phone out of his pocket and strode to the door. There was a taxi waiting right in front, the bistro being a popular hangout and a good spot to collect a fare. Esteban flung open the door and jumped in.

"Which is the nearest hospital with an emergency room?"

"Beth Israel North," provided the cabbie as he pulled out.

"Take me there, pronto."

"You got it!" and he sped away.

As soon as the taxi arrived at the emergency room entrance, Esteban instructed him to wait, just in case. He ran inside and seeing the reception desk, approached holding out his badge so the security guard wouldn't argue with him.

The woman at the reception post was a large black woman, whose smile dissipated in the face of Esteban's grim visage. This was going to be a serious encounter. "May I help you?"

"I hope so, ma'am. This is an urgent situation. I need to know if a patient was brought in within the last hour. Her name is Debra Chorister. She's a petite black woman in her thirties." He stood there, looming above the woman as he awaited a response.

"We haven't had any emergency arrivals in over three hours. And that was an elderly man who had fallen in his tub," she was apologetic but certain.

"Are there any other emergency rooms where an ambulance might deliver a patient from the area of 86th and Third Ave.?"

"There's always a possibility that a patient would be delivered to a different hospital if they requested it," she offered.

"No, Ms. Chorister was unconscious and unable to communicate a preference, nor did she likely have any insurance information on her that would describe specifics for care. She was visiting the area."

"In that case, Agent," she obviously couldn't recall his name from the credentials, all she remembered was FBI and she knew they were called agents instead of detectives, "I don't know where to direct you. There are three other hospitals with emergency rooms in the area."

"You don't seem to be overly burdened at the moment, would you mind calling the other ERs to see if Ms. Chorister was admitted?" As harried as he was, he tugged out that charmer of a smile and used it now on the kindly hospital matron.

"Certainly, it'll just take a few moments... I hope." She started calling. Each of the hospitals was on speed dial. "You never know how swamped they are at any given time."

"I understand, and, thank you,"

"You are most welcome."

The next ten minutes were the longest of Esteban's life. The receptionist dutifully called each hospital and each time, after she'd held while they checked their logs, she came up with a blank.

"I'm so sorry, Agent, but Debra Chorister has not been admitted to any of the local emergency rooms. If I can help in any other way…" she let the question lie, not knowing what else to say.

"No, thank you so much," and he finally read her nametag, "Marta. You have been a great help." With that he loped back to the cab, hopped in and told the driver, "Downtown. Federal Plaza."

CHAPTER 47

He awakens out of a stupor more than a dream. Abandoning the tour group that he joined in their drive to Dogubeyazit, the scientist stayed the night in the same hotel as they, but parted company upon arrival in the city... their quest and his diverging. The last days and weeks have left him blank yet hopeful as he tries to put the pieces together from the stirring conclusions that he is being forced to accept. Oddly, the acceptance is much easier than he'd expected. Acknowledging the divinity of creation, the design that has escaped his detection all these years, is a great hurdle that has simply dissolved by witnessing the life-changing evidence under the microscope lens. It is taking him through a humbling analysis of what he has believed, pulling it apart piece by piece as he grasps the wonder that he's over - looked in his study of the tiniest particles of organic nature. The maxim of not seeing the forest for the trees reveals to him how blind he has been to the obvious so that he wonders how he ever missed it.

But he's getting it now.

The dawn brings him to his feet. Scrubbing his eyes with his balled fists, he feels like a child viewing the world for the first time as some - thing incredibly grand and beyond his ken. A new wonder pervading his thoughts, he quickly goes through his ablutions, dressing for a day of personal discovery that, if he approaches this correctly, can affect humanity. But are they ready for it? *The question is moot. He must tackle the challenge.*

Lunch packed in a tucker bag he'd acquired in Australia during his youthful explorations, he is ready for the road. Striking out on his own, he has engaged a car and driver, realizing that he needs a local to direct him, perhaps even save him from making a grave blunder as he embarks to visit area landmarks, some that are not even recognized as such by the locals.

Becoming lost in this region would be a death-defying act of pure stupidity. A few well-placed questions to the hotel clerk has fueled him with information about the border that gives him a healthy fear of the politics. Life changes slowly in the Kurdish area of Üzengili where the research scientist is bound, seeking the place of the excavation all those years past. He is told that he must not dither after the sun sets and that he must be aware of roving men who are armed and danger - ous. He is also warned away from the hills as he could encounter Turkish Border Patrols, Iranian Border Patrols or insalubrious char - acters that have ill intent at their core. None of the options engender a great deal of confidence, and although he had been here in even more treacherous times, traveling alone when no one knew where he has gone, he has a certain amount of healthy trepidation.

The driver meets him in the lobby of the hotel and, to the scientist, he appears a trustworthy fellow. The hotel manager had spoken high - ly of him as one who has grown up in the surrounding highlands and shares his knowledge of the region forthrightly and amiably. They shake hands and, the driver's smile beaming through a dark complex - ion tanned from years of working outdoors, age-worn lines crinkling at the corners of his eyes, is familiar to the scientist. They each study one another closely and then the driver slaps the researcher on the back and pulls him into a bearhug.

At first the scientist is shocked but then the smell of the driver's jacket, laden with wood smoke, and his breath, redolent of fennel seed that he constantly chews, brings his memory flooding back.

"Garip!"

"Doctor Ari!"

They hold each other by the shoulders and look into faces that have changed over two decades, but not enough to hamper recogni - tion.

"I cannot believe that you have come again! It is more than pleas - ure that makes me offer my car for you!"

"Garip," Dr. Ari is completely off kilter by this amazing bit of luck. No, he rephrases this in his mind, it is a destiny of sorts, and one that eases his heart so greatly he is nearly overwhelmed with emotion. "Never would I have thought that I would have the good fortune of

seeing you again! And to once more have you as my guide. I am amazed."

"I am not. God has His plan. This is why you are here, yes?"

"Yes, I can truly say that He brought me here. And He led me to the most revered tour guide in the region." The smile that lit both their faces was almost unreal. Dr. Ari hefts his pack and the two walk out to the waiting car.

Garip opens the door of his vehicle proudly, "You like my car?" He pats the roof. "A Volkswagen. Very popular and good for gas. I just bought last year."

"Business has been good, then?"

Garip nods his head as he closes the door for the researcher and goes around to settle himself into the driver's seat. "Very good. Even the brigands do not keep the tourists away." He looks over the back of the seat at the doctor. "Everyone wants to visit the place of the flood."

"You mean Mt. Ararat. I met some young people going to hike its slopes expecting to find evidence of the receding floodwaters."

"Then they go to the wrong place," says Garip as he turns over the ignition and drives through town. "The government, it was clever to make a park around the right place, and many visitors come to see it."

"You mean the ark?" Dr. Ari has been reading up on the Durupinar formation. He never visited the area when he was here two decades ago, his mission clearly defined to help supervise the opening of the grave. But he remembers Garip well. As one of the men who had been hired to help with the dig, he had been a wealth of information about the folklore of the site and had spent many hours with Dr. Ari telling him about the past. In an odd way they had bonded and that bond was evident now, never having dissipated over time and their complete separation by years and miles.

"You know about it, but I never took you there. It was protected, special permission must be granted then," says Garip.

"And, if I recall, there was much turmoil and danger in the hills. Is there still?"

"Enough that we will not linger after dark if you wish to go there."

He asks over his shoulder, "Where do you go today?"
  "Durupinar."

CHAPTER 48

When the call was placed to 911, it was intercepted by an ambulance that was parked just around the corner, the emergency techs having stopped to get a snack while continuing to monitor their radio. It was an unusual call as it was routed directly to them and not through a dispatch center. Jumping into the cab, they circled the block to double-park in front of the restaurant that had placed the emergency call, opened the rear doors and unloaded the gurney.

It didn't take five minutes from receiving the call to their rushing through the front door, the restaurant's patrons moving out of the way, even helping by shifting some of the tables to make room for the EMTs to wheel out the patient. The whole operation was completed in less than eight minutes from call to loading the patient and barreling up 3rd Avenue, which is when the taxi bearing Esteban had pulled toward the curb to allow it passage.

The ambulance didn't go toward any of the hospitals with emergency wards in the area. It headed straight out of Manhattan to the Bronx to pick up I-87 and points north. The patient, secured to the gurney in the back, was completely unaware of her journey. Both straps and a drug immobilized Debra, impairing her to the point of oblivion.

The trek took nearly an hour, long enough for her to begin to reclaim her senses, but keep her from being able to independently move her limbs. As Debra's eyelids fluttered open, an effort that was close to impossible at first, she was aware that she couldn't move anything but her eyes, and her vision was clouded, unfocused. All that was visible were shining instruments of such vague proportions she couldn't make out their shape or purpose. She was struggling to breathe, something hindering her innate ability, though she hadn't quite lost the involuntary capacity. Working hard, she took one deep breath followed by another, wondering at the exertion necessary for such a simple function.

Although her sight was still fuzzy, her mind was clearing and she began to go through each of her physical abilities. She couldn't open her mouth, try as she would. Her hands, arms, feet and legs were inert. However much effort her mind applied to the task of initiating any kind of physical movement, other than her eyes opening and labored breathing, nothing budged.

What is going on? Where am I and why? The questions went unvoiced as her vocal chords would not work, frustrating her deeper. Debra tried to piece things together but all she recalled was turning at the sound of the door opening and being disappointed at the entrance of a biker couple decked out in their leathers. She remembered thinking how hot they must have been, practically covered from head to toe on a warm summer's eve, but she also knew that the gear could be life saving were they to take a tumble on their motorcycle. She had watched them come over to the bar right beside her and order drinks when she had been distracted by the door again which, once more, did not yield the form of Esteban. After that, all she remembered was drinking a little wine and then she realized why it had tasted off, the bikers must have put something in her glass.

Why on earth would they do that? She couldn't think of one reason why anyone would be interested in drugging her. Even if it had anything to do with the missing patient case, it would make no sense. They had nothing. For all intents and purposes, their hands were tied by a lack of real evidence of any wrongdoing. All they had were conjecture and supposition, albeit good ones. She tried to shake her head in disbelief, but the muscles would not respond.

The ambulance, she finally figured out that she was strapped to a gurney in the back of one, was slowing down and this time it didn't seem to be to accommodate traffic, which she could hear. Thankfully, the drug had not impaired her hearing. Debra was actually able to hear more clearly than she could see, but control of her muscles was not returning and that was beginning to fire her temper, futile as it was to get angry at her current circumstances.

As the vehicle rolled to a stop, Debra realized that she was in virtually the same pickle that her friend Allie had experienced just over a year ago. *Ell is going to have it in for Roy for certain,* she thought. Ell had been worried about his penchant to get his unofficial "partners" embroiled in some kind of trouble. This was different. Debra had not gone undercover with potential bad guys harboring absolutely evil intent – not that Allie had expected such a scenario either.

Shoving the thought away as being irrelevant now, Debra tried to concentrate on what was happening around her. She had to make a quick decision whether she should play unconscious. It wouldn't take much effort. All she had to do was close her eyes because she couldn't move anything anyway.

She chose her course as the doors swung open. Play dead.

❧❧❧

Paying off the taxi driver, Esteban climbed out and rode the elevator up to the 23rd floor. Exiting the lift, he strode down the aisle of darkened cubicles. There were a few agents on duty, of course. This was the FBI and there needed to be bodies available at all times, but the night crew was not as numerous. He went directly to his desk and sat down, pulling the hard copy file out of the drawer and proceeding to look through every bit of data that was stored therein. He fired up the computer terminal and compared the digital files with what he knew, which was abysmally little.

The last thing he wanted to do was call Ell to let her know that Debra had somehow suffered some kind of seizure and been hauled off by an ambulance that no one could find. He'd already been on the phone with 911 dispatch to back-check the log. Somehow, they had no account, no recording of a call taken at that time from that address. Evidently, the ersatz EMTs had intercepted the call and answered it themselves. They had been prepared for this. But how?

How could they have known where they were meeting or who would arrive first? As he thought on it, he realized that the likelihood was that both of them were being followed. Their activities weren't exactly a secret and anyone in the clinic network would have been able to track one or both of them.

They probably didn't care which one of us they got. Either one would suffice, though they'd have been better off to get me than Debra. He began to think that they might have assumed he would be the first one there, usually the man is. But because he had detoured to get the flowers, he arrived second, sealing Debra's fate. If they couldn't get him, they'd take her.

Wonderful, just wonderful. Now she's suffering what was probably meant for me. Damn my good intentions! The difference, he realized, was that he had the resources to find her when she would not have had that advantage to locate him. Fact was, his ASAC would have happily written him off as a thorn in his side permanently removed.

Okay, he had the tools at his fingertips, all he needed to do was center his mind on retrieving Debra from a certified disappearance. They found so many of the others, he can find her, too.

After calling dispatch, he'd looked up every midtown and uptown hospital with an emergency room using his cell phone. While the taxi drove him to Federal Plaza, he'd then proceeded to call all the ones that Marta had not, and he'd come up empty. Debra hadn't been admitted to any one of them.

So, where was the ambulance taking her?

Locking the file back in his desk, he shot out of his chair and ran back to the elevator. There was only one possible place.

Lord, please don't let me be wrong.

CHAPTER 49

Garip drives the 15 kilometers toward the Kurdish village of Üzengili where border clashes along the disputed Turkish-Iranian boundary are commonplace. A native of the province, Garip is accus - tomed to the ongoing conflict but is always aware of reports as he transports tourists back and forth to the national park that encom - passes the Durupinar formation, mindful of keeping them safe. The road to Üzengili wends through a wide valley flanked by Agri Dagh, a volcano rising more than 16,000 feet in elevation, the escarpment long associated with the three nations, Turkey, Iran and Armenia. The long-lost kingdom of Urartu has left its mark in the name of that volcanic peak as Ararat, by which the area is referred in biblical text.

The spring green of the pastures turning to amber as the heat of the year beats down upon the region, the barren highlands climb sharply from the valley floor creating a channel that the road follows south toward the border with Iran. Just two miles from that embattled line there lies a boat-shaped formation on the dry slope, a splash of verdure surrounding the base of the exposed sides. Named for the Turkish pilot Ilhan Durupinar, who snapped the photo of the oddly shaped geology in 1959, the Turkish government recognized the research done on the formation and set the acreage aside as a nation - al park. As Garip drives up the road toward a rose-colored stucco building, Dr. Ari and his guide are greeted by a sign that plainly reads, "Noah's Ark National Park Visitor Center."

The vista is one of a desert plain, skirted by a jagged crestline. Eroded terraces stretching into the horizon, the white cap of Ararat rises in the distance. Climbing out of the car, the scientist asks himself, Is this where it all began again? *He is well-versed in the tale of Noah, having pored over the Book of Genesis repeatedly since beginning work on the anomalous bone extracted from a forgotten grave not but a few kilometers from this spot.*

Garip visits this place regularly, ushering tourists, both scoffers and believers, to view the unusual structure jutting up from the soil. He directs the researcher to follow him to the contoured form, where they walk the circumference, gazing up at the sides standing taller than either of them.

"You have been here many times, Garip. What do you believe of this formation?"

"It is not natural," answers the guide. "I have heard all kind of people say "yes" this is the great boat and many who mock the name of this place." He looks directly at the scientist. "I believe this was placed here by God for us to see." He sweeps his hand across the panorama of gullies, hills and mountain backdrops, "There is much that speaks to the truth of the flood. The many stones across the plain, they are not usual. The stories come down to us from ancient times of the man who built a great ship filled with all manner of living things. Even receipts of food cooked by the wife of the mariner." He wags his head in incredulity that so many overlook the evidence. "Fables tell truth among the words handed down. Me? I think this is truth."

Dr. Ari nods his head in acceptance of the belief of Garip. The fact that he is even now in the company of the one man he had come to know when he sojourned here briefly on a quest two decades before, is a confirmation of strange maneuverings around him. Dogubeyazit is a city of more than 60,000 people and he meets Garip from among the hundreds of local tour guides? Accident is not the explanation. He has read through as much information about this site as he's been able to gather, both pro and con about the veracity of this as Noah's Ark, built to the specifics detailed in biblical passages. Rounding the struc-ture, skepticism leaves him. This formation is too atypical, standing peculiarly among the dried watercourses. No, he is not ready to dis-miss the stories that have descended through time about the great flood, the massive seaworthy craft and the single family that is told to have survived the upheaval surpassing all cataclysms in the annals of time.

Dr. Ari has spent his life following data compiled, and continuing to be compiled over centuries, that unveil the structure of the smallest of organisms, down to the most basic of elements. The supernatural, the spiritual, he has always relegated to the province of nonsense. That is, until he began dissecting the assembly of cells that were so far outside the norm that he could not reconcile its function – and he knew that it functioned because it still harbored life – its very existence with what he thought he knew to be fact.

He shakes his head as he looks upon the vast structure before him, wondering if he has indeed lost his mind.

BLOOD BARONS

CHAPTER 50

The gurney was on the ground and rolling before Debra realized it. Closing her eyes to feign unconsciousness ended up occurring in fact. The jarring of the wheels rapidly turning over the uneven surface, of first a concrete apron in front of the rear entrance to a building and then the threshold of a wide doorway, shook her out of the momentary doze. She heard the whoosh of pneumatic doors opening and closing as she was wheeled down a hall, discerning the confined area by the increase in the echoing sound bouncing off the walls, and into a larger space. Keeping her eyes closed, she had to rely on sound and the slight sensation she had across her skin of the ambient air temperature. She was unable still to actually move any of her limbs, partially from the after-effects of the drug, but also because she was secured tightly to the gurney with wide straps across her shoulders, midsection and legs. Unwilling to allow her captors knowledge of her awareness, who at first awakening she had thought might be rescuers, she made no attempt to wriggle fingers or toes. The more she could learn when their guard was down, the better.

Upon delivering her to the open room that left her cold, even under the cover of a light blanket, she was abandoned for a time. Hearing nothing except the whir of electrical appliances and the periodic rush of air through a vent as the air conditioner came on, Debra concluded that she was indeed alone and opened her eyes. At least she tried to. It was a struggle to blink and finally open them wide enough to focus on the ceiling, which, being immobilized, was all that was in her field of vision. The place was softly lit by overhead banks of fluorescent tubes that were obviously turned to the lowest intensity, keeping her from seeing much anyway. The feeling of the area was like a hospital recovery room although she'd never occupied one as a patient before, only having visited family and friends after they'd undergone surgery. It was at this point that she realized she was no longer wearing her dress.

For some reason, her clothes had been changed and she was only now awake enough to note the different feel of the fabric on her skin. Slowly, she was becoming more and more alert and the fact that she now wore what appeared to be a hospital gown sent a shiver of panic down her spine.

What in God's name am I doing here? And where is here? Knowing she was alone, she attempted to move her extremities and other than a slight stirring in her fingertips, nothing answered her mental directives. *Well, I'm stuck now and I have no idea why I'm here, but it can't be a good thing.* Silently she prayed that Roy would figure things out and rescue her.

What was it I'd told him about not comparing me to Dudley Do-right's Nell? And here I am, the epitome of her tied to the rails wait-ing for the train to come chugging down the track. Only, what did the unstoppable steam engine have in store for Debra? She didn't want to contemplate the possibilities.

Esteban had just rounded the on-ramp for the interstate heading north, away from Manhattan. He'd visited the clinic in Nyack but, for some stupid reason he'd blown off the one that he knew was in Scarsdale, an upscale suburb of the most populous city in the United States. Never having been there before, he was flying by the seat of his pants, and the GPS in the Marquis, to find his way to the place where he suspected Debra had been transported. He didn't have an ounce of proof upon which he'd stacked his assumption, but he didn't have any other leads, either. He'd watched the ambulance hurtle uptown as he'd come south, and after checking every emergency room in the path north, it struck him that he needed to climb out of his box.

Leafing back through the files, he arrived at the conclusion that Debra's abduction absolutely was related to their literal fly-by-night investigation and that he had been the intended quarry. The only thing that could possibly save Debra from whatever these people had planned was the fact that they'd gone off script. They took the weaker link who would not have had the resources to locate the other partner. Praying that he was right, he zoomed north toward the turnoff that would take him to the sleepy village and a facility that should be closed for the night.

BLOOD BARONS

CHAPTER 51

The doctor was standing by his phone waiting for news about the latest developments. He had given the go-ahead to pick-up the offender that was creating such havoc at the San Rafael extension.

Out of the blue, a health inspector from Marin County had appeared with a warrant at a warehouse near the waterfront. He had been informed that the organization that rented the space was not directly affiliated with the clinic network, only that it was contracted to dispose of their medical waste. The surprise was that another inspector from the county Environmental Health Services simultaneously appeared at the San Rafael Surgery Center with a warrant to examine their records of biohazard disposal and to inspect the whole facility.

He had received a call from Dr. Parven, who was abnormally distressed by the incursion conducted by offensive public health employees. Parven was generally even tempered if blunt in his dealings with officials, having a self-righteous attitude about the calling of his clinic regarding the research. However, public employees, particularly those who wield an autocratic authority and enjoy throwing it around, quickly lit the doctor's fuse and his response to the invasive force, warrant in hand, was not a pretty one. In fact, Parven had been quickly warned by the deputy sheriff, who had accompanied the EHS representative, that any interference with the lawful execution of the warrant would result in jail time. Dr. Parven unhappily backed off and allowed the inspector access to records and the facility, which included every corner and cupboard.

When the doctor asked if there was anything that could be considered a problem, Parven answered in the negative as all questionable waste had been collected the night before. He was not as certain when it came to the data banks, there may still be reference to a couple of individuals who were no longer considered patients but had not been purged from the records.

The doctor considered Dr. Parven's disclosure with care. There may be a problem and then there may not. As an afterthought, Dr. Parven, quite out of character as generally being a cool customer, said that he'd been informed that the warrant was approved partially because of photographic substantiation.

That was enough for the doctor to decide that measures must be initiated to counter the possibility of an escalation to practical charges being laid against one of his clinics. He thanked Dr. Parven, told him to keep composure and that he would handle the situation, then unceremoniously hung up.

This was a development that could be serious and the only credible witness was the FBI special agent who had lodged the complaint with the EHS, which had left nothing to chance and received the warrant within hours. He had to admire the agent for going to the one agency that would not vacillate when it came to a serious question of improper handling of environmentally hazardous waste materials. Leave it to zealous bureaucrats to imply wrongdoing by established businesses. He, more than anyone, understood the revenue factor.

The problem now, however, was how to handle the dilemma. This was something that could be blown out of proportion and take down the whole operation. Pictures or not, what was always needed in bringing a case to court, which is where this will be headed if the inspector uncovers anything unhygienic, is a witness to testify to the veracity of the evidence. Hence, it was necessary for him to come up with a solution and fast.

He did.

Unfortunately, the solution was misapplied and the incorrect subject was now laying on a gurney in one of the network clinics. Being rid of the black researcher would be useful, yes, but she was not the more dangerous one of the pair. The doctor had endorsed the plan to apprehend the special agent, it being fairly believable that a man of 50 could collapse from a heart issue, as opposed to a woman in her late 30s, though the latter was not out of the question. More and more women were suffering from heart attacks due to the highly stressful lives they lead.

No matter. It was a moot point at this juncture as the woman was lying inert in a pre-op room, awaiting the next, and last, surgical procedure of her life. If it worked, terrific, he thought, one last person to be able to detail their work. He shrugged, *If it didn't, well, same dif - ference.*

BLOOD BARONS

CHAPTER 52

A surgical team entered the room. She wouldn't have known that except for the fact that they had taken her blood pressure and other vital signs and while wrapping the cuff for the sphygmomanometer (Debra gave herself a pat on the back for recalling the medical term) one of them caught her out.

"Awake now, are you?" The voice had an inflection that was either South African or Australian, she couldn't tell. Not that it really mattered where the guy was from, his intention was not a wholesome one as far as she was concerned, having been drugged, bound and transported to an unknown location. And what the plan was for her now, she had no idea, nor was she sure that she wanted to know.

"Good thing, dear," he said, soothingly. "We're just going to take care of that mitralvalve problem. It's amazing that you've been able to function as well as you have all these years with this, but your little emergency has called us to take care of this as soon as possible. Thank goodness they got you here right away. The prolapsed valve to your left atrium is beyond help so we'll be installing a prosthetic valve within a couple of hours."

No!!! Debra tried to scream but her vocal chords were completely inoperable, anesthetized by whatever drug had been administered in her wine hours ago. At least she thought it was hours ago. If the doctor had any indication of her extreme distress, he gave no indication of it, continuing to evaluate her vitals.

"Just in case you'd had anything to eat before you were brought in, we're going to keep you sedated until its time for surgery. We want to be certain that nothing can go wrong," he kept his voice calming as he administered another dose of a drug, though she didn't know which one and she was unable to ask. In her mind she was screaming negatives to the whole scenario.

I don't have a heart problem!! What's the matter with you idiots!

I'm perfectly healthy!! All the yelling in her mind was not getting through to the anesthesiologist, as he had finally admitted to the occupation, and the words she so wanted to screech began to fade as she went under one more time.

One thing Esteban had done, before he went roaring off to the suburbs, was access the security camera system of the city. This city probably had the most surveillance of any population center on earth. Practically every business, street corner and mass transit depot had been outfitted with a camera. Operational for nearly six months, the Domain Awareness System hadn't even been officially announced to the media yet, and Esteban tapped into it as soon as he'd arrived at Federal Plaza. Knowing the time and place of the supposed emergency call to the restaurant, he was able to enter the information into the system and work with the NYPD to follow the ambulance to its destination. It would take time for them to track the route and he was in a hurry, knowing that Debra's life hung in the balance.

Certain in his mind what the final location was for the fake EMTs, he was following the GPS directions when he received a call from the counterterrorism bureau at the police department. Immediately after speaking with the tech, he checked the e-mail showing the route that the ambulance followed on its way out of Manhattan.

Just in time, he veered back onto the interstate from his previously intended turn-off to Scarsdale, nearly clipping the rear quarter panel of a refrigerator truck as he swerved out of the exit lane. The truck's dash lights illuminated the driver who was swearing a blue streak until he noticed the flashing lights in the Mercury's grill, not that the angry look dissipated any as Esteban shot back onto the freeway and out of sight.

Almost made the mistake of my life, and Debra's, thought Esteban as he floored it up I-87. Realizing how critical assumptions can be, he was caught in his own wrong thinking, presuming that the one clinic that he hadn't investigated was the obvious place where they'd take

Debra. It was uncertain if he would get to her in time but had he followed his first impression there would have been no way he could have made it back across the Hudson before the damage was done. Even now he may too late, and all because he disregarded his training, presupposing that the one clinic he'd visited where the reception had been warm and fuzzy presented no threat.

How could he have been so stupid? *Mensó!* He berated himself. Of course the personnel would appear glib and genial. What better way to divert suspicion? Laying aside his self-scorn, he called the one other agent who didn't treat him as a pariah. *Though he will now.*

Special Agent Swift Dusenberry wasn't thrilled to receive an SOS from Esteban but he wasn't one to mock the one-time golden boy, either. They hadn't exactly become bosom buddies, but the two of them had hit it off all right when Esteban had been transferred from the Denver office. Swift – he'd picked up the moniker as a star receiver playing college football – respected his colleague for having cracked the eco-terrorism case in the Plains, particularly because Esteban wasn't the kind of guy to back down. Swift also did what he believed he must to get the job done as long as it wasn't too far out of bounds, making them more blood brothers than adversaries. It was Swift's wife, Tanya, however, who had really closed the deal for him. She'd taken a shine to the older agent as one whom she felt was a good role model for her man, reinforcing his conviction to stand up for what was right. So when the call came late in the evening, she was all-in for him to backup Esteban, even more so because she knew no one else in that office would. Within minutes Swift was in his vehicle following Esteban's lead from his home on the Jersey side of the Hudson River.

⚜⚜⚜

Esteban had given Dusenberry detailed directions to the Nyack Central Surgery Center and, checking his watch, calculated that Swift was only a matter of twenty minutes behind him if he'd put the pedal to the metal. At this time of night traffic wasn't impossible to negotiate on the Parkway, though it was always busy. Being a Jersey boy,

Swift knew the roads in and around New York like no one else. He was just the kind of man Esteban would want to have at his back, which is why he'd called him. He needed a team player, not a player.

Having been to the location before, Esteban had an edge that he wouldn't have if he'd still been working on the assumption that Scarsdale was his target. He prayed that he'd deduced the situation correctly, because there were no third shots. He'd already played his second chance and this had better be it. Having nothing else to run on except God's will and assumption, Esteban flew toward the exit in Nyack.

⚜⚜⚜

For some reason, the anesthesiologist was keeping her on the edge of consciousness. She had no idea how long she'd been held in pre-op, only that she'd slide into a base level of awareness and a nurse would call over the foreign doctor. He'd hold her eyes open and check the pupils for dilation, and Lord knows what else, because Debra didn't. She was just trying to hang on to some awareness in order to figure a way out of this. She'd already seen what had happened to the research "subjects" where the experiment had succeeded and she wanted no part of the mind-numbing "new" life of government-directed drudgery. There was no other way of looking at the after-effects of these driven, productive individuals that had sunk into an existence, as she could find no other word to describe it. *I can't go through life with no purpose, especially no recognition of any higher authority but govern - ment programs.* That is how she envisioned those people's lives, as empty automatons leading others through an empty subsistence, a soulless survival.

Debra tried again to move some digit, some muscle, make a whimper, but nothing came forth, not even a sigh. It was still hard to breath, her chest felt constricted and outside of her conscious ability to move.

I'm stuck and these people are going to put some unnatural, unnecessary object in my heart! All right, be calm. Screaming in your mind is going to help nothing, girl. Think, think, think!

As soon as she felt as though she was getting back control of some of those thought processes, here came the doctor with a hypodermic, adding a little something more to the drug cocktail that was already flowing through her veins.

She began slipping under again.

BLOOD BARONS

CHAPTER 53

Esteban found his way back to the surgery center where he'd been so congenially received last week. Parking on the street at some distance away from the clinic in an attempt to keep a low profile, he wondered about the personnel at this place.

That gal, Jeanne, she'd been the nicest of the bunch. Payaso! Shouldda known better. Makes you wonder, though, who the master - mind really is, here. Her or the pleasant old doctor. Or... none of the above.

He got out of the car and phoned Swift as he went around to the trunk. Seeing no lights inside, Esteban questioned again whether he was at the right place. *They could have taken her anywhere.* Then he reasoned that wasn't true. An ambulance barreling toward anyplace except for a medical facility might cause a ruckus, and if he was right, they couldn't very well conduct a surgical procedure in someone's kitchen. *Well, they could, but the logistical problems would probably outweigh the benefits. No, they have to be here.*

Getting Swift on the phone was easy. The hard part was the fact that his ETA was still another fifteen to twenty minutes away. Digesting the fact that he'd have to wait was the worst of all. Esteban knew very well that if these guys could carry out a sophisticated kidnapping, they were perfectly capable of holding the fort against a lone FBI agent, whether or not the element of surprise was on his side. *I need an army, not a jack-in-the-box.*

This was a highly complex batch of criminals, mostly because they probably didn't consider themselves to be working in opposition to the law, they considered themselves researchers who were improving the human condition. Though how removing someone's past to create a practical simpleton that is capable of only the most superficial appreciation of life would be an improvement, he couldn't get. Having all the physical needs met leaves the whole spiritual realm in limbo.

Esteban had read about the fact that humans were naturally wired for a spiritual connection, so the question was now, if that is so and nanobot technology virtually re-wired the neurons in the brain to accept a new reality, does that mean that the spiritual is overridden?

Esteban shook his head to evict the thought that having no knowledge of the deeper things of life, that makes the experience worth the effort, is precisely what this new technology appears to be promoting. The concept was anti-human, if not anti-God. Although he'd shunned those values for so many years in an effort to avoid pain – *yeah, and how's that workin' for ya?* – he realized that this one aspect, the spirit connection, was essential in life. No physical experience can outweigh or overshadow that because it holds no energy, no power. It's the epitome of barrenness.

As he opened the trunk and took off his jacket and holster in order to don his bulletproof vest, he realized why all these thoughts were flooding him now. He had been as dead to the spirit as were those newly remade human robots, reconfigured in the image of *their* god... until now. As much as he mourned their utter loss of what was their essence, he knew that he'd gone through a rebirth, a reconfiguring of his, and it was inexorably tied to the woman who was being held inside this building.

Slipping back into the shoulder holster and leaning in to grab the standard issue shotgun, he hoped that he was indeed in the right place. If not, all that wonderful growth will have been for the acceptance of yet more pain because he will have missed his opportunity to save Debra, and, in a fashion, himself.

Knowing that if he waltzed into the situation alone he'd probably blow the whole deal, he impatiently waited for his backup to arrive.

⚜⚜⚜⚜

This time when Debra was brought around, the nurse was slapping her hand, trying to get her attention.

"Can you feel anything, honey?"

Expecting to have no sound emanating from her attempt to exercise her vocal chords, Debra was shocked at the croaking sound of her own voice for the fact that she was able to vocalize anything, and that it sounded more like a toad than human. How the nurse understood her effort to say "no" was beyond Debra's ability to comprehend, but the woman did and proceeded to inject some other drug into the IV tube.

It only took a few moments until Debra had some feeling return to her hand where the nurse had been tapping its back. She then tried to move her toes and found that she could.

"Give it a minute, honey, and we'll have you up."

Debra didn't ask why but she felt an urge to use the bathroom and began to push her legs over the side of the hospital bed to get to the facilities and empty her bladder.

"Careful, careful. I'll help you up so you can get to the restroom. No, I can't read your mind," she said in response to the odd look Debra gave her. "I knew that you'd need to go by now which is why we brought you out of your sleep."

The nurse helped her sit up on the bed and keep her upright, the dizziness walloping her perception and nearly knocking her over.

"It's okay, I'll hold on to you to get you to the toilet and then you can take it from there." She placed her hands under Debra's upper arms, assisting her to her feet and as Debra moved forward she became stronger and self-propelled. It didn't take too long to negotiate the six or so feet to the bathroom and Debra made it clear that she could handle the rest without assistance.

Taking her time to clutch every countertop and handhold, Debra guided herself into the room and managed to close the door. There was no lock so she chucked the thought that she could gain time by locking herself in the room. There being nothing for it, she went ahead and relieved herself, got cleaned up and then, dropped the seat and planted herself on it for a few minutes of restoration and solitude. Unfortunately, she wasn't given long to try to pull her scattered thoughts together when the nurse opened the door slightly and asked if she needed help.

"No. No, I can manage. I just need a few minutes."

"That's fine. You take your time and then I'll help you get back into bed."

But what if I don't want to get back into bed? What I want is out of here! She desperately tried to think of how she could buy some time besides acting as if she had a bladder the size of Lake Superior, and that would only stave off the nurse for a couple of minutes. *Now what?*

She wasn't allowed the opportunity to come up with a plan. Debra heard another male voice through the door and it sounded commanding in getting the patient back to a prone position. *You mean, captive, bub.* The panic began to supersede her anger as she realized her complete helplessness. Virtually naked, barefoot and hardly able to walk under her own power, the terror rolled over her like a tidal wave. As the door again opened, the nurse came in and asked if Debra could stand on her own, only to find her already on her feet.

⚜⚜⚜

Swift pulled up behind Esteban, who was leaning against the passenger side of the Mercury, staring at the lifeless building, carefully camouflaging his grip on the shotgun from anyone who might drive past. He didn't move from his watch position, seeing the driver's side door open up and Swift stepping out, but he nearly jumped out of his skin when the passenger door opened and the other agent who stepped into the street was no other than ASAC Harry Bestner.

Spinning on his heel, Esteban shot Swift a glare that would take down a howitzer. "What the hell's going on?"

"You need backup so I brought it," Swift replied coolly.

Turning his attention to Bestner, Esteban asked, "Are you here to help or hinder?" As an afterthought he added, "Sir."

Bestner was not in a mood to tangle with the singularly biggest pain-in-the-ass agent that he'd ever supervised. He corrected that in his head, *tried to supervise.* "This is not my idea of a date night, but we'll see whether you're on the mark or a complete screw-up."

"Ah, so you're here to witness my flame-out," Esteban shrugged his shoulders. "Well then, welcome to the party. We'll know soon enough if I'm right or you finally have your documentation to boot me." Looking over at Swift, he asked, "Ready, Benedict?"

"Believe it or not, Esteban, I am your friend. Bestner is here to back you up and make sure these guys are put away for good."

"Or, that I'm put away for good. Either way, this will be a major score for the FBI or a total fubar to support the ASAC's opinion of my incompetence." He shrugged again, "I have nothing to lose. Let's go."

Bestner had agreed to accompany Dusenberry for two reasons. If he'd been right and Esteban had gone over the edge, he could personally uphold the decision to cash him out without allowing the situation to become an intra-agency mess. If Esteban was right, then the FBI would have a win and he'd be on site to make sure procedure was followed. All three were outfitted in bulletproof vests, handguns and agency issue shotguns. Assuming that the majority of the bad guys would be medical professionals, Esteban thought, and frankly hoped, that the now three musketeers would outnumber any armed criminals.

They went around the back of the building first to ascertain what vehicles were present. They found three cars, one a Lamborghini.

"Snazzy ride, even for this neighborhood," whispered Esteban.

"Yeah, someone has an ego," added Swift.

"And a bank account to match," put in Bestner, getting his wind up. The adrenaline of a takedown was a reminder to what life had been before he'd landed behind a desk, and how much more he'd preferred it to the endless reams of paperwork and slew of official e-mails and meetings. He'd taken the ASAC position because he'd needed the raise to put his kids through college and support a wife with a serious health issue. It didn't matter what the benefits of the job were, she still suffered and he had never adjusted to the political role. Most days, he hated life, missing being on the front lines with the glory hounds like Esteban. But now, he questioned his decision to be out in the field again. It had been too long and he was afraid that his skills had grown rusty.

Too late to back out now, and he unsnapped his holster. Extracting his gun, he instantly recalled the feel of it in his hand and allowed instinct to take over.

As they circled the building, they checked the security cameras to keep out of direct view, only to find that there was just one camera perched at the front entrance. That fact made Esteban wonder again if he'd come to the right place, not that he had any leads that would direct them to an alternate location. Whatever the clinic owners' rationale for not using more security, they were committed now.

After noting the vehicles in the lot, they passed by the garage door to the loading bay and saw that it had not been completely closed. It hovered a mere two or three inches above the ground. Just enough of a rift to allow a meager strip of light to peep out from under the metal lip. Getting down on his hands and knees, Esteban peered under the door. With one eye he could see the tires of a large vehicle and just enough of it to identify an ambulance.

Dusting off his pants and hands he told his cohorts what he'd seen. "It doesn't guarantee that this is the same vehicle I saw rushing out of town, but it's a strong possibility. Most private clinics like this don't have their own private EMT service." He looked over at Bestner. "I don't suppose you brought a warrant with you."

Without answering, Bestner dropped down to his knees to take a look for himself. He tried to get his arm through the aperture but finding that he couldn't reach, he used the end of a telescoping baton to sweep something out under the door. Standing up with a pastel woven scarf or shawl in his hand, he said, "but I do have this."

Esteban took it and held it to his nose. He'd never seen it before but he knew Debra's perfume. "It's hers. It's Debra's."

"Then we must be in the right place," said Bestner, his usually dour expression cut by a sinister looking grin. "Keep the evidence safe because now we don't need no *steenkeeng* warrant."

Esteban nodded and they advanced on the rear entrance.

⚜⚜⚜⚜

Weak as she was, Debra confronted the nurse with the only thing she could find in one of the bathroom drawers, a catheter. The container was hard plastic and if she stabbed with it, she could inflict some damage. Wielding her new weapon, Debra was not about to go down without a fight.

The nurse was a kindly woman in her fifties who did not laugh at Debra, standing there, pathetic in her determination to fight her way out. "You can put that down, honey, I'm not going to hurt you."

"No, you're just going to make it possible for them to cut me open and destroy my life," Debra called up every once of energy she had to brandish the plastic tube menacingly.

"No, no, that's not going to happen. Who do you think is the one who insisted on bringing you around?" She didn't move closer knowing that Debra was on the brink of causing a disturbance and the doctor had already jumped down her throat about allowing the patient to clear her bladder. "I don't know what's going on around here. They called me in for an emergency procedure which is highly out of the ordinary, but I need this job so I came. I had no idea what was happening until I overheard the doctors in the other room." She peered out the door to be sure that they were alone. "Try to relax and let me help you."

"Why would you want to help me? What did you hear?"

"Of course, I heard the doctor tell you that they were preparing to do a valve replacement and that is just not what we do here, and certainly not in the middle of the night. So I had to double check that I was right."

She came just a bit closer and Debra was wavering between wanting to believe the nurse and trying to stand her ground. "Keep your distance," she managed to get through gritted teeth.

"Look, we have to get you out of here. I've bought us a little time by telling them you had a problem in here. He grumbled about it but backed off." The nurse moved a little closer and snatched the instrument out of Debra's hand. She could see the patient was about to howl so she immediately clamped her hand over Debra's mouth. Pulling her close to her surgical scrubs, she whispered in her ear. "Shhh. We have to be quiet. My car is outside."

Debra relaxed and the nurse said, "My name is Rose. Can you walk now?"

"Yes." Rose had pulled her hand away from Debra's mouth to hear her muffled answer.

"Good. We don't have time to find your clothes, we just have to get out of here." She looked at the frightened woman shivering in a hospital gown. "Are you with me?"

Debra nodded and allowed Rose to put her arm around her and move as quickly as they could out of the prep room and down the hall. Muffled voices filtered out from one of the closed doors and Rose moved Debra hurriedly in the opposite direction toward the back door.

Just as Rose was about to put her hand on the doorknob, hugging Debra close to her to keep her upright, the door flew open, being pulled wide by men with guns and bulletproof vests. The door being breached without a proper key set off an alarm inside and immediately the men swarmed past the two frightened women. All the two ladies heard as they rushed by was, "Get outside, find a safe place and wait for us."

The women went through the door, which, had the agents arrived a minute later, Rose's opening the door from the inside would have overridden the alarm.

The damage was done and the two fled to Rose's car, climbing in and turning on the heat for the benefit of Debra who was coming down from the drug-induced paralysis. Reaching around and grabbing a throw that she always kept in the car, Rose wrapped Debra up for warmth and modesty.

What happened inside the building was a blur to the men who were apprehended. The agents quickly cuffed them and led them into the parking lot, Bestner calling for local support.

Debra and Rose didn't see anything of what occurred inside the clinic. They were safely ensconced in the Toyota waiting for their rescuers to emerge. When Debra saw Roy pushing out one of the surgical team, the others leading out two other men, she just crumpled in her seat, tears of mixed joy and relief silently streaming down her face.

After getting the three men seated on the asphalt in the back of the clinic, Bestner and Swift took over the follow-up while Esteban strode over to the car that had Rose and Debra encamped in the front seats.

Rose wound down the power windows so he could talk to them.

Crouching down by the passenger door, Esteban looked first at Rose, nodding his thanks, then at Debra, "Are you okay?"

"I wouldn't have been, given another half hour for them to retool my heart," she'd regained much of her attitude and quick tongue thanks to the adrenaline pumping through her system that fought off the residue of the drugs' symptoms.

"Thank God." He reached his hand in to take hold of hers. "I don't know what I would have done if anything had happened to you."

"You and me both since I wouldn't have remembered any of it anyway."

Rose looked a little puzzled by the last statement, chalking it up to anesthesia being a culprit of memory loss. When she had said she didn't know what was going on at the clinic, she had meant it.

Esteban ignored the other occupant of the sedan, not for lack of interest, but his intense concern for Debra took precedence. He answered her flip comment. "That is if you had survived."

At that, Rose's eyebrows climbed skyward. *Not survive? This may not have been a usual surgery but there's no reason to think anyone would die.* She sat back and tried to digest the bits and pieces she was gathering from their conversation. She knew that this was an abnormal situation and had obviously picked up on the fact that the patient was not there by choice, but the fact that her boss had been unceremoniously seated on the ground in his scrubs, hands cuffed behind his back, added to her confusion getting worse, not better.

After a few more minutes, Esteban rose from squatting by the car, leaned in and kissed Debra's cheek while Rose watched, further bewildered by events.

Turning to face the woman who had probably secured her memory, maybe even her survival, Debra was drawn and exhausted by the ordeal. "I must apologize for not trusting you, Rose. And thank you for saving my life."

"I don't understand," said the nurse. "I got that there was something not quite right going on, but we do procedures here all the time and nobody dies."

"I think that this clinic is not centrally involved, that they just refer or are part of a research network. Other than that, I really can't tell you much. I'm sorry." Debra sighed and sank further into the seat.

"Don't apologize to me. You've been through something that I don't understand. Frankly, we need to get you someplace where you can recover properly." Rose looked over at Debra, "You stay here. I'm going to check on something," and she climbed out of the car.

Rose walked over to where the FBI agent who had come over to talk to Debra was standing near the surgeon, the other doctor and assistant. He was a tall man, who appeared to be severe and punctilious, but who now looked faded.

"Agent?" Rose came up to him directly and he turned to greet her with a brooding expression.

"Yes? Oh, Ms., I'm sorry I haven't even gotten your name, but I want to thank you for taking care of Ms. Chorister. What can I do for you?"

"Well, I'm concerned for Ms. Chorister. She's had a number of different drugs administered over the past hours and really is in need of proper care, not to mention clothes."

"You are absolutely right," said Esteban. "I'm trying to get things set so we can release the witnesses. It's been a matter of getting these three to booking and asking a few questions." He looked down at her with sympathy. "I understand you were the nurse that was there to assist with surgery?"

"Yes. I'm Rose Treading and I was called in for an emergency procedure, which is completely abnormal. But, when I'm called to help," she shrugged her shoulders as if to say, *you know how it is.* "And it was overtime, which I can really use with a daughter having just moved in with me. She's going through a terrible divorce and has two little ones."

"It looks like something didn't sit well with you about this," Esteban wanted more details.

"We do mostly outpatient surgeries and certainly not late night procedures. That in itself was out of the ordinary, then the fact that the patient, Ms. Chorister, was so drugged that she was suffering paralysis," Esteban cut her off.

"How did you know that it was drug-induced?"

"At first, I didn't, but then I heard the anesthesiologist talking with the surgeon about how much longer they wanted her "immobilized." They were talking about her like an enemy agent, not a patient. It was really strange and made my hair stand on end."

"Is that why you decided to help her?"

"That and a few other oddities, like the third man who you've arrested. Though he was one of the med techs, he didn't seem to have anything to do with the surgical team, kind of more like a "heavy?" You know, what they might call muscle in crime movies. I'd never seen him before and he gave me the willies." Rose visibly shivered at the thought.

"Thank you, Rose," Esteban softened his tone. "The locals have just arrived and we'll be able to clean this up so you can go home. There's an officer there who will take all your information so you can come to the station to make a statement tomorrow," he looked at his watch, "later today. There will be someone there from the FBI who will talk to you along with the Nyack Police." He shook her hand with both of his, "Again, thank you for helping Debra, Ms. Treading." He led her over to the officer that would get all of her information then went to Rose's car to get Debra.

"Has anyone been over here to take your statement yet?" Esteban opened the door to the Toyota and put his hand tenderly on Debra's arm. She was wrapped tightly in the throw, trying to keep warm despite the outside temperature hanging in the 70s.

"No, I guess they figured I'm in your care." She looked up at him. "What now? Can I go?"

"Yes, I'm going to take you back to the city. We really should take you to get checked at a hospital first."

"No! I have seen enough of *healthcare* in the last two weeks to last me a lifetime and I don't want *anybody* to touch me," she lashed out vehemently.

"Not even me?" though he didn't remove his hand from her arm.

Debra was getting her fire back and gave him solid stinkeye. "Of course I don't mean you. Ell may really have it in for you after this, but you're the only one I can trust." She looked at him imploringly, "Can we go now?"

"As a matter of fact, we can," he leaned in to stabilize her so she could stand. "Let me help you."

Debra's first instinct was to rebuff his offer, but as she tried to get her legs under her, she found the power wasn't there and she relented, allowing him to half-lift her out of the car. Esteban started leading her toward the blue tank but even in her weakened state, she pushed him toward Rose, who was still talking to the uniformed officer.

"Where are you going?" he asked.

"I need to talk to Rose."

"So be it," and he led her to where the nurse was standing.

He stood back as Debra hugged the woman and thanked her for saving her life. Esteban could see that the nurse was perplexed by the incident, and her eyes reflected her weariness. But her mouth twitched upward when Debra offered her gratitude and she returned the hug. Debra then tried to remove the blanket from around her body and hand it back to Rose who gently refused it, wrapping it tighter around her shoulders and kindly shoving her off into Esteban's arms. He accepted his charge and took Debra to his car and home.

CHAPTER 54

"What do you see?" Garip is watching the bewildered look on Dr. Ari's face.

"Something I never thought that I'd see or understand. This is an amazing artifact."

"So you think this is the great boat?" Garip knows what he thinks for himself, but recalling what this man was like years ago, he is try-ing to reconcile that memory with the man standing beside him, the uncertainty he sees replacing the past confidence. Two decades had elapsed and the researcher is obviously struggling with something that challenges who he had been, a man of science who had eschewed the possibility of God's direction and design.

"I have learned too much in the last few weeks to deny the possi-bility that this is indeed the great boat, as you call it," affirms the sci-entist.

"Good. There is much buried here that cannot be false. But many men have come here just to call it a lie." Garip stands tall and looks up at the side of the formation rising from the grassy foundation. "They are fools who cannot see the wonders of God."

After a few moments of silence contemplating the structure and its grandiosity when considered in perspective to the far distant past, the guide regards his companion.

Finally, Garip speaks, feeling that Dr. Ari has reached a conclu-sive point. "Where do we go now?"

"Back to the site of the excavation."

Garip weighs his answer, the recent history of the embattled region is a travel consideration. "You know that it is no longer. What was left is destroyed."

"I know," replies the scientist with remorse underlying his words. "But it is imperative that I visit the place."

"Then we will go."

⚜ ⚜ ⚜ ⚜

Coming back from the national park, they drive up the hillside toward the village, only to turn off at a point where some tumbledown ruins are barely visible from the road. As Garip steers the car up a rut - ted dirt track, a large standing stone comes into view, one that Dr. Ari recognizes from his earlier visit and the photographs that captured its image for posterity. As they come closer, the rock, six feet or more in height, has pictographs engraved on its face that the scientist recalls seeing, not only in his pictures but in one of the archaeologist whose work they had followed and subsequently destroyed. Guilt pangs come again as he remembers his own passive role in disparaging the man's name. On the stone are eight crosses ranging in size from one that overshadows all the others, a second that is half its size followed by three smaller, and three more that are smaller yet.

They exit the car and the scientist walks over to the massive stone that is pierced at the top with a round hole that is easily eight inches in diameter, an aperture through which a thick and sturdy rope had been knotted at one time in the distant past, creating a sea anchor to match the size of anchors used by modern cargo ships. He runs his hand across the surface, feeling the indentations of the incised cross - es that Byzantine Christians had carved to represent the family of Noah, the only antediluvian patriarch to survive the Great Flood. Dr. Ari is familiar with many of the flood legends that cultures around the world have told for centuries, including the one that the student in the van had mentioned – the Epic of Gilgamesh.

The great warrior Gilgamesh who was despondent, despite all his riches, wives and the kingdom he ruled, even as the son of a god he was afraid of death, and went seeking the one man who had lived beyond all others, the flood survivor. And he searched for the one thing that he believed would give him peace: everlasting life. In quest of this he sought out the old man, who even in this mythic tale appeared to be God's seafarer, Noah.

As Dr. Ari brushes his fingers across the largest cross, he realizes

334

that the warrior king was seeking something that would be attainable, but not until millennia later. For what did he seek but what the Messiah promises? Everlasting life, but not the life that Gilgamesh understood which was one of glorying through battles won, women ravished, raiment donned and feasts consumed for time immemorial. It is the enduring life of the spirit, of peace and being in the presence of God after corporeal existence is finished. This the temporal king never understood as did the character in the story that symbolized Noah.

He thinks on the young college student hunting corroboration of a myth that, were he to give it consideration, would see the underlying truth of the tale, that there is a basis in fact, and here, touching this anchor stone, the research scientist sees the proof of it that the archae - ologist, who was once photographed with this very stone, discovered.

Garip stands by the side, looking again at the stone that is much taller than he. He has visited this, and stones like it, many times, show - ing tourists the wonders of antiquity. He knew its significance, most of the indigenous folk did, they'd grown up with the story of the flood survivor who had landed here, in the mountains of Ararat. But he won - ders at the man whom he has not seen for decades, his solemnity at studying a stone that all around here have seen and take for granted.

Wiping his eye of moisture, Dr. Ari turns to Garip and says, "Let's visit the site of the farmhouse."

"There is nothing there anymore. I told you before, yes?"

"Yes, that is what you said, Garip, but I need to go and see it again."

"Very well. We will go," he says cheerfully, getting back into the car to head further up the rough road.

It takes another fifteen minutes to go a mile up what was little more than a goat trail. The scientist worries for the undercarriage of Garip's prized Volkswagen and says as much.

"Do not worry, this is a great car. She will climb mountains if I must go. But I am careful."

"I imagine that you are, Garip, and I am grateful that you are will - ing to drive out to the old site. Have you been out there since that

time?"

"Only once. A man and his friends who had visited the place some time before you came. He came back again after you were gone and said that the graves and old house were ruined. I thought, how can that be? They are already ruins. So I came out to look and, you know?" He glances briefly over his shoulder at the scientist, *"He was right. It had been a ruin before, but now it was all gone,"* he adds sadly. *"That is why I wonder you want to see it."*

"I understand, but it is something I must do," answers Dr. Ari.

A few minutes later, Garip drives up to what was once a fieldstone fence, but now is nothing more than a few strewn rocks along a bro - ken line delineating a large property. The homestead is nothing but random piles of stones. Some had obviously been hauled off for use elsewhere by the modern neighbors. What hurt most of all was the sight of obvious gravestones thrown down in disrespect for those whose bones had been laid beneath. Dr. Ari had been there for the excavation of what was left of the bodies that had been buried there, but he had not personally seen all the destruction that had been ordered after their leaving. Garip had been there, too, working as one of the diggers. He had not seen that part of the desecration of the site either as he was the one who had driven the scientist back to Dogubeyazit, along with the carefully guarded specimen.

Dr. Ari walks over to where the tombstones had been knocked down. The graves were no longer open, having been filled in both by the elements and scavengers, and he kneels down beside the place where they had exhumed the bones, bits of fabric and artifacts. He places his open hand across the sparse grass that covers the clods of earth that had half-dissolved under seasons of snows, rains and winds over twenty long years. He is beginning to have an understanding of whose bones he has been dissecting in the laboratory and they aren't those of Noah or any of his immediate family.

As he continues to examine the pillaged graves, he removes the two cherished photos from his breast pocket, comparing the long ago scene with what he now sees. Garip has been hanging back, watching this man whom he has not seen or heard from in 20 years, the anguish *he feels is almost palpable. The extraction of the photos draws him forward to look.*

"You have pictures of the dig?" asks Garip.

"Yes. I just brought these two with me," he says as he holds them out for the driver to see.

"Oh!" Garip almost yelps with surprise and delight. "The man! You have pictures of the man!"

Dr. Ari is instantly pulled out of his trance. "What do you mean, the man?"

"The man who was here when you took the bones out of the grave. He just watched and then he left."

"You saw him? Other than in these photos, I mean?"

"Oh yes! He was very, uh, sad, but he did not speak. It was as if he was not really here, but, oh, he was here." Garip's head bobs in affirmation. "I could not take my eyes from him because his coat was so white. I thought, how could he be so clean with all the dirt?" He pauses his narrative for a moment. "I even asked him how that could be. Was he not digging with the rest?" Garip looks intently at Dr. Ari, "I did not think he would answer, but he did. He said, "I come to grieve. Pray with me." And I nodded and closed my eyes to pray for those in the grave. When I open my eyes? He is gone." A slight shiv - er goes through the burly man recalling the incident.

The scientist says nothing at first, realizing the significance of the experience for this simple, wholehearted man. Then he is compelled to ask, "Do you know who it was?"

Without hesitation, Garip says, "Who but Christ?"

CHAPTER 55

Bringing Debra up the steps, she was dressed in a pair of woolen socks and an oversized FBI jacket halfway hiding the hospital gown, Esteban felt sheepish as Ell buzzed them in. He had Debra call Ell on his cell, her own things being held as evidence for forensic examination, and give her the rundown knowing that had he been the one to tell the story, he wouldn't have gotten a word in for the dressing down he'd receive. Climbing the stairs, Debra was weak from the drugs so he easily lifted her to take her to the elevator. She complained that she could make it under her own steam until he shushed her with a kiss, taking her by surprise and shutting her up.

The vision that confronted Ell when she opened the front door to her flat was a tired Esteban carrying a strangely clad Debra, grey wool socks twice the size of her feet, her legs hanging over his arms. Ell's mouth opened as if to give him a tongue-lashing but his glare clamped her mouth closed, thinking better of the harangue she had planned.

"Down the hall and to the right," said Ell instead, seeing the wiped-out Debra, eyes glazed from her ordeal.

Esteban followed direction and sat Debra on the side of the bed, feet dangling a few inches above the floor, socks flopping at the toes. "Ell, can you help Debra get dressed for bed? She's been through the wringer and needs to sleep. I'll get some water."

"I can take care of myself," Debra declared with a feeble flash of anger.

"Uh-huh," was all Roy said as he exited the room, leaving the two women to get Debra situated. He could tell that Ell was just biding her time before lighting into him when she got him alone, but he sloughed it off as being inevitable and went to the kitchen.

A few minutes later, he came back to the bedroom and knocked, opening the door just enough to put his arm through with a bottle of water. "Debra, you need to drink as much fluid as you can to flush your system," before she could argue, he added, "doctor's orders."

"Hah! Like I'll ever listen to another doctor again!"

But the bottle disappeared from his hand and Ell said, "Thank you." To Debra, she commanded gently, "Debra you know you need water."

Esteban closed the door and left the apartment before Ell had her chance to corner him. It was coming up on 3 a.m. and he was thoroughly bushed. Debra was in competent hands and he was no longer needed.

⚜⚜⚜⚜

Hoping that Ell had had enough time to calm herself, though he much doubted it, Esteban arrived at the apartment late the next morning expecting to be assaulted with well-earned epithets. Not that Ell was malicious by nature, she was just overly protective of her family and friends, having a tendency to splutter her indignation when she perceived danger. Esteban understood the reaction as being one borne from helplessness. He'd suffered the feeling innumerable times, including last night when he'd been unsure whether he would arrive in time to save Debra. Prepared for the worst, he pressed the button for entry.

The buzzer went off and he entered the building and bypassed the elevator, climbing the stairs with little more enthusiasm than he'd felt hours earlier. The difference being that he'd at least gained a few hours sleep and the tiredness wasn't due to physical exhaustion as much as an emotional drain.

The door to Ell's apartment was open for him to come in and he did so with the slightest trepidation, wondering when Ell would give him his deserved what-for. What he heard was some clattering around in the kitchen and smelled the savor of breakfast. Bacon frying, muffins baking and coffee brewing. Until now he hadn't realized he was hungry.

Closing the door behind him, he followed his nose to be greeted by a not quite smiling Ell, handing him a cup of fresh-brewed coffee.

340

Something of a surprise because he'd learned that she was a tea drinker. Debra, like him, enjoyed coffee and he saw that she was up, dressed casually and seated at the glass top table that served as a dining set.

"Well, are you going to sit down or not?" asked Ell as she dished up the eggs and bacon, making plates for all three.

"Uh, sure, thanks," he said accepting plates for himself and Debra. He walked over with the handful of two plates and a mug, setting them down gingerly before taking a seat.

Ell brought her own plate over and sat down. "Nice play, you'd have made a good waiter."

"We'll see if that isn't going to be my next career move after last night."

"What I heard, that doesn't sound too probable," said Ell. "I'd think you're more likely to be promoted than aced out."

"Depends on who you talk to," he said, masticating a mouthful. "The ASAC seems satisfied that we went in with enough ammo to make kidnapping charges stick, if nothing else."

"By "ammo" I'm guessing you mean evidence and not bullets," said Debra, speaking for the first time while she moved food around on her plate. Her stomach was still in an uproar after being fed all the pharmaceuticals the night before.

"No appetite yet, huh?" observed Esteban.

"Not really, though I know that I need to eat. Whatever drug cocktail they gave me left me with a nasty headache."

"That's why you need to drink a lot of water," pointed out Esteban.

"And you are the medical guru?" she said snidely. "I'm sorry, evidently the drugs affected my charming temperament, too."

"What I understand, drugs and alcohol bring out one's true disposition," he smirked as he ate another forkful. "And yes, I do know something about coming out of drug-induced hazes."

Ell gave him a questioning look, "Then how did you get into the FBI if you had *experience* with drugs?"

"That's not what I said. I said that I know something about it. We do go through special agent training. I think they call the place

Quantico?"

"Okay, rub it in. I'm just your average auntie who worries about my friends."

"And no better worrier have I ever encountered," he said sincerely.

"Enough already," said Debra. "I have a headache and you all are aggravating it."

"Does that mean you're not going sight-seeing today?" Esteban jibed.

"Nope. It's been put it off for a few days, that is if Debra is recovered enough," interjected Ell.

"Good, maybe I can come along," said Esteban. "Today, however, I'm going to have to get a full statement from the victim of a reprehensible crime." He looked at Debra over the rim of his coffee mug, "Can you handle it?"

"If I have to, and I know that it's necessary. I want these guys to go away for the rest of their lives."

"If I have anything to say about it, they will," declared Esteban in a low, ominous voice.

"I believe you," said Debra.

"I wish I could," said Esteban unconvinced.

⚜⚜⚜

As the evidence was collected and statements digitally recorded, some of the pieces began to fall into place. The three culprits detained from the Nyack Central Surgery Center included one of the staff surgeons at the clinic. He traveled as a specialist for a number of clinics, including Scarsdale-Midtown and Darrington, a name that Esteban recalled from the first missing patient they located in NYC. Having investigated, he found it to be another outpatient clinic like Nyack, referring to Scarsdale for the major procedures. Rose Treading had referred to him as her "boss" because she had assisted in the operating room with him many times in the past and he was the man in charge, as far as she understood, the night of Debra's abduction.

He and the anesthesiologist had lawyered-up immediately, a private foundation providing their legal counsel. The man whom Rose had called "muscle" had an attorney provided by another organization. Whether the two legal groups were related wasn't apparent but none of them were talking much. In fact, the two doctors maintained their assertion that they'd been called in for an emergency procedure by someone whom they claimed to be the patient's physician.

How that could be, Esteban had no answers thus far. He had turned over everything to the ASAC from the investigation that he and Debra had executed on his vacation, including all the evidence of illegal dumping of medical waste in California, and the follow-through from Marin County Environmental Health Services. They'd turned up evidence of improper biohazard disposal, though no actual bodies, which was what Debra and Esteban had hoped for and halfway expected. But they had uncovered records of three patients at the San Rafael clinic who had ultimately disappeared. The San Francisco field office had been called in when a database connection to the Scarsdale clinic was also found and they located the crew of the boat that Esteban had photographed. Interrogations of the captain and his henchmen, as Debra called them, were underway.

It looked like the structure of the intricately complex plot was still unfolding, the FBI tracing some association between the clinics that Debra and Esteban had identified. Esteban, however, was unsatisfied at how the investigation was being handled by the FBI. It was beginning to look like politics was rearing its ugly head. ASAC Harry Bestner was firmly on Esteban's team in terms of presenting the evidence and making an effort to bring all the field offices together to assemble the facts, but even he quickly came up against some resistance from Washington. Was there a cover-up brewing? The why of it eluded them both.

What they did have were all the digital and photographic connectors, including the clinic network with the one individual serving in some capacity on all boards. Esteban had been given clearance to go into the background of the research grants from the AHRQ, but stonewalling was instantaneous from that agency and the legal counsel for GSF Research, which manufactured the experimental medical devices. It was obvious that this was a deeply rooted scheme, possibly with illicit aspects, that would be under investigation for a good long while. In the meantime, Esteban was hoping that the experimental usage of the medical devices could be halted. U.S. attorneys were heading toward an injunction to stop them. Problem was, they would only be able to discontinue them at the clinics so far identified by Debra's research, maybe. The likelihood that there were many other unidentified clinics involved was great, and if these six had been hard to discover, the others will be that much more vigilant in concealing their ties and records.

As to the concept that neuron replacement was part of the medical device research, the Justice Department was either being blocked from acquiring the AHRQ and GSF Research records by both governmental agencies (the term "national security" was getting bandied about) and/or by the Justice Department itself, neither of which scenario surprised Esteban. The whole Wyoming affair had been submerged by the very same arm of the administration that now had oversight of this investigation, which didn't instill much confidence that results would be forthcoming anytime soon.

It wasn't looking so great for the good guys, but then, Esteban was hard-pressed to determine who the "good guys" really were anymore.

⚜⚜⚜

Within hours of their arrest, there was one snafu for the clinic trio, a little snippet of information that just happened to slip out of one of the Nyack detainees' lips. The South African doctor owned a rather sumptuous sailing vessel that was registered in his home country and he kept moored at a Long Island yacht club as a second residence. He didn't take it out often but it was apparently made available to the board of directors of both the Nyack and Scarsdale clinics. Other than that, and the fact that both he and the surgeon were on contract at both surgical centers, there wasn't much in the way of intersecting business between clinics. Referrals appeared to be the only other connection.

Bestner rapidly obtained a search warrant as soon as the anesthesiologist made mention of the boat in hopes that something, *anything* of interest, perhaps even incriminating, might have been left on board. The file of photos and witness accounts Esteban and Debra had supplied from San Rafael urged him to jump on the information as soon as it surfaced. If there had been any body dumps, which the reports they made implied, this could be the only lead. Or another dead end.

By this time ASAC Bestner was supportive of the theory of research gone bad. The two maverick investigators had documented a number of individuals who had undergone medical device implantation and had subsequently suffered partial or complete memory loss, altering their personality. What was still lacking was the motive behind it all.

BLOOD BARONS

CHAPTER 56

She has just pressed the button on her desk console to end the phone call with the one person she is least inclined to have a conver-sation. Even her ex-husband doesn't come close to this man's callous disregard for any other individual's well-being, creating a quandary for her as to why he funds a project that would benefit the human con-dition. For once she was able to hang up without having borne the usual ridicule for not meeting his expectations, giving her the chance to breathe a sigh of relief.

The doctor had informed her of a problem that had arisen with some of the clinics involved in the medical device research, and being one to worry incessantly, panic had at first set in. He had been, how-ever, able to explain that it was a temporary setback, no real harm has been done other than inspections by a couple of county agencies and a minor law enforcement brush-up. No wrongdoing has been commit-ted and there will be no adverse consequences, all of which soothed her initial alarm. Because each of the clinics came under her purview to some degree, he did send an actual report about the arrest in Nyack, which had no direct impact on the research as it was not immediately associated with the clinic network. Nyack was only a referral facility and did not participate in the studies. Thereby, he had reassured, if there is found to be some illegal activity it will not reflect on the research facilities.

What the doctor hadn't told her was that the device they had meant to use in Nyack had been collected as evidence. Luckily, in his think-ing, the FBI didn't know what to look for and the miniscule difference between this and other manufacturers' devices would go undetected.

She whisks hair away from her face with her fingers as she exam-ines both the information the doctor has provided, who supplies gen-eral oversight for all the clinics, and the correspondence that she has just received.

The contents of the latter document offers her the most comfort, as this is what, fortunately, she has just shared with the last caller, the sponsor who so generously underwrites the trust.

Weighing the two reports and what they represent is just another unanswerable reservation she carries about her work. On the one hand, two of the clinics are undergoing scrutiny for malpractice, neg- ligence in medical waste handling and an arm's length connection to a criminal charge of kidnapping with malicious intent. But it appears that, at this juncture, there are no indictments for her organization and no direct evidence that could result in any. This is a relief to her though she has pressed the doctor to resolve any and all accusations. They could endanger the government grants.

Yet here, lying in front of her, is the letter that has just arrived and she was overjoyed to be able to share it with the donor. Either infor- mation regarding the hiccup on both coasts hasn't yet reached the ears of the Agency for Health Research and Quality, or they have disre- garded it, finding it irrelevant. What matters to her is that the award has been renewed, the Administration's discretionary fund covering the lion's share of these costly quality improvement technical assis- tance and implementation grants.

Hallelujah! Her job is secure for another three years... if, and that's a big if, the doctor can make certain nothing again occurs that will jeopardize the research funding.

CHAPTER 57

Throwing his bags on the floor of the office/library where he keeps a cot for those intense hours of research at the lab, Dr. Ari flops into the chair at his desk. Exhaustion is an understatement of his physical condition. If traveling to Turkey was supposed to alleviate some of his anguish regarding the work he's under contract to produce, it com - pletely backfired. If anything, he is even more distressed by what he is now convicted. In his mind and his conscience he is satisfied that he has been shown facts that are undeniable, all of which leaves him in a worse predicament than when he began his sojourn east.

The experiments were virtually completed before he even left to test his theory of the specimen's nativity against the evidence left in this material world, a place and circumstances that he knows once existed and has been since destroyed in the name of science.

He doesn't know whether to laugh with derision at the arrogance of himself, his archaeologist colleague and his benefactor, or in utter joy at what he has proven to be true. The tears flow in any case, out of elation, total fatigue and painful knowledge that he is complicit in attempting to subvert God. Though he hasn't understood his function in this until now, the insight is almost more than he can bear, but he has a grave decision to make... will he deliver or not?

⚜⚜⚜

Hours later, Dr. Ari finds himself slumped at his desk, exactly where he collapsed upon arrival from the airport. Oddly, he feels rest - ed and more assured of what he must do.

Before leaving for Turkey he had successfully, to a degree, created the serum combining DNA from the bone specimen into the DNA from the donor. The problem, after numerous attempts, arose from the newly merged strand cohering at first but only managing to remain intact for

*a period of just 24 hours before it would begin to disintegrate. No mat-
ter what he's tried, nothing has worked to counter the devitalizing
process.*

*He had worked with a team of geneticists that began the tri-
umphant experimentation in gene modification such as the famed
combining of specific DNA facets of the fruit fly with tomatoes,
improving the altered vegetable for disease resistance. This is the reason he was tapped for this research. At the time he had no clue why
the benefactor was interested in delving into this particular bone specimen, a fascinating sample of humanity for more than one reason, the
first being the great age of the bone itself. The second is the fact that
this portion of the bone is comprised of the cells that are still vital
despite being surrounded by cells that had undergone petrification.
Third, he found that the cells carried a unique version of the DNA that
controlled aging. Not only has he found this anomaly, but there are
more, including the fact that the person to whom this bone belonged
had lived in excess of 900 years.*

*The implausible facts cascaded one after another until he had to
make the journey to the easternmost part of provincial Turkey. It did-
n't matter to him that the Kurdish region is suffering constant conflict
with the Iranians and roaming bandits, he had been impelled to make
the trip.*

*The final inconsistency with average human cells is the practical
absence of mitochondrial DNA, indicating the lack of a physical mother for this man of antiquity. Dr. Ari, the scientist, could find no other
explanation for the missing component of the organelle. All these factors had pressed him to fly halfway around the world to seek confirmation of what he now believes to be fact.*

*His years dissecting and scrutinizing the basic components of liv-
ing matter has only served to strengthen his faith... faith that he had
been raised to shun. The only child of a medical doctor whose own
father had escaped the horror of Nazi death camps, fleeing Germany
to settle in the pre-nation of Israel, still called Palestine at that time,
Dr. Ari had been told that God doesn't exist. How can there be a god
that would allow the brutalization of his chosen people and millions of*

others by a monster born in human skin? And for much of his life, he accepted that explanation, which pursued him as he worked to dis - prove God.

Bowing his head again on the desk, the scientist begins to under - stand why he is being pulled through this ordeal of exploration and ultimate discovery. God is proving to him not only His existence, but the tiniest scintilla of His plan.

The deeper he has gone into this experiment, the more he sees the contradiction of who he has become and the institution for which he is working. It has taken 20 years, but the puzzle is coming together.

As Dr. Ari has been uncovering facts piece by piece, he feels com - pelled to contact the organization that continues to archive the evi - dence of the archaeological detective who has since passed on, the man who suffered slander by many, including the Foundation that employs him. After speaking with the man's widow, the enormity of what the Foundation, and the benefactor in particular is attempting to reconstruct, with his collusion, is finally striking home. The archaeol - ogist had discovered the elements that the benefactor found a way to exploit long before that explorer had appreciated all of the implica - tions of his conclusions.

The ultimate purpose of his work overwhelms him as his eyes fly open to see that it is the effort to recreate antediluvian man's longevi - ty for the benefactor's personal application. This is the epitome of megalomania and he has been in the service of it all along!

For centuries individuals have sought the secret to eternal life and many institutions have been applying genetic research to accomplish what could not be found in a legendary fountain of youth, or by mak - ing a deal with the devil. They have moved to analyzing the genetic code in hopes of solving the riddle, but none had gone so far as to steal the DNA of a man whom science does not believe to have ever exist - ed.

The utter paradox was that this man, whose power and wealth had purchased Dr. Ari's every breath for 20 years, entirely rejects all speech, allusion to, and concept of the Creator, disavowing the exis - tence of an almighty God... the very same and only God in who he, *even as a scientist, now places all his faith. The benefactor, this very man who has referred to himself as god, just as his father before him (what irony in that alone), now relies on the tale of something he rejects to build his future?*

Cradling his head in his hands, the research scientist is baffled by this revelation. How it can be that someone would deny God yet believe that he could use His creation and twist it to his own diabolic purpose is unimaginable. Yet that's precisely what this manipulator believed he could do, no, CAN do.

Here he is, a lowly, and now humbled, scientist tinkering with the very bones of Adam, the first man, for there could be no other expla-nation for the nonconformity of certain elements in the ancient speci-men's DNA. That this man functioned despite the lack of normal mtDNA molecules, let alone living more than 900 years, as was con-firmed by the tests conducted, is beyond the ken of accepted science. This man had no mother, only a Father, who breathed life into his nos-trils, and whose bones were exhumed, carried in the Ark and again interred by Noah after the floodwaters had subsided. This is the pat-tern that was followed by the Israelites who carried Joseph's bones with them to the Promised Land when Moses led them to freedom from Egyptian slavery.

Dr. Ari is distraught considering his participation in engineering what the heir of the Scirras' legacy believes can give him enormous longevity, perhaps even the immortality that Adam enjoyed before his fall from grace. And now Ari is at the crossroads of seeing the fruition of decades of duplicitous research.

Falling to his knees, he prays for forgiveness and guidance.

CHAPTER 58

Insisting he be left alone, the research benefactor turns off his tele - phones, essentially barricading himself in his office. Now he can allow an hour, for that is all the leeway available, to contemplate what will be an irrevocable decision.

Having already dealt with the trustee of GSF Research, he has heard that the grants had been approved to continue the medical device experimentation. Should everything continue as he expects, the implementation can proceed which will ultimately create a new citi - zenry of compliance. No more dissention, anger and frustration exhib - ited by the body politic. It can and will be a world of acceptance, peaceful coexistence over which he will enjoy influence and the supreme benefits. What is most astounding to him is the acquiescence of the government to partner with him, albeit most all the bureaucra - cies are operating without full awareness of the program. Even his trustee has limited knowledge of the full scope of the research though she views all the results and knows that, at this point in the studies, the outcomes have been abysmal. However, he has confidence in his research scientists both in the medical device development and stud - ies, and in his genetic engineer who has delivered this vial to him... the realization of the most crucial element of his strategy.

Before taking that next step he turns to scanning page after page of financial statements, market reports, and investment assessments. Taking in all the data in a flash, his mind thoroughly attuned to eco - nomic trends and manipulations, he finally turns to peer out his win - dow, a full wall of glass with a sweeping view of the bay. Pleasure craft weave around the few behemoth tankers slowly chugging up the channel, giving them wide berth as they approach the marine terminal to offload their liquid gold – oil. He watches as the ship anchors in deep water, bringing the commodity that he has maneuvered to record high values, creating even more wealth than he had projected, wealth that was being pumped into establishing a new domain to be under his control, not that anyone would notice... for a while. The shift will come incrementally as people become less and less aware, even unable to hold on to their own thoughts, their individual histories gradually being replaced with complacency. Even without implement - ing the technology research that he sponsors, they are already well on their way to desensitizing the population. The educational system has done an exemplary job over the past 150 years, and all his father and he had left to do was piggyback on to someone else's diligent effort, usurping it for themselves. Amazingly, those educators and agitators still have not recognized that their hard work has already been appro - priated, much like leveraging other people's money to increase one's own fortune. Those activists and ideologues should have paid more attention to their own lessons, losing sight of the prize in their zealotry they've permitted the theory to be turned back on themselves.

Shaking his head at the foolishness of the "elite," he checks his watch. It's time.

He calls the nurse into his sanctuary. After she inserts the needle into the vial that has been his focal point for the last hour, she lifts it to expel the air from the hypodermic. She then swabs his arm with an alcohol-soaked cotton ball and inserts the needle through the subcu - taneous layer of skin and into his vein pulsing with life that he envi - sions being elongated by decades, perhaps centuries beyond man's normal lifespan. All with the help of a being whose existence he disal - lows.

He waves her off and out of the room, insisting on pressing the plunger himself, injecting the recombined DNA into his arm, his mind now warring with itself. How can this work if he doesn't believe in God or Creation?

Although the research scientist has warned him of the possibility of the engineered DNA strands unraveling once the serum enters his bloodstream, he ignores the caution, unable to deny his ambition of creating a supra-mortal dynasty to subjugate and outlast generations of lesser beings.

The serum working its way through his veins, he settles back into his leather chair and continues his work. Whatever the outcome of this experiment, he has no reason to abandon his duties.

Within a couple of hours he begins to feel a little odd, not ill or pain... different. There is some dynamic change occurring in his body. Good or bad, he can't discern. The scientist hadn't told him what to expect, in fact, there would have been no way to foresee what the reaction would be. All he can do now is wait and see what happens. The plan is to perpetuate his life by ten times that of an ordinary man. Being extraordinary suits him.

The internal sensations were growing more pronounced as time passed, drawing his attention away from the papers and computer monitor dominating his desk.

His thoughts begin to turn to how he is placing confidence to reach incredible longevity in the attributes of an ancient bone fragment. His expectations are reliant on a relic exhibiting inexplicable anomalies that appear to point directly to a Maker. As the irony of his denial of God, a God who must have created the man from whom this DNA was extracted, swims before his eyes, he feels life as he knows it slipping away.

He begins to glimpse God's plan, the brief proof of which he has pumping through his corruptible veins, that what he's been grasping to achieve is not God's notion of immortality.

CHAPTER 59

Recovered from her near-surgery experience, Debra was ready to take advantage of what vacation time she had left. Esteban had been buried under a literal ton of paperwork, sorting through financial statements, patient records, even waste management documents from the clinics where the Justice Department had served warrants. He'd given Bestner warning that he was taking a couple of days to escort his "partner" around the city before her departure, and today was the day. A promised tour of New York was in order.

Hunting down parking in a city that houses more than eight million people with millions more daily residents working the offices, businesses and myriad other jobs, was not on Esteban's agenda. It was to be a taxi tour and Ell, being called to work, planned to meet them for dinner later.

Unable to leave the investigation completely to the professionals on the 23rd floor of 26 Federal Plaza, Esteban found himself being interrogated by Debra, who was keen to know what had transpired while she recuperated from the Nyack ordeal.

"You have to give me the scoop," she urged as he paid the cabbie, leaving them to stroll around Battery Park.

"You sound more like a reporter than a researcher," he hoped he could redirect the conversation.

"All this running around after nefarious doctors and illegitimate garbage collectors has gotten the best of me. No longer am I the mousey bookworm."

"Talk about mixed metaphors."

She poked him in the side with a narrow and very sharp elbow, "Don't give me no guff, Roy. I've earned the right to see the underbelly of this medical mystery," she said insistently. "As long as you bypass any disgusting details, not that we'd come across any before my, uh, mishap." She looked up at him as they strolled to the waterside to view the Statue of Liberty guarding the gate of New York Harbor. "Whenever medicine is involved things could get nasty, what with body parts, blood and possible gore."

"You were right to begin with. This has been an administrative investigation. Anything to do with operating room niceties haven't come up except in what procedures were planned, etc."

"Good, now talk."

"You have become a demanding individual. What has Ell been teaching you?"

"Just a little assertive behavior. Nothing much," dissented Debra.

"Right." They walked in silence until coming up to the rail where they could look across at Ellis and Liberty Islands. "Actually, you've already gotten most of the information because you obtained a lot of it in your research. Nothing yet has come up to disprove any of it. You connected the dots on GSF Research and AHRQ funding of research awards, but we haven't been able to divide out anything in the grant applications that directly denote the kind of research you and I suspect."

"Like that's any surprise. I'm sure you got a good look at how those things read, vague upon vaguer language. I've had to read through stuff like that and half the time I'm not sure what the purpose is because of the liberal use of generalities, particularly if it has anything to do with education."

"They can't all be like that," argued Esteban.

"Oh, they're not," she relented. "It's just some of the things that are funded make so little sense that you wonder at the waste. For example, while I was living in L.A. there was this county arts grant that was given to a woman choreographing a dance about conjoined twins. They said it was an important diversity issue."

"You're kidding. Siamese twins is a social problem? In what way? People don't respect them or they're discriminated against?" He was astounded. "What's the fractional population factor of individuals suffering from this "diversity" circumstance, I wonder."

"I did too, and even looked it up, about one in one hundred thousand births. Go figure," said Debra. "Point being, things that are funded can be obscure or even ambiguous. Depends on the wording and how well the grant writer addresses the funding agency's guidelines."

"So, we can't find anything that addresses the possible nanobot neuron replacement concept except for language that discusses "healthcare improvements.""

"I suspect that's all you'll get other than wording that would discuss improved mobility, medical device function, mental acuity or overall recuperation time, or some such," clarified Debra.

"You may have missed your calling."

"I've already had enough career changes, thank you, and spending even more time at the computer isn't something I relish." She looked out over the grey chop of New York Bay, seeing the gallant symbol of liberty holding aloft her beacon to the masses seeking hope and freedom from oppression.

"It is hugely sad to realize that what that statue stood for is rapidly being undermined," said Debra soberly. "The funny thing is that the downhill slide had already begun when Lady Liberty was erected in 1886."

"Don't tell me you're one of those illuminati conspiracy theorists," Esteban teased.

"No. It has to do with the growing trend toward public education in the late 19th century. Did you know the first teachers' association was formed here in New York in 1857 and that it incorporated bits and pieces from the Communist Manifesto published just nine years before?"

"I had no idea."

"Frankly, I hadn't either until Toddy tracked it down for one of his articles on ChangingWind.Org. You'd be surprised what facts and solutions to many of the problems people complain about he addresses."

"The most recent damage done to independent thought and volition, we have just witnessed," said Esteban.

"And can't prove, even after all that cross-country travel to interview witnesses and, for all intents and purposes, victims," she sighed. "What I've been waiting for is your theory as to motive. Seems like that's our missing link. You said you were formulating one, and I'm ready to hear it."

"Yeah, so was Bestner. I'll have to admit, I sounded like a complete fool, because the concept is so beyond belief it sounds asinine."

"That I will not accept. There again, I'm the one who had you read Toddy's version of life by government," she admitted.

"Considering all we've seen and documented, your pal Toddy's not so far off the mark, which was what garnished the rolling eyes of the ASAC. Not that I blame him."

"So, you do think there's something to this nanobot theory."

"Look at the evidence," said Esteban. "Either these patients, or victims depending how you view things, have been utterly brainwashed, hypnotized, suffered pharmaceutically-induced amnesia or, and I'll grant you it's off-the-wall, they've had neuron replacement therapy, or neuronal, as it was also referred to. Most of the technology has been with stem cell work in Parkinson's, but I'm not convinced that someone hasn't already gone into the nanotech area with it."

"Looks like you've been doing your homework," smiled Debra, "and I've become obsolete."

"That's what you think," and he took the opportunity to steal a kiss.

"Oh my," she blushed. "Another role change is coming."

"Could be," he said without blinking an eye and continued with his narrative. "I think you were leading us down the right track. The biggest problem was the "why" of it." He paused and scratched his chin. "Not being certifiable, it's hard to put yourself in the shoes of someone who is."

"And who would that be?"

"You're the one who targeted him. The heir and current currency and commodity manipulator extraordinaire…"

"David Scirras."

"What a mind. That's what I love about you, always a step ahead," he grinned. "It comes down to what we saw in action, compliant behavior, a form of mind control."

"Okay, I'll grant you that, but, as you said, why?"

"That's exactly what Bestner asked, and this is the crazy part." He took a breath before plunging ahead. "We already know that the Scirras Foundation has tentacles in more than fifty countries, all with the intent of manipulating the politics to create an atmosphere amenable to his world view."

"Which is that he should be in charge," interrupted Debra.

"By and large. He wields his financial empire like a mace in battle, swinging it to topple who he deems unworthy but bypassing those he can influence to his way of thinking."

"Nice imagery."

He caught her eye and she saw the seriousness of his point. "To him we are all enemy combatants. He just deals with us through economic terrorism, couched in acceptable or harmonizing phraseology. Euphemistic, if you'd rather."

"I wouldn't. I like to hear the unvarnished truth."

"That's another thing I love about you, no B.S."

"I do sound loveable when you put it that way."

He had to laugh at that. "So what does a guy like this want but as much control as he can manage?"

"Which in his mind is everything," added Debra.

"Exactly. He has already proven himself to be a manipulator of the environmental movement, the Occupy Wall Street types who want something for nothing, and the so-called peaceniks, who are anything but. All of it is to cause upheaval in order to propel people that he can influence, and even control, their way to power. Which makes me wonder about the president. How much is he being directed, manipulated, or, in some instances, undermined? Scirras is the ultimate outside operator."

"I saw the "Wizard of Oz," too. Smoke and mirrors."

"Except our guy really does have power through the marketplace, well-placed funding to obtain the results he wants. That is what the Foundation does here and his Free States Foundation does overseas. What's so very sad is that the people who run his operations are all expendable as far as he is concerned. That's where the nanotechnology comes in. It's a devious way to achieve complacency among the general populace. Think of how this can be done, we saw the beginnings of the experimentation, or we believe that we have. It would take time to execute the intricate details, integrate the nanotechnology into medical devices of every kind, even dental implants, obliging just about every individual to eventually receive a medical apparatus of some kind. How many older people do you know who have had lens implants after removal of cataracts? The technology can be in virtually anything artificial that we take for granted as a health improvement."

"Which brings you all the way back to the grants for "quality improvement technical assistance implementation." I can't believe I still remember that," she said.

"What else could be behind this? I don't know, but having followed the one who's behind the grants and in the forefront of economic manipulation that we've seen bring down currencies and shoot up commodity prices to unaffordable levels," Esteban shrugged his shoulders as if to give up, it was so far outside the norm. "And then…"

"There's more?"

"Yeah. In my hunting around I decided to give your buddy Toddy a call."

"I'm impressed if he actually talked to you. He's not big on government lackeys," she taunted.

"The honor was all mine," he grinned back. "He brought up the whole concept of replicating nanobots."

"As if replacing brain cells with nanoneurons isn't enough."

"Even you brought up the Michael Crichton book that went into nanotechnology, and replicating science, ten years ago. He was prophetic in other ways, could be this one, too."

"Great, like I need more nightmare material," Debra said bleakly. "Leave it to Toddy to think of the bright side."

"Well there is a bright side, in a way. This kind of technology would replicate cells to do things like rebuild a pancreas or a kidney."

"Now wouldn't that be something. Patients like that young girl, Kara, who I told you about. She'd be able to produce her own kidney rather than having to go through a transplant and all the immune-suppressing drugs that come with their own form of side effects."

"Like Toddy said, it could be great, or it could be disastrous for the independent human mind."

"Progress doesn't come without it's perils, does it," she said as they walked back to Broadway to flag a taxi to see more of New York–Times Square, Rockefeller Center, St. Patrick's Cathedral, most of the usual tourist stops and then back to lower Manhattan. The final destination for the day was to be Ground Zero.

BLOOD BARONS

EPILOGUE

The memorial at Ground Zero wasn't to be dedicated until September 11, about two months away when the underground museum would be opened to the public. The square fountains, that hold the place where the foundations of the twin towers stood, have been flowing for nearly a year, a gossamer veil of water raining over the sides. The names of those who had lost their lives here, in Shanksville, Pennsylvania and at the Pentagon on 9/11 ring each reflecting pool, inscribed in bronze.

Esteban and Debra had obtained passes. Though it may not have been a necessity with his credentials, they wanted to go the route that every other visitor would have to follow. Strolling among the forest of white oak trees that had been planted around the memorial park, they enjoyed the lengthening shadows as the day stretched toward evening.

"Years ago, when I first contemplated coming to New York I never thought it would include a visit to pay tribute to innocent individuals lost in a terrorist attack on our soil," observed Debra as she and Roy gazed at the flowing waterfalls encircling the roots of each building that had once occupied that space.

"Neither did I," said Roy, running his fingers over the name of one person whom he would never have the opportunity to meet. "I drive near here all the time and have not had the chance to come by. You almost don't need to see the memorial to feel the loss. This city is filled with it."

"How do you mean?"

"I was here in the nineties. The place was burgeoning with energy, an underlying feeling of optimism, something that I immediately noticed was lacking when I came back into town."

"Really," she sounded perplexed and not thoroughly convinced there could be such a dynamic change in a city's atmosphere.

"I know it seems kind of strange to make an observation like that, but that is what I felt. I guess the old '60s folks would call it "vibes." Anyway, something was gone out of the verve I'd encountered before."

"People don't realize how tragedy pervades everything and everyone associated with it, and this tragedy, this was an unexpected act of such malicious violence that I think, even now, it's hard to believe. I understand what you're saying, it still suffuses the very air, long after the smothering dust has settled. If I can still see the images so clearly, it's certain those who lived here and experienced it would never forget it." She was quiet for a few moments.

"Now, put that into context of what we saw of people who had lived fast-paced, energetic, purposeful lives, and when we met them, none of that survived after their surgeries. In fact, they were in survival mode, left with nothing more than plodding through day-by-day, which is basically the difference between pre-9/11 and post-9/11. They are both heartbreaking, one on a personal level, the other, a national tragedy."

"What worries me is whether we can manage to come back to who we were as a nation, not just before 9/11 but far more than a hundred years ago when we still understood the tenets of the Constitution," said Debra somberly.

"You realize that either one of us, because of our ethnicity and color, would be considered 'traitors to the cause' in thinking this way."

"You know what? If more people would study the facts of his nation and think for themselves maybe we wouldn't be in the mess we're in, trying to dig out of a hole that people, who worry more about so-called race than individual liberty, have been digging deeper because of group-think."

"Whoa," he laughed. "You're not likely to be invited to the next NAACP convention," smiled Esteban.

"Nor you to La Raza." She looked up at him, offended by the whole concept of race designating politics. "You know, sometimes I hate black people."

"I can't believe you just said that," Esteban was shocked at her bluntness.

"I grew up with all kinds of people, but those of color who use race as a crutch - that we've been "kept down" by white folk - tick me off." She steamed for a few seconds. "This is one nation. What happened in this place was horribly catastrophic yet it actually pulled us together for a season, the same way that the Israelites would come together when they were beset by the pagan nations around them. You know what's really appalling? That it would take a national tragedy for us to forget our differences, because there are none. We are, every one of us, Americans. Of that, I passionately understand."

"Just another reason I love you, that unbridled passion for what's right." He pulled her close.

"Do I get the idea that you don't mean that in the platonic, buddy kind of way?" She looked up at him dubiously.

"I knew you were smart," and he kissed her.

-30-

23 AND IT SHALL COME TO PASS, THAT IN WHAT TRIBE THE STRANGER SOJOURNETH, THERE SHALL YE GIVE HIM HIS INHERITANCE, SAITH THE LORD GOD.

EZEKIEL 47

In memoriam for my dearly missed friend, Debra H., who was always a true and compassionate companion with a giving spirit and a gentle heart too easily broken in this broken world.

Afterword

Blood Barons, as well as being a good yarn, is an exercise in realizing the implications of scientific advances in today's society. These are not the plain explanations of natural laws such as the discovery of gravity, or even the mapping and naming of heavenly bodies, these scientific applications can change the natural world, whether or not one believes in God. It is a matter of redirecting nature to suit singular man's purposes, particularly to evil intent. Again, some may like to argue what prescribes evil. To those of us who understand right and wrong - and many do not have this ability of simple discernment as being educated out of it - the insertion or intrusion of unnatural technology that can, or is meant to, change native thought, is an unconscionable usage.

This is simply a tale of what is possible, not what has (or has yet) occurred. It is also meant to present how an unleashed and unrepentant governmental agency(cies) may usurp the individual's free will, which, has already been affected through overbearing legislation and administrative regulation.

If you find it frightening... good. We were forewarned by our Founding Fathers that despotism stands at the door ready to slip in and bind a free people if ever we abdicate our vigilance.

The following is a vastly abbreviated list of references regarding some of the issues presented in *Blood Barons*. Research these issues for yourself.

A.D.K.

Affordable Care Act
Affordable Care Act Full Text. Retrieved June 2012 from
http://www.healthcare.gov/law/full/

Supreme Court of the United States, Syllabus: National Federation of Independent Business ET AL v. Sibelius, Secretary of Health and Human Services, ET AL. Retrieved July 2012 from
http://www.supremecourt.gov/opinions/11pdf/11-393c3a2.pdf

IPAB, Obama, and Socialism. Stanley Kurtz. National Review.

Retrieved June 2012 from
http://www.nationalreview.com/corner/264988/ipab-obama-and-socialism-stanley-kurtz#

AHRC
Agency for Health Research and Quality. U.S Department of Health and Human Resources. Retrieved September 2012 from
http://www.ahrq.gov/
http://www.ahrq.gov/about/ataglance.htm
http://www.ahrq.gov/fund/cefarra.htm
http://www.ahrq.gov/fund/arrafaq.htm

Genetics
'Better' DNA out of fossil bones. Alison Ross. Retrieved August 2012 from
http://news.bbc.co.uk/2/hi/science/nature/4260334.stm

James D. Watson. Retrieved August 2012 from
http://en.wikipedia.org/wiki/James_D._Watson

'Longevity Gene' Common Among People Living To 100 Years Old And Beyond. Retrieved August 2012 from
http://www.sciencedaily.com/releases/2009/02/090203081624.htm

'Longevity Gene' Helps Prevent Memory Decline and Dementia. Retrieved August 2012 from
http://www.sciencedaily.com/releases/2010/01/100112165234.htm

Mapping and Sequencing the Human Genome. Human Genome Project Information. Retrieved August 2012 from
http://www.ornl.gov/sci/techresources/Human_Genome/publicat/primer/prim2.html#f7

The Retrieval of Ancient Human DNA Sequences.
Oliva Handt, Matthias Krings, R. H. Ward, and Svante Paabo. Retrieved August 2012 from
http://www.ncbi.nlm.nih.gov/pmc/articles/PMC1914746/pdf/ajhg00021-0095.pdf

Species determination of ancient bone DNA from fossil skeletal remains of Turkey using molecular techniques. Hasibe Cingilli Vural and Ahmet Adil Tirpan. Retrieved August 2012 from http://www.academicjournals.org/sre/pdf/pdf2010/18%20Aug/Vural%20and%20Tirpan.pdf

General Motors
General Motors Chapter 11. Retrieved August 2012 from http://en.wikipedia.org/wiki/General_Motors_Chapter_11_reorganization

Sherk and Zywicki: Obama's United Auto Workers Bailout. James Sherk, Todd Zywicki. Retrieved September 2012 from http://online.wsj.com/article/SB10001424052702303768104577462650268680454.html

Holocaust
Holocaust Encyclopedia, Josef Mengele. United States Holocaust Memorial Museum. Retrieved August 2012 from http://www.ushmm.org/wlc/en/article.php?ModuleId=10007060

Nanotechnology
Nanobots: Report on Nanobots (Nanotechnology Robots). Retrieved 2010 and August 2012 from http://nanobot.info/

UCSF unveils model for implantable artificial kidney to replace dial - ysis. Nanotechnology Now. Retrieved August 2012 from http://www.nanotech-now.com/news.cgi?story_id=39929

Noah's Ark
Wyatt Archeological Research. Retrieved August 2012 from http://wyattmuseum.com/

Discovered: Noah's Ark. Ron Wyatt. Retrieved September 2012 from http://www.ronwyatt.com/noahs_ark_book.html

Ron Wyatt Talking About Jesus' Blood Sample. Retrieved September

2012 from
http://www.youtube.com/watch?v=EGLPADW_kUw

ABOUT THE AUTHOR

Former newspaper publisher and editor, A. Dru Kristenev has more than three decades of experience in periodicals. Kristenev grew up in the publishing industry working every angle of a paper, from ad sales and production to writing and overseeing editorial content. The author carries a Bachelor of Arts degree, a Master of Science and a California Community Colleges Lifetime Teaching Credential and taught at the foremost colleges and universities in the Inland Northwest.

Since 2010, Kristenev has been on the road as an independent Christian missionary, crossing the United States more than ten times. She has also been a columnist for CanadaFreePress.com since 2014.

THE BARON SERIES

Four books in the series of stand-alone novels based on current, factual occurrences, the relationship of characters leads from one story to the next, weaving an ongoing tale of journalists running across criminally tainted philanthropy and politics. Caught by their own curiosity to uncover the truth, they are pulled deeper and deeper into the investigations, unexpectedly putting their lives at risk...

Land Barons- the first book in the Baron Series of romantic suspense novels that rely on solid research of environmentalist influence on American lifestyles, touching on the long reach of government regulation and media/corporate power. Anthea Keller is seeking a peaceful place to ply her trade as a PR agent. Instead, she finds herself in the center of a land scam, drawn in by Gary Mathers, an ex-cop who just can't reconcile the deadly misfortunes of local property owners forced to sell off assets. And who is waiting in the wings to snap up the firesale deals?

Gold Baron- the second work in the series. Fact meets fiction in the election process of the 2008 presidential campaign season, drawing on the reality driving the candidacies - who's influencing who and to what end with global markets and politics as the backdrop. Solana Greyfisher returns home to Idaho only to be snagged by a fascinating story that leads her to Toddy Littman, researcher extraordinaire. Together they dig through the morass of campaign funding paper trails only to attract the murderous ire of power brokers working the system to their own benefit.

Energy Barons - the third novel, whirls around political manipulation of the environmental movement causing economic upheaval in the West and endangering lives of the innocent. Ambitious Allie Maitland is caught by surprise while investigating what appears to be anything but an accident at the new power plant. Sawyer Aleman, former marine, wheedles his way into the FBI inquiry, under Allie's skin and into the role of guardian. Before they know it, the story rolls from Wyoming to Alaska and everyone involved is walking a perilous tightrope of greed, murder and mayhem.

BLOOD BARONS - the fourth novel in the Baron Series brings the tale full circle.

NYC: a metropolis of 8 million people; 500 disappear each year. Of those, three dead end case files lie open on Special Agent Roy Esteban's desk. Who are they? Why doesn't anyone know they're gone and why does no one care?

Lack of leads and an ASAC that wants the cases closed drives the FBI agent to take on an unorthodox partner in Researcher Debra Chorister. Together they track an unwholesome alliance between corporate science and government healthcare. And those three lone individuals? They're not the only ones who can't be found.

UNKNOWN PREDATOR

Hands tied by regulations, what does a rancher do to forestall the concocted destruction of a traditional way of life by officials cowering behind an "unknown predator?" Not what you'd think.

When neighboring landowners take action, dropping them into the middle of a legal quagmire, individuals obsessed with their own righteous cause threaten the ranchers' livelihood… and their lives.

A. Dru Kristenev
ChangingWind Ministries
changingwind@earthlink.net

Scripture Led Politics:
Mutual Exclusivity Be Damned

Wonder how Scripture relates to the political atmosphere in which we live?

Numerous legislative, judicial and regulatory decrees have altered life in America to a degree that our parents' generation would find it unrecognizable. To what end? Who benefits from the draconian coding that now cages the free thinker, particularly the faithful?

As government draws each new line in the sand, Author A. Dru Kristenev has taken a scriptural view of the cascading legal enactments, noting how they are fundamentally changing the American Dream. These commentaries open a deep discussion of how believers must tap their intellect and view the shifting political landscape in the historical light of the Bible, contemplating its significant lessons and their application.

....

Read all of A.Dru Kristenev's books available on Amazon.com...

THE BARON SERIES Political Suspense novels:

Land Barons

Gold Baron

Energy Barons

BLOOD BARONS

Unknown Predator

Non-fiction Books:

Scripture Led Politics: Mutual Exclusivity Be Damned

Pay Attention!! ...your life, family and nation depend on it

www.ingramcontent.com/pod-product-compliance
Lightning Source LLC
Chambersburg PA
CBHW071246250626
47163CB00002B/349